IMAGE COMICS
PRESENTS

THE DEAD

IMAGE COMICS, INC.
Robert Kirkman–Chief Operating Officer / Erik Larsen–Chief Financial Officer
Todd McFarlane–President / Marc Silvestri–Chief Executive Officer
Jim Valentino–Vice President
Eric Stephenson–Publisher/Chief Creative Officer / Corey Hart–Director of Sales
Jeff Boison–Director of Publishing Planning & Book Trade Sales
Chris Ross–Director of Digital Sales / Jeff Stang–Director of Specialty Sales
Kat Salazar–Director of PR & Marketing / Drew Gill–Art Director
Heather Doornink–Production Director / Nicole Lapalme–Controller
IMAGECOMICS.COM

HAND

VOLUME 1: COLD WAR RELICS

KYLE HIGGINS
WRITER

STEPHEN MOONEY
ARTIST

JORDIE BELLAIRE
COLOURIST

CLAYTON COWLES
LETTERER

DEANNA PHELPS
PRODUCTION ARTIST

CREATED BY KYLE HIGGINS AND STEPHEN MOONEY

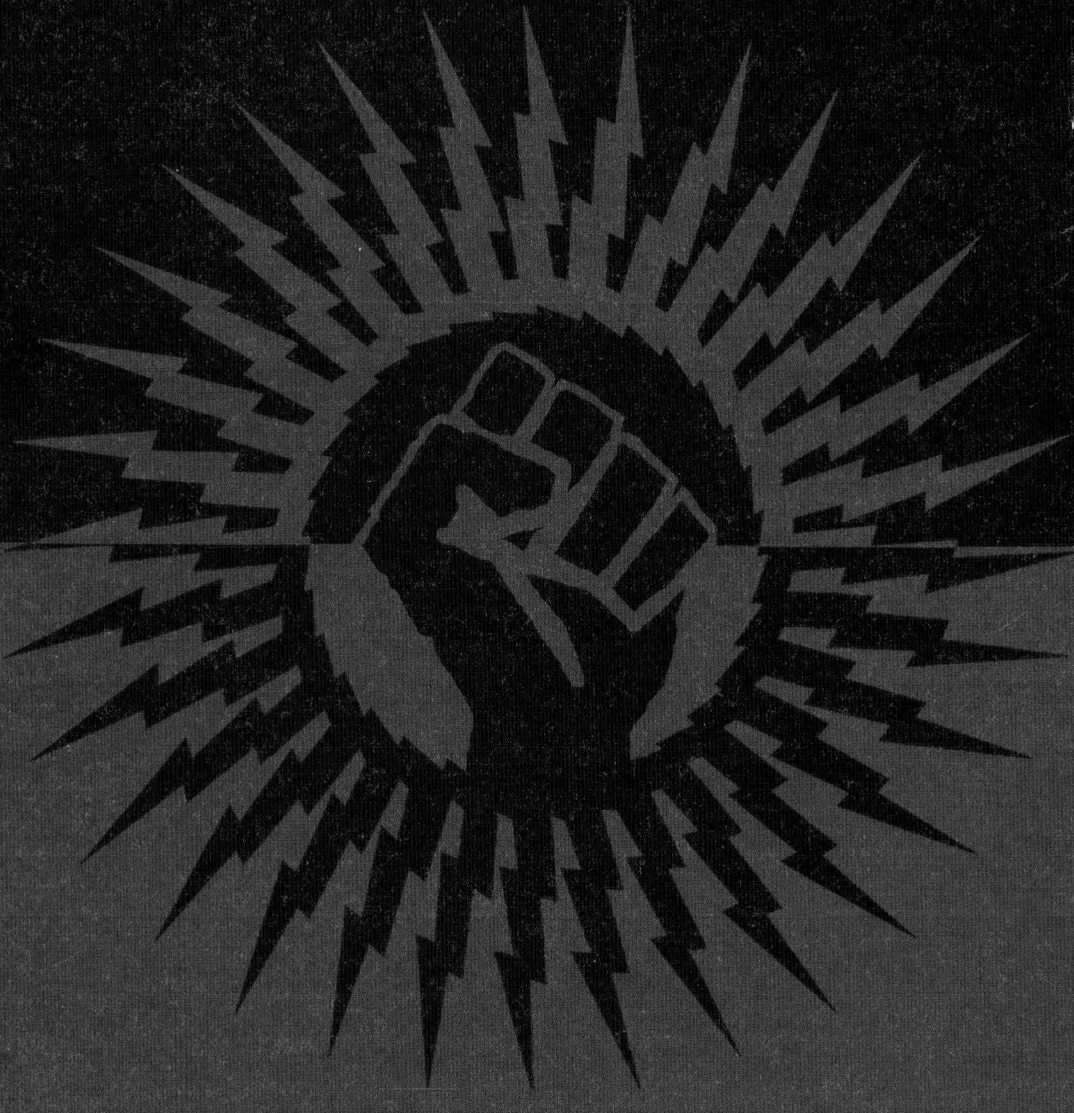

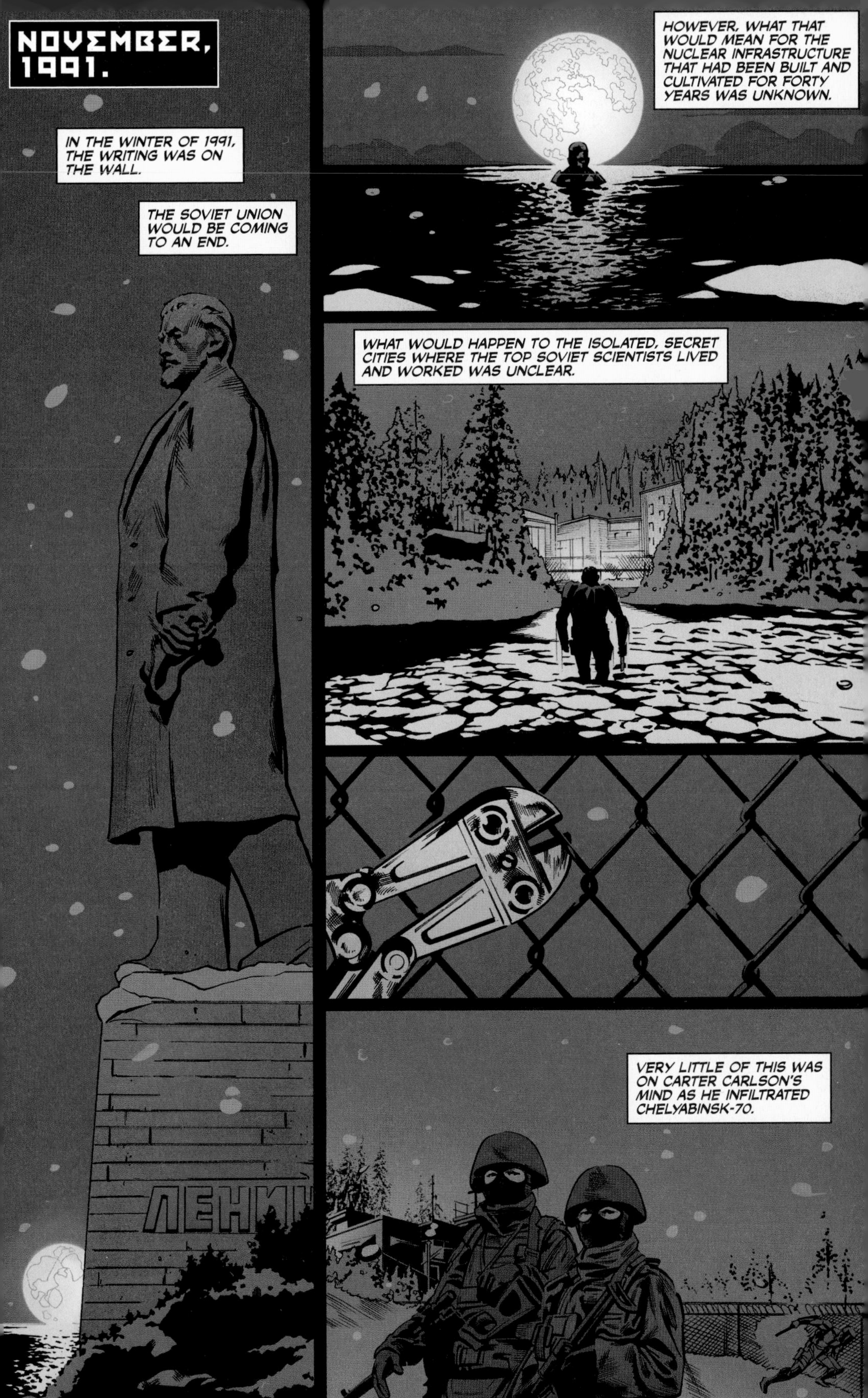
NOVEMBER, 1991.
IN THE WINTER OF 1991, THE WRITING WAS ON THE WALL.
THE SOVIET UNION WOULD BE COMING TO AN END.
ЛЕНИН
HOWEVER, WHAT THAT WOULD MEAN FOR THE NUCLEAR INFRASTRUCTURE THAT HAD BEEN BUILT AND CULTIVATED FOR FORTY YEARS WAS UNKNOWN.
WHAT WOULD HAPPEN TO THE ISOLATED, SECRET CITIES WHERE THE TOP SOVIET SCIENTISTS LIVED AND WORKED WAS UNCLEAR.
VERY LITTLE OF THIS WAS ON CARTER CARLSON'S MIND AS HE INFILTRATED CHELYABINSK-70.

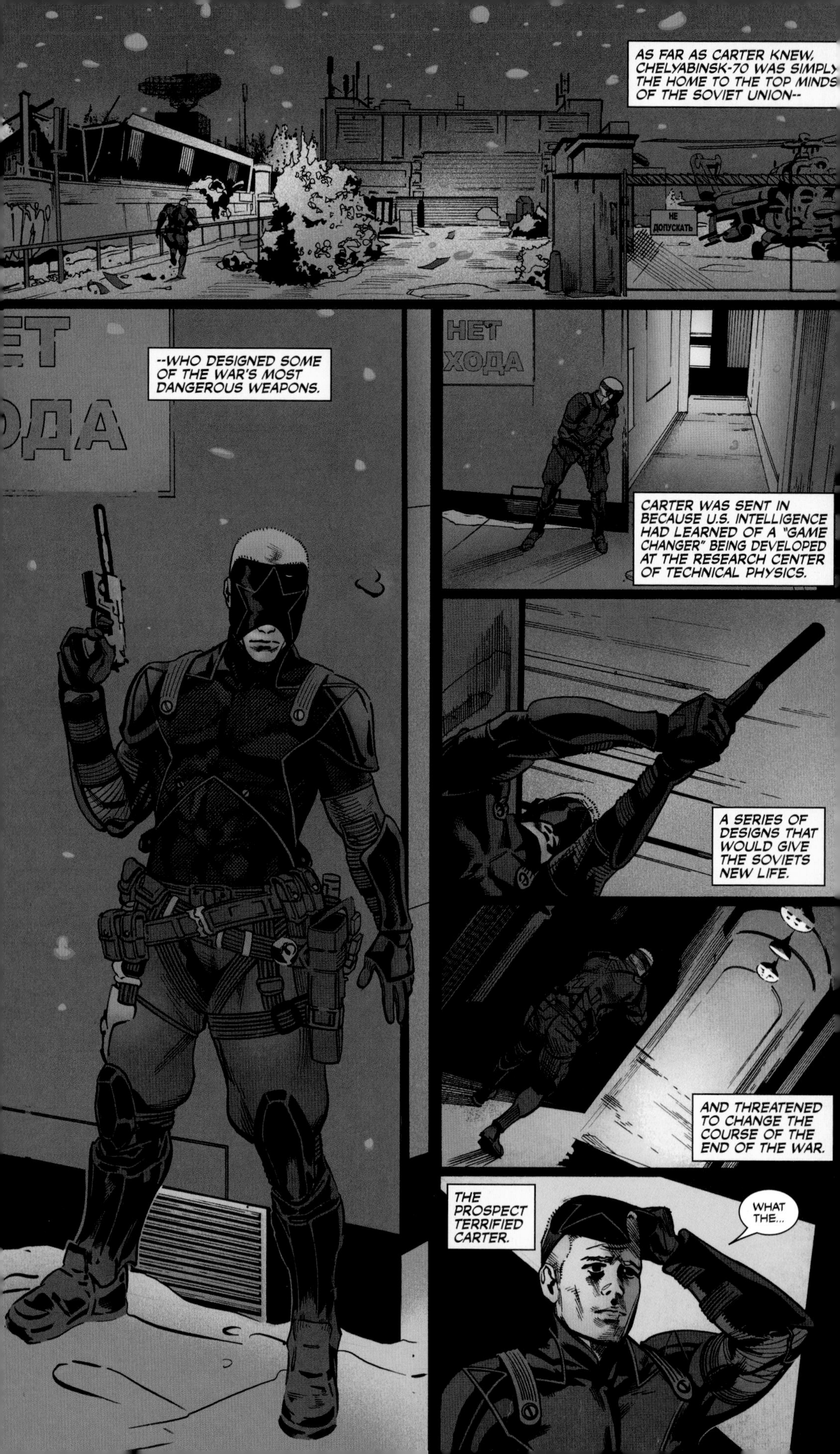
AS FAR AS CARTER KNEW, CHELYABINSK-70 WAS SIMPLY THE HOME TO THE TOP MINDS OF THE SOVIET UNION--
НЕ ДОПУСКАТЬ
НЕТ ХОДА
--WHO DESIGNED SOME OF THE WAR'S MOST DANGEROUS WEAPONS.
НЕТ ХОДА
CARTER WAS SENT IN BECAUSE U.S. INTELLIGENCE HAD LEARNED OF A "GAME CHANGER" BEING DEVELOPED AT THE RESEARCH CENTER OF TECHNICAL PHYSICS.
A SERIES OF DESIGNS THAT WOULD GIVE THE SOVIETS NEW LIFE.
AND THREATENED TO CHANGE THE COURSE OF THE END OF THE WAR.
THE PROSPECT TERRIFIED CARTER.
WHAT THE...

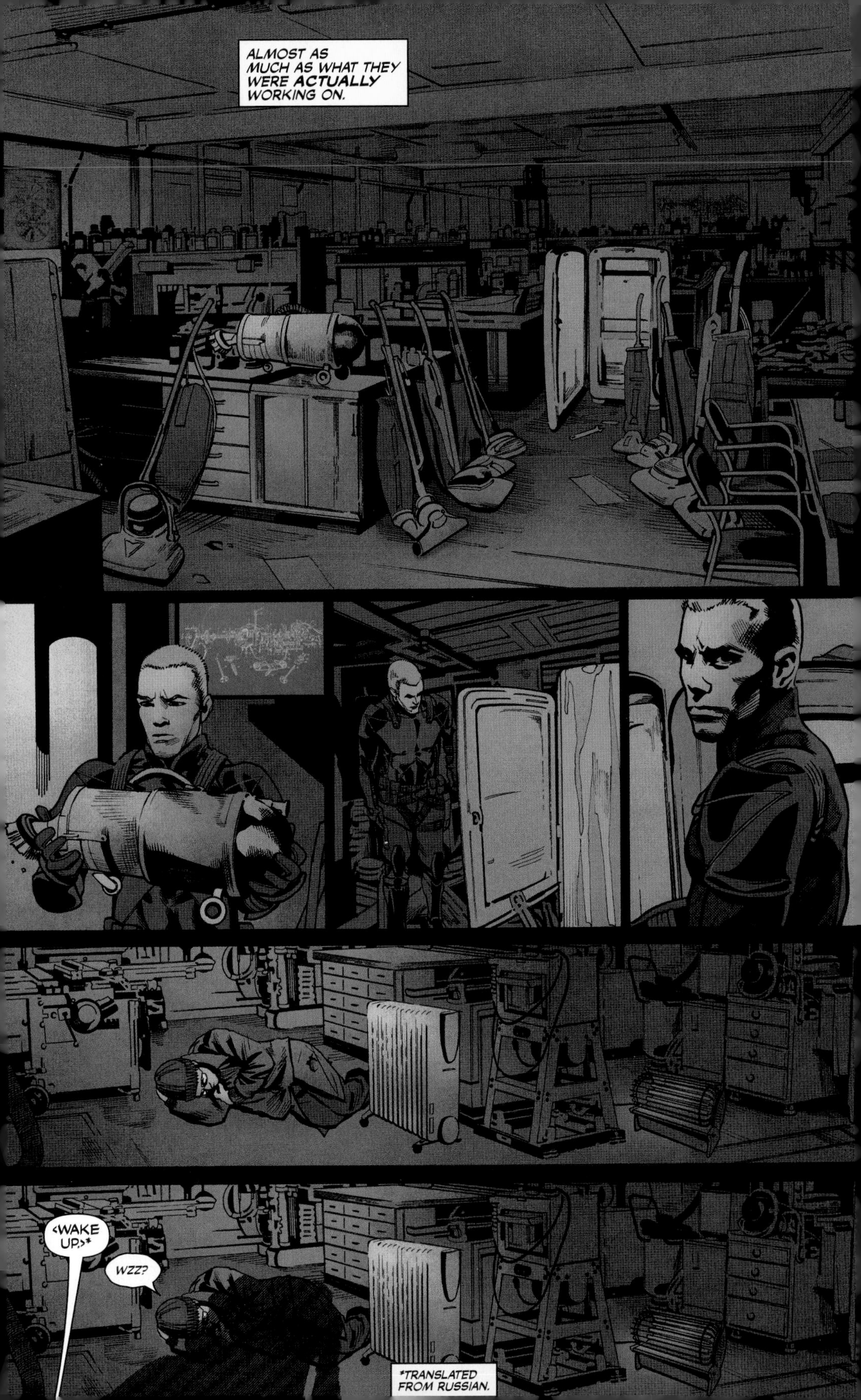
ALMOST AS MUCH AS WHAT THEY WERE **ACTUALLY** WORKING ON.
<WAKE UP.>*
WZZ?
*TRANSLATED FROM RUSSIAN.

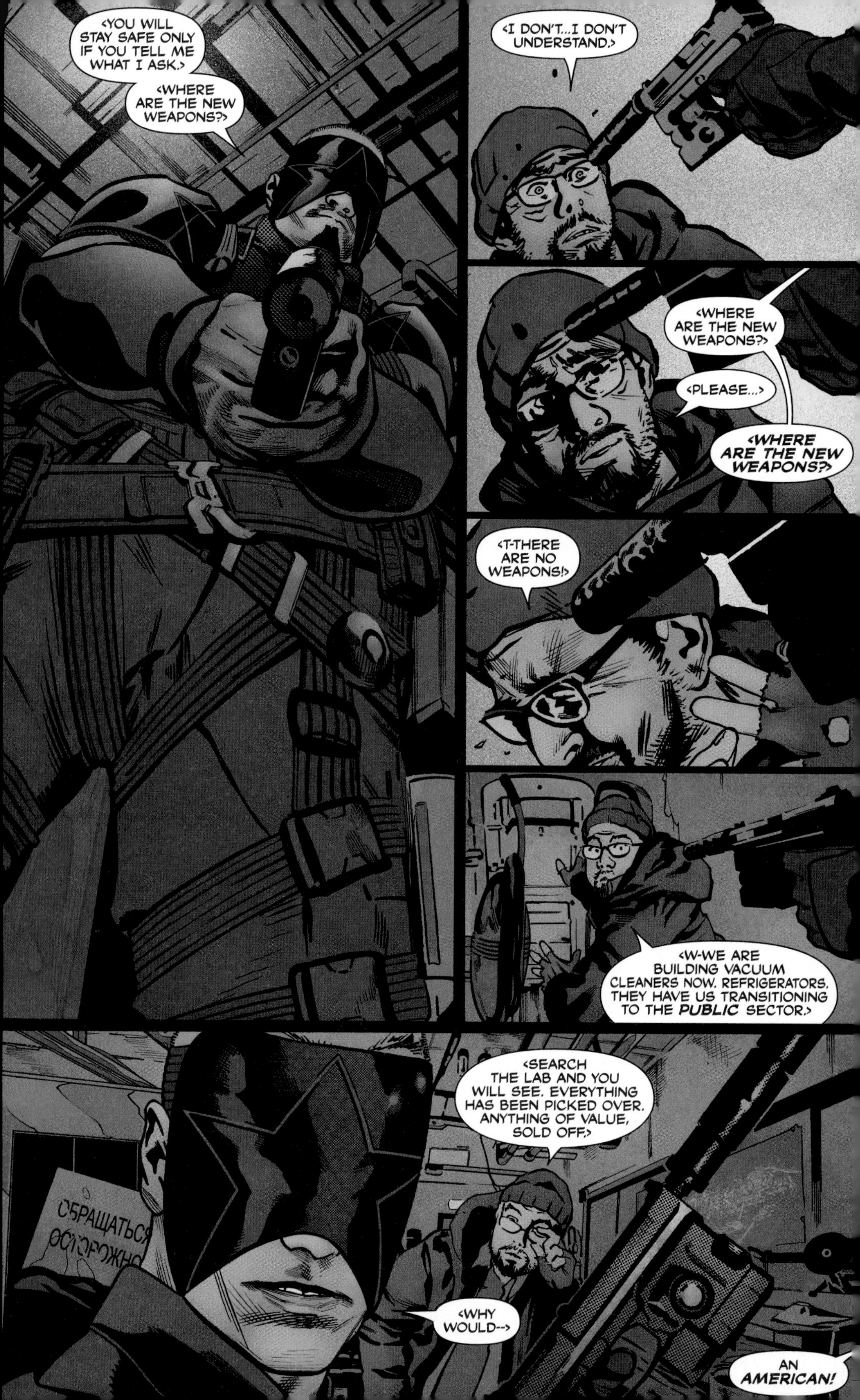
‹YOU WILL STAY SAFE ONLY IF YOU TELL ME WHAT I ASK.›
‹WHERE ARE THE NEW WEAPONS?›
‹I DON'T...I DON'T UNDERSTAND.›
‹WHERE ARE THE NEW WEAPONS?›
‹PLEASE...›
‹WHERE ARE THE NEW WEAPONS?›
‹T-THERE ARE NO WEAPONS!›
‹W-WE ARE BUILDING VACUUM CLEANERS NOW, REFRIGERATORS. THEY HAVE US TRANSITIONING TO THE *PUBLIC* SECTOR.›
‹SEARCH THE LAB AND YOU WILL SEE. EVERYTHING HAS BEEN PICKED OVER. ANYTHING OF VALUE, SOLD OFF.›
ОБРАЩАТЬСЯ ОСТОРОЖНО
‹WHY WOULD--›
AN *AMERICAN!*

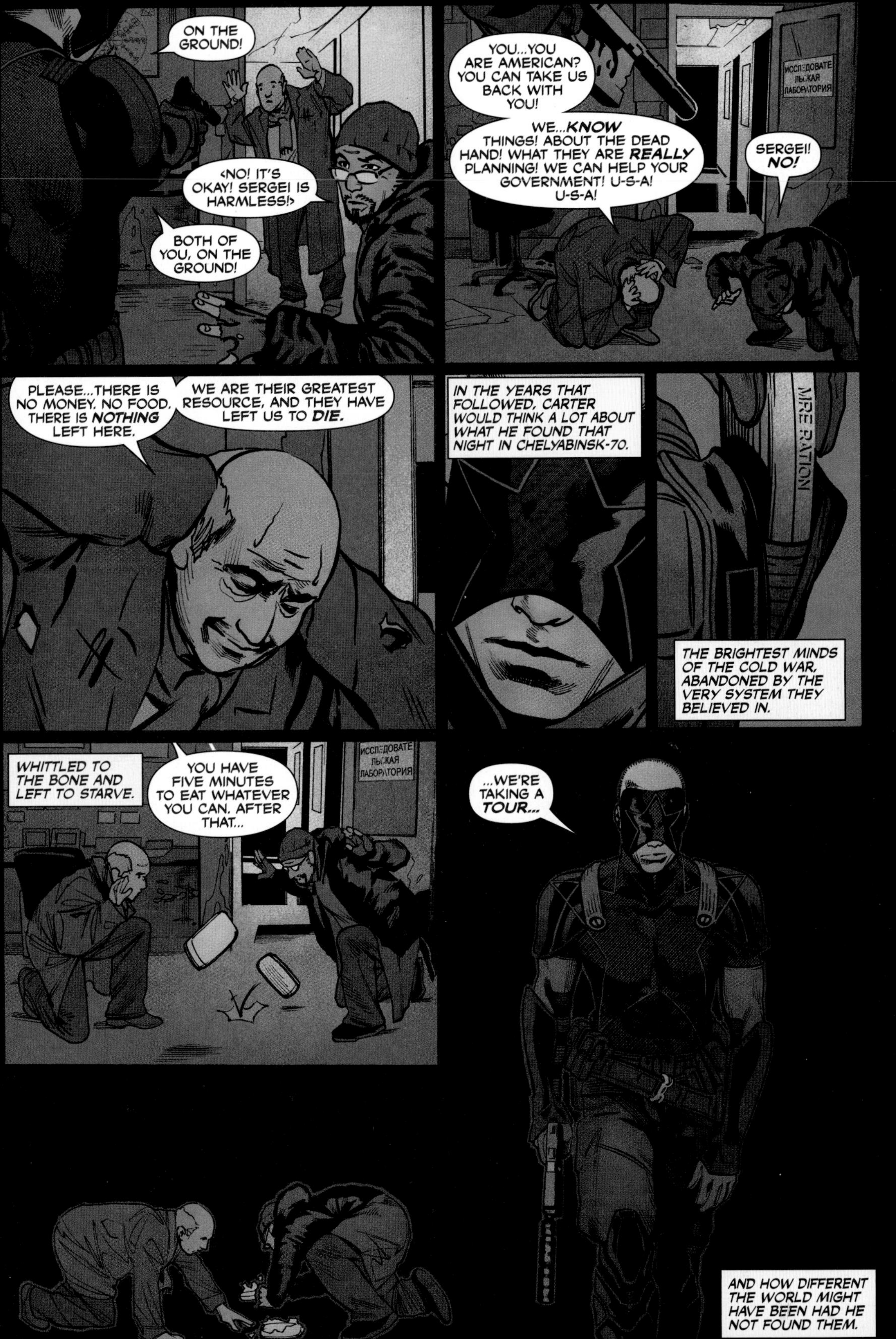

ON THE GROUND!
‹NO! IT'S OKAY! SERGEI IS HARMLESS!›
BOTH OF YOU, ON THE GROUND!
YOU...YOU ARE AMERICAN? YOU CAN TAKE US BACK WITH YOU!
WE...KNOW THINGS! ABOUT THE DEAD HAND! WHAT THEY ARE REALLY PLANNING! WE CAN HELP YOUR GOVERNMENT! U-S-A! U-S-A!
SERGEI! NO!
ИССЛЕДОВАТЕЛЬСКАЯ ЛАБОРАТОРИЯ
PLEASE...THERE IS NO MONEY, NO FOOD. THERE IS NOTHING LEFT HERE.
WE ARE THEIR GREATEST RESOURCE, AND THEY HAVE LEFT US TO DIE.
IN THE YEARS THAT FOLLOWED, CARTER WOULD THINK A LOT ABOUT WHAT HE FOUND THAT NIGHT IN CHELYABINSK-70.
MRE RATION
THE BRIGHTEST MINDS OF THE COLD WAR, ABANDONED BY THE VERY SYSTEM THEY BELIEVED IN.
WHITTLED TO THE BONE AND LEFT TO STARVE.
YOU HAVE FIVE MINUTES TO EAT WHATEVER YOU CAN. AFTER THAT...
...WE'RE TAKING A TOUR...
AND HOW DIFFERENT THE WORLD MIGHT HAVE BEEN HAD HE NOT FOUND THEM.

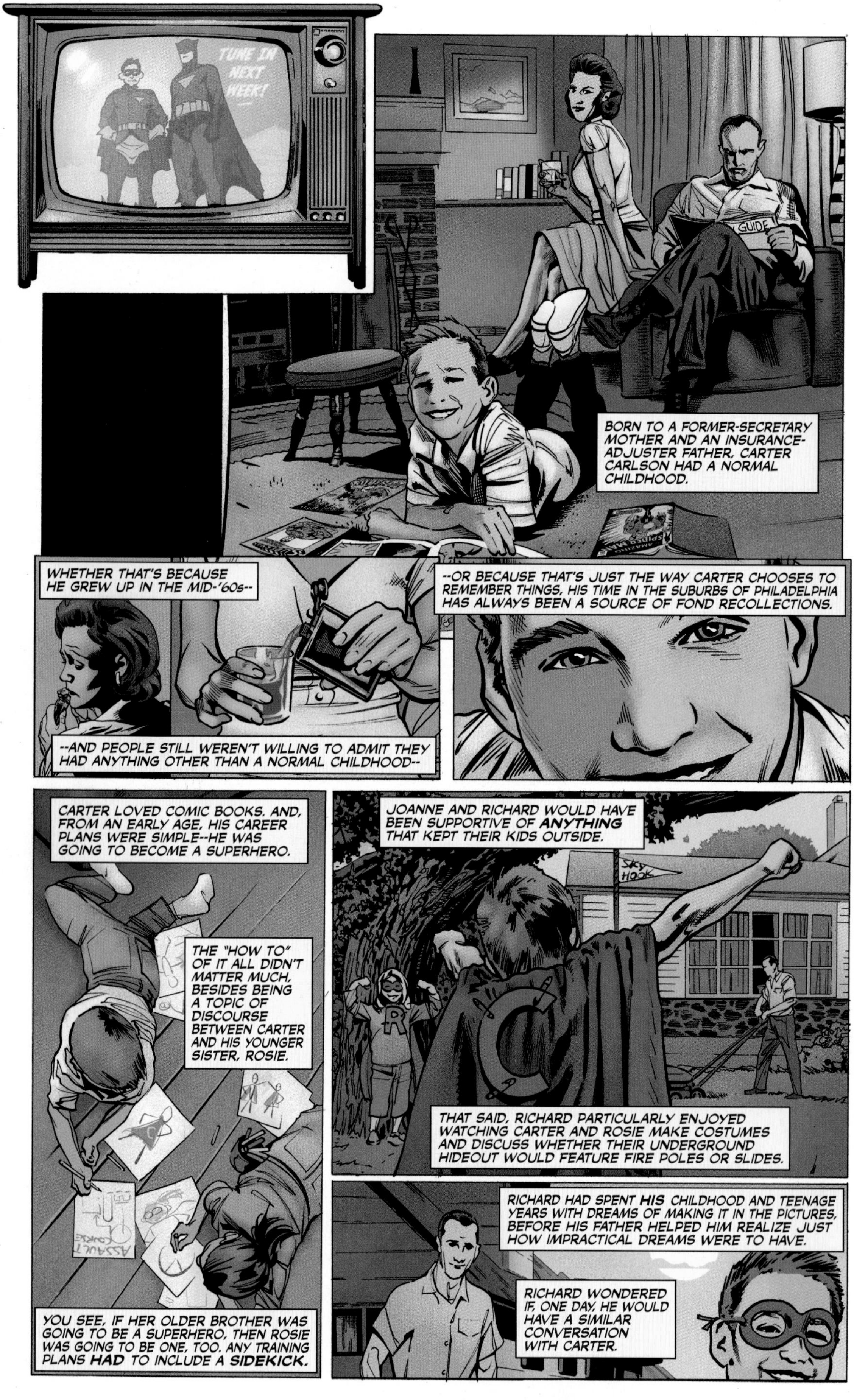

TUNE IN NEXT WEEK!
GUIDE
BORN TO A FORMER-SECRETARY MOTHER AND AN INSURANCE-ADJUSTER FATHER, CARTER CARLSON HAD A NORMAL CHILDHOOD.
WHETHER THAT'S BECAUSE HE GREW UP IN THE MID-'60s--
--AND PEOPLE STILL WEREN'T WILLING TO ADMIT THEY HAD ANYTHING OTHER THAN A NORMAL CHILDHOOD--
--OR BECAUSE THAT'S JUST THE WAY CARTER CHOOSES TO REMEMBER THINGS, HIS TIME IN THE SUBURBS OF PHILADELPHIA HAS ALWAYS BEEN A SOURCE OF FOND RECOLLECTIONS.
CARTER LOVED COMIC BOOKS. AND, FROM AN EARLY AGE, HIS CAREER PLANS WERE SIMPLE--HE WAS GOING TO BECOME A SUPERHERO.
THE "HOW TO" OF IT ALL DIDN'T MATTER MUCH, BESIDES BEING A TOPIC OF DISCOURSE BETWEEN CARTER AND HIS YOUNGER SISTER, ROSIE.
ASSAULT COURSE
YOU SEE, IF HER OLDER BROTHER WAS GOING TO BE A SUPERHERO, THEN ROSIE WAS GOING TO BE ONE, TOO. ANY TRAINING PLANS HAD TO INCLUDE A SIDEKICK.
JOANNE AND RICHARD WOULD HAVE BEEN SUPPORTIVE OF ANYTHING THAT KEPT THEIR KIDS OUTSIDE.
SKY HOOK
THAT SAID, RICHARD PARTICULARLY ENJOYED WATCHING CARTER AND ROSIE MAKE COSTUMES AND DISCUSS WHETHER THEIR UNDERGROUND HIDEOUT WOULD FEATURE FIRE POLES OR SLIDES.
RICHARD HAD SPENT HIS CHILDHOOD AND TEENAGE YEARS WITH DREAMS OF MAKING IT IN THE PICTURES, BEFORE HIS FATHER HELPED HIM REALIZE JUST HOW IMPRACTICAL DREAMS WERE TO HAVE.
RICHARD WONDERED IF, ONE DAY, HE WOULD HAVE A SIMILAR CONVERSATION WITH CARTER.

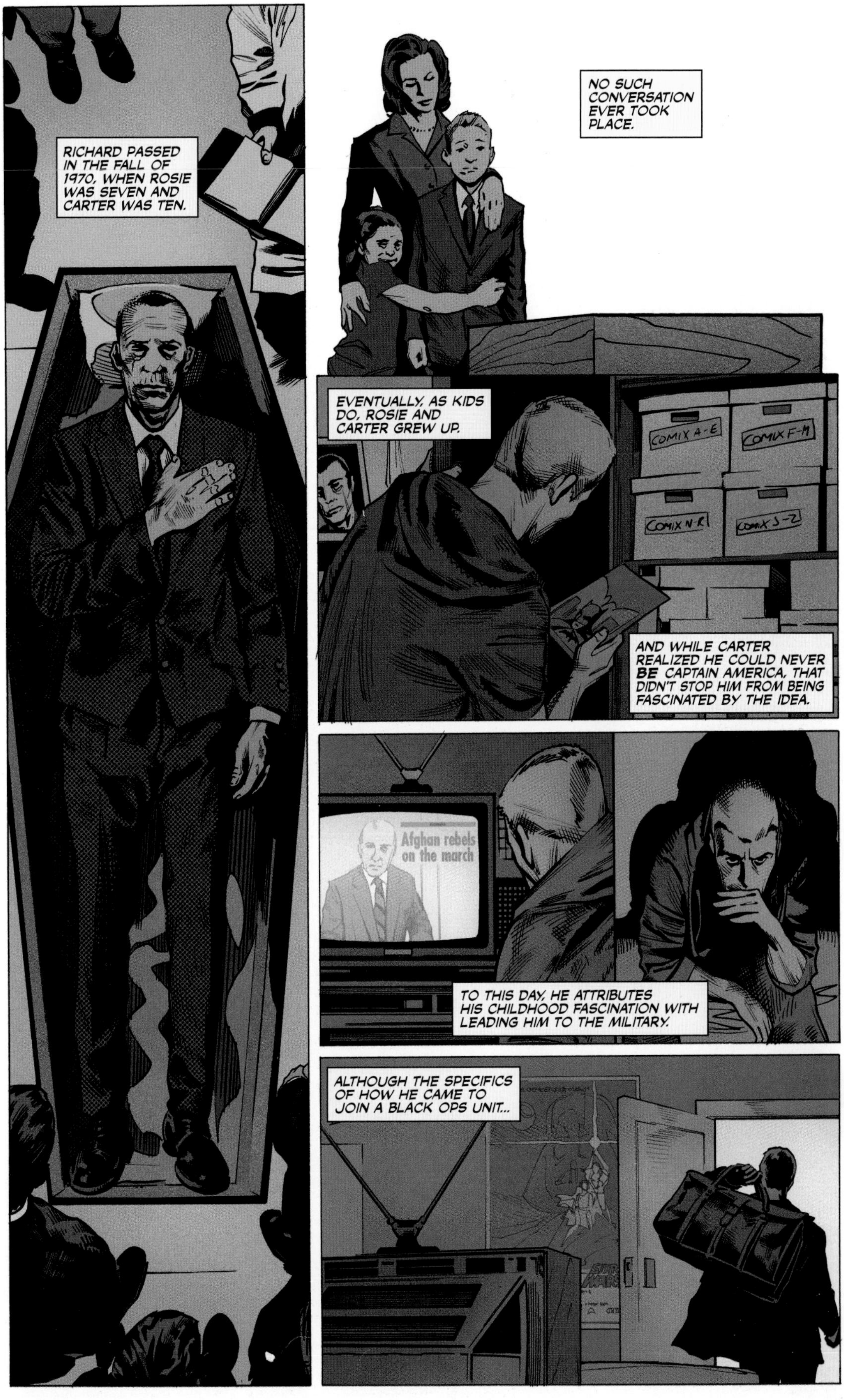
RICHARD PASSED IN THE FALL OF 1970, WHEN ROSIE WAS SEVEN AND CARTER WAS TEN.
NO SUCH CONVERSATION EVER TOOK PLACE.
EVENTUALLY, AS KIDS DO, ROSIE AND CARTER GREW UP.
COMIX A-E
COMIX F-M
COMIX N-R
COMIX S-Z
AND WHILE CARTER REALIZED HE COULD NEVER BE CAPTAIN AMERICA, THAT DIDN'T STOP HIM FROM BEING FASCINATED BY THE IDEA.
Afghan rebels on the march
TO THIS DAY, HE ATTRIBUTES HIS CHILDHOOD FASCINATION WITH LEADING HIM TO THE MILITARY.
ALTHOUGH THE SPECIFICS OF HOW HE CAME TO JOIN A BLACK OPS UNIT...

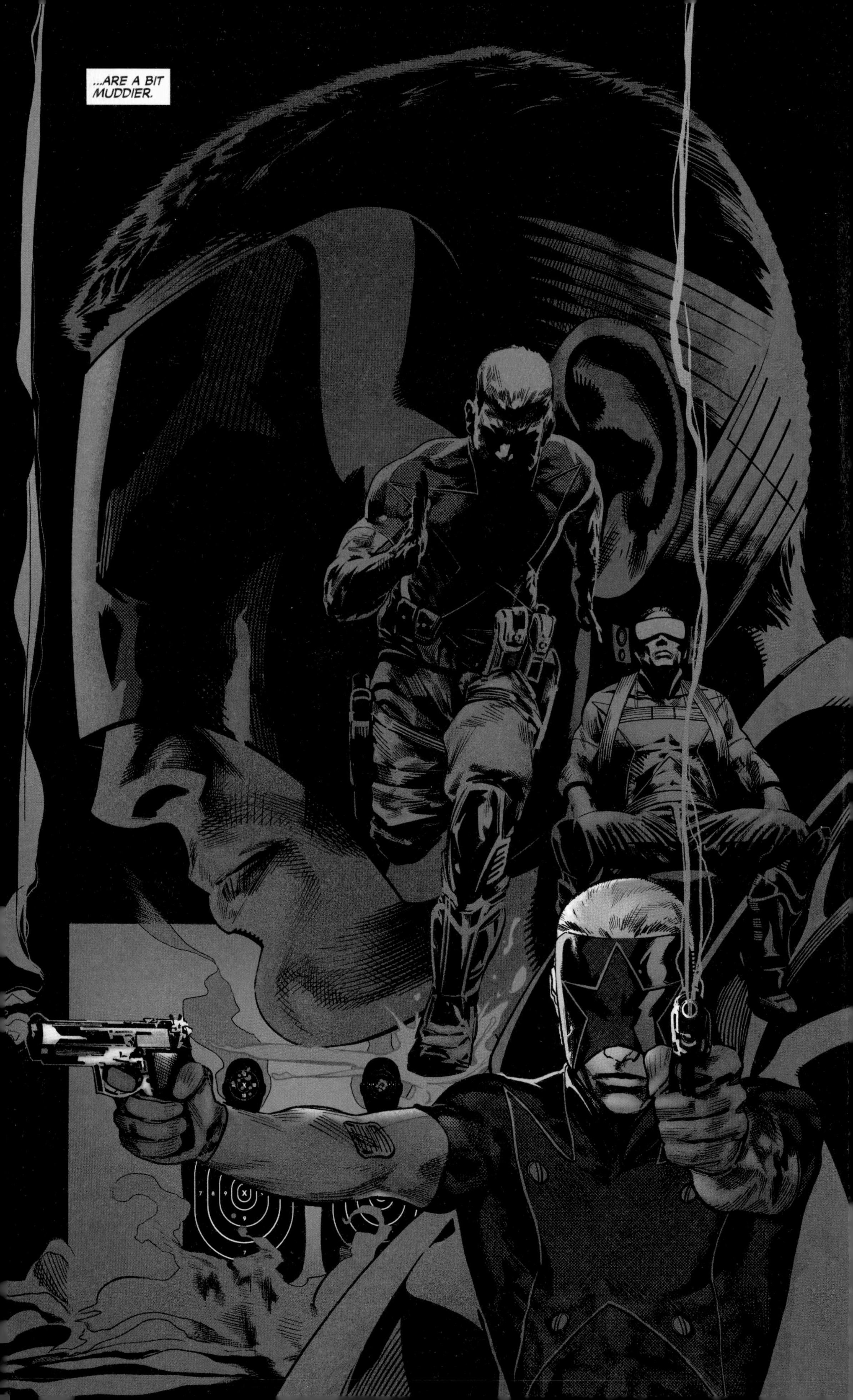
...ARE A BIT MUDDIER.

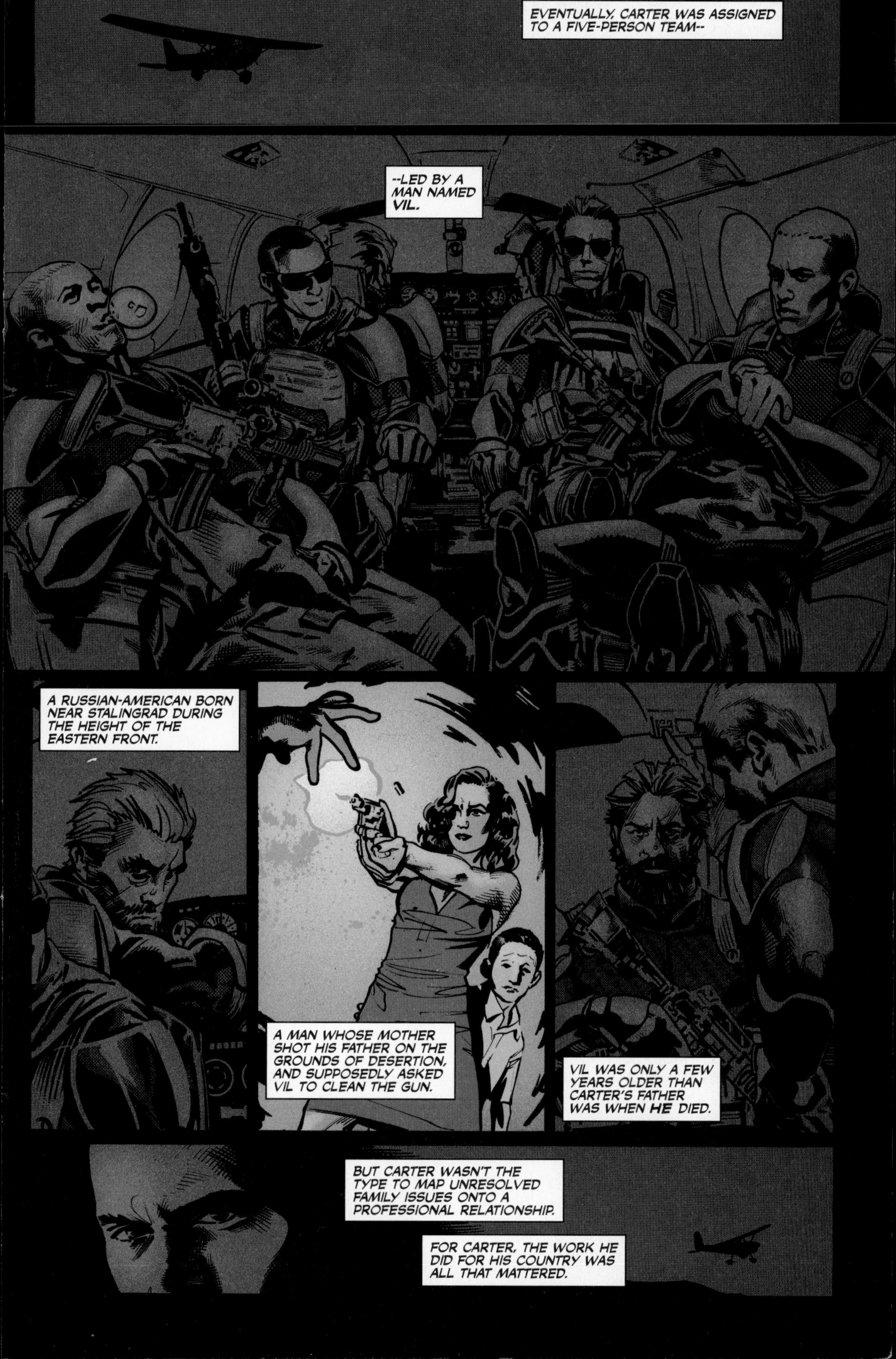
EVENTUALLY, CARTER WAS ASSIGNED TO A FIVE-PERSON TEAM--
--LED BY A MAN NAMED VIL.
A RUSSIAN-AMERICAN BORN NEAR STALINGRAD DURING THE HEIGHT OF THE EASTERN FRONT.
A MAN WHOSE MOTHER SHOT HIS FATHER ON THE GROUNDS OF DESERTION, AND SUPPOSEDLY ASKED VIL TO CLEAN THE GUN.
VIL WAS ONLY A FEW YEARS OLDER THAN CARTER'S FATHER WAS WHEN HE DIED.
BUT CARTER WASN'T THE TYPE TO MAP UNRESOLVED FAMILY ISSUES ONTO A PROFESSIONAL RELATIONSHIP.
FOR CARTER, THE WORK HE DID FOR HIS COUNTRY WAS ALL THAT MATTERED.

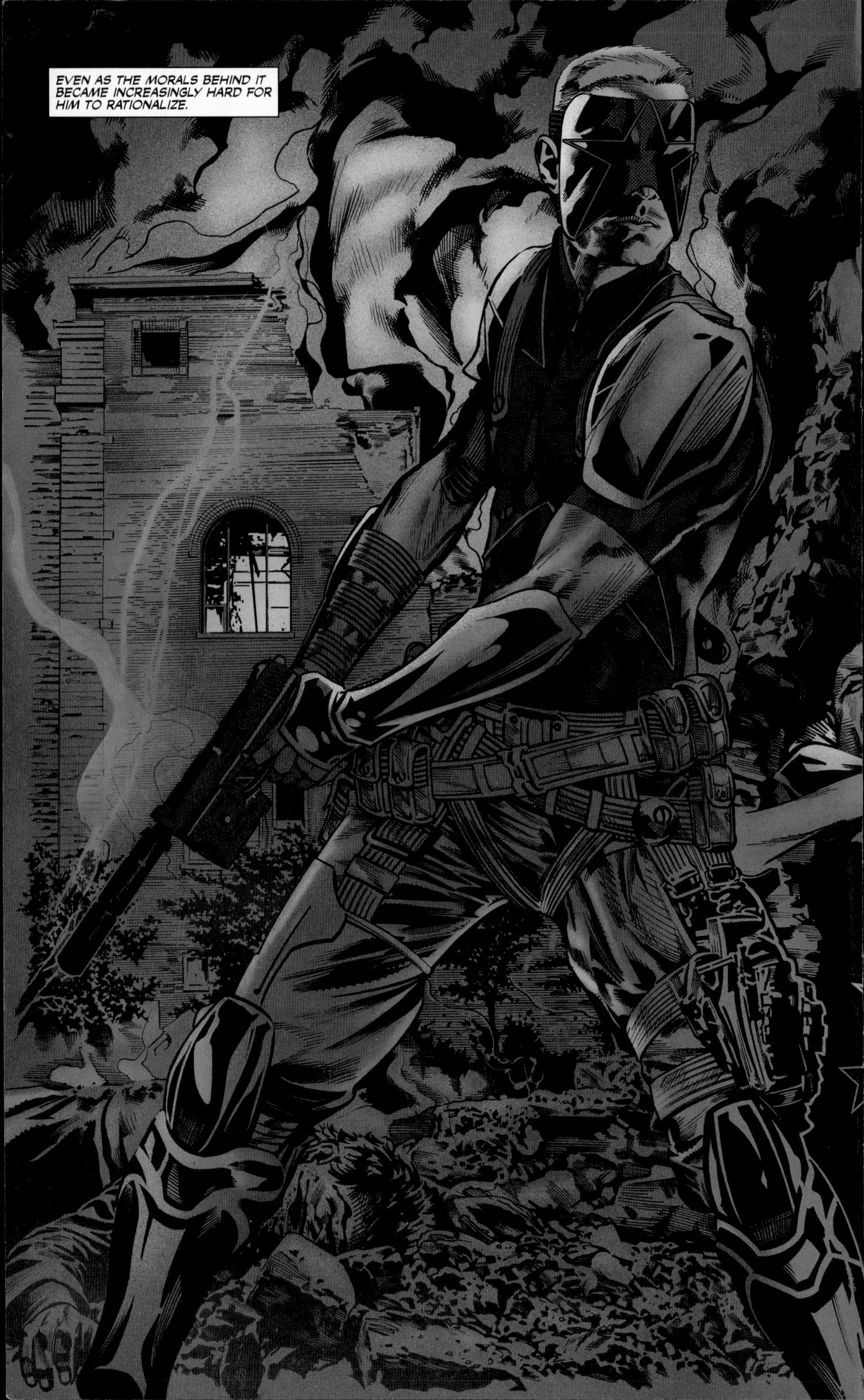
EVEN AS THE MORALS BEHIND IT BECAME INCREASINGLY HARD FOR HIM TO RATIONALIZE.

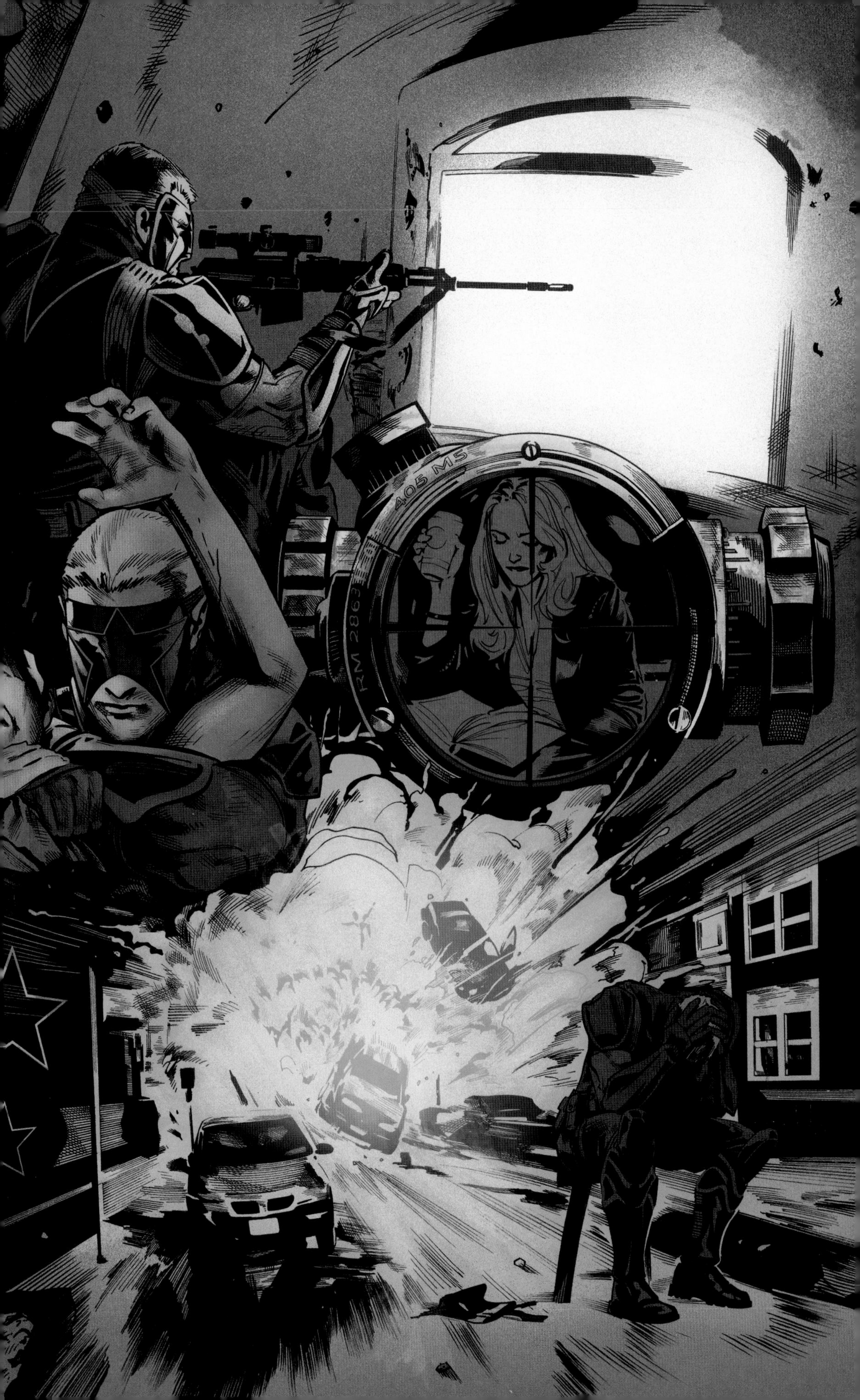
405 M5
RM 2863

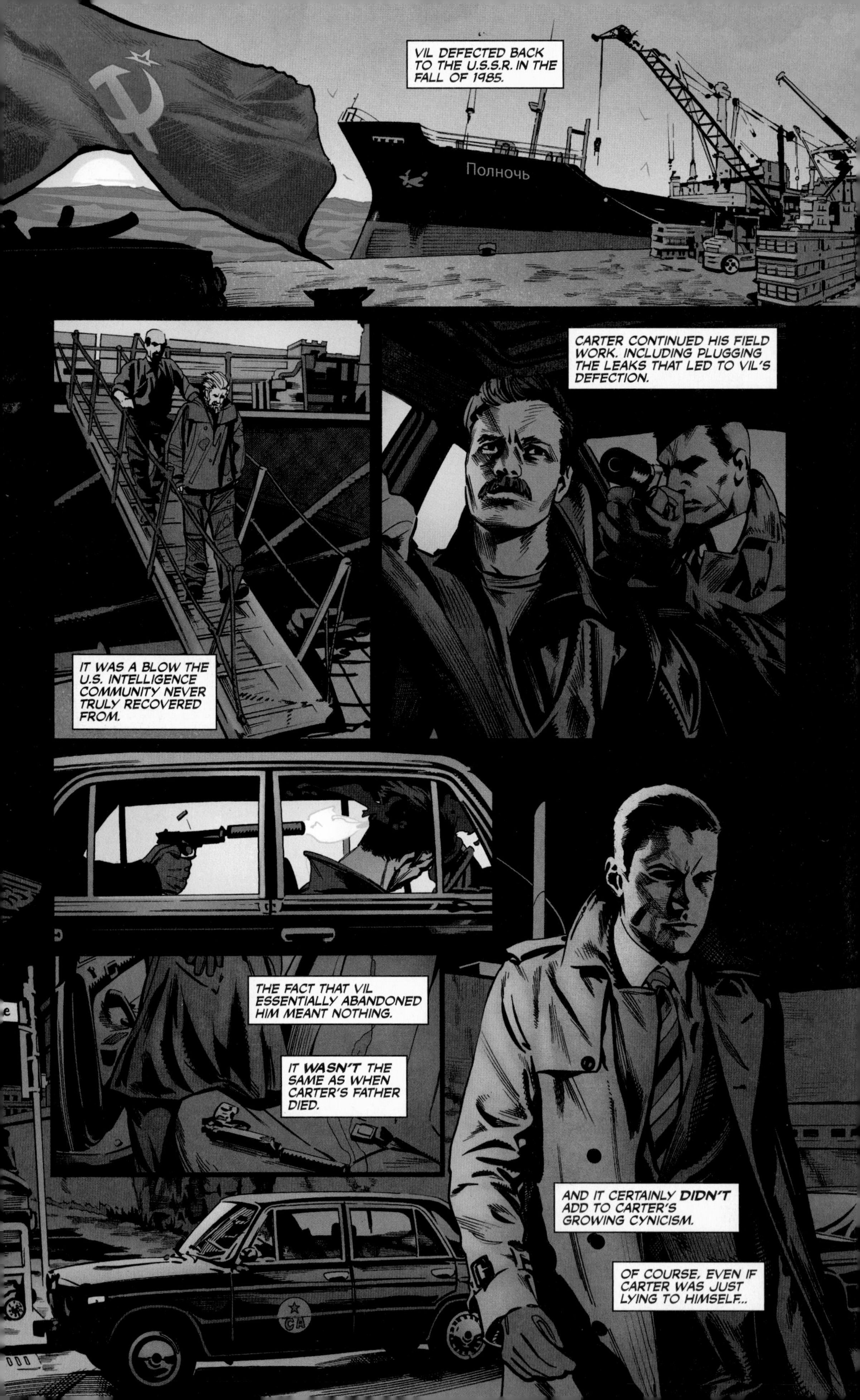
VIL DEFECTED BACK TO THE U.S.S.R. IN THE FALL OF 1985.
Полночь
IT WAS A BLOW THE U.S. INTELLIGENCE COMMUNITY NEVER TRULY RECOVERED FROM.
CARTER CONTINUED HIS FIELD WORK. INCLUDING PLUGGING THE LEAKS THAT LED TO VIL'S DEFECTION.
THE FACT THAT VIL ESSENTIALLY ABANDONED HIM MEANT NOTHING.
IT **WASN'T** THE SAME AS WHEN CARTER'S FATHER DIED.
AND IT CERTAINLY **DIDN'T** ADD TO CARTER'S GROWING CYNICISM.
OF COURSE, EVEN IF CARTER WAS JUST LYING TO HIMSELF...

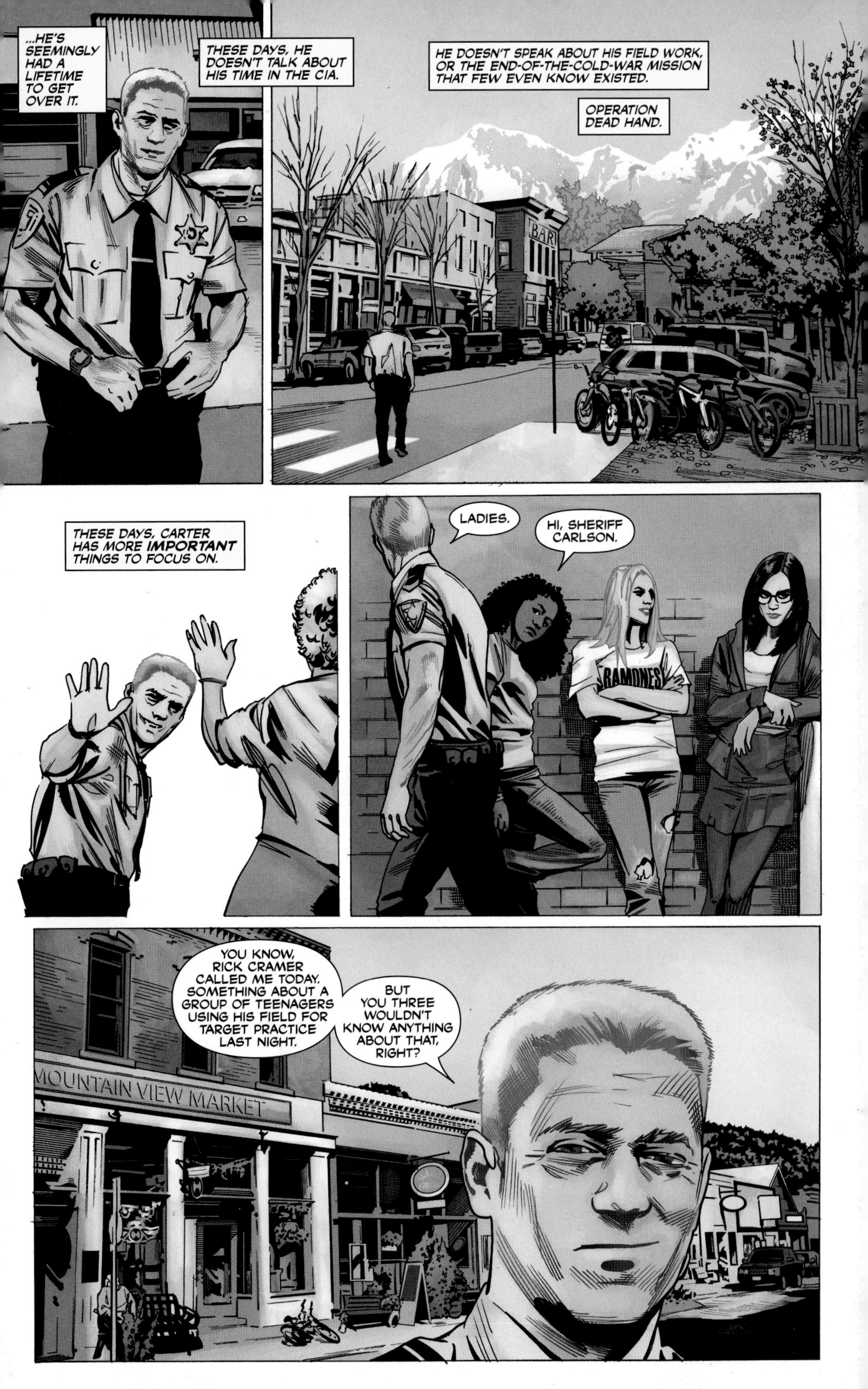
...HE'S SEEMINGLY HAD A LIFETIME TO GET OVER IT.
THESE DAYS, HE DOESN'T TALK ABOUT HIS TIME IN THE CIA.
HE DOESN'T SPEAK ABOUT HIS FIELD WORK, OR THE END-OF-THE-COLD-WAR MISSION THAT FEW EVEN KNOW EXISTED.
OPERATION DEAD HAND.
BAR
THESE DAYS, CARTER HAS MORE IMPORTANT THINGS TO FOCUS ON.
LADIES.
HI, SHERIFF CARLSON.
RAMONES
YOU KNOW, RICK CRAMER CALLED ME TODAY. SOMETHING ABOUT A GROUP OF TEENAGERS USING HIS FIELD FOR TARGET PRACTICE LAST NIGHT.
BUT YOU THREE WOULDN'T KNOW ANYTHING ABOUT THAT, RIGHT?
MOUNTAIN VIEW MARKET

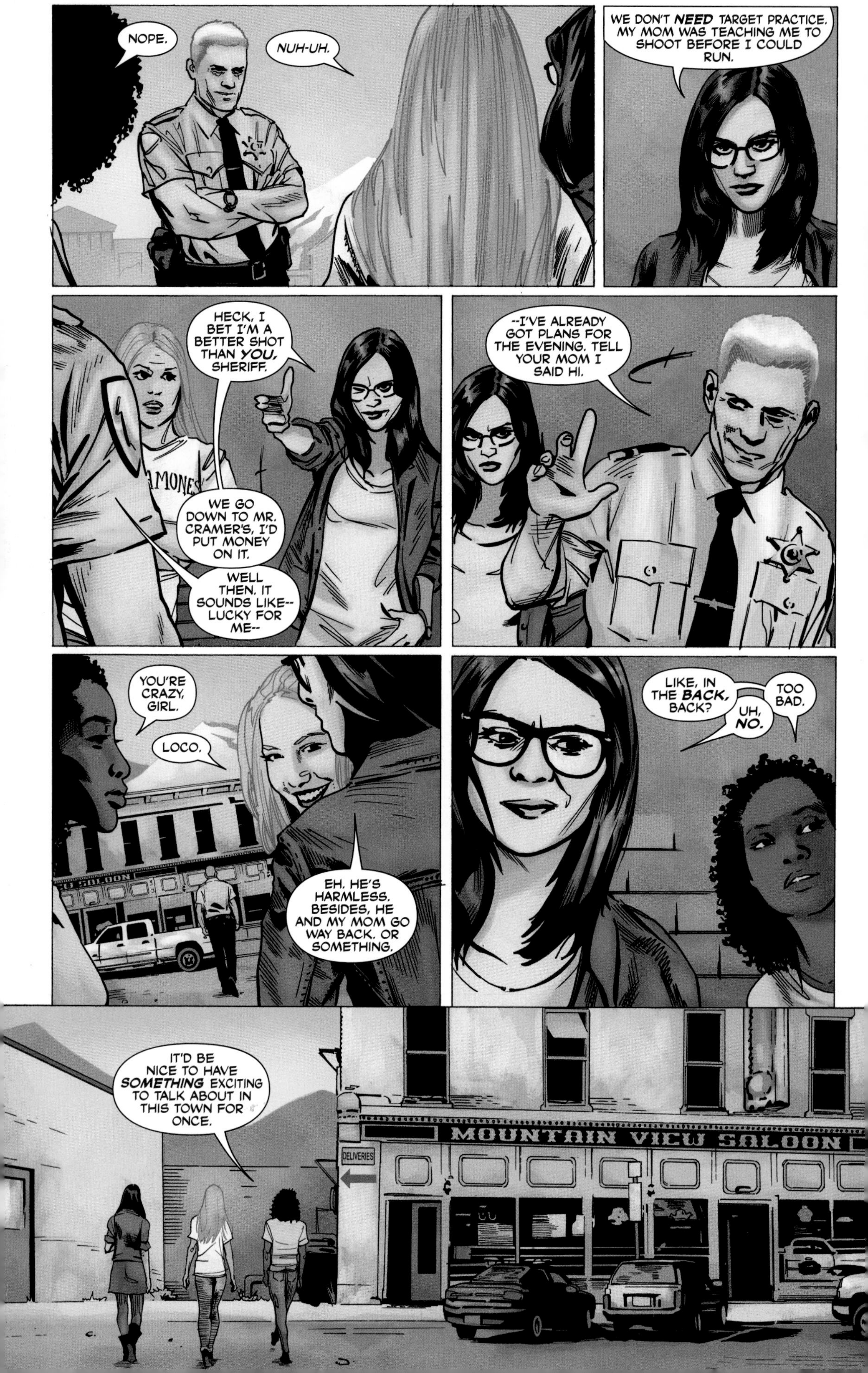
NOPE.
NUH-UH.
WE DON'T NEED TARGET PRACTICE. MY MOM WAS TEACHING ME TO SHOOT BEFORE I COULD RUN.
HECK, I BET I'M A BETTER SHOT THAN YOU, SHERIFF.
WE GO DOWN TO MR. CRAMER'S, I'D PUT MONEY ON IT.
WELL THEN. IT SOUNDS LIKE--LUCKY FOR ME--
--I'VE ALREADY GOT PLANS FOR THE EVENING. TELL YOUR MOM I SAID HI.
YOU'RE CRAZY, GIRL.
LOCO.
EH. HE'S HARMLESS. BESIDES, HE AND MY MOM GO WAY BACK. OR SOMETHING.
LIKE, IN THE BACK, BACK?
TOO BAD.
UH, NO.
IT'D BE NICE TO HAVE SOMETHING EXCITING TO TALK ABOUT IN THIS TOWN FOR ONCE.
DELIVERIES
MOUNTAIN VIEW SALOON

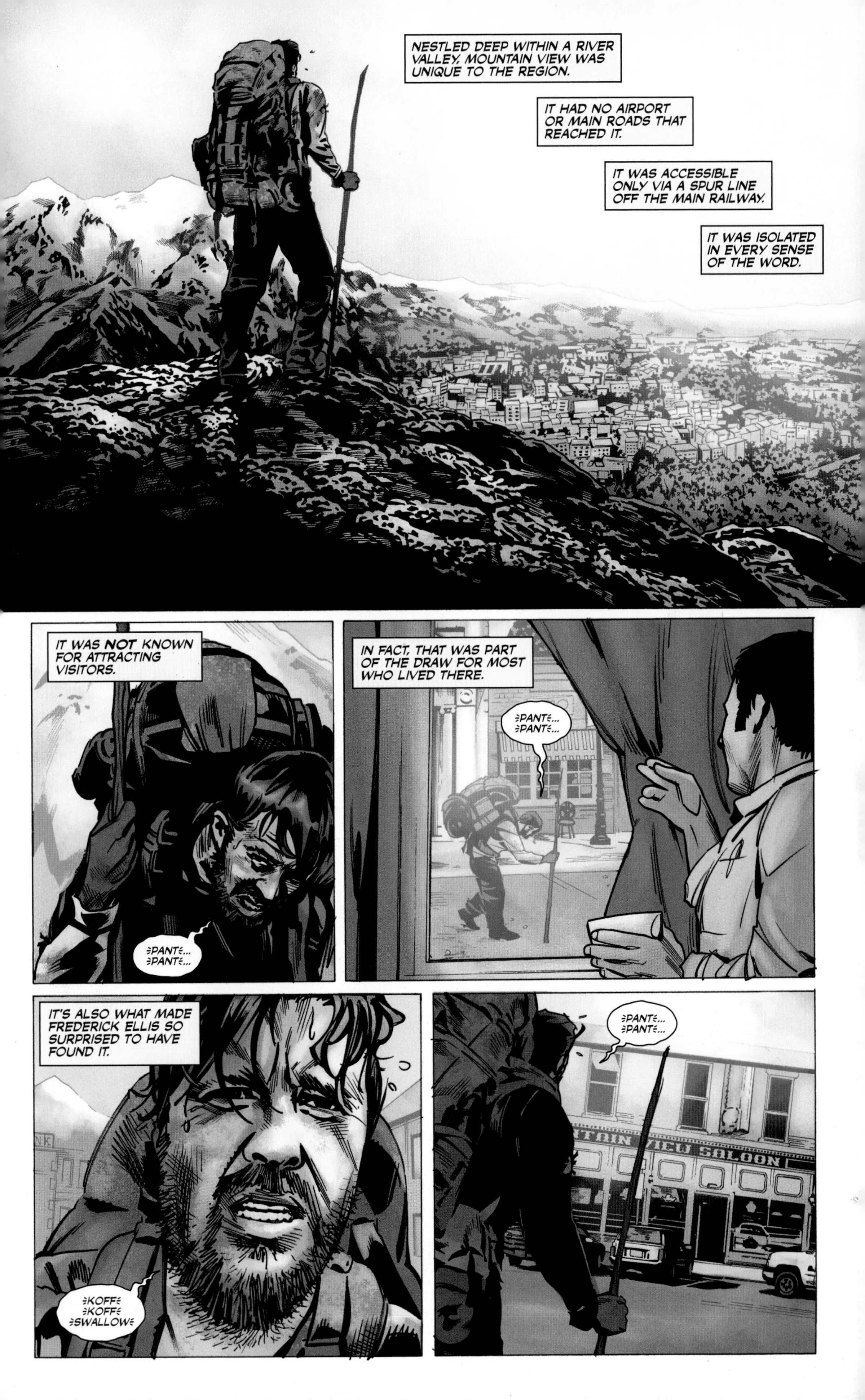

NESTLED DEEP WITHIN A RIVER VALLEY, MOUNTAIN VIEW WAS UNIQUE TO THE REGION.
IT HAD NO AIRPORT OR MAIN ROADS THAT REACHED IT.
IT WAS ACCESSIBLE ONLY VIA A SPUR LINE OFF THE MAIN RAILWAY.
IT WAS ISOLATED IN EVERY SENSE OF THE WORD.
IT WAS **NOT** KNOWN FOR ATTRACTING VISITORS.
PANT... PANT...
IN FACT, THAT WAS PART OF THE DRAW FOR MOST WHO LIVED THERE.
PANT... PANT...
IT'S ALSO WHAT MADE FREDERICK ELLIS SO SURPRISED TO HAVE FOUND IT.
KOFF KOFF SWALLOW
PANT... PANT...
SALOON

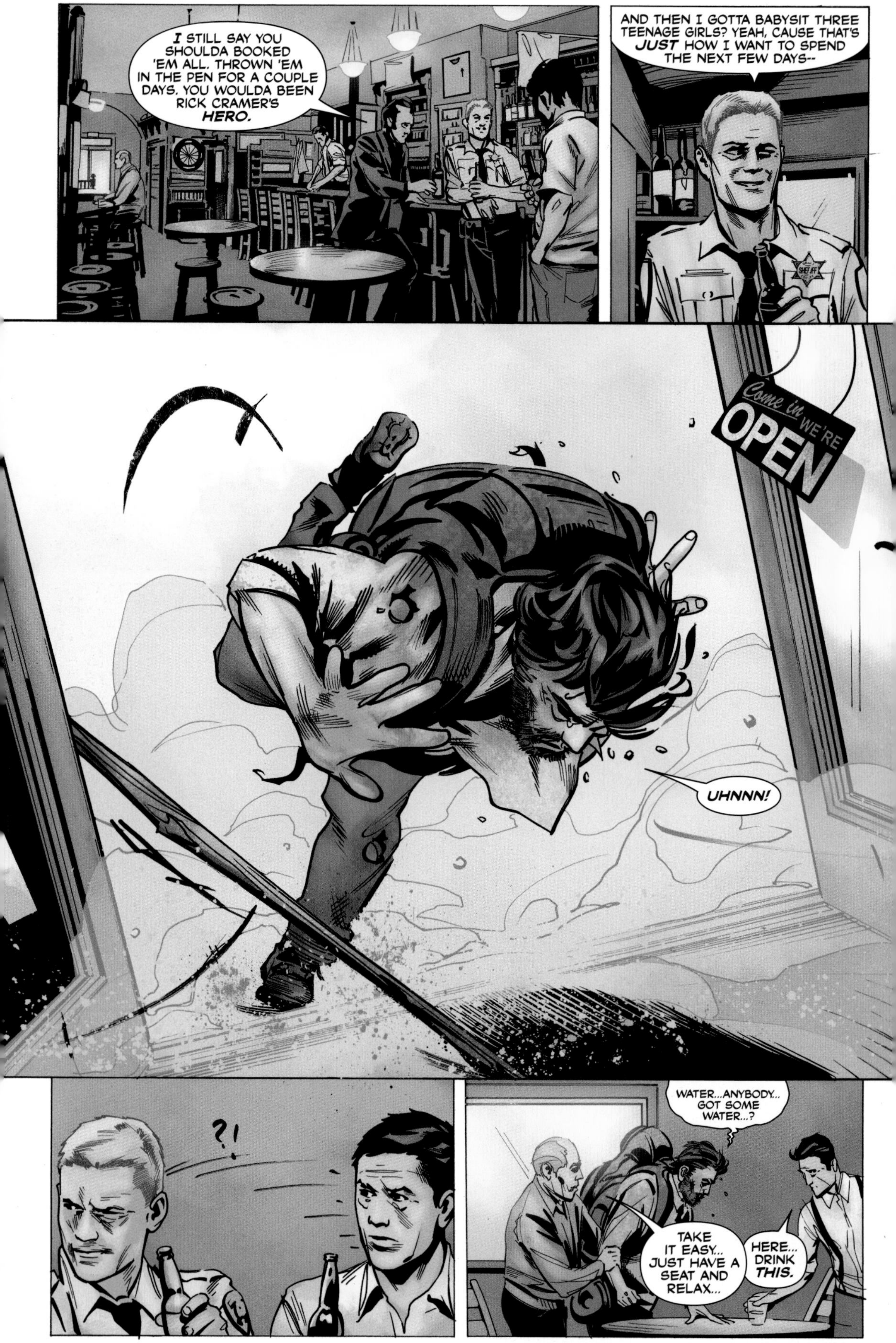
I STILL SAY YOU SHOULDA BOOKED 'EM ALL. THROWN 'EM IN THE PEN FOR A COUPLE DAYS. YOU WOULDA BEEN RICK CRAMER'S HERO.
AND THEN I GOTTA BABYSIT THREE TEENAGE GIRLS? YEAH, CAUSE THAT'S JUST HOW I WANT TO SPEND THE NEXT FEW DAYS--
Come in WE'RE OPEN
UHNNN!
?!
WATER...ANYBODY... GOT SOME WATER...?
TAKE IT EASY... JUST HAVE A SEAT AND RELAX...
HERE... DRINK THIS.

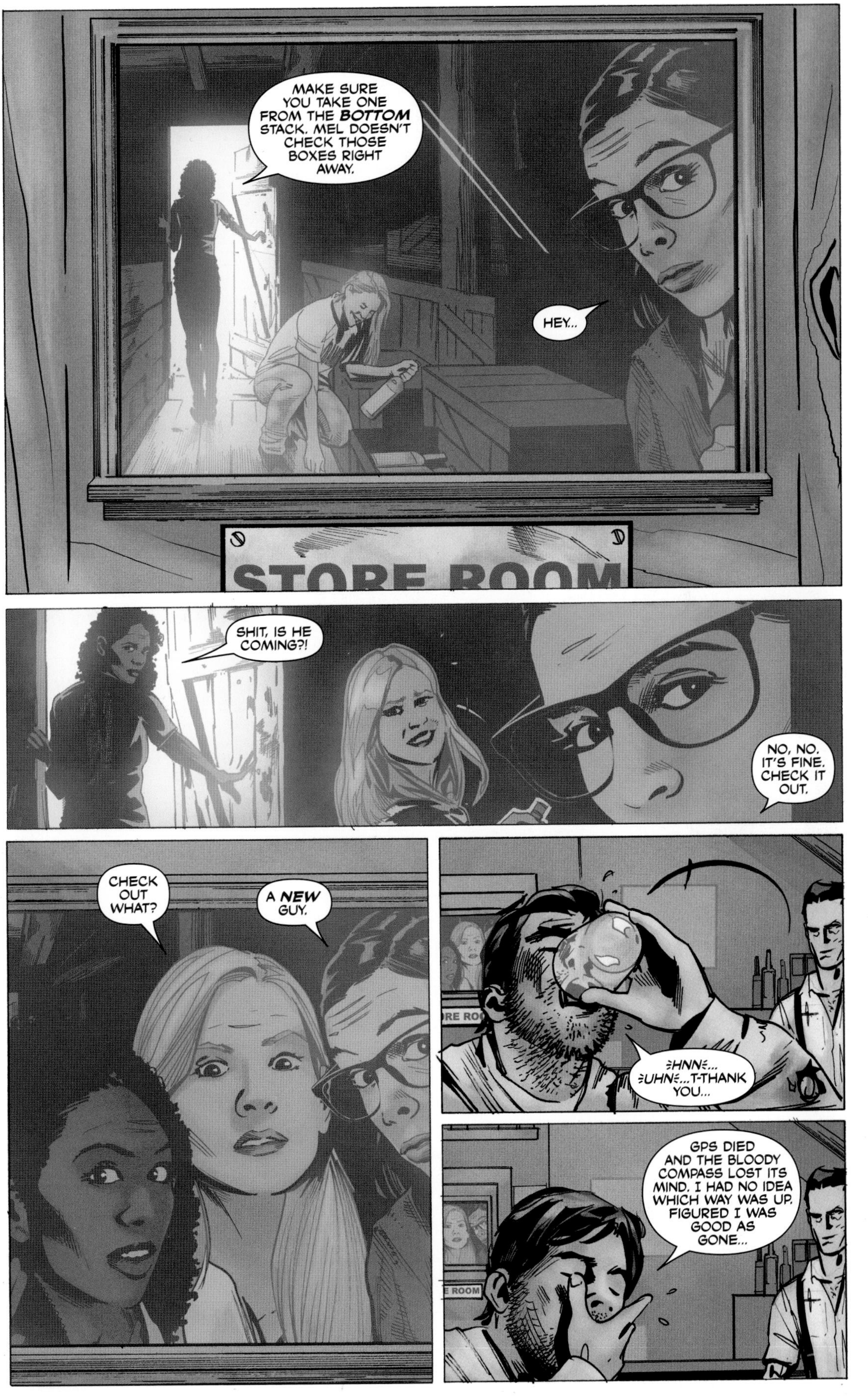
MAKE SURE YOU TAKE ONE FROM THE *BOTTOM* STACK. MEL DOESN'T CHECK THOSE BOXES RIGHT AWAY.
HEY...
STORE ROOM
SHIT, IS HE COMING?!
NO, NO. IT'S FINE. CHECK IT OUT.
CHECK OUT WHAT?
A *NEW* GUY.
HNN... UHN... T-THANK YOU...
GPS DIED AND THE BLOODY COMPASS LOST ITS MIND. I HAD NO IDEA WHICH WAY WAS UP. FIGURED I WAS GOOD AS GONE...

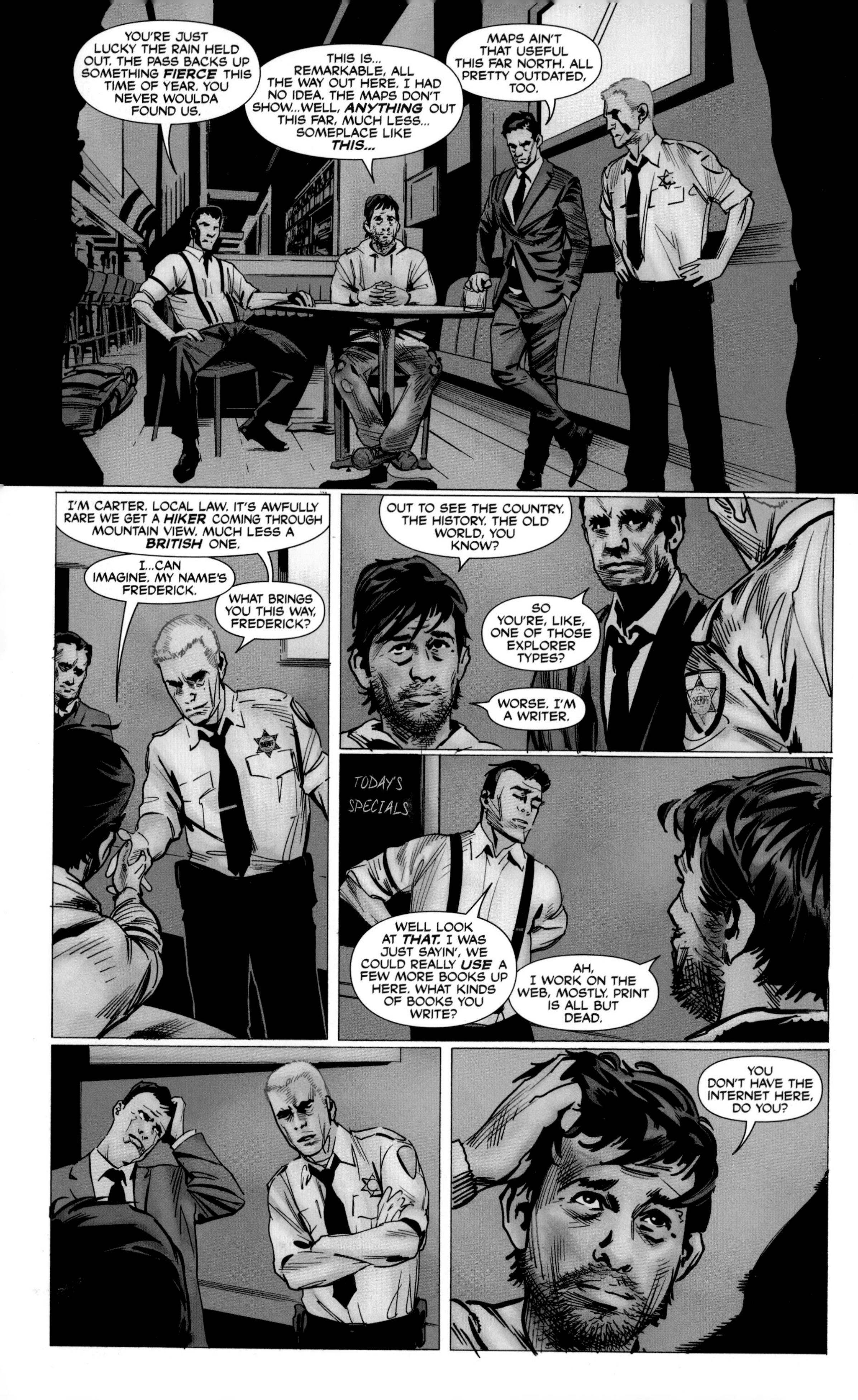
YOU'RE JUST LUCKY THE RAIN HELD OUT. THE PASS BACKS UP SOMETHING **FIERCE** THIS TIME OF YEAR. YOU NEVER WOULDA FOUND US.
THIS IS... REMARKABLE, ALL THE WAY OUT HERE. I HAD NO IDEA. THE MAPS DON'T SHOW...WELL, **ANYTHING** OUT THIS FAR, MUCH LESS... SOMEPLACE LIKE **THIS...**
MAPS AIN'T THAT USEFUL THIS FAR NORTH. ALL PRETTY OUTDATED, TOO.
I'M CARTER. LOCAL LAW. IT'S AWFULLY RARE WE GET A **HIKER** COMING THROUGH MOUNTAIN VIEW. MUCH LESS A **BRITISH** ONE.
I...CAN IMAGINE. MY NAME'S FREDERICK.
WHAT BRINGS YOU THIS WAY, FREDERICK?
SHERIFF
OUT TO SEE THE COUNTRY. THE HISTORY. THE OLD WORLD, YOU KNOW?
SO YOU'RE, LIKE, ONE OF THOSE EXPLORER TYPES?
WORSE. I'M A WRITER.
SHERIFF
TODAY'S SPECIALS
WELL LOOK AT **THAT.** I WAS JUST SAYIN', WE COULD REALLY **USE** A FEW MORE BOOKS UP HERE. WHAT KINDS OF BOOKS YOU WRITE?
AH, I WORK ON THE WEB, MOSTLY. PRINT IS ALL BUT DEAD.
YOU DON'T HAVE THE INTERNET HERE, DO YOU?

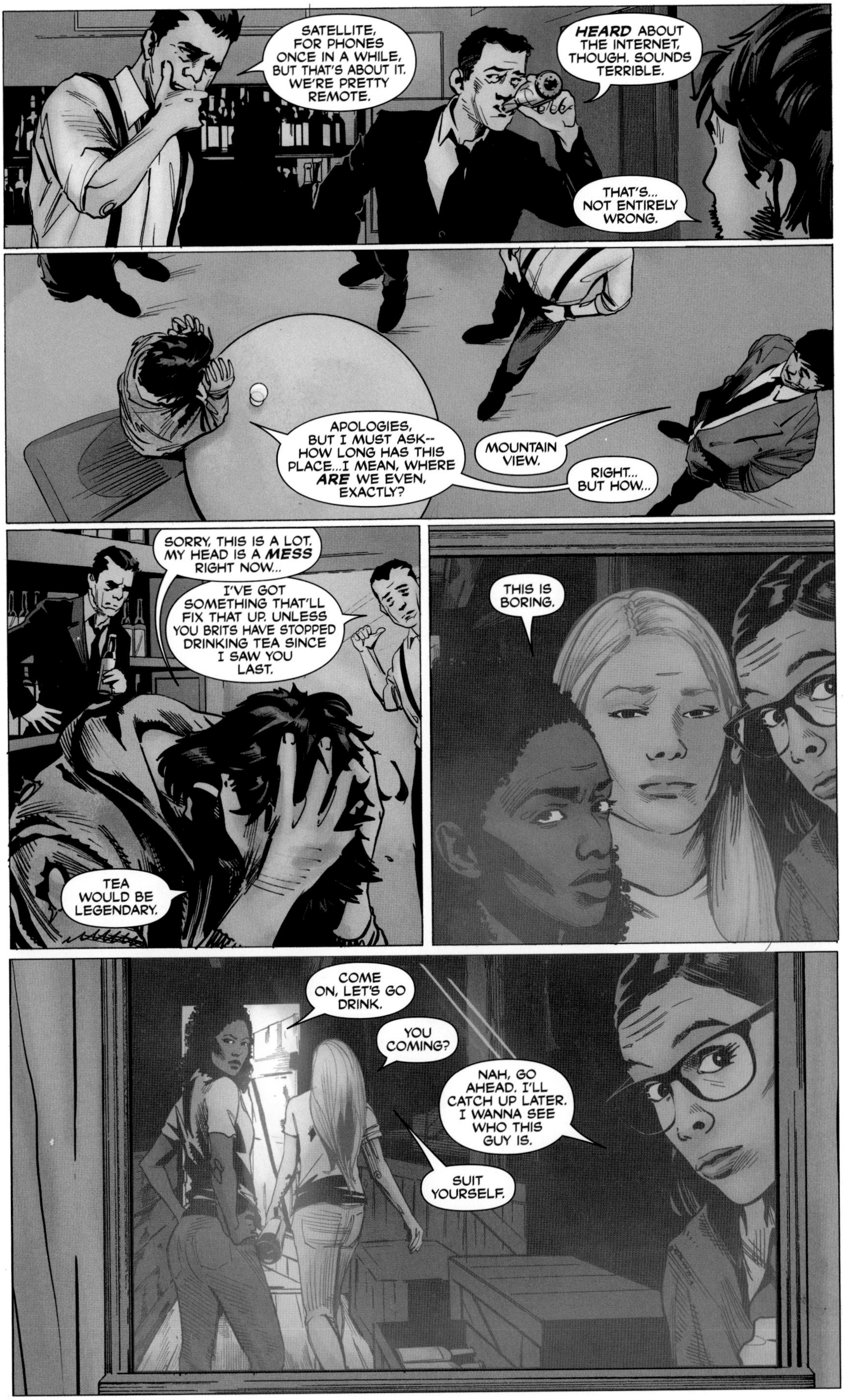
SATELLITE, FOR PHONES ONCE IN A WHILE, BUT THAT'S ABOUT IT. WE'RE PRETTY REMOTE.
HEARD ABOUT THE INTERNET, THOUGH. SOUNDS TERRIBLE.
THAT'S... NOT ENTIRELY WRONG.
APOLOGIES, BUT I MUST ASK-- HOW LONG HAS THIS PLACE...I MEAN, WHERE ARE WE EVEN, EXACTLY?
MOUNTAIN VIEW.
RIGHT... BUT HOW...
SORRY, THIS IS A LOT. MY HEAD IS A MESS RIGHT NOW...
I'VE GOT SOMETHING THAT'LL FIX THAT UP. UNLESS YOU BRITS HAVE STOPPED DRINKING TEA SINCE I SAW YOU LAST.
TEA WOULD BE LEGENDARY.
THIS IS BORING.
COME ON, LET'S GO DRINK.
YOU COMING?
NAH, GO AHEAD. I'LL CATCH UP LATER. I WANNA SEE WHO THIS GUY IS.
SUIT YOURSELF.

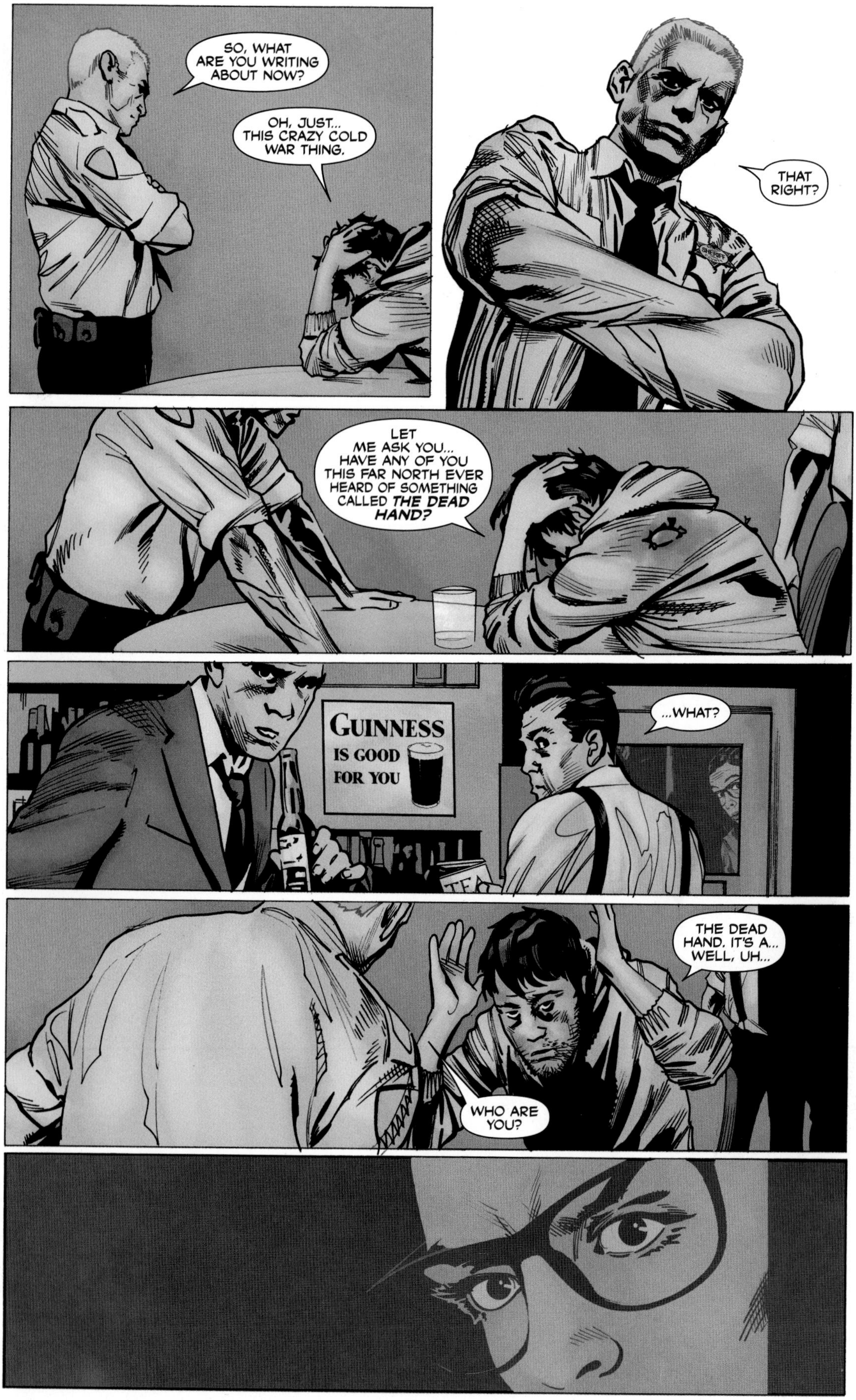
SO, WHAT ARE YOU WRITING ABOUT NOW?
OH, JUST... THIS CRAZY COLD WAR THING.
THAT RIGHT?
LET ME ASK YOU... HAVE ANY OF YOU THIS FAR NORTH EVER HEARD OF SOMETHING CALLED ***THE DEAD HAND?***
GUINNESS IS GOOD FOR YOU
...WHAT?
THE DEAD HAND. IT'S A... WELL, UH...
WHO ARE YOU?

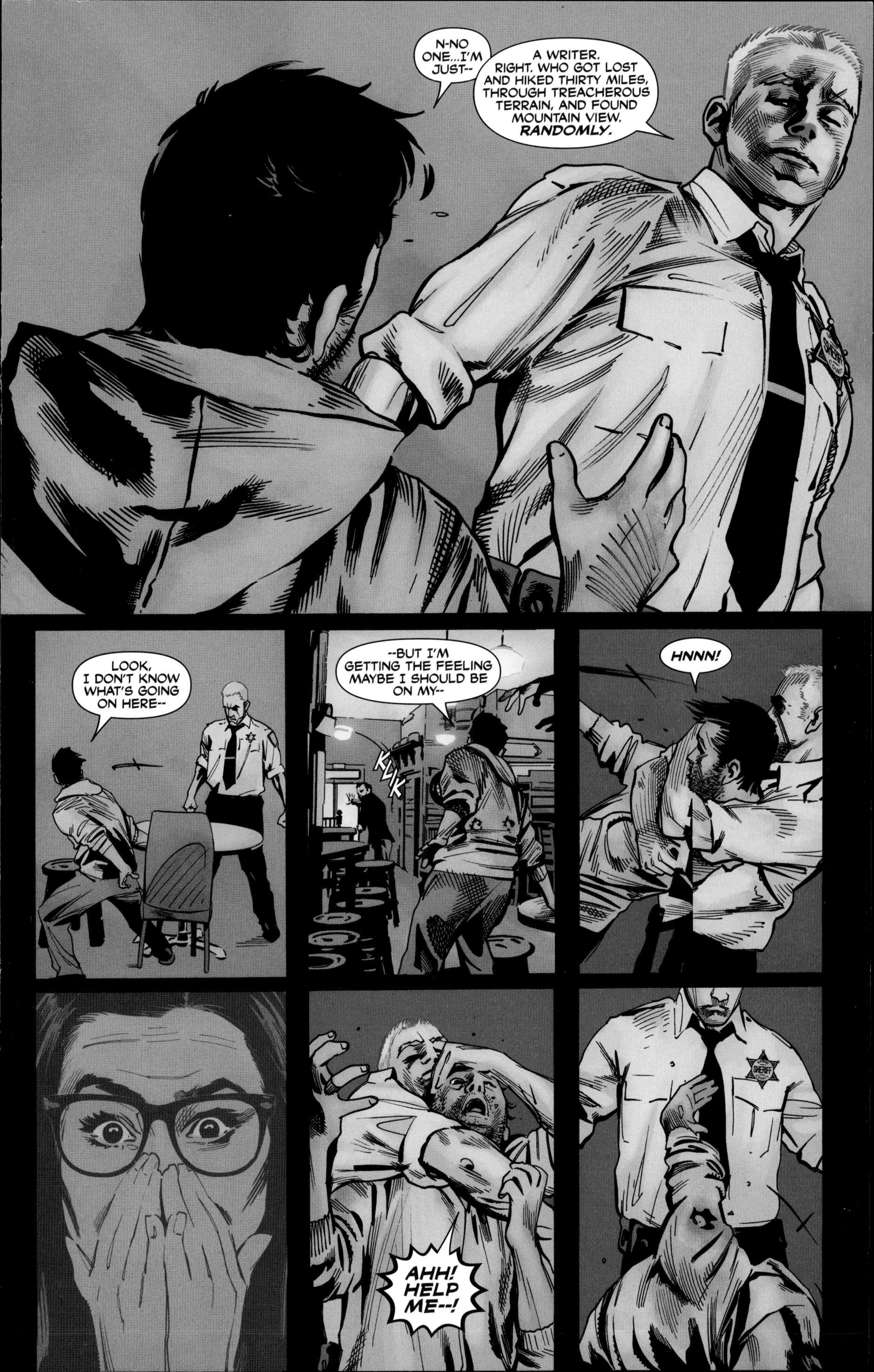
N-NO ONE...I'M JUST--
A WRITER. RIGHT. WHO GOT LOST AND HIKED THIRTY MILES, THROUGH TREACHEROUS TERRAIN, AND FOUND MOUNTAIN VIEW. RANDOMLY.
LOOK, I DON'T KNOW WHAT'S GOING ON HERE--
--BUT I'M GETTING THE FEELING MAYBE I SHOULD BE ON MY--
KLIK
HNNN!
SHERIFF
AHH! HELP ME--!

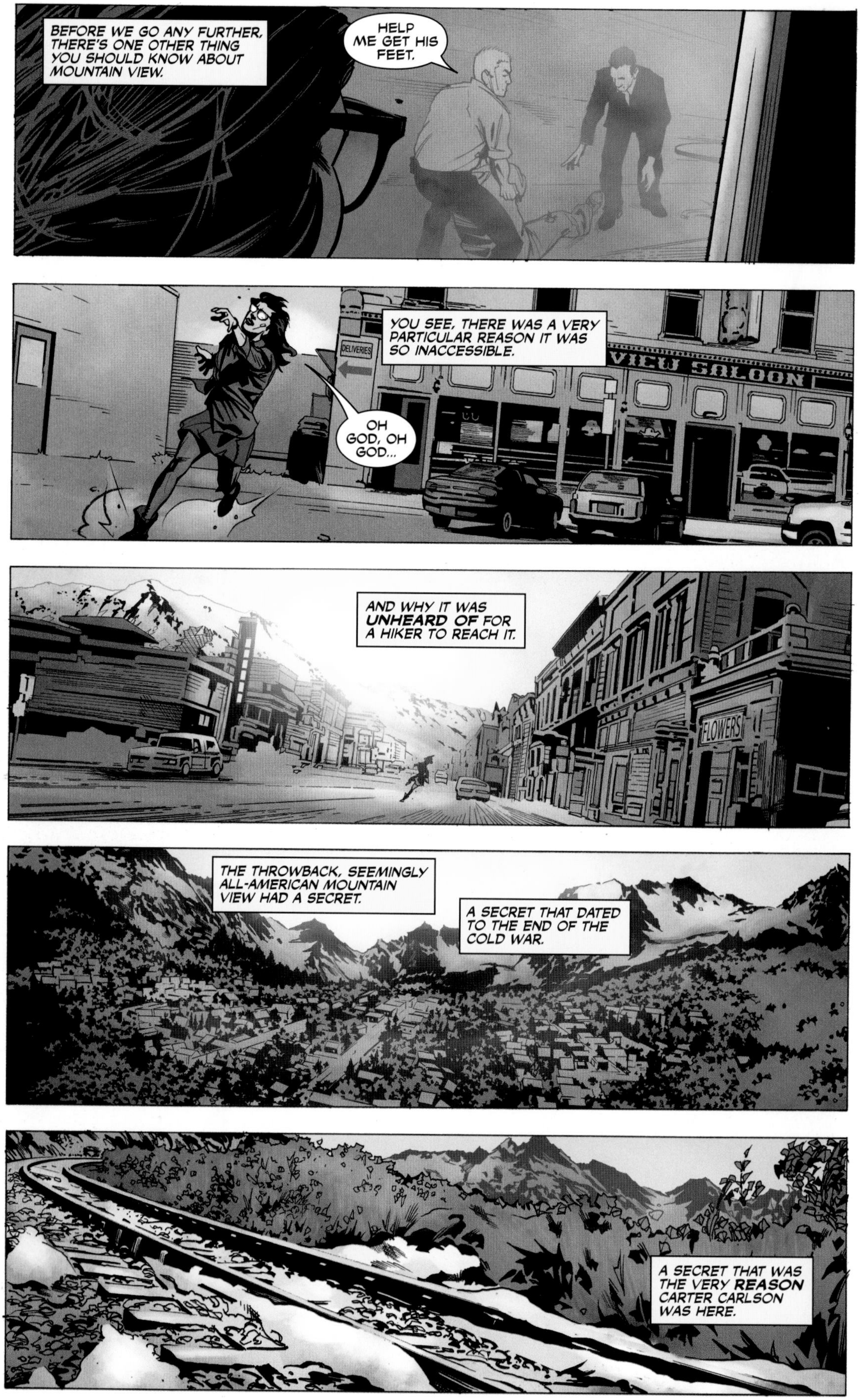
BEFORE WE GO ANY FURTHER, THERE'S ONE OTHER THING YOU SHOULD KNOW ABOUT MOUNTAIN VIEW.
HELP ME GET HIS FEET.
DELIVERIES
YOU SEE, THERE WAS A VERY PARTICULAR REASON IT WAS SO INACCESSIBLE.
VIEW SALOON
OH GOD, OH GOD...
AND WHY IT WAS **UNHEARD OF** FOR A HIKER TO REACH IT.
FLOWERS
THE THROWBACK, SEEMINGLY ALL-AMERICAN MOUNTAIN VIEW HAD A SECRET.
A SECRET THAT DATED TO THE END OF THE COLD WAR.
A SECRET THAT WAS THE VERY **REASON** CARTER CARLSON WAS HERE.

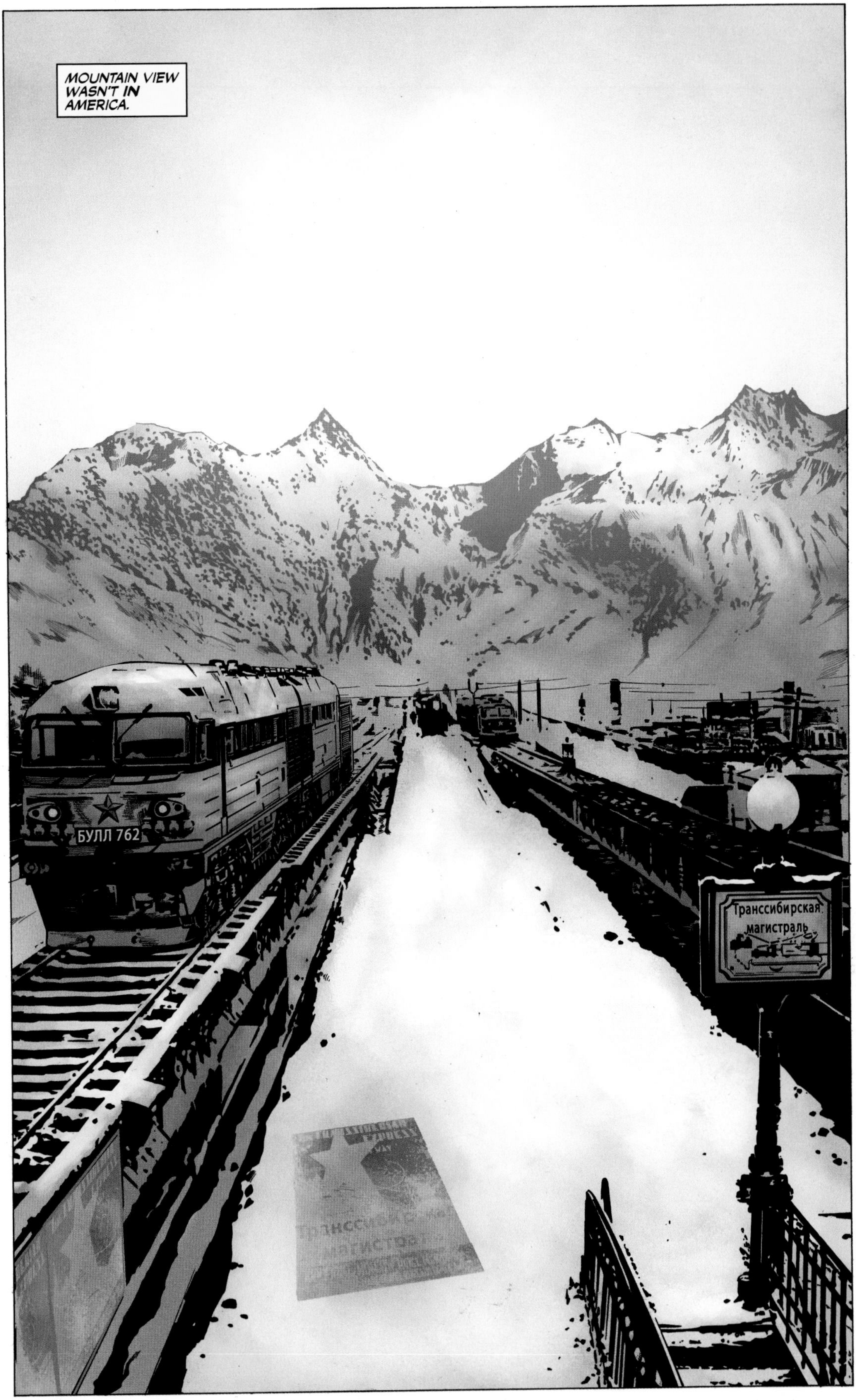
MOUNTAIN VIEW WASN'T IN AMERICA.
БУЛЛ 762
Транссибирская магистраль

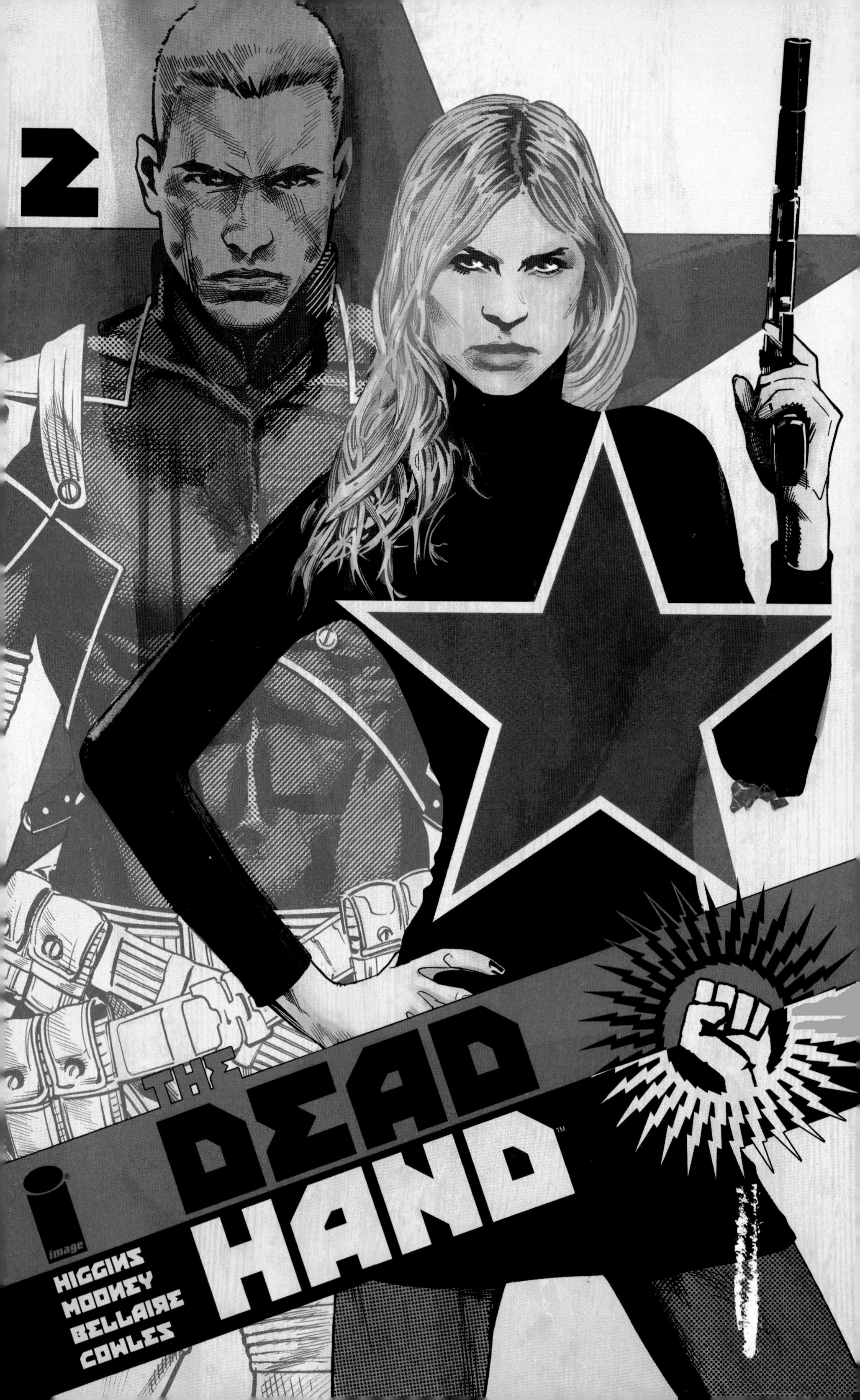
2
THE DEAD HAND™
image
HIGGINS
MOONEY
BELLAIRE
COWLES

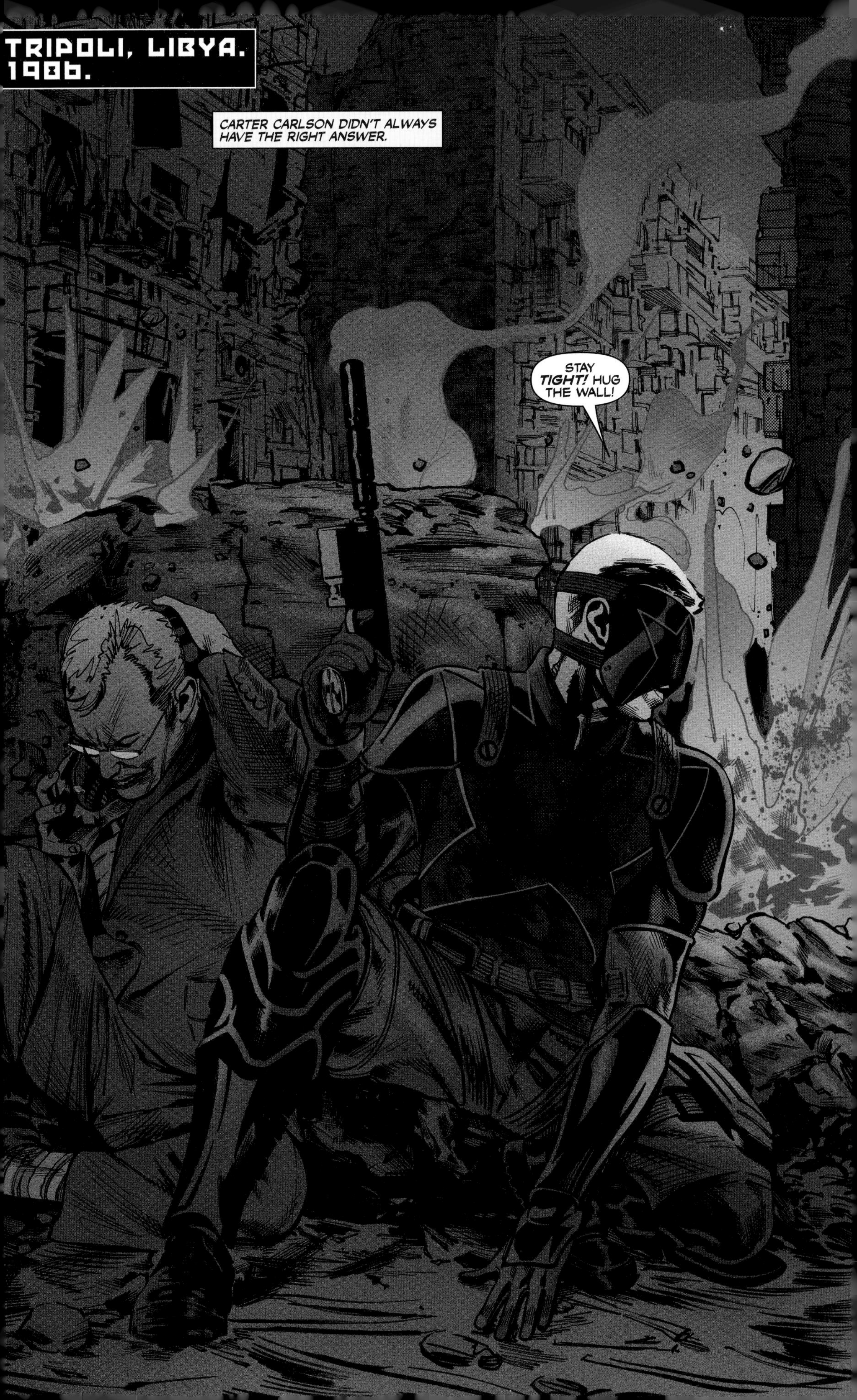
TRIPOLI, LIBYA. 1986.
CARTER CARLSON DIDN'T ALWAYS HAVE THE RIGHT ANSWER.
STAY TIGHT! HUG THE WALL!

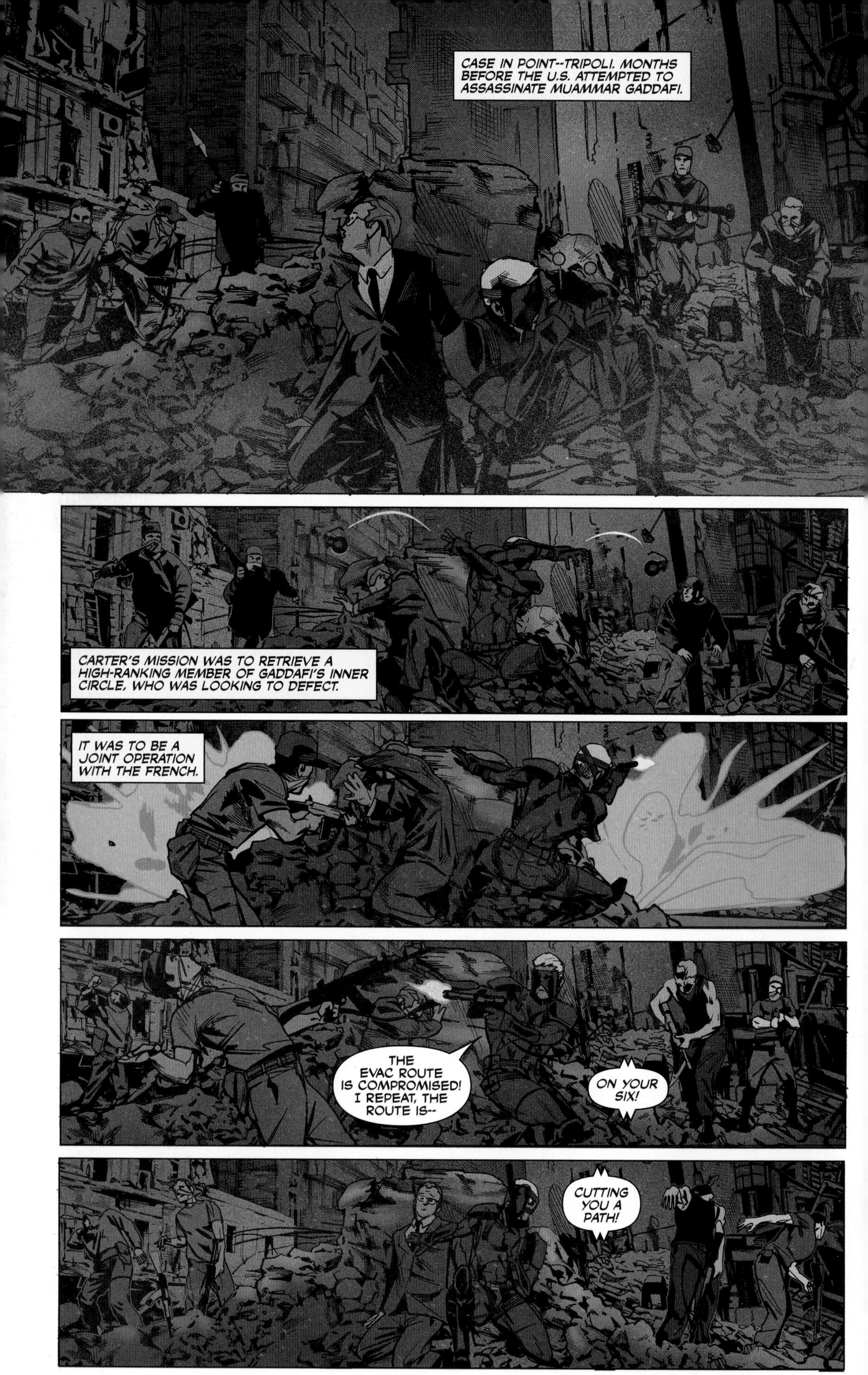
CASE IN POINT--TRIPOLI. MONTHS BEFORE THE U.S. ATTEMPTED TO ASSASSINATE MUAMMAR GADDAFI.
CARTER'S MISSION WAS TO RETRIEVE A HIGH-RANKING MEMBER OF GADDAFI'S INNER CIRCLE, WHO WAS LOOKING TO DEFECT.
IT WAS TO BE A JOINT OPERATION WITH THE FRENCH.
THE EVAC ROUTE IS COMPROMISED! I REPEAT, THE ROUTE IS--
ON YOUR SIX!
CUTTING YOU A PATH!

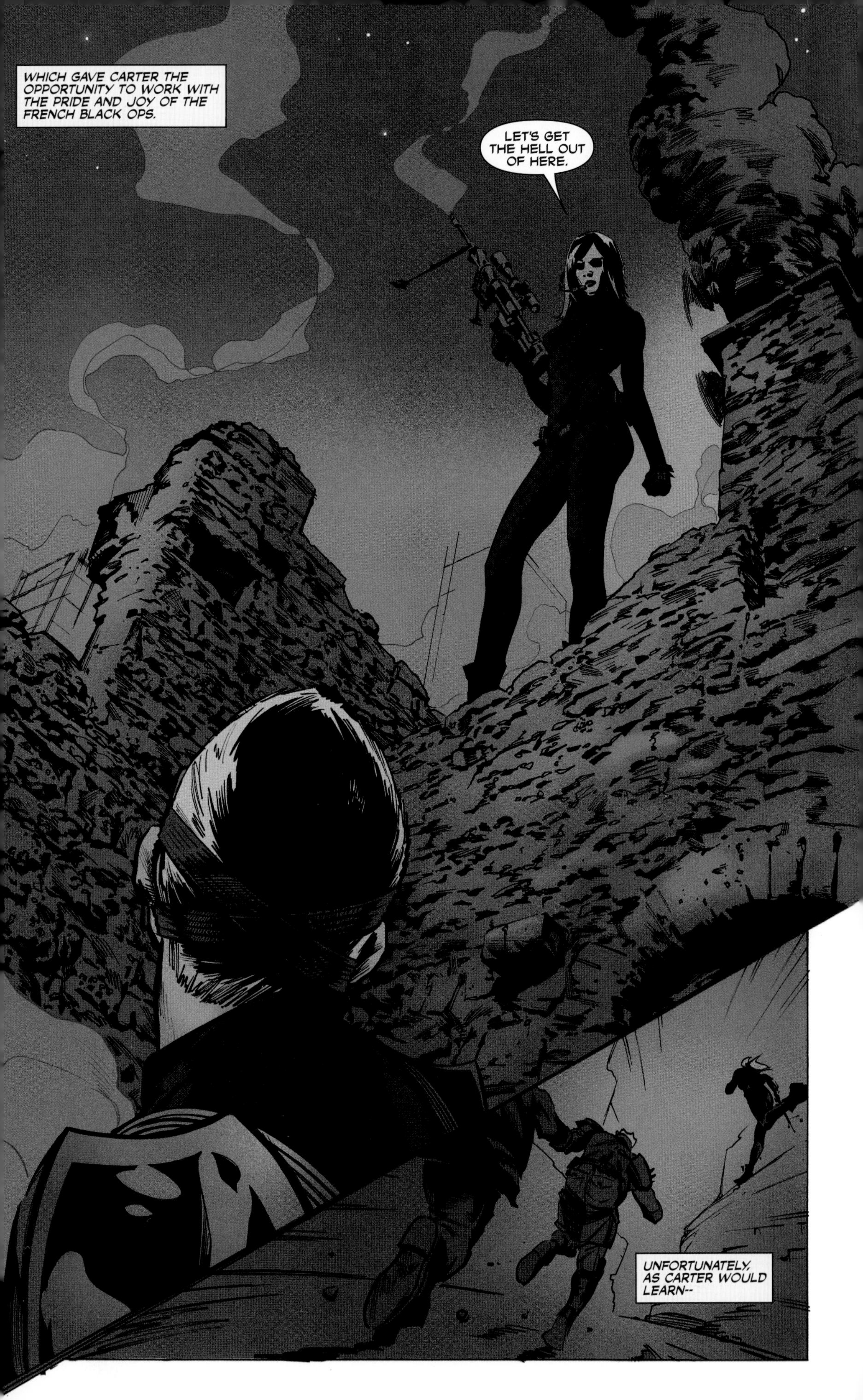
WHICH GAVE CARTER THE OPPORTUNITY TO WORK WITH THE PRIDE AND JOY OF THE FRENCH BLACK OPS.
LET'S GET THE HELL OUT OF HERE.
UNFORTUNATELY, AS CARTER WOULD LEARN--

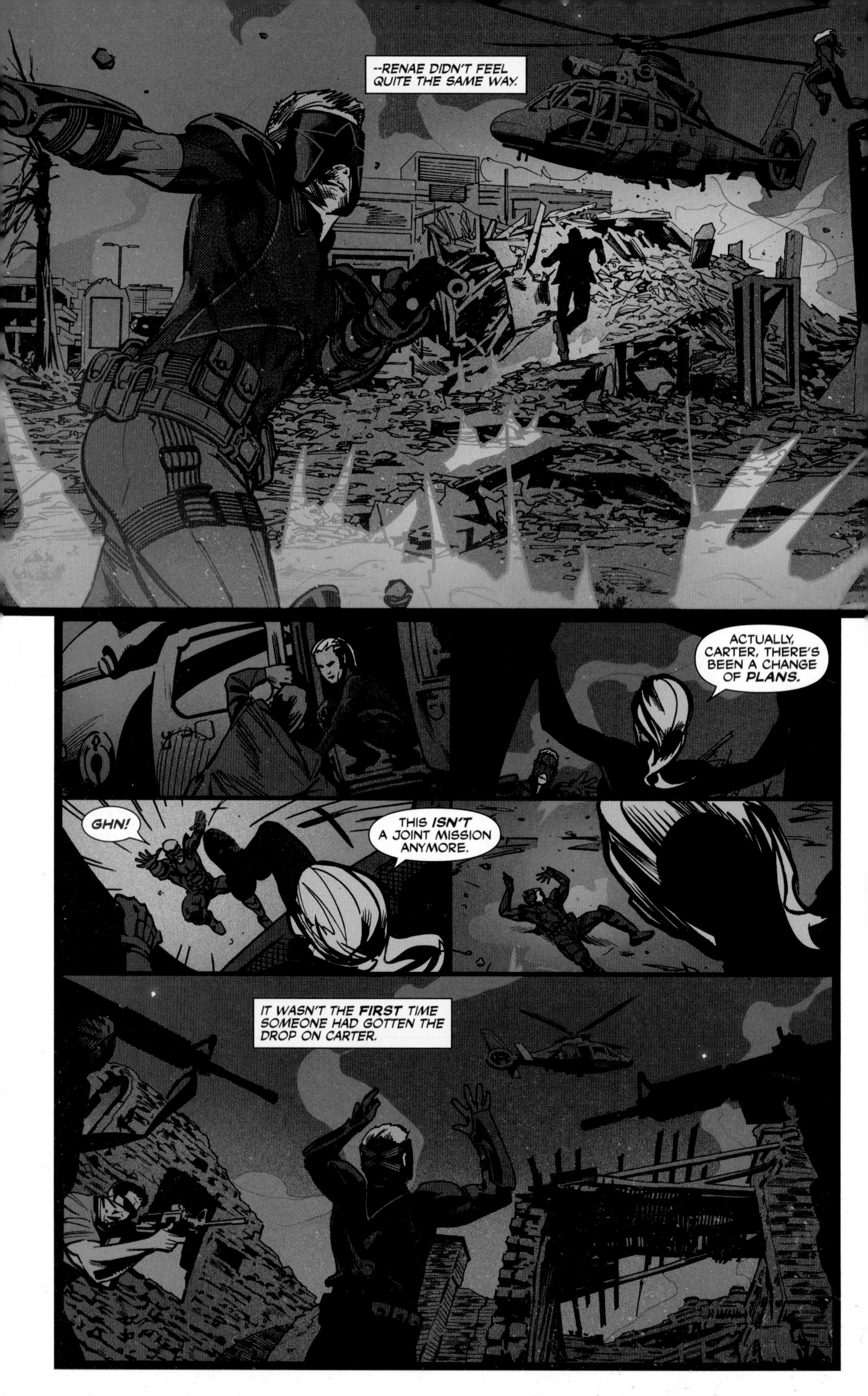
--RENAE DIDN'T FEEL QUITE THE SAME WAY.
ACTUALLY, CARTER, THERE'S BEEN A CHANGE OF PLANS.
GHN!
THIS ISN'T A JOINT MISSION ANYMORE.
IT WASN'T THE FIRST TIME SOMEONE HAD GOTTEN THE DROP ON CARTER.

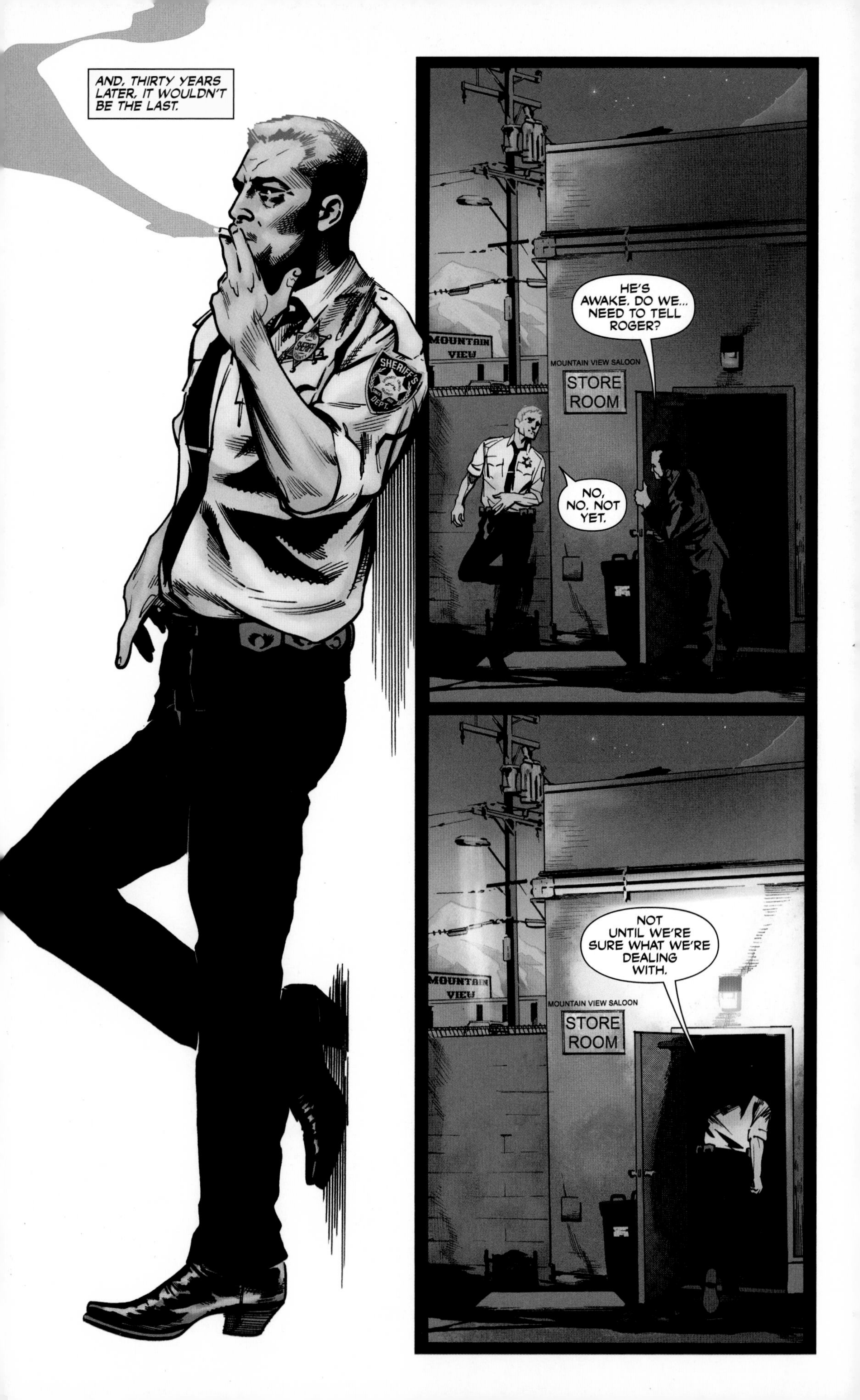
AND, THIRTY YEARS LATER, IT WOULDN'T BE THE LAST.
SHERIFF'S DEPT.
MOUNTAIN VIEW
MOUNTAIN VIEW SALOON
STORE ROOM
HE'S AWAKE. DO WE... NEED TO TELL ROGER?
NO, NO. NOT YET.
MOUNTAIN VIEW
MOUNTAIN VIEW SALOON
STORE ROOM
NOT UNTIL WE'RE SURE WHAT WE'RE DEALING WITH.

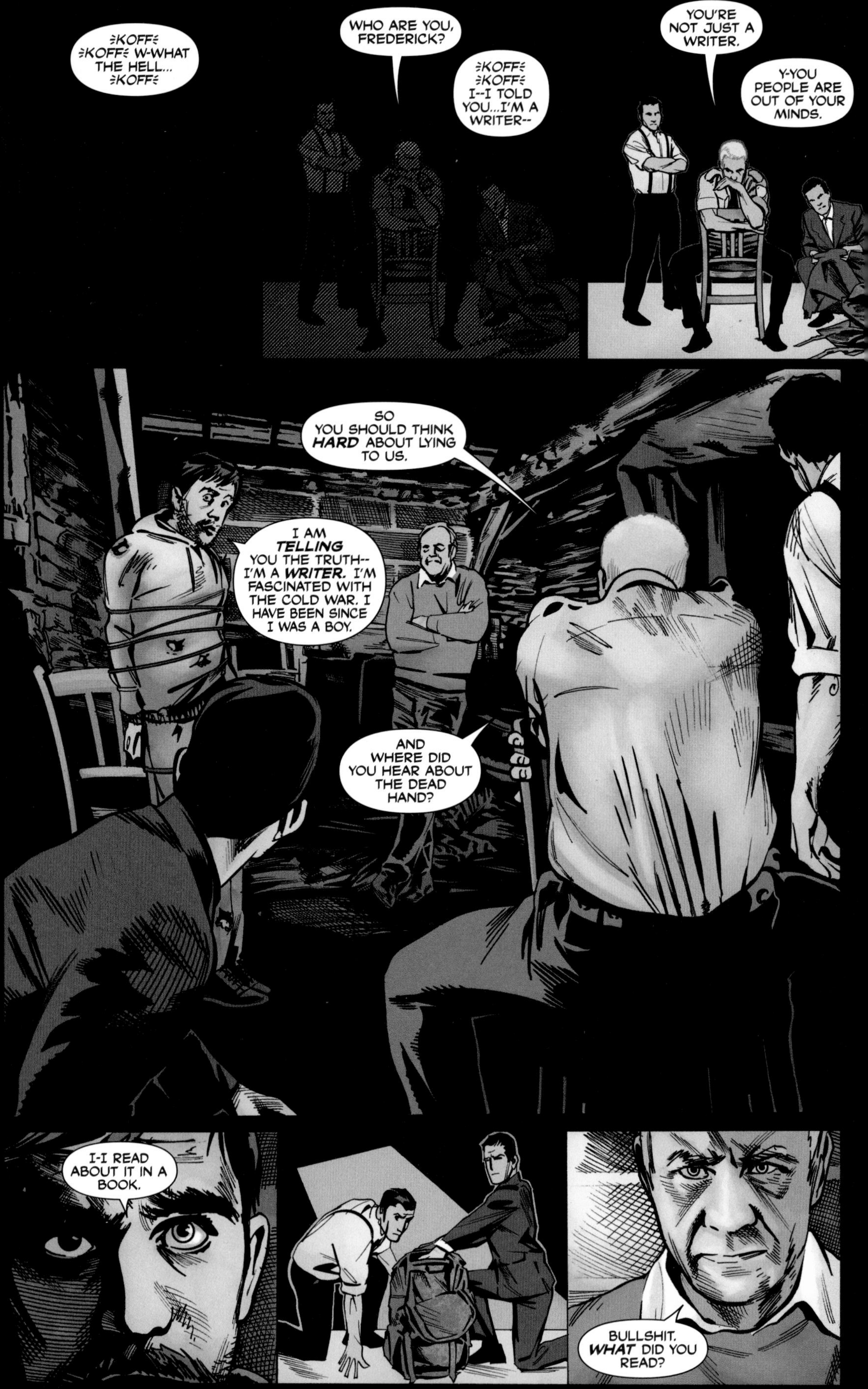

KOFF *KOFF* W-WHAT THE HELL... *KOFF*
WHO ARE YOU, FREDERICK?
KOFF *KOFF* I--I TOLD YOU...I'M A WRITER--
YOU'RE NOT JUST A WRITER.
Y-YOU PEOPLE ARE OUT OF YOUR MINDS.
SO YOU SHOULD THINK **HARD** ABOUT LYING TO US.
I AM ***TELLING*** YOU THE TRUTH-- I'M A ***WRITER.*** I'M FASCINATED WITH THE COLD WAR. I HAVE BEEN SINCE I WAS A BOY.
AND WHERE DID YOU HEAR ABOUT THE DEAD HAND?
I-I READ ABOUT IT IN A BOOK.
BULLSHIT. ***WHAT*** DID YOU READ?

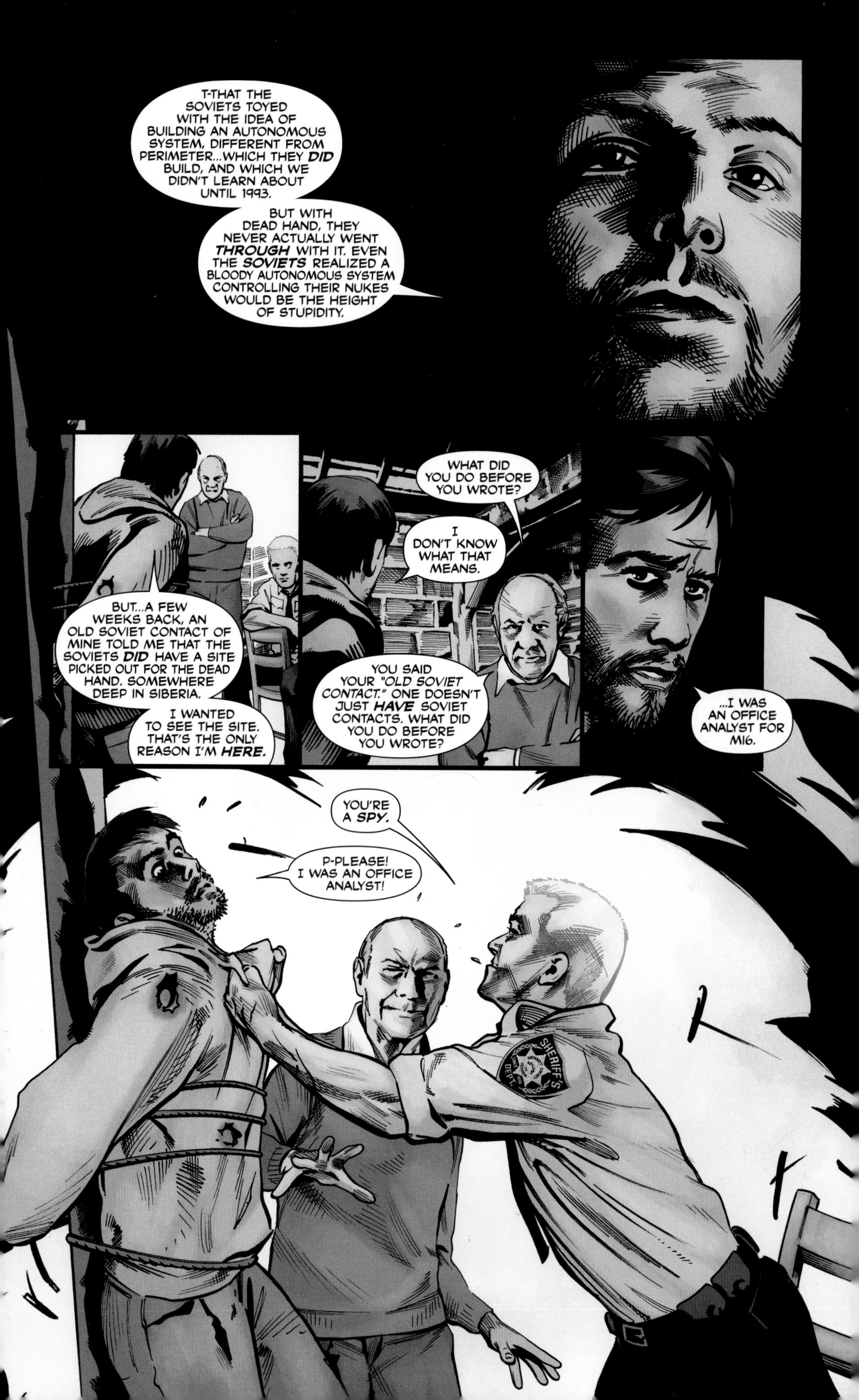
T-THAT THE SOVIETS TOYED WITH THE IDEA OF BUILDING AN AUTONOMOUS SYSTEM, DIFFERENT FROM PERIMETER...WHICH THEY DID BUILD, AND WHICH WE DIDN'T LEARN ABOUT UNTIL 1993.
BUT WITH DEAD HAND, THEY NEVER ACTUALLY WENT THROUGH WITH IT. EVEN THE SOVIETS REALIZED A BLOODY AUTONOMOUS SYSTEM CONTROLLING THEIR NUKES WOULD BE THE HEIGHT OF STUPIDITY.
BUT...A FEW WEEKS BACK, AN OLD SOVIET CONTACT OF MINE TOLD ME THAT THE SOVIETS DID HAVE A SITE PICKED OUT FOR THE DEAD HAND. SOMEWHERE DEEP IN SIBERIA.
I WANTED TO SEE THE SITE. THAT'S THE ONLY REASON I'M HERE.
YOU SAID YOUR "OLD SOVIET CONTACT." ONE DOESN'T JUST HAVE SOVIET CONTACTS. WHAT DID YOU DO BEFORE YOU WROTE?
I DON'T KNOW WHAT THAT MEANS.
WHAT DID YOU DO BEFORE YOU WROTE?
...I WAS AN OFFICE ANALYST FOR MI6.
YOU'RE A SPY.
P-PLEASE! I WAS AN OFFICE ANALYST!
SHERIFF'S DEPT.

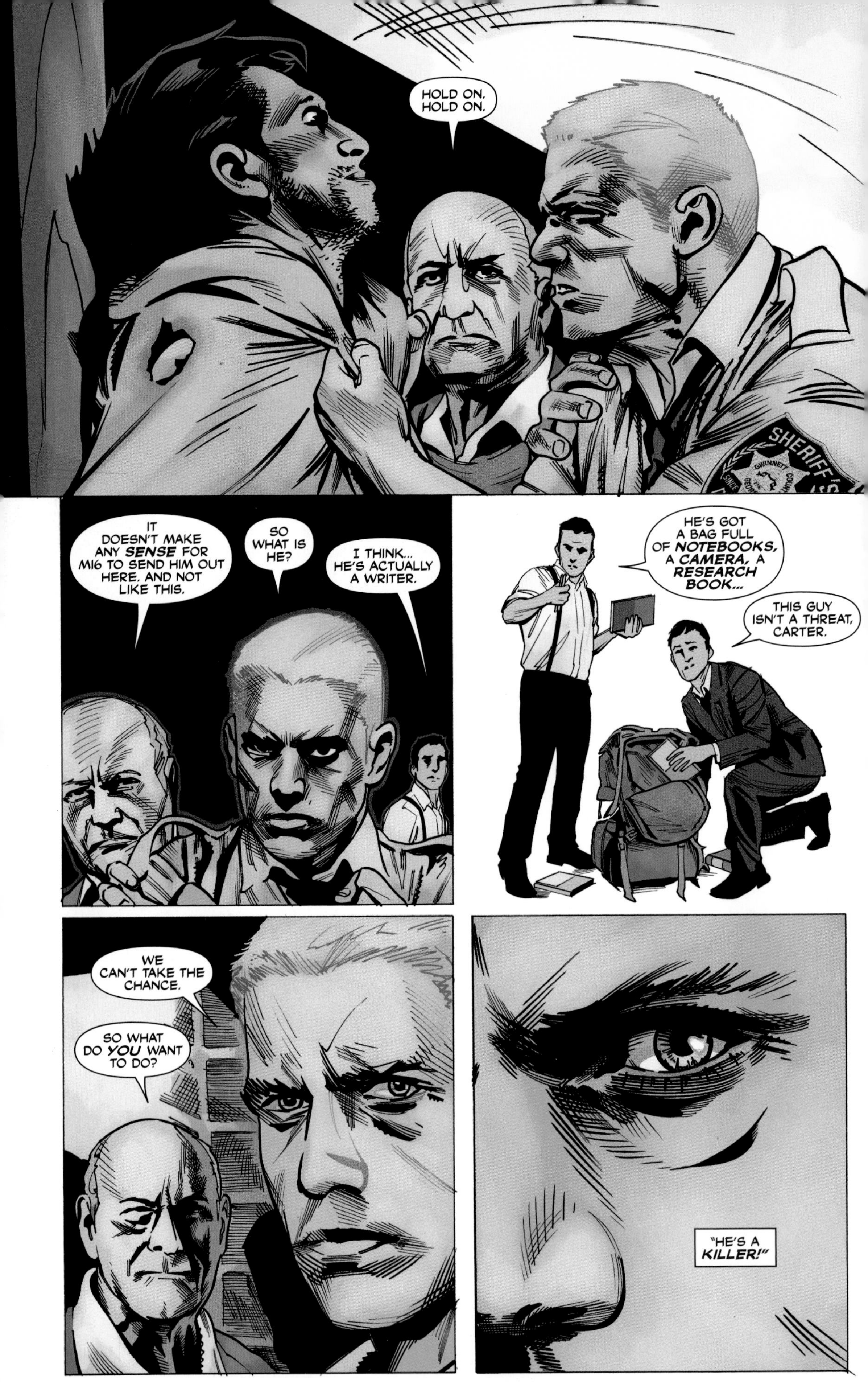
HOLD ON. HOLD ON.
IT DOESN'T MAKE ANY SENSE FOR MI6 TO SEND HIM OUT HERE. AND NOT LIKE THIS.
SO WHAT IS HE?
I THINK... HE'S ACTUALLY A WRITER.
HE'S GOT A BAG FULL OF NOTEBOOKS, A CAMERA, A RESEARCH BOOK...
THIS GUY ISN'T A THREAT, CARTER.
WE CAN'T TAKE THE CHANCE.
SO WHAT DO YOU WANT TO DO?
"HE'S A KILLER!"

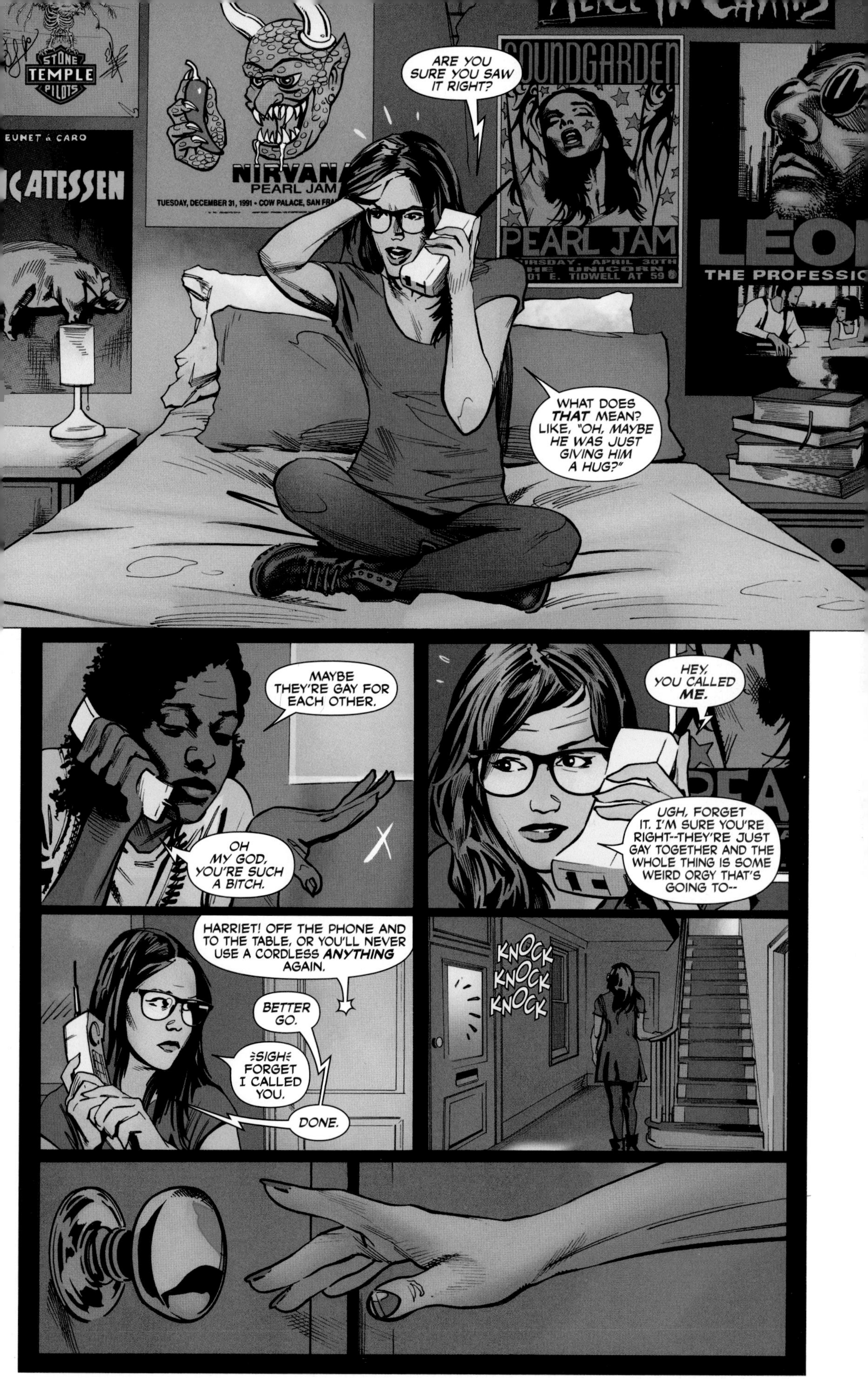
ARE YOU SURE YOU SAW IT RIGHT?
WHAT DOES THAT MEAN? LIKE, "OH, MAYBE HE WAS JUST GIVING HIM A HUG?"
MAYBE THEY'RE GAY FOR EACH OTHER.
OH MY GOD, YOU'RE SUCH A BITCH.
HEY, YOU CALLED ME.
UGH, FORGET IT. I'M SURE YOU'RE RIGHT--THEY'RE JUST GAY TOGETHER AND THE WHOLE THING IS SOME WEIRD ORGY THAT'S GOING TO--
HARRIET! OFF THE PHONE AND TO THE TABLE, OR YOU'LL NEVER USE A CORDLESS ANYTHING AGAIN.
BETTER GO.
SIGH FORGET I CALLED YOU.
DONE.
KNOCK KNOCK KNOCK

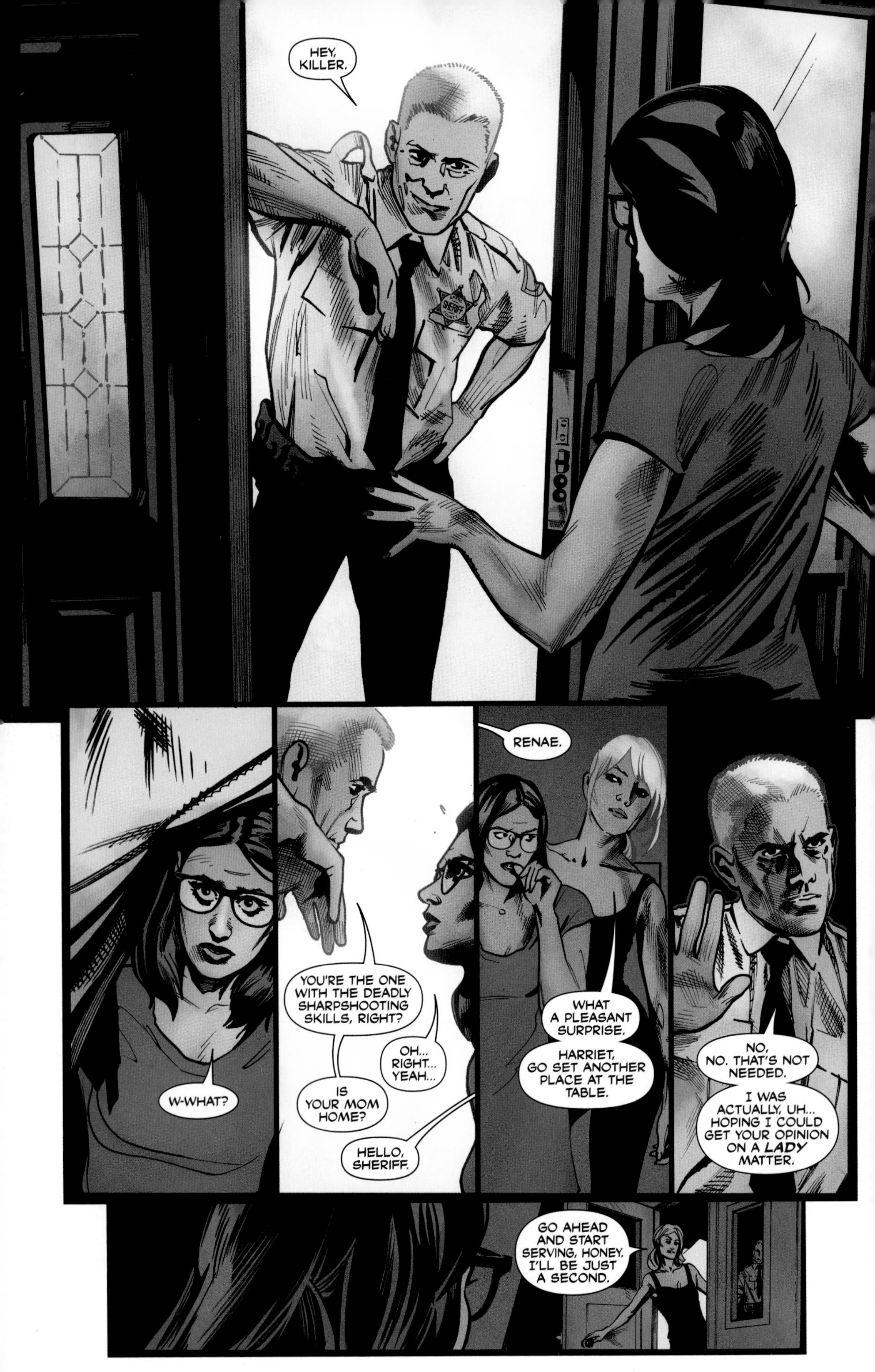
HEY, KILLER.
W-WHAT?
YOU'RE THE ONE WITH THE DEADLY SHARPSHOOTING SKILLS, RIGHT?
OH... RIGHT... YEAH...
IS YOUR MOM HOME?
HELLO, SHERIFF.
RENAE.
WHAT A PLEASANT SURPRISE.
HARRIET, GO SET ANOTHER PLACE AT THE TABLE.
NO, NO. THAT'S NOT NEEDED.
I WAS ACTUALLY, UH... HOPING I COULD GET YOUR OPINION ON A *LADY* MATTER.
GO AHEAD AND START SERVING, HONEY. I'LL BE JUST A SECOND.

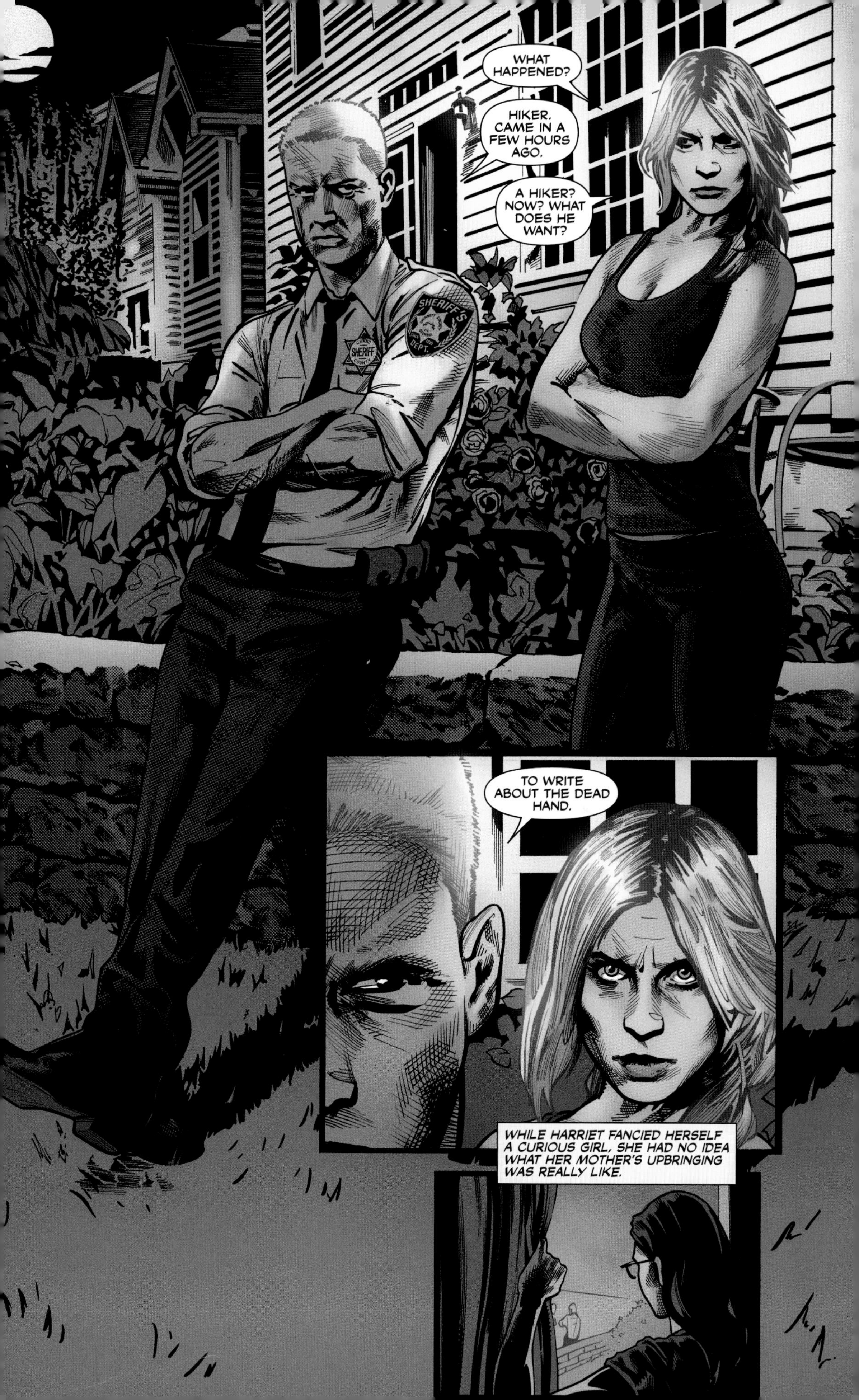
WHAT HAPPENED?
HIKER. CAME IN A FEW HOURS AGO.
A HIKER? NOW? WHAT DOES HE WANT?
TO WRITE ABOUT THE DEAD HAND.
WHILE HARRIET FANCIED HERSELF A CURIOUS GIRL, SHE HAD NO IDEA WHAT HER MOTHER'S UPBRINGING WAS REALLY LIKE.

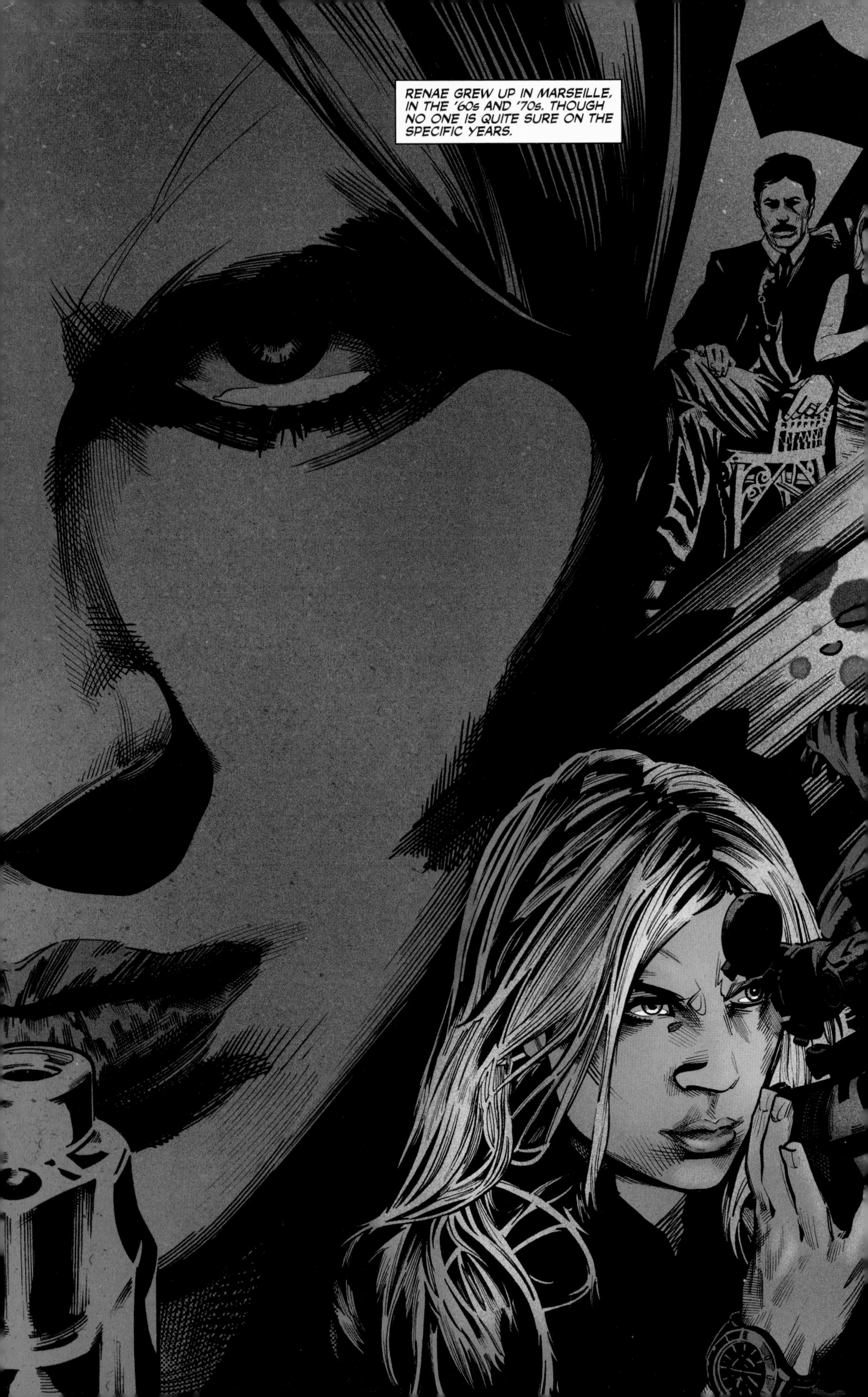
RENAE GREW UP IN MARSEILLE, IN THE '60s AND '70s. THOUGH NO ONE IS QUITE SURE ON THE SPECIFIC YEARS.

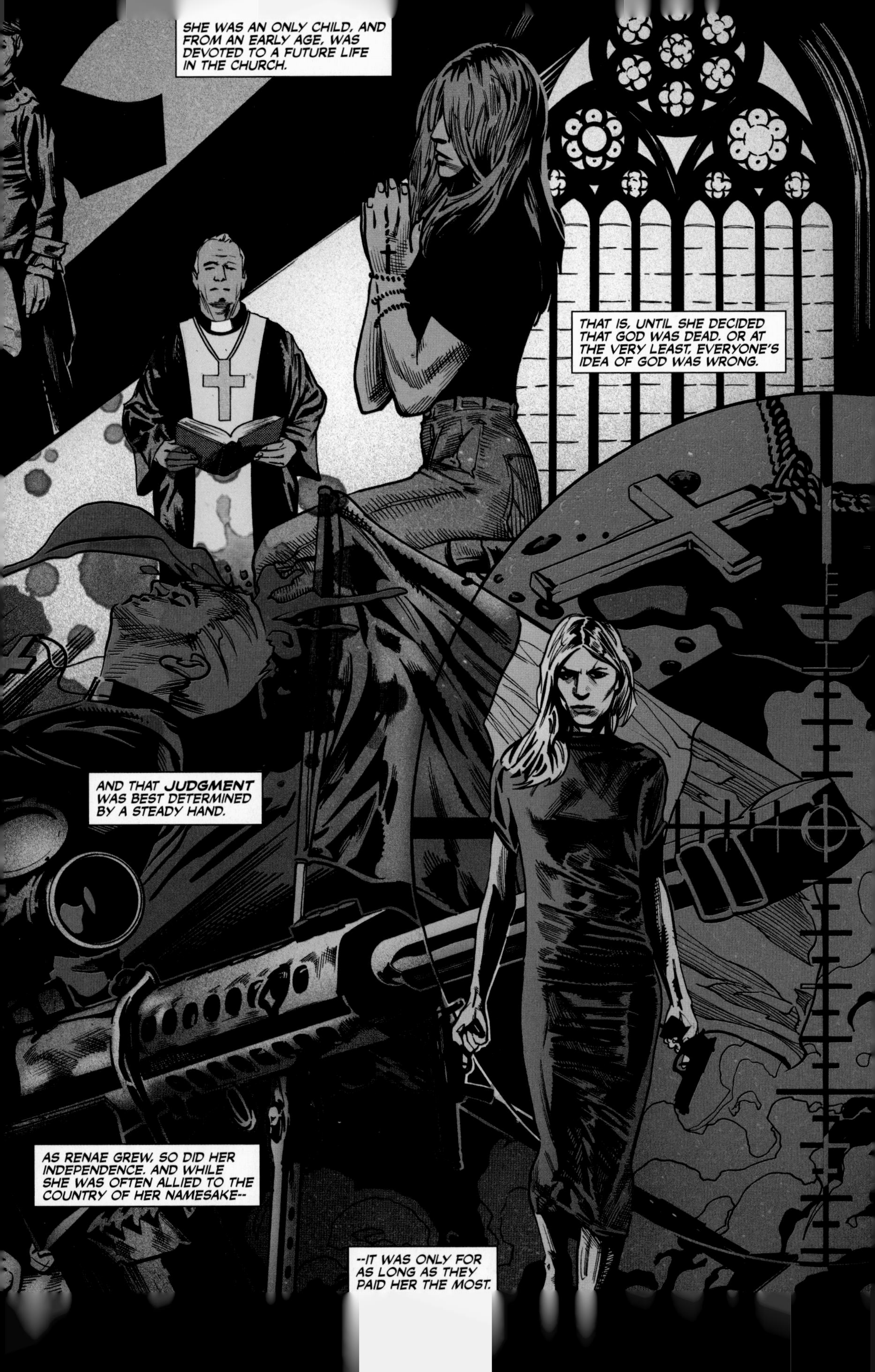
SHE WAS AN ONLY CHILD, AND FROM AN EARLY AGE, WAS DEVOTED TO A FUTURE LIFE IN THE CHURCH.
THAT IS, UNTIL SHE DECIDED THAT GOD WAS DEAD. OR AT THE VERY LEAST, EVERYONE'S IDEA OF GOD WAS WRONG.
AND THAT JUDGMENT WAS BEST DETERMINED BY A STEADY HAND.
AS RENAE GREW, SO DID HER INDEPENDENCE. AND WHILE SHE WAS OFTEN ALLIED TO THE COUNTRY OF HER NAMESAKE--
--IT WAS ONLY FOR AS LONG AS THEY PAID HER THE MOST.

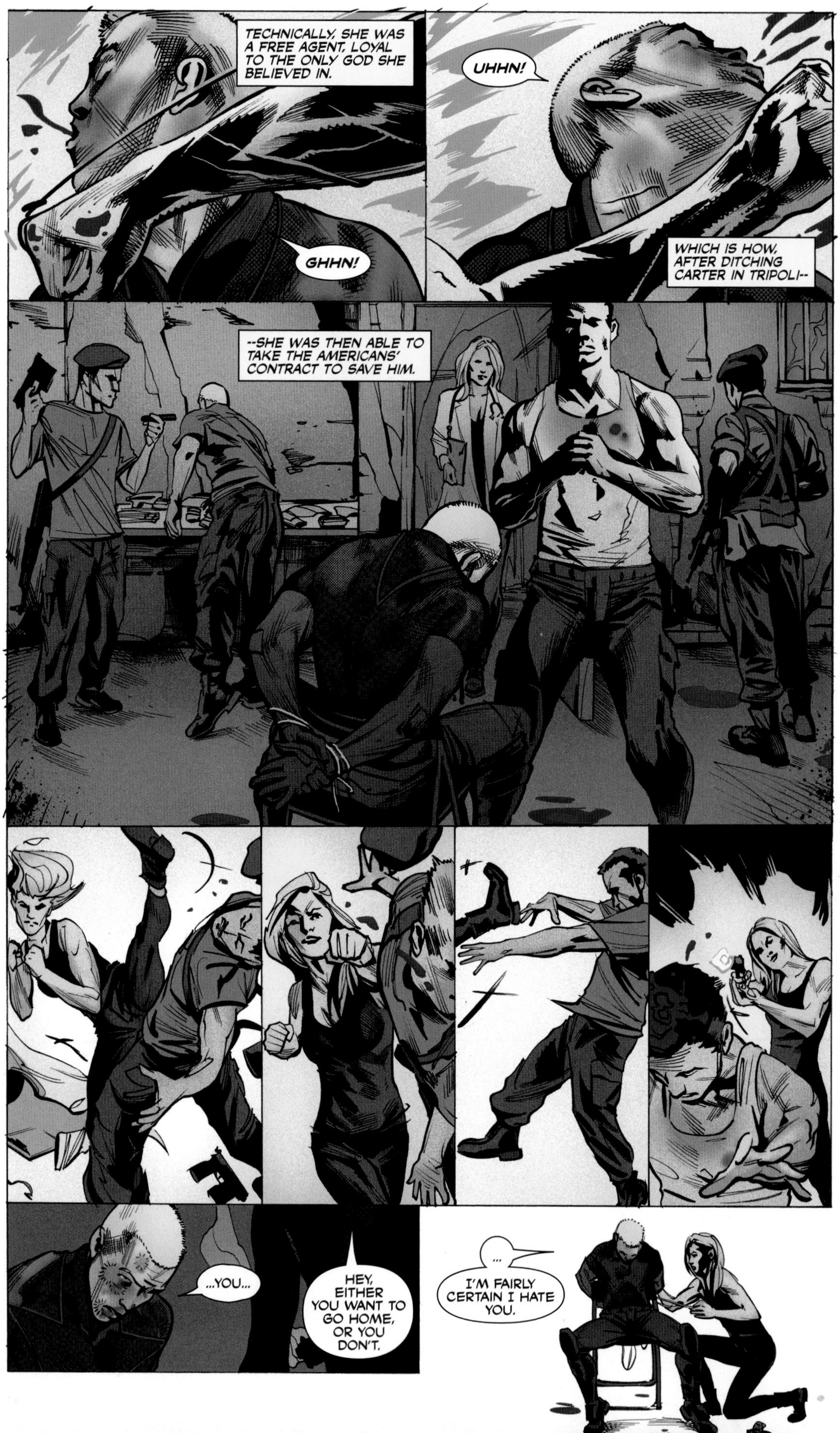
TECHNICALLY, SHE WAS A FREE AGENT, LOYAL TO THE ONLY GOD SHE BELIEVED IN.
GHHN!
UHHN!
WHICH IS HOW, AFTER DITCHING CARTER IN TRIPOLI--
--SHE WAS THEN ABLE TO TAKE THE AMERICANS' CONTRACT TO SAVE HIM.
...YOU...
HEY, EITHER YOU WANT TO GO HOME, OR YOU DON'T.
...
I'M FAIRLY CERTAIN I HATE YOU.

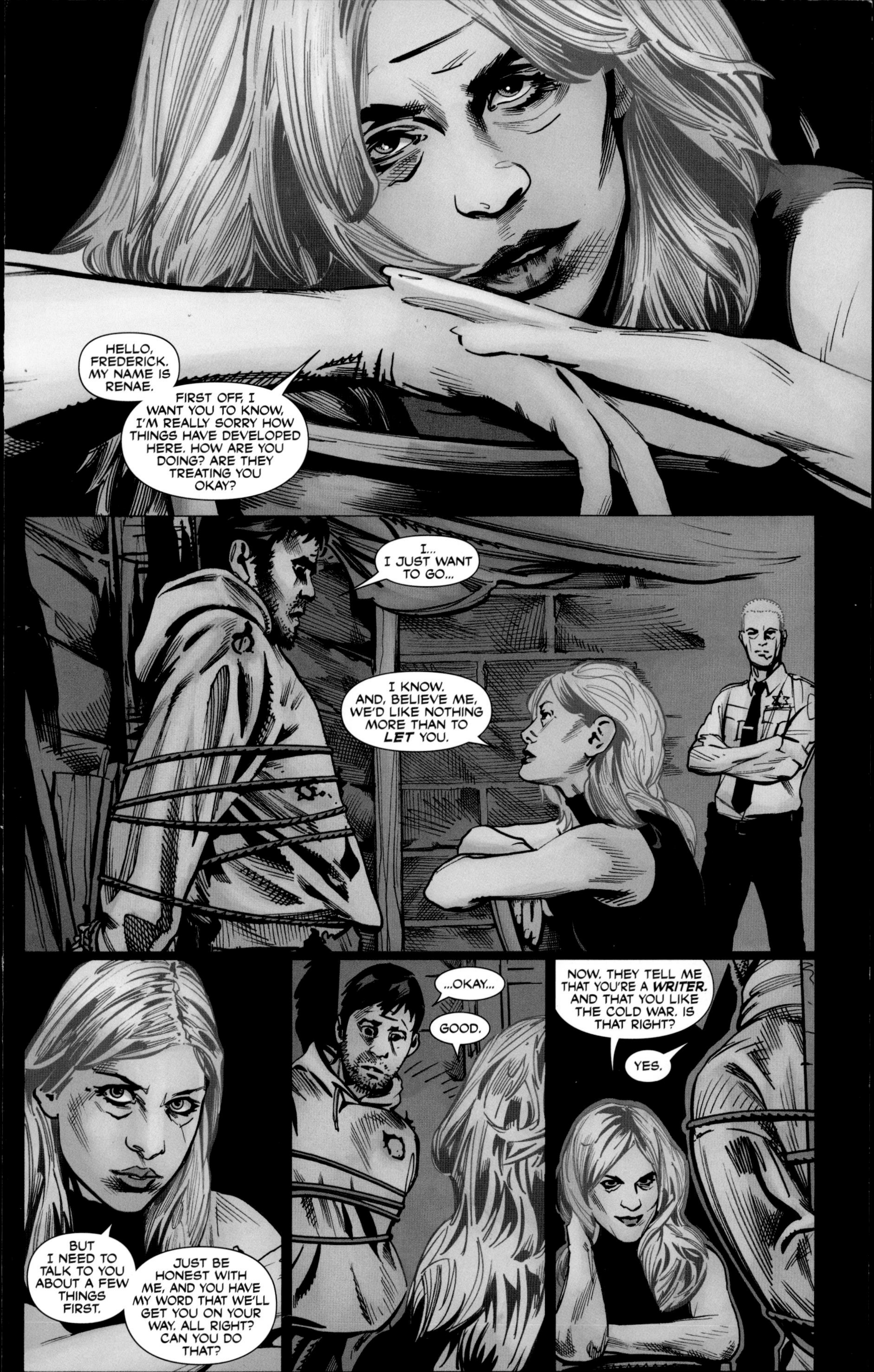
HELLO, FREDERICK. MY NAME IS RENAE.
FIRST OFF, I WANT YOU TO KNOW, I'M REALLY SORRY HOW THINGS HAVE DEVELOPED HERE. HOW ARE YOU DOING? ARE THEY TREATING YOU OKAY?
I... I JUST WANT TO GO...
I KNOW. AND, BELIEVE ME, WE'D LIKE NOTHING MORE THAN TO LET YOU.
BUT I NEED TO TALK TO YOU ABOUT A FEW THINGS FIRST.
JUST BE HONEST WITH ME, AND YOU HAVE MY WORD THAT WE'LL GET YOU ON YOUR WAY. ALL RIGHT? CAN YOU DO THAT?
...OKAY...
GOOD.
NOW, THEY TELL ME THAT YOU'RE A WRITER. AND THAT YOU LIKE THE COLD WAR. IS THAT RIGHT?
YES.

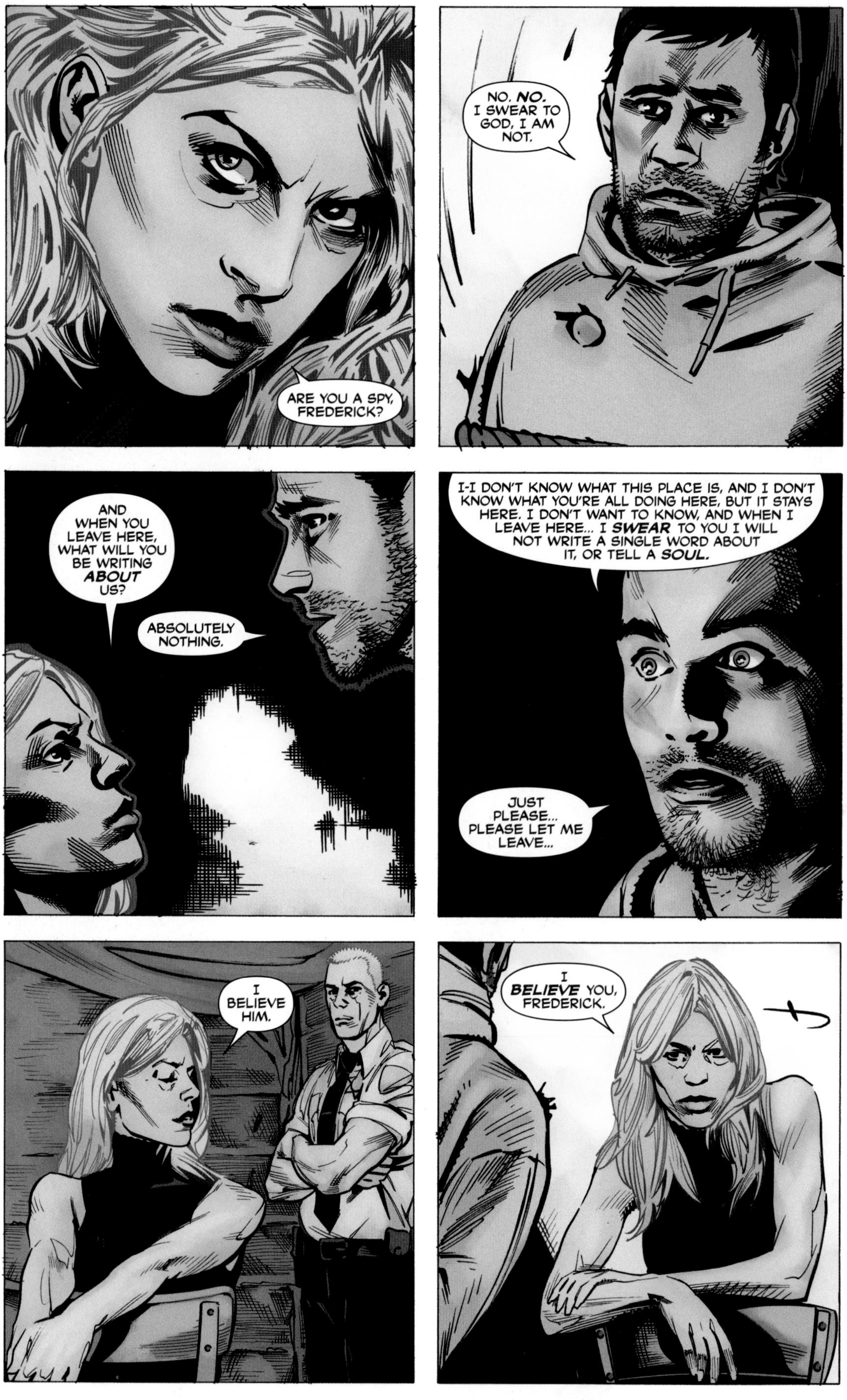
ARE YOU A SPY, FREDERICK?
NO. NO. I SWEAR TO GOD, I AM NOT.
AND WHEN YOU LEAVE HERE, WHAT WILL YOU BE WRITING ABOUT US?
ABSOLUTELY NOTHING.
I-I DON'T KNOW WHAT THIS PLACE IS, AND I DON'T KNOW WHAT YOU'RE ALL DOING HERE, BUT IT STAYS HERE. I DON'T WANT TO KNOW, AND WHEN I LEAVE HERE... I SWEAR TO YOU I WILL NOT WRITE A SINGLE WORD ABOUT IT, OR TELL A SOUL.
JUST PLEASE... PLEASE LET ME LEAVE...
I BELIEVE HIM.
I BELIEVE YOU, FREDERICK.

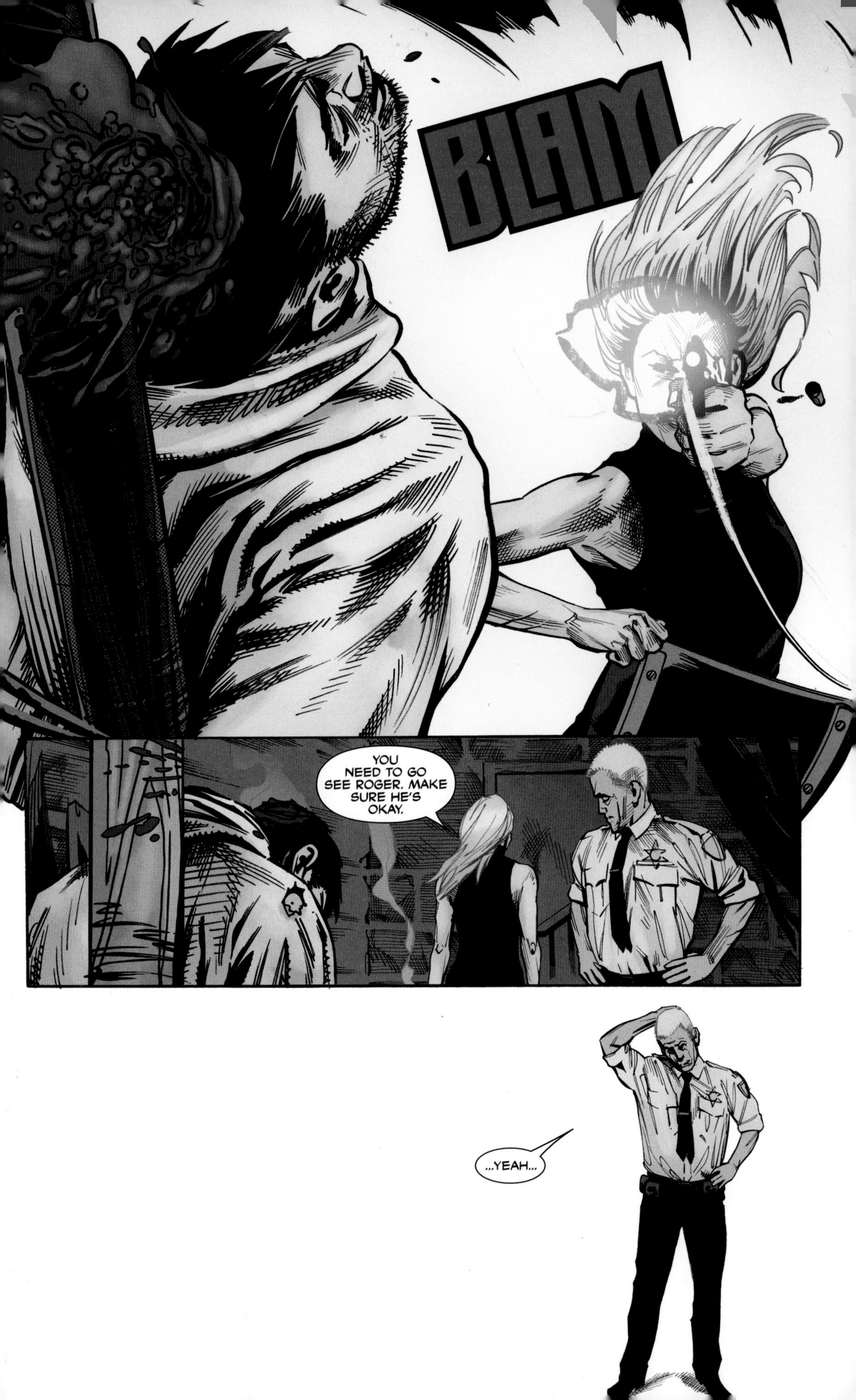
BLAM
YOU NEED TO GO SEE ROGER. MAKE SURE HE'S OKAY.
...YEAH...

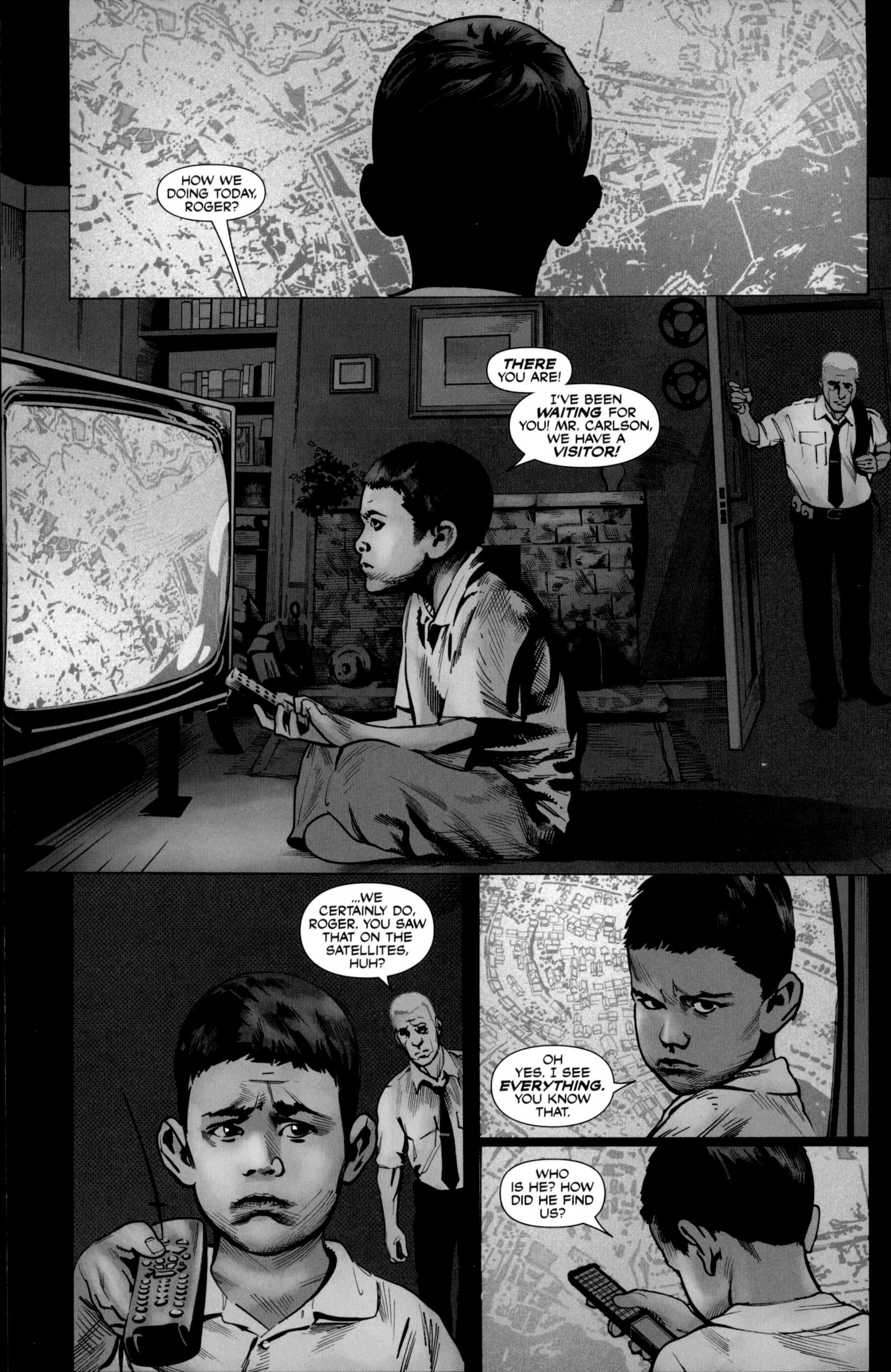
HOW WE DOING TODAY, ROGER?
THERE YOU ARE!
I'VE BEEN WAITING FOR YOU! MR. CARLSON, WE HAVE A VISITOR!
...WE CERTAINLY DO, ROGER. YOU SAW THAT ON THE SATELLITES, HUH?
OH YES. I SEE EVERYTHING. YOU KNOW THAT.
WHO IS HE? HOW DID HE FIND US?

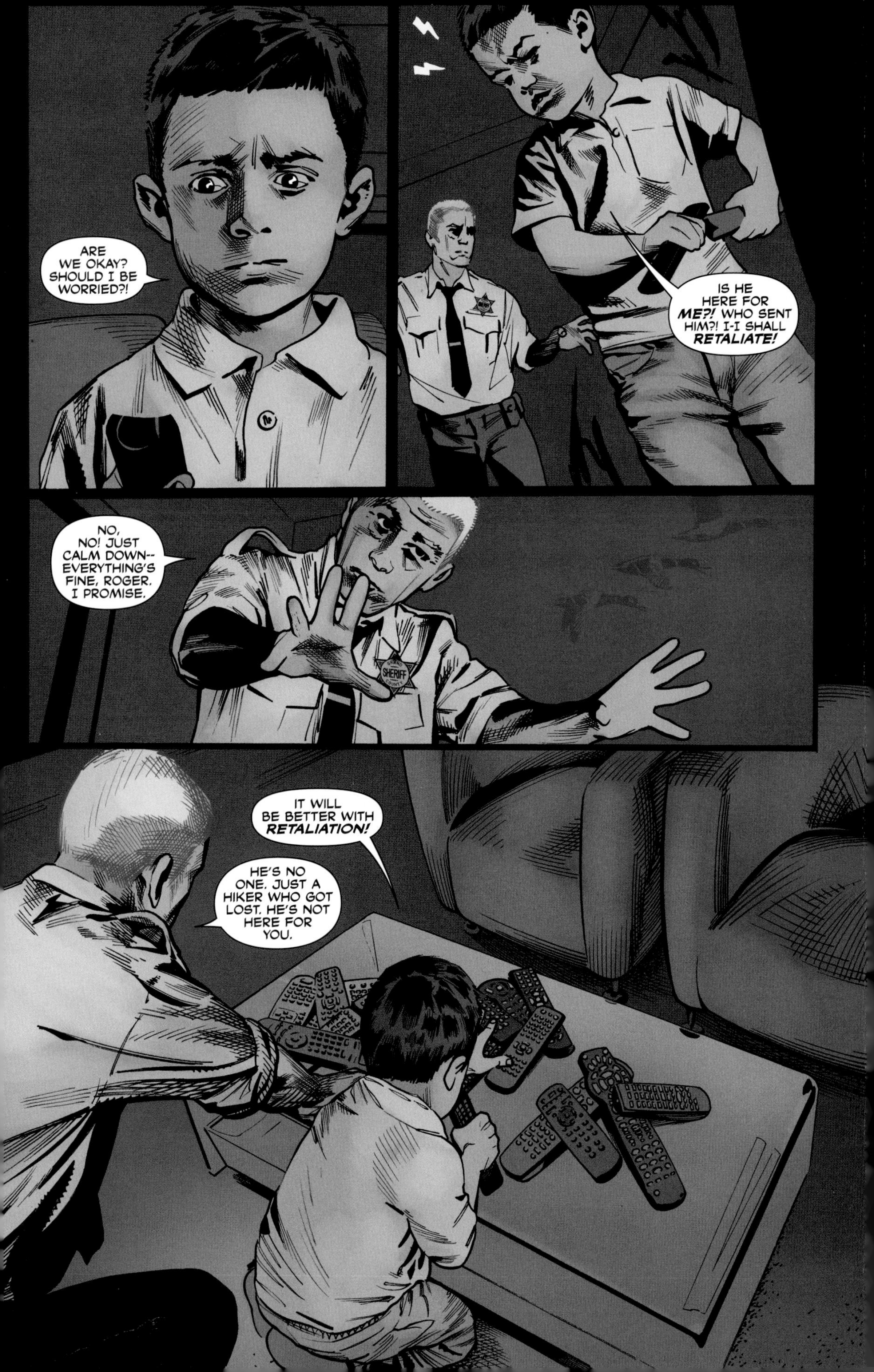
ARE WE OKAY? SHOULD I BE WORRIED?!
IS HE HERE FOR ME?! WHO SENT HIM?! I-I SHALL RETALIATE!
NO, NO! JUST CALM DOWN-- EVERYTHING'S FINE, ROGER. I PROMISE.
SHERIFF
IT WILL BE BETTER WITH RETALIATION!
HE'S NO ONE. JUST A HIKER WHO GOT LOST. HE'S NOT HERE FOR YOU.

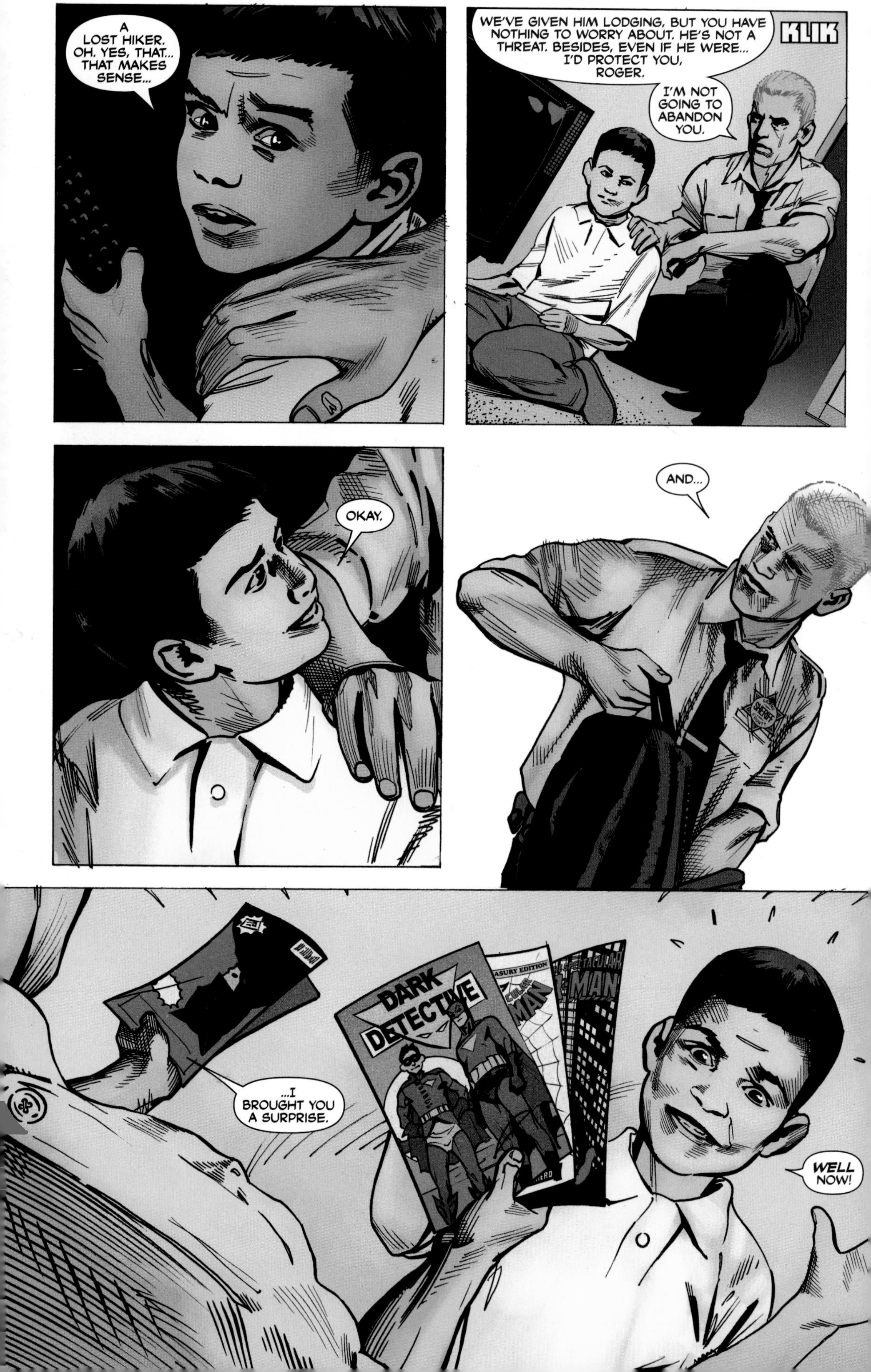
A LOST HIKER. OH. YES, THAT... THAT MAKES SENSE...
KLIK
WE'VE GIVEN HIM LODGING, BUT YOU HAVE NOTHING TO WORRY ABOUT. HE'S NOT A THREAT. BESIDES, EVEN IF HE WERE... I'D PROTECT YOU, ROGER.
I'M NOT GOING TO ABANDON YOU.
OKAY.
AND...
...I BROUGHT YOU A SURPRISE.
DARK DETECTIVE
WELL NOW!

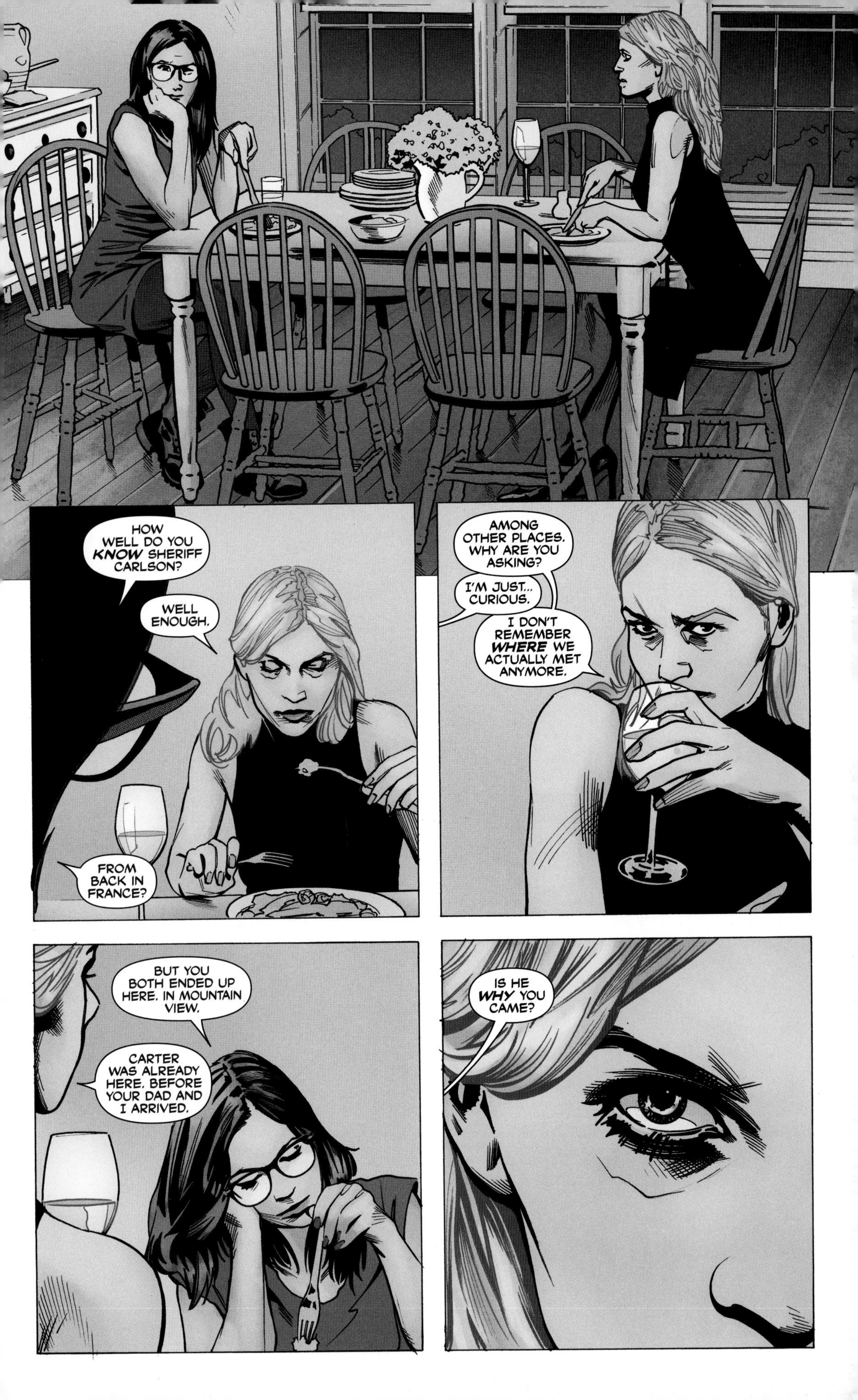
HOW WELL DO YOU *KNOW* SHERIFF CARLSON?
WELL ENOUGH.
FROM BACK IN FRANCE?
AMONG OTHER PLACES. WHY ARE YOU ASKING?
I'M JUST... CURIOUS.
I DON'T REMEMBER *WHERE* WE ACTUALLY MET ANYMORE.
BUT YOU BOTH ENDED UP HERE. IN MOUNTAIN VIEW.
CARTER WAS ALREADY HERE. BEFORE YOUR DAD AND I ARRIVED.
IS HE *WHY* YOU CAME?

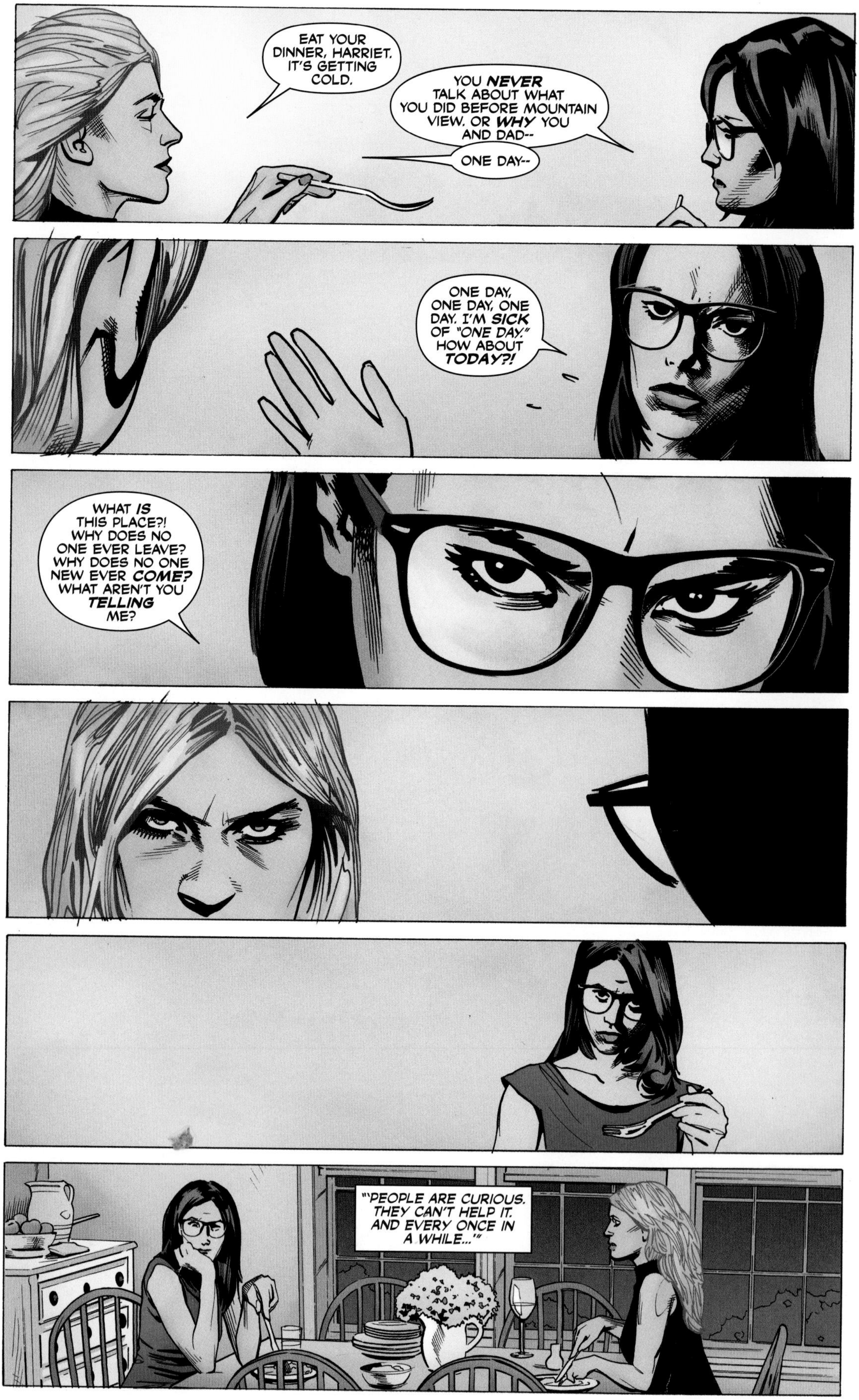
EAT YOUR DINNER, HARRIET. IT'S GETTING COLD.
YOU NEVER TALK ABOUT WHAT YOU DID BEFORE MOUNTAIN VIEW. OR WHY YOU AND DAD--
ONE DAY--
ONE DAY, ONE DAY, ONE DAY. I'M SICK OF "ONE DAY." HOW ABOUT TODAY?!
WHAT IS THIS PLACE?! WHY DOES NO ONE EVER LEAVE? WHY DOES NO ONE NEW EVER COME? WHAT AREN'T YOU TELLING ME?
"PEOPLE ARE CURIOUS. THEY CAN'T HELP IT. AND EVERY ONCE IN A WHILE..."

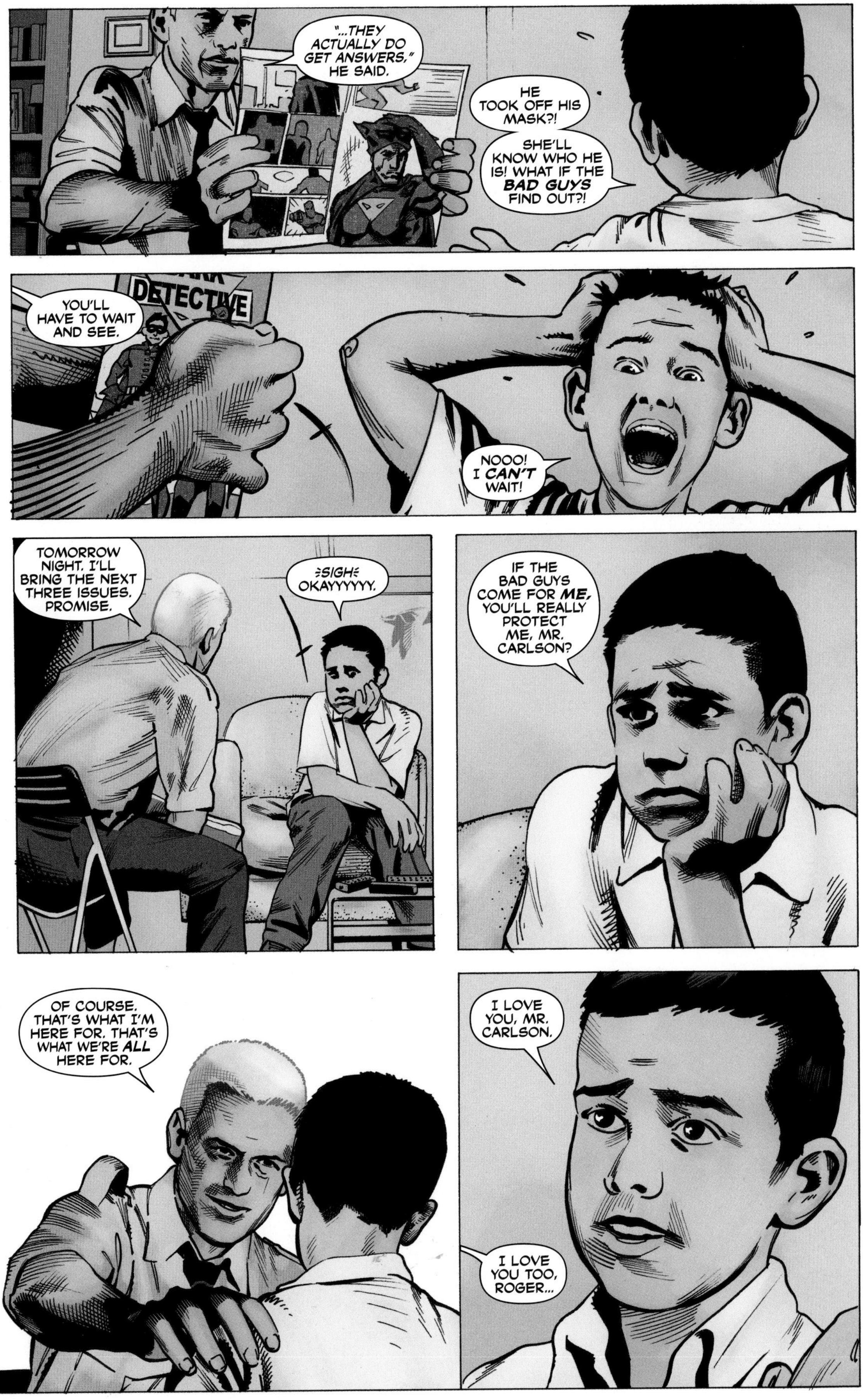
"...THEY ACTUALLY DO GET ANSWERS," HE SAID.
HE TOOK OFF HIS MASK?!
SHE'LL KNOW WHO HE IS! WHAT IF THE BAD GUYS FIND OUT?!
DETECTIVE
YOU'LL HAVE TO WAIT AND SEE.
NOOO! I CAN'T WAIT!
TOMORROW NIGHT. I'LL BRING THE NEXT THREE ISSUES. PROMISE.
SIGH OKAYYYYYY.
IF THE BAD GUYS COME FOR ME, YOU'LL REALLY PROTECT ME, MR. CARLSON?
OF COURSE. THAT'S WHAT I'M HERE FOR. THAT'S WHAT WE'RE ALL HERE FOR.
I LOVE YOU, MR. CARLSON.
I LOVE YOU TOO, ROGER...

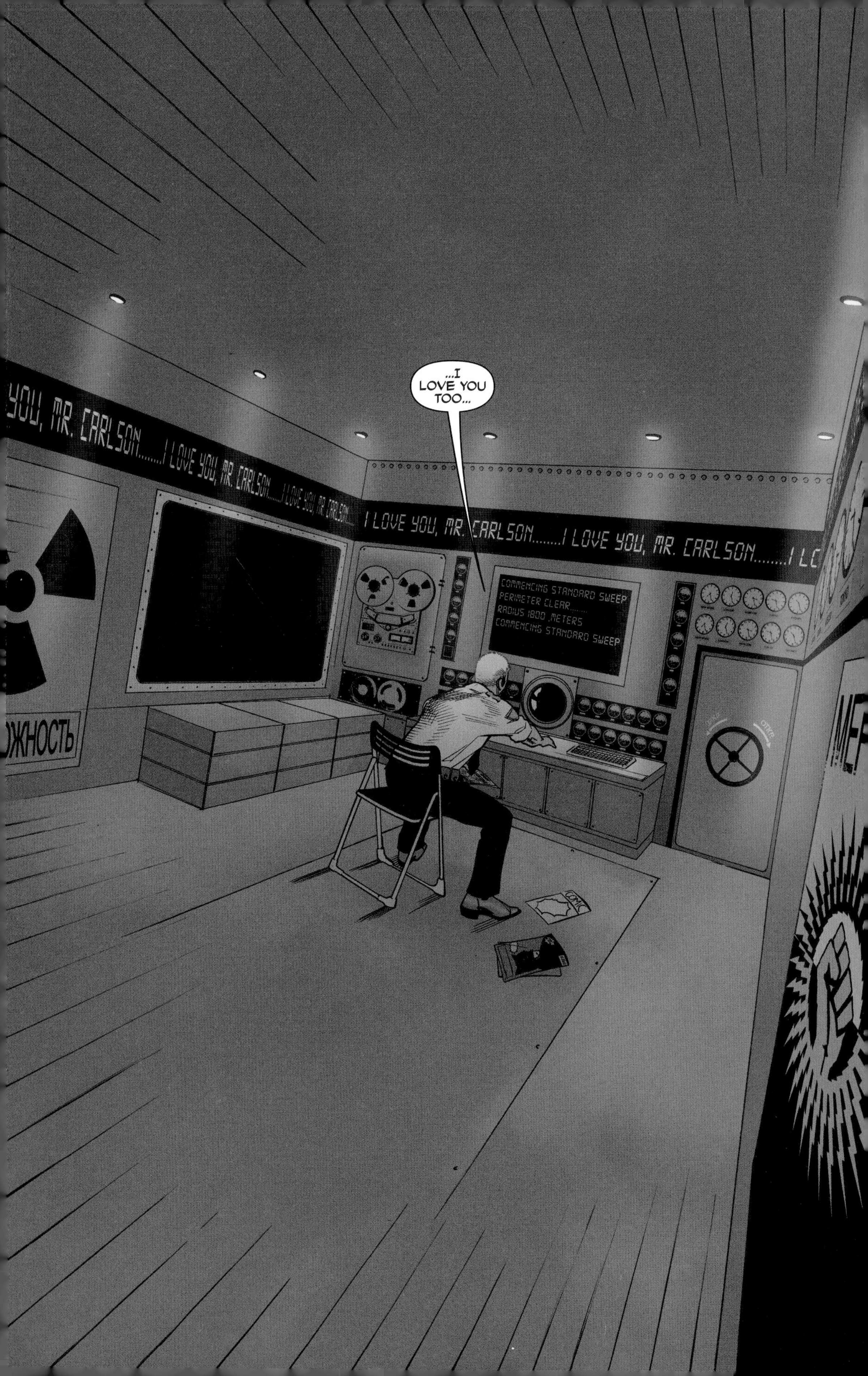

...I LOVE YOU TOO...
I LOVE YOU, MR. CARLSON........I LOVE YOU, MR. CARLSON........
COMMENCING STANDARD SWEEP
PERIMETER CLEAR........
RADIUS 1800 METERS
COMMENCING STANDARD SWEEP

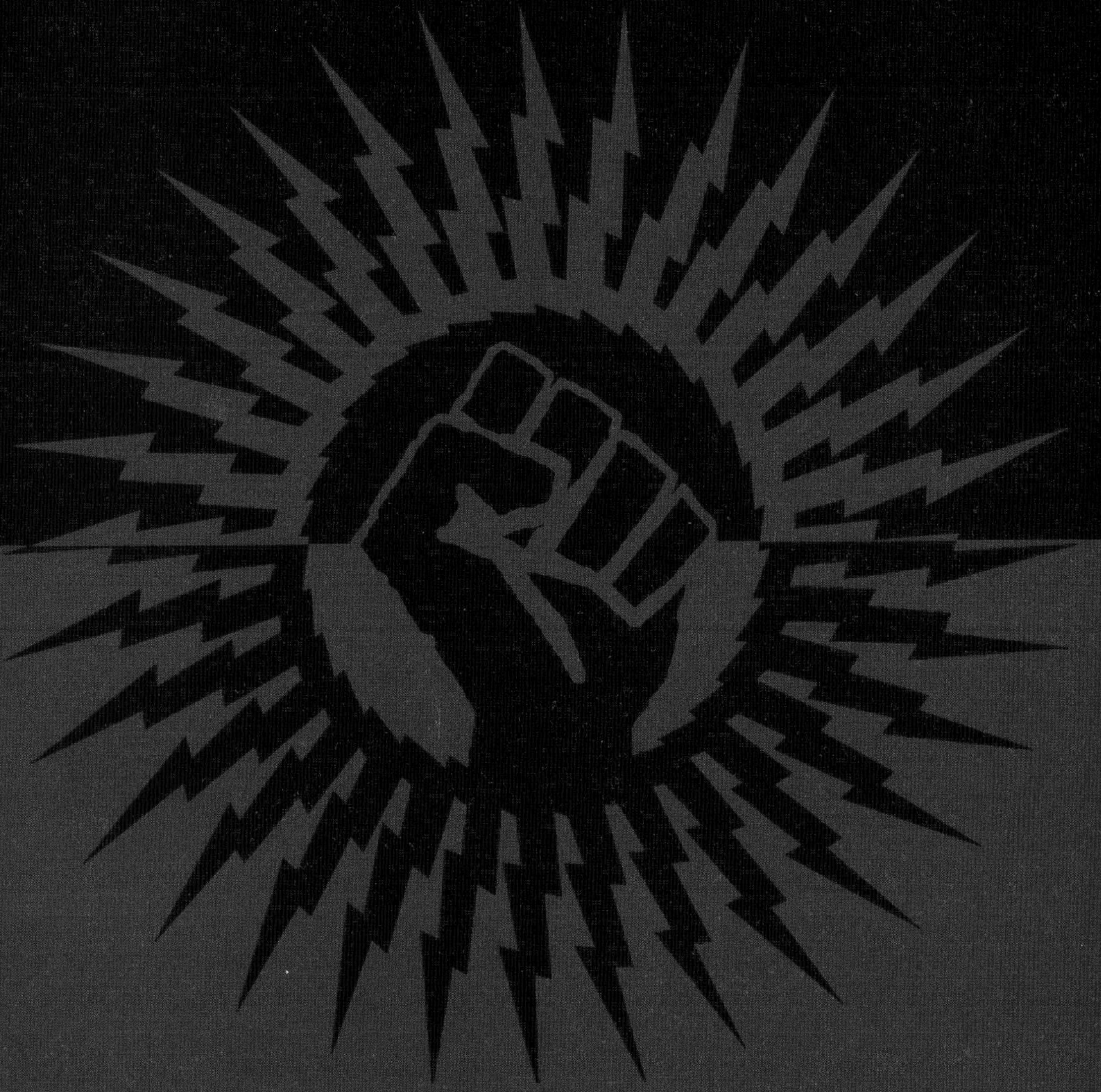

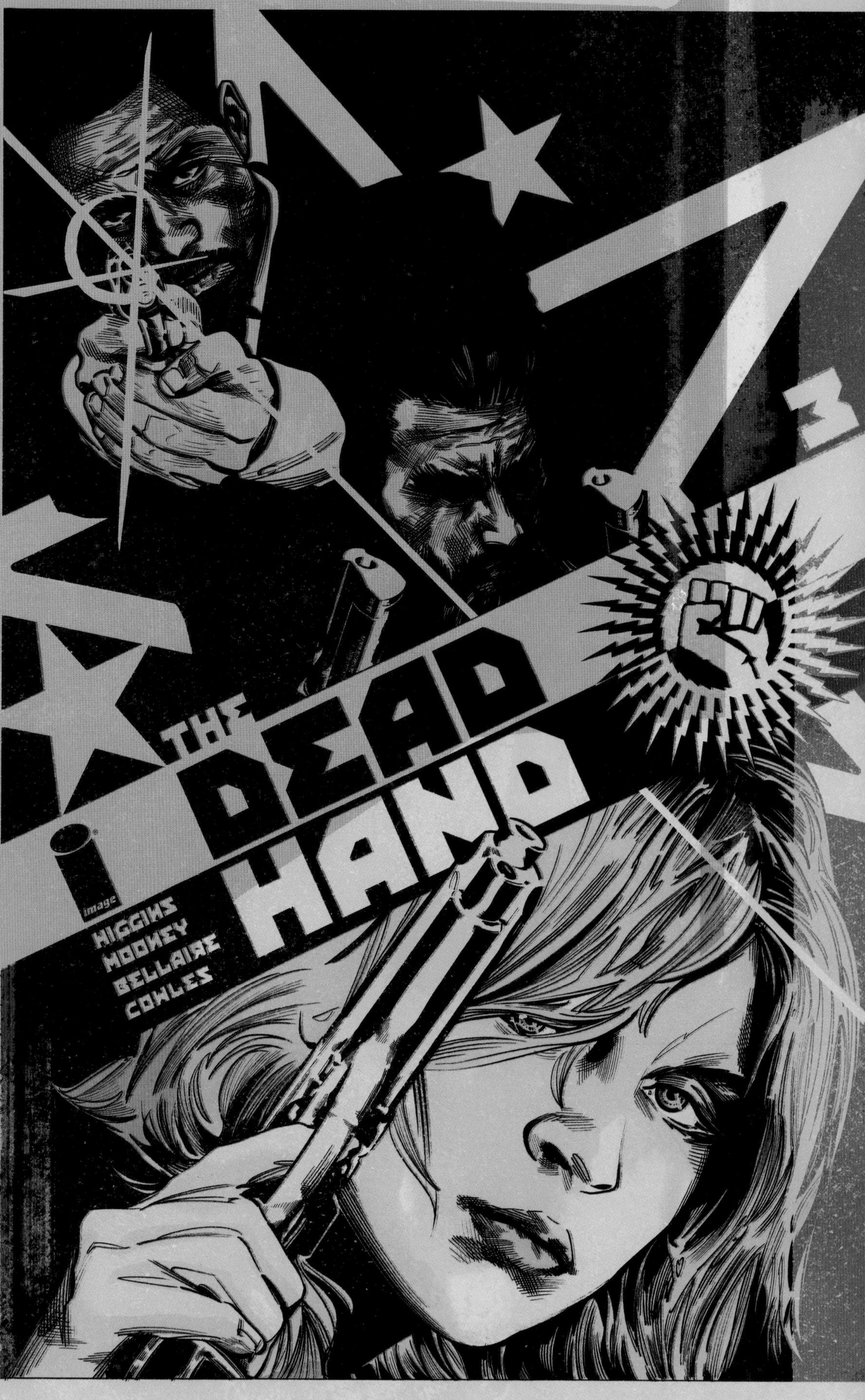

3
THE DEAD HAND
image
HIGGINS
MOONEY
BELLAIRE
COWLES

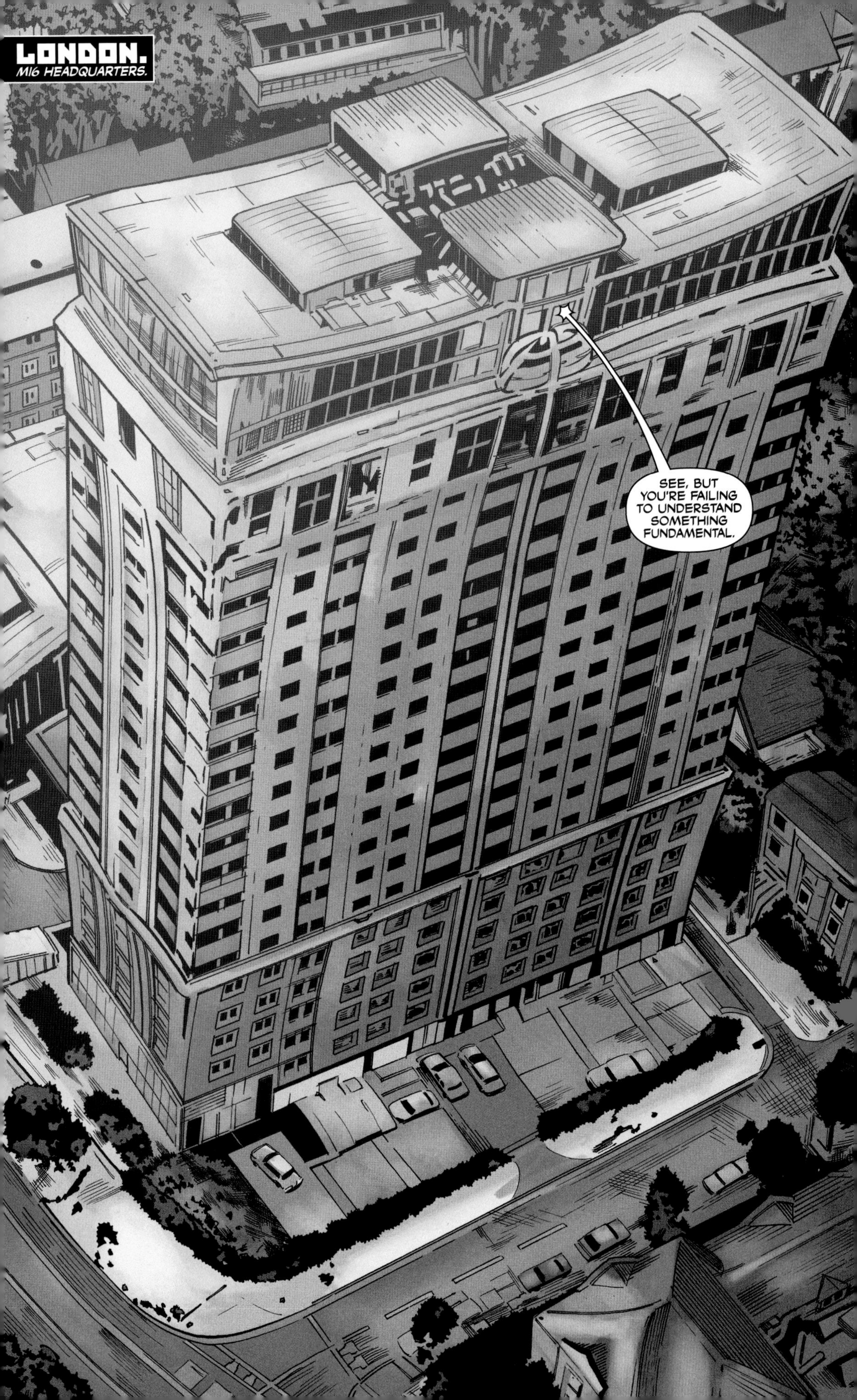
LONDON.
MI6 HEADQUARTERS.
SEE, BUT YOU'RE FAILING TO UNDERSTAND SOMETHING FUNDAMENTAL.

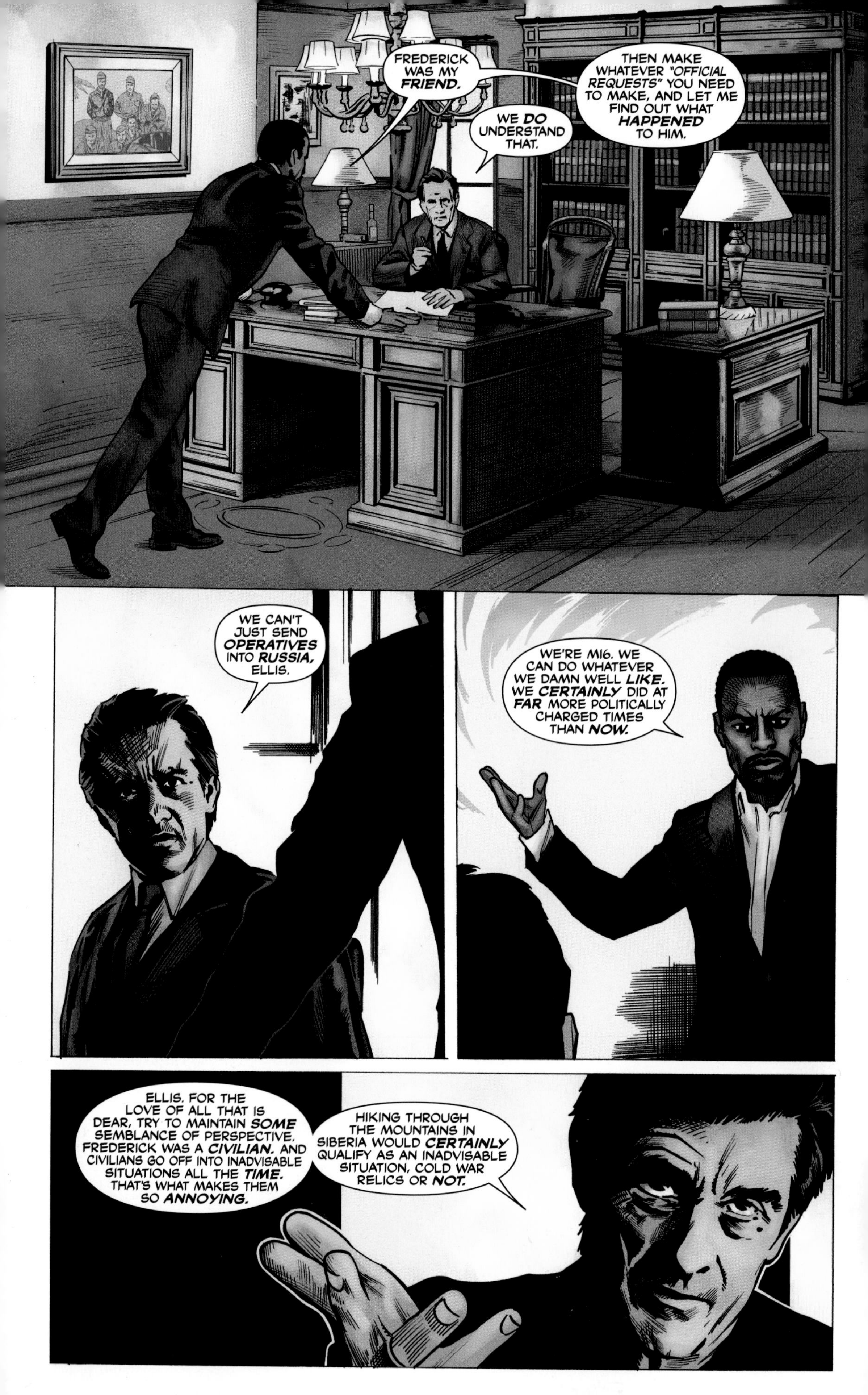
FREDERICK WAS MY FRIEND.
WE DO UNDERSTAND THAT.
THEN MAKE WHATEVER "OFFICIAL REQUESTS" YOU NEED TO MAKE, AND LET ME FIND OUT WHAT HAPPENED TO HIM.
WE CAN'T JUST SEND OPERATIVES INTO RUSSIA, ELLIS.
WE'RE MI6. WE CAN DO WHATEVER WE DAMN WELL LIKE. WE CERTAINLY DID AT FAR MORE POLITICALLY CHARGED TIMES THAN NOW.
ELLIS, FOR THE LOVE OF ALL THAT IS DEAR, TRY TO MAINTAIN SOME SEMBLANCE OF PERSPECTIVE. FREDERICK WAS A CIVILIAN. AND CIVILIANS GO OFF INTO INADVISABLE SITUATIONS ALL THE TIME. THAT'S WHAT MAKES THEM SO ANNOYING.
HIKING THROUGH THE MOUNTAINS IN SIBERIA WOULD CERTAINLY QUALIFY AS AN INADVISABLE SITUATION, COLD WAR RELICS OR NOT.

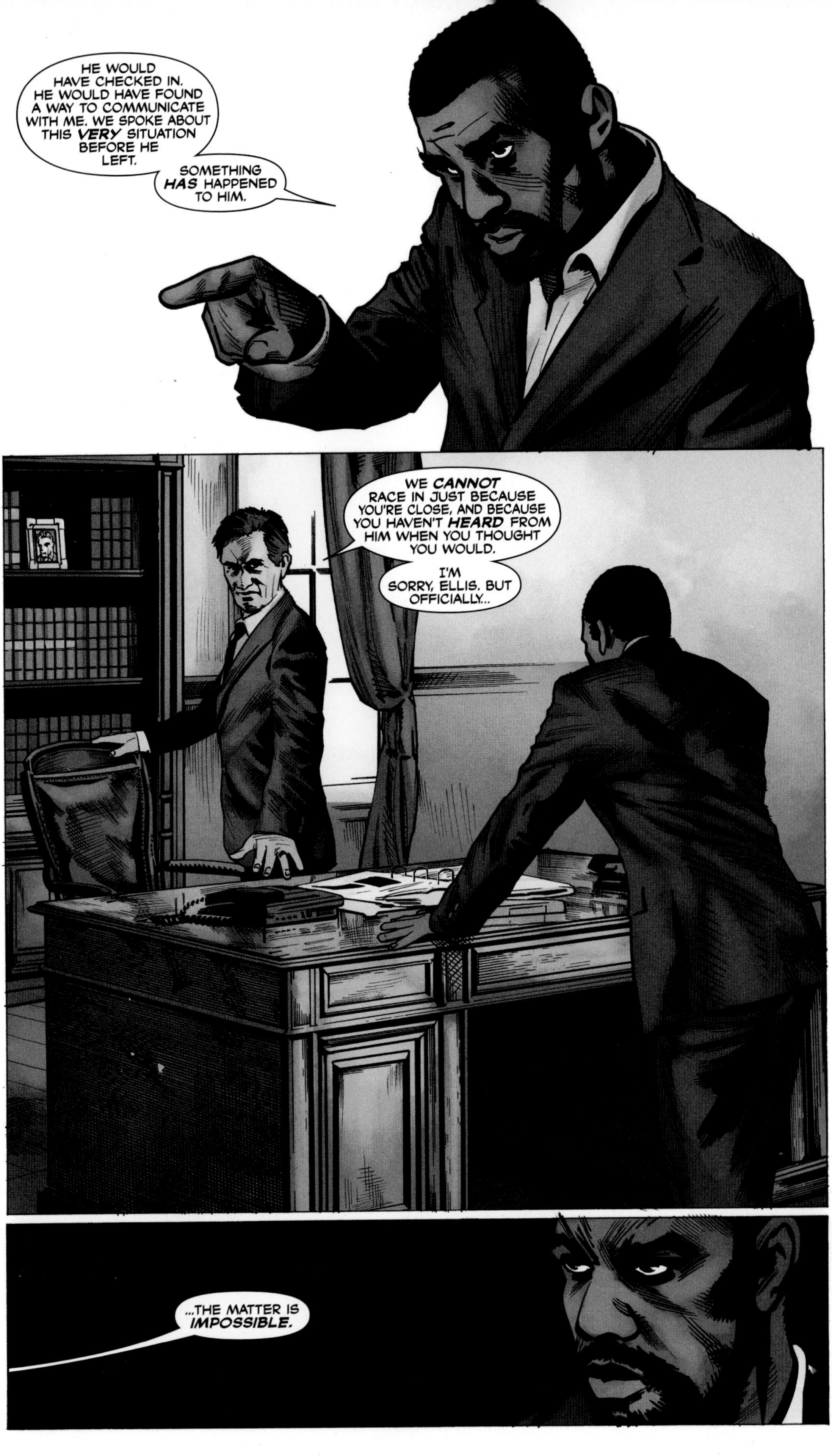
HE WOULD HAVE CHECKED IN. HE WOULD HAVE FOUND A WAY TO COMMUNICATE WITH ME. WE SPOKE ABOUT THIS VERY SITUATION BEFORE HE LEFT.
SOMETHING HAS HAPPENED TO HIM.
WE CANNOT RACE IN JUST BECAUSE YOU'RE CLOSE, AND BECAUSE YOU HAVEN'T HEARD FROM HIM WHEN YOU THOUGHT YOU WOULD.
I'M SORRY, ELLIS, BUT OFFICIALLY...
...THE MATTER IS IMPOSSIBLE.

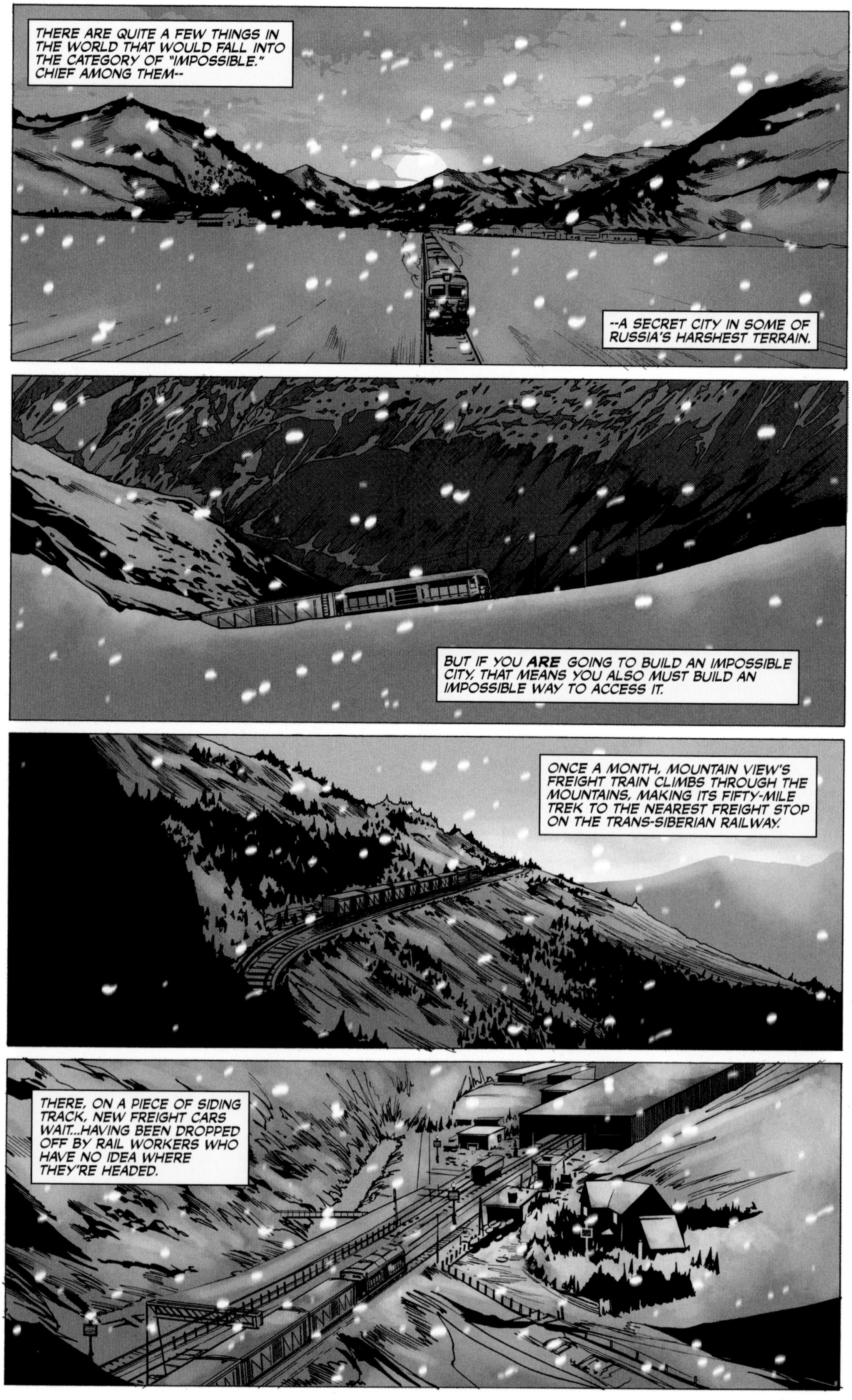
THERE ARE QUITE A FEW THINGS IN THE WORLD THAT WOULD FALL INTO THE CATEGORY OF "IMPOSSIBLE." CHIEF AMONG THEM--
--A SECRET CITY IN SOME OF RUSSIA'S HARSHEST TERRAIN.
BUT IF YOU **ARE** GOING TO BUILD AN IMPOSSIBLE CITY, THAT MEANS YOU ALSO MUST BUILD AN IMPOSSIBLE WAY TO ACCESS IT.
ONCE A MONTH, MOUNTAIN VIEW'S FREIGHT TRAIN CLIMBS THROUGH THE MOUNTAINS, MAKING ITS FIFTY-MILE TREK TO THE NEAREST FREIGHT STOP ON THE TRANS-SIBERIAN RAILWAY.
THERE, ON A PIECE OF SIDING TRACK, NEW FREIGHT CARS WAIT...HAVING BEEN DROPPED OFF BY RAIL WORKERS WHO HAVE NO IDEA WHERE THEY'RE HEADED.

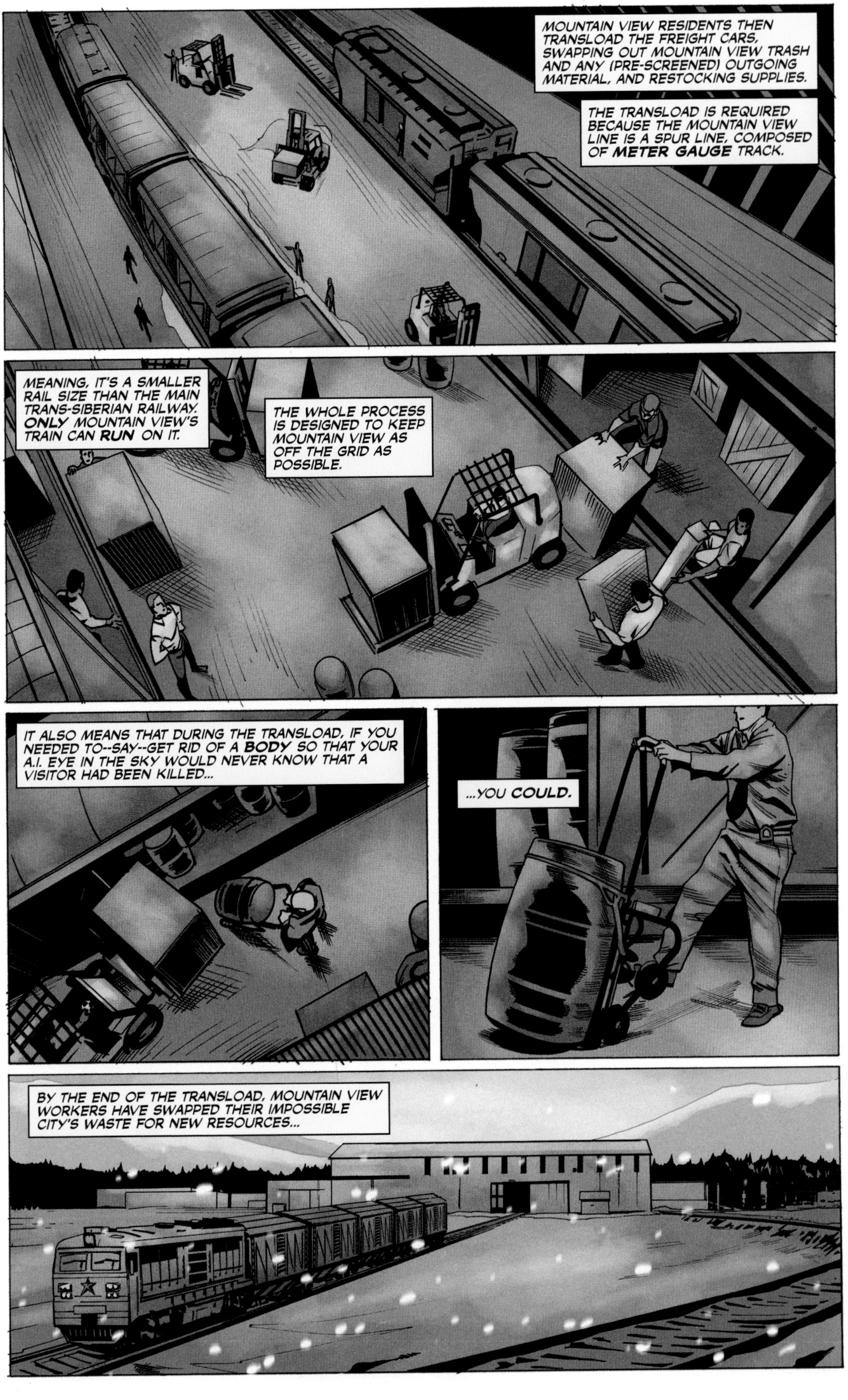
MOUNTAIN VIEW RESIDENTS THEN TRANSLOAD THE FREIGHT CARS, SWAPPING OUT MOUNTAIN VIEW TRASH AND ANY (PRE-SCREENED) OUTGOING MATERIAL, AND RESTOCKING SUPPLIES.
THE TRANSLOAD IS REQUIRED BECAUSE THE MOUNTAIN VIEW LINE IS A SPUR LINE, COMPOSED OF METER GAUGE TRACK.
MEANING, IT'S A SMALLER RAIL SIZE THAN THE MAIN TRANS-SIBERIAN RAILWAY. ONLY MOUNTAIN VIEW'S TRAIN CAN RUN ON IT.
THE WHOLE PROCESS IS DESIGNED TO KEEP MOUNTAIN VIEW AS OFF THE GRID AS POSSIBLE.
IT ALSO MEANS THAT DURING THE TRANSLOAD, IF YOU NEEDED TO--SAY--GET RID OF A BODY SO THAT YOUR A.I. EYE IN THE SKY WOULD NEVER KNOW THAT A VISITOR HAD BEEN KILLED...
...YOU COULD.
BY THE END OF THE TRANSLOAD, MOUNTAIN VIEW WORKERS HAVE SWAPPED THEIR IMPOSSIBLE CITY'S WASTE FOR NEW RESOURCES...

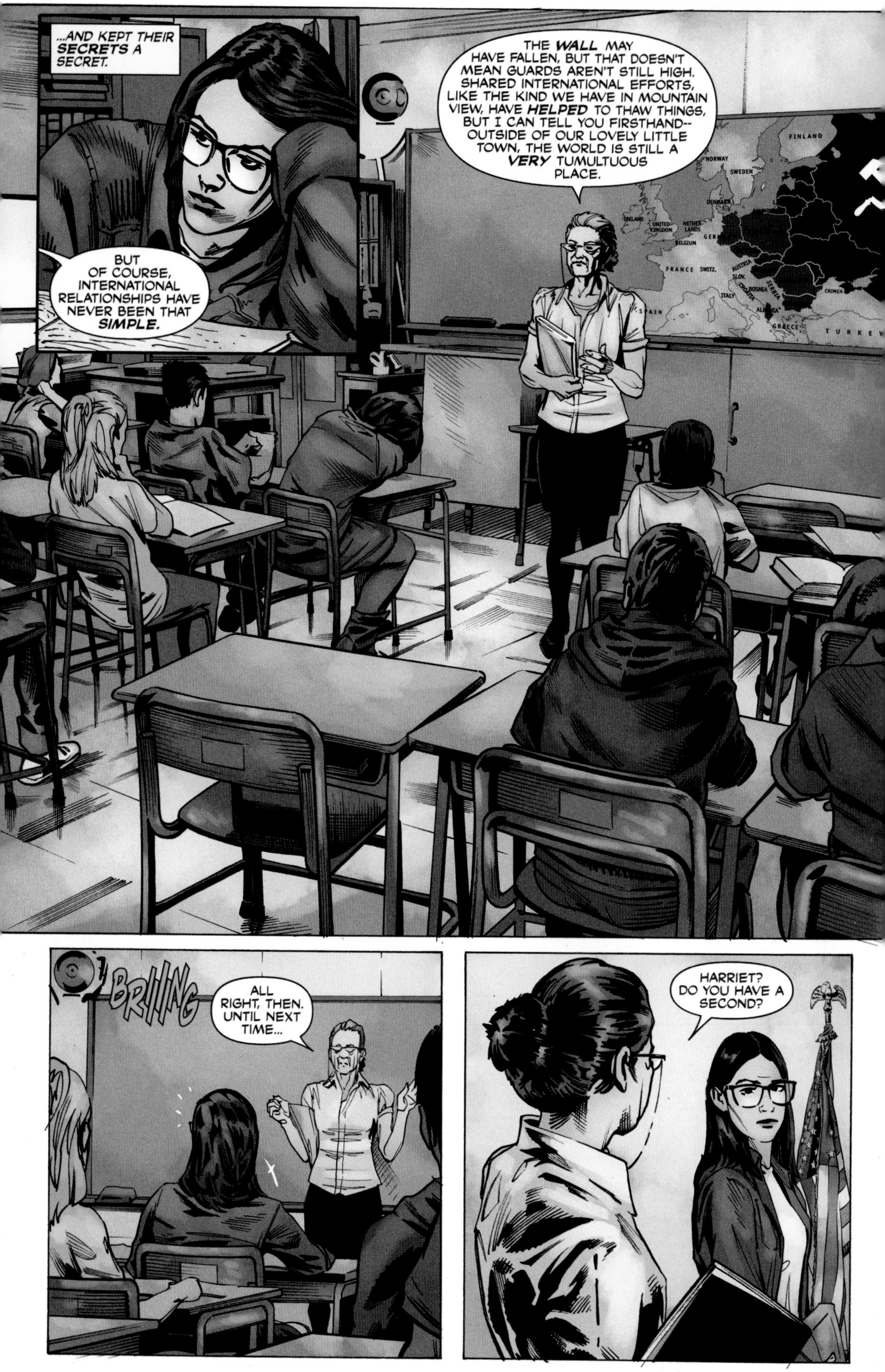
...AND KEPT THEIR SECRETS A SECRET.
BUT OF COURSE, INTERNATIONAL RELATIONSHIPS HAVE NEVER BEEN THAT SIMPLE.
THE WALL MAY HAVE FALLEN, BUT THAT DOESN'T MEAN GUARDS AREN'T STILL HIGH. SHARED INTERNATIONAL EFFORTS, LIKE THE KIND WE HAVE IN MOUNTAIN VIEW, HAVE HELPED TO THAW THINGS, BUT I CAN TELL YOU FIRSTHAND--OUTSIDE OF OUR LOVELY LITTLE TOWN, THE WORLD IS STILL A VERY TUMULTUOUS PLACE.
FINLAND
NORWAY
SWEDEN
IRELAND
UNITED KINGDOM
NETHERLANDS
BELGIUM
FRANCE
SWITZ.
AUSTRIA
ITALY
BOSNIA
CRIMEA
TURKEY
BRIIING
ALL RIGHT, THEN. UNTIL NEXT TIME...
HARRIET? DO YOU HAVE A SECOND?

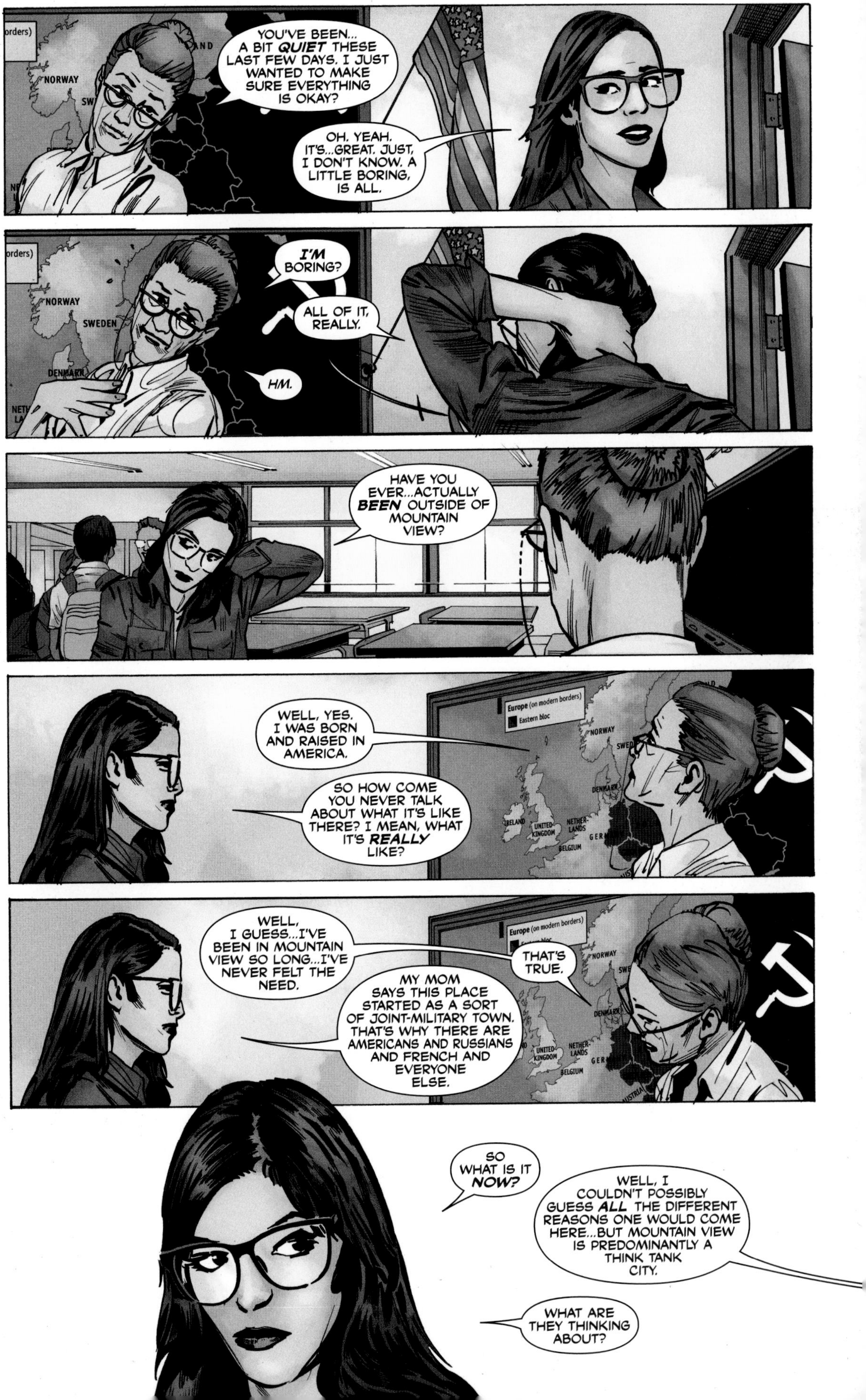

orders)
NORWAY
YOU'VE BEEN... A BIT QUIET THESE LAST FEW DAYS. I JUST WANTED TO MAKE SURE EVERYTHING IS OKAY?
OH. YEAH. IT'S...GREAT. JUST, I DON'T KNOW. A LITTLE BORING, IS ALL.
orders)
NORWAY
SWEDEN
DENMARK
I'M BORING?
ALL OF IT, REALLY.
HM.
HAVE YOU EVER...ACTUALLY BEEN OUTSIDE OF MOUNTAIN VIEW?
Europe (on modern borders)
Eastern bloc
NORWAY
IRELAND
UNITED KINGDOM
NETHER-LANDS
BELGIUM
DENMARK
WELL, YES. I WAS BORN AND RAISED IN AMERICA.
SO HOW COME YOU NEVER TALK ABOUT WHAT IT'S LIKE THERE? I MEAN, WHAT IT'S REALLY LIKE?
Europe (on modern borders)
NORWAY
UNITED KINGDOM
NETHER-LANDS
BELGIUM
DENMARK
AUSTRIA
WELL, I GUESS...I'VE BEEN IN MOUNTAIN VIEW SO LONG...I'VE NEVER FELT THE NEED.
THAT'S TRUE.
MY MOM SAYS THIS PLACE STARTED AS A SORT OF JOINT-MILITARY TOWN. THAT'S WHY THERE ARE AMERICANS AND RUSSIANS AND FRENCH AND EVERYONE ELSE.
SO WHAT IS IT NOW?
WELL, I COULDN'T POSSIBLY GUESS ALL THE DIFFERENT REASONS ONE WOULD COME HERE...BUT MOUNTAIN VIEW IS PREDOMINANTLY A THINK TANK CITY.
WHAT ARE THEY THINKING ABOUT?

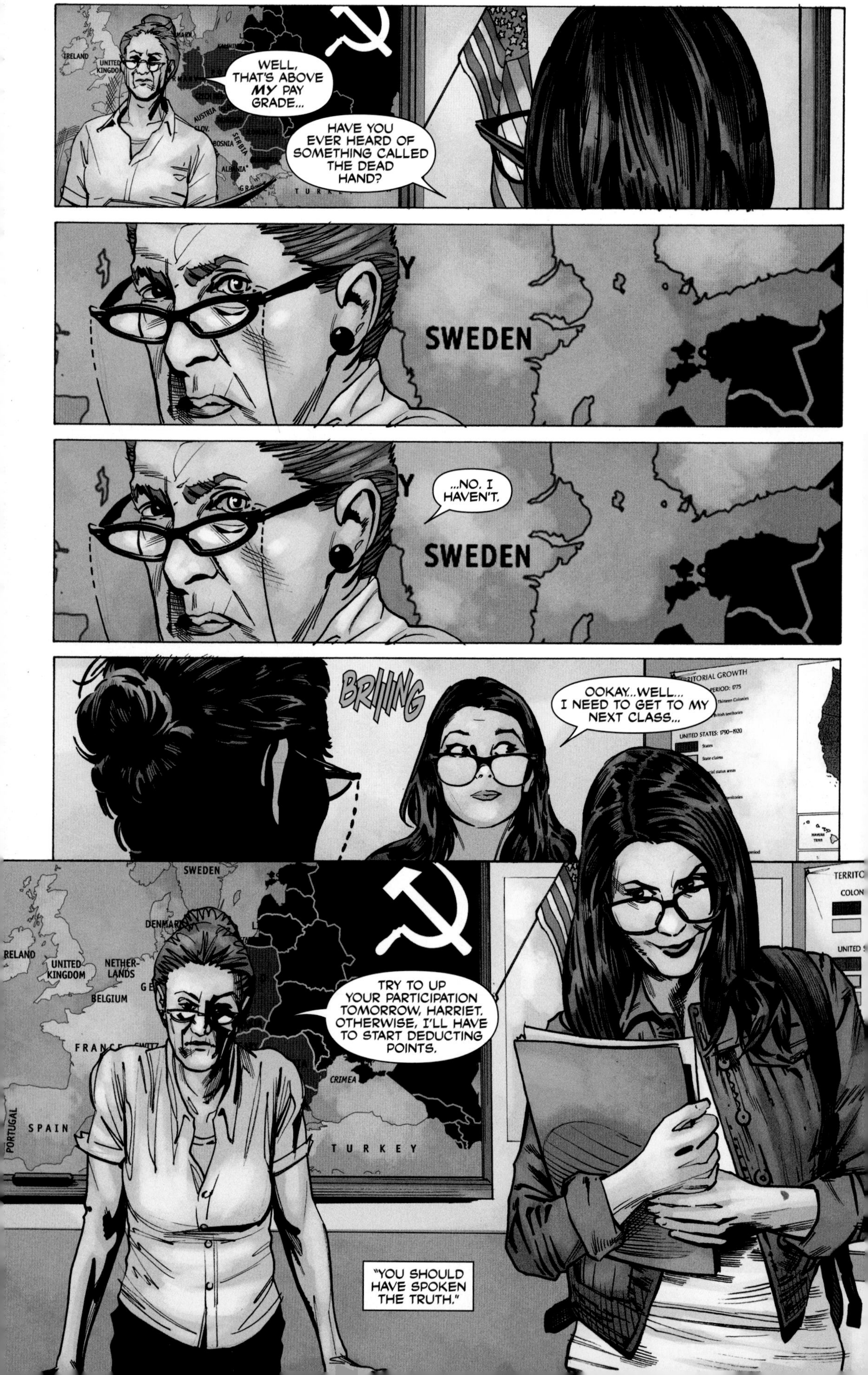
WELL, THAT'S ABOVE MY PAY GRADE...
HAVE YOU EVER HEARD OF SOMETHING CALLED THE DEAD HAND?
SWEDEN
SWEDEN
...NO. I HAVEN'T.
BRIIING
OOKAY...WELL... I NEED TO GET TO MY NEXT CLASS...
TERRITORIAL GROWTH
TRY TO UP YOUR PARTICIPATION TOMORROW, HARRIET. OTHERWISE, I'LL HAVE TO START DEDUCTING POINTS.
"YOU SHOULD HAVE SPOKEN THE TRUTH."

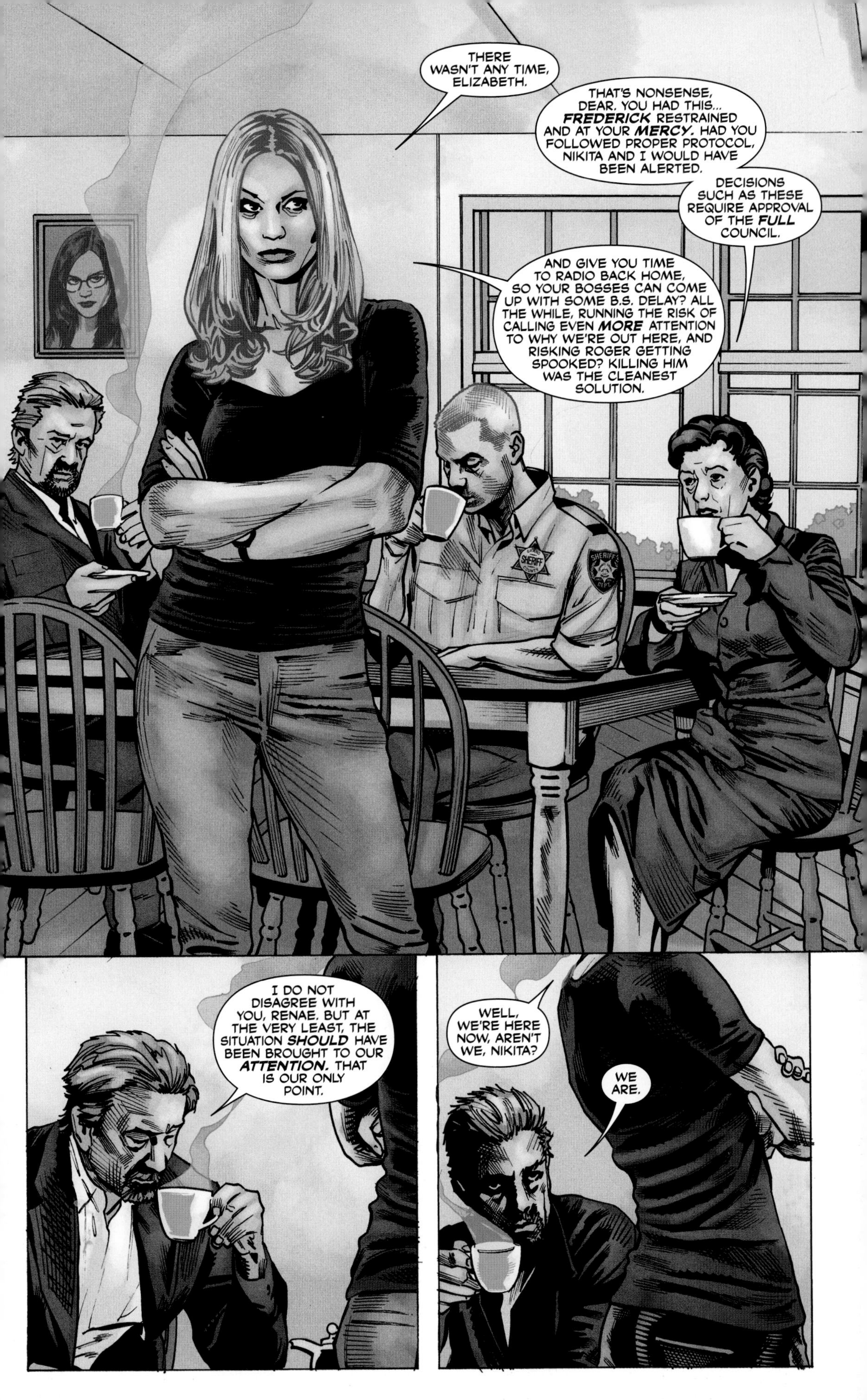

THERE WASN'T ANY TIME, ELIZABETH.
THAT'S NONSENSE, DEAR. YOU HAD THIS... ***FREDERICK*** RESTRAINED AND AT YOUR ***MERCY.*** HAD YOU FOLLOWED PROPER PROTOCOL, NIKITA AND I WOULD HAVE BEEN ALERTED.
DECISIONS SUCH AS THESE REQUIRE APPROVAL OF THE ***FULL*** COUNCIL.
AND GIVE YOU TIME TO RADIO BACK HOME, SO YOUR BOSSES CAN COME UP WITH SOME B.S. DELAY? ALL THE WHILE, RUNNING THE RISK OF CALLING EVEN ***MORE*** ATTENTION TO WHY WE'RE OUT HERE, AND RISKING ROGER GETTING SPOOKED? KILLING HIM WAS THE CLEANEST SOLUTION.
I DO NOT DISAGREE WITH YOU, RENAE. BUT AT THE VERY LEAST, THE SITUATION ***SHOULD*** HAVE BEEN BROUGHT TO OUR ***ATTENTION.*** THAT IS OUR ONLY POINT.
WELL, WE'RE HERE NOW, AREN'T WE, NIKITA?
WE ARE.

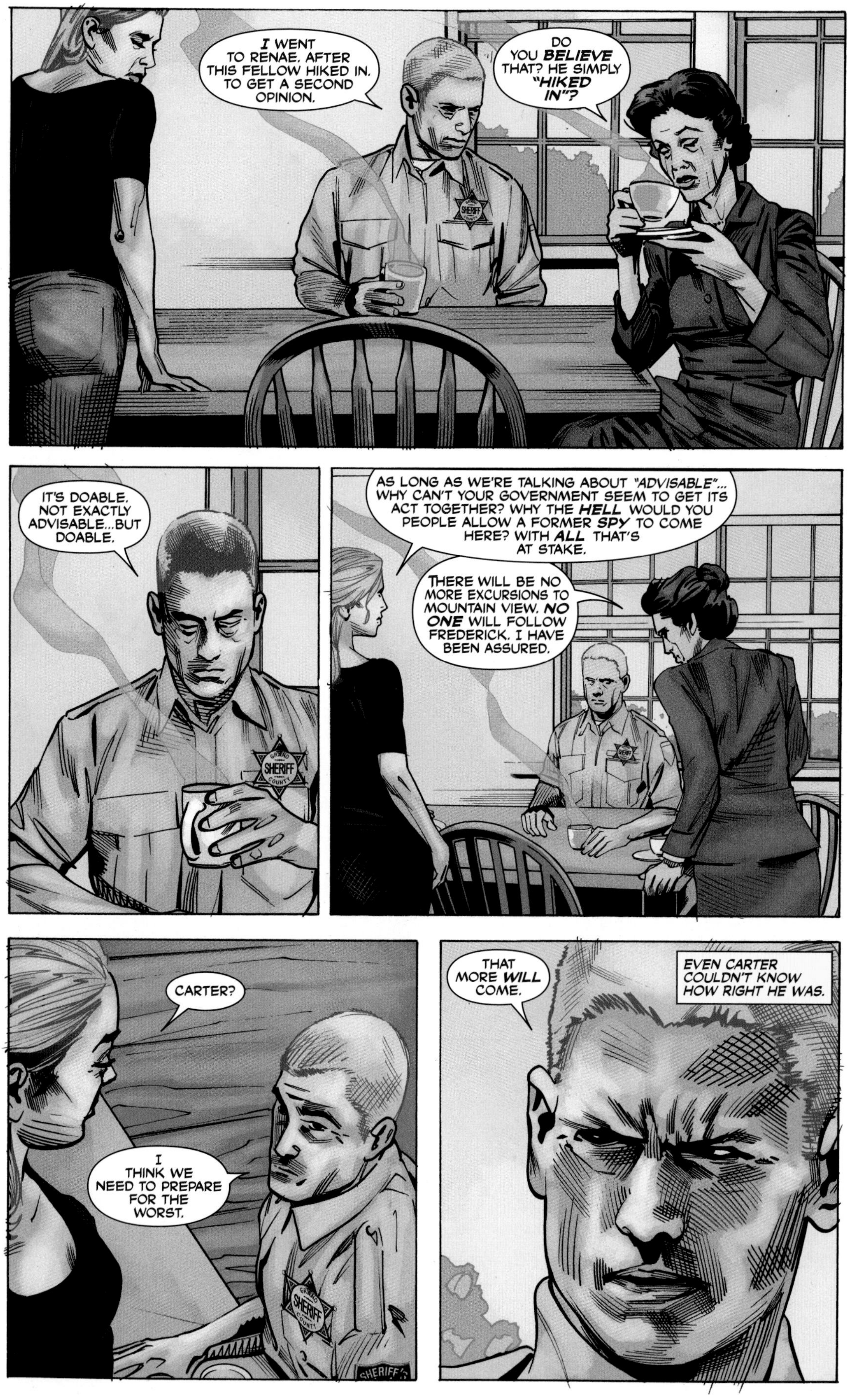
I WENT TO RENAE, AFTER THIS FELLOW HIKED IN, TO GET A SECOND OPINION.
DO YOU BELIEVE THAT? HE SIMPLY "HIKED IN"?
IT'S DOABLE. NOT EXACTLY ADVISABLE...BUT DOABLE.
AS LONG AS WE'RE TALKING ABOUT "ADVISABLE"... WHY CAN'T YOUR GOVERNMENT SEEM TO GET ITS ACT TOGETHER? WHY THE HELL WOULD YOU PEOPLE ALLOW A FORMER SPY TO COME HERE? WITH ALL THAT'S AT STAKE.
THERE WILL BE NO MORE EXCURSIONS TO MOUNTAIN VIEW. NO ONE WILL FOLLOW FREDERICK. I HAVE BEEN ASSURED.
CARTER?
I THINK WE NEED TO PREPARE FOR THE WORST.
THAT MORE WILL COME.
EVEN CARTER COULDN'T KNOW HOW RIGHT HE WAS.

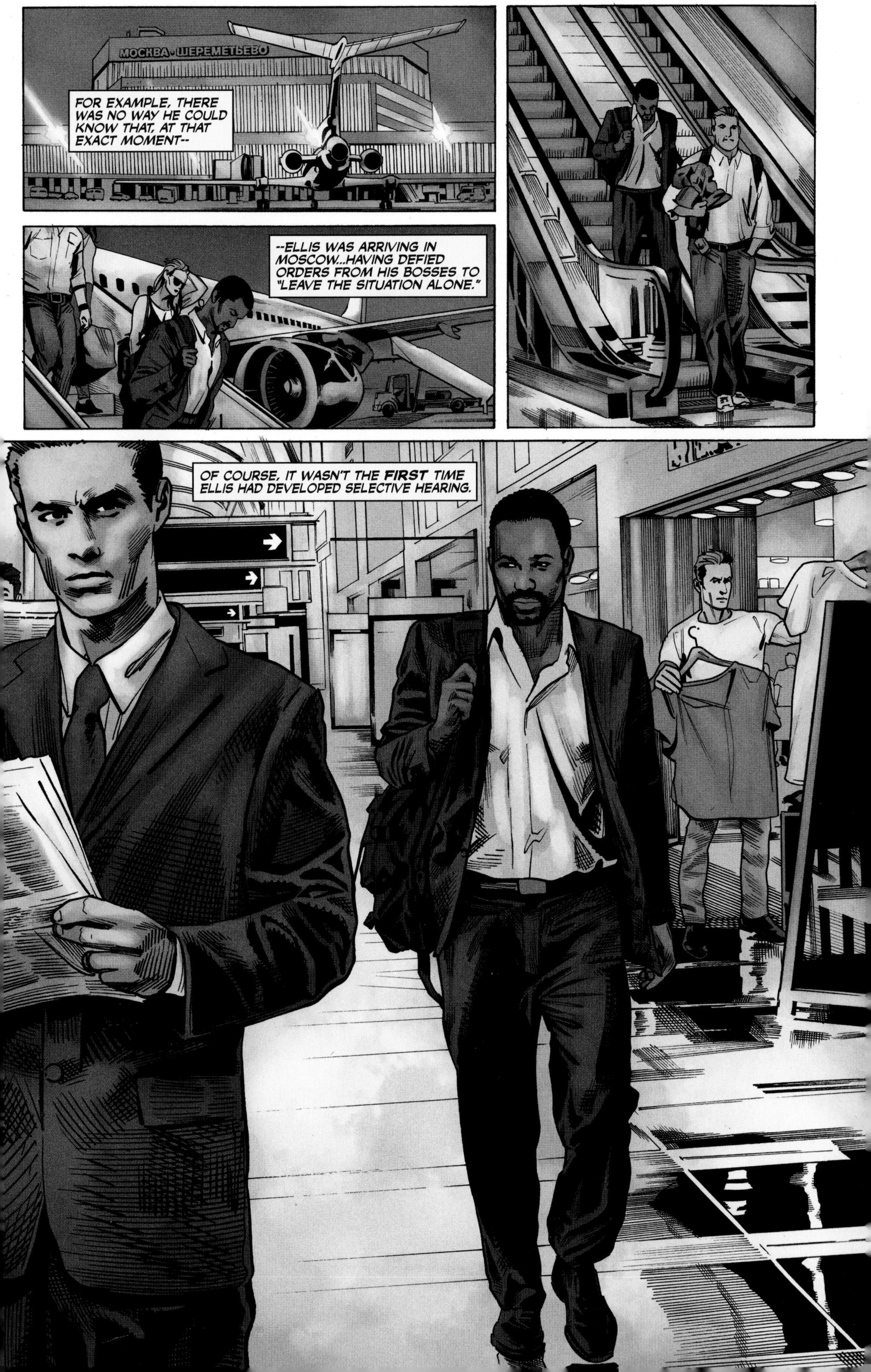
МОСКВА · ШЕРЕМЕТЬЕВО
FOR EXAMPLE, THERE WAS NO WAY HE COULD KNOW THAT, AT THAT EXACT MOMENT--
--ELLIS WAS ARRIVING IN MOSCOW...HAVING DEFIED ORDERS FROM HIS BOSSES TO "LEAVE THE SITUATION ALONE."
OF COURSE, IT WASN'T THE **FIRST** TIME ELLIS HAD DEVELOPED SELECTIVE HEARING.

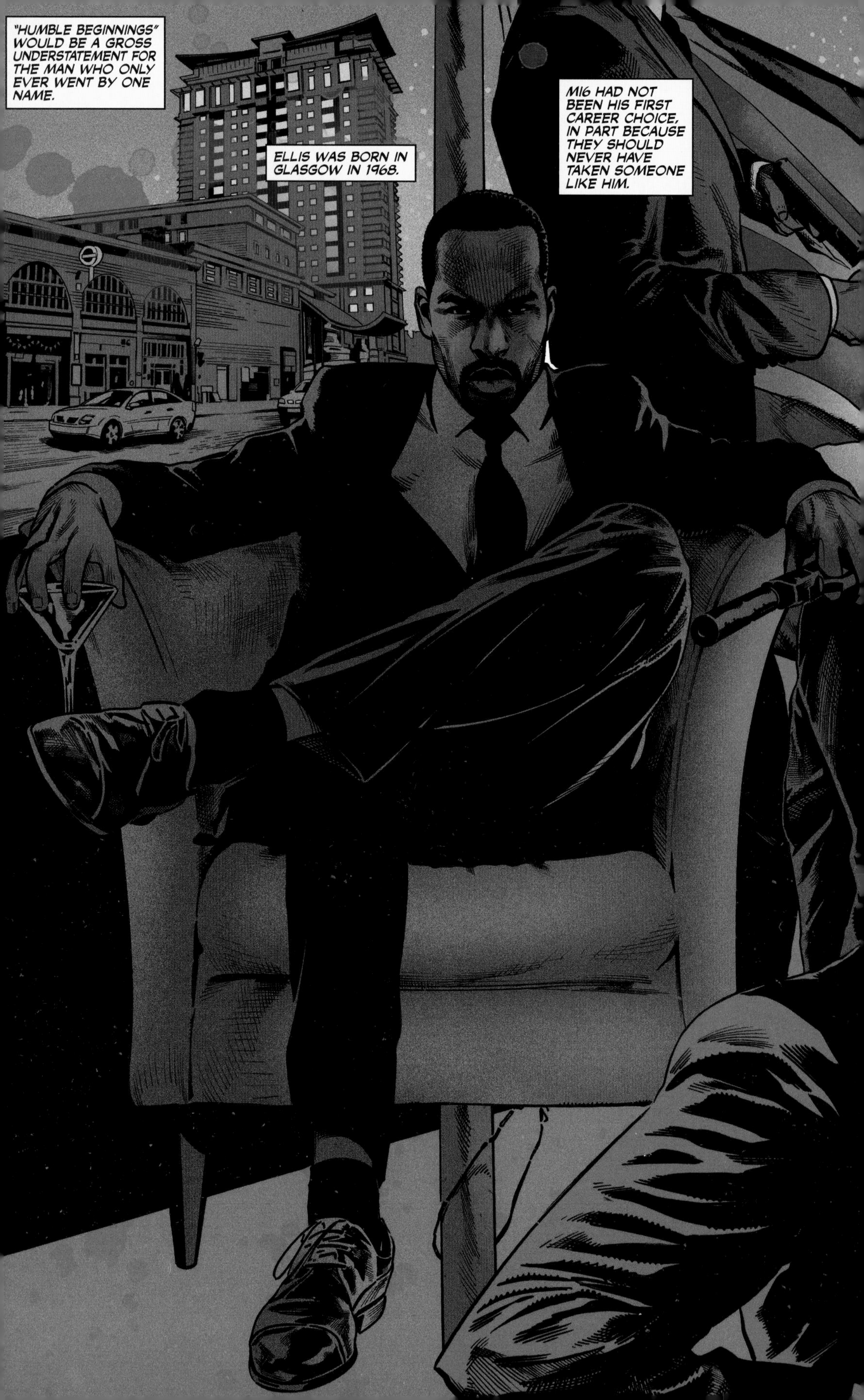
"HUMBLE BEGINNINGS" WOULD BE A GROSS UNDERSTATEMENT FOR THE MAN WHO ONLY EVER WENT BY ONE NAME.
ELLIS WAS BORN IN GLASGOW IN 1968.
MI6 HAD NOT BEEN HIS FIRST CAREER CHOICE, IN PART BECAUSE THEY SHOULD NEVER HAVE TAKEN SOMEONE LIKE HIM.

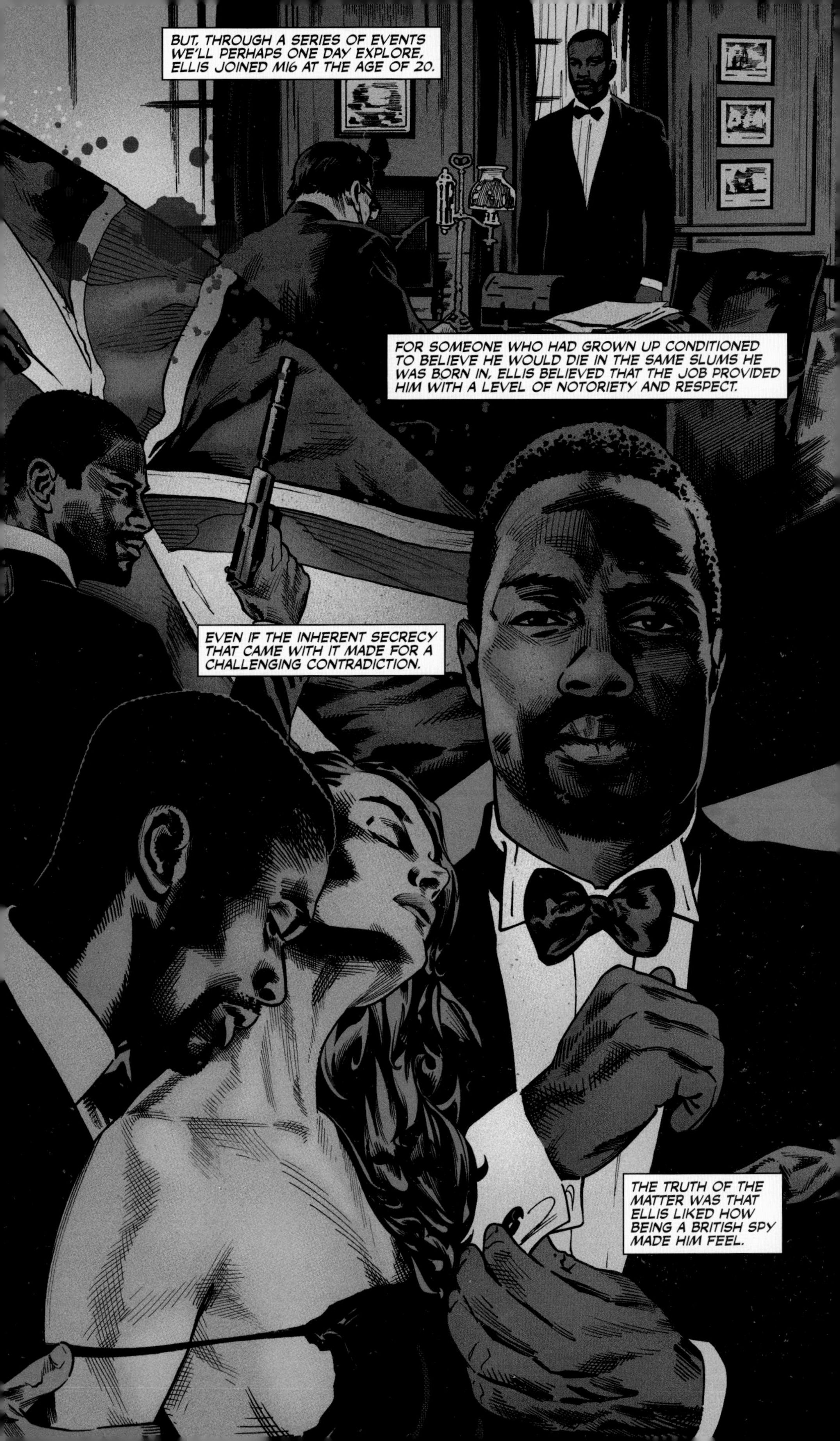
BUT, THROUGH A SERIES OF EVENTS WE'LL PERHAPS ONE DAY EXPLORE, ELLIS JOINED MI6 AT THE AGE OF 20.
FOR SOMEONE WHO HAD GROWN UP CONDITIONED TO BELIEVE HE WOULD DIE IN THE SAME SLUMS HE WAS BORN IN, ELLIS BELIEVED THAT THE JOB PROVIDED HIM WITH A LEVEL OF NOTORIETY AND RESPECT.
EVEN IF THE INHERENT SECRECY THAT CAME WITH IT MADE FOR A CHALLENGING CONTRADICTION.
THE TRUTH OF THE MATTER WAS THAT ELLIS LIKED HOW BEING A BRITISH SPY MADE HIM FEEL.

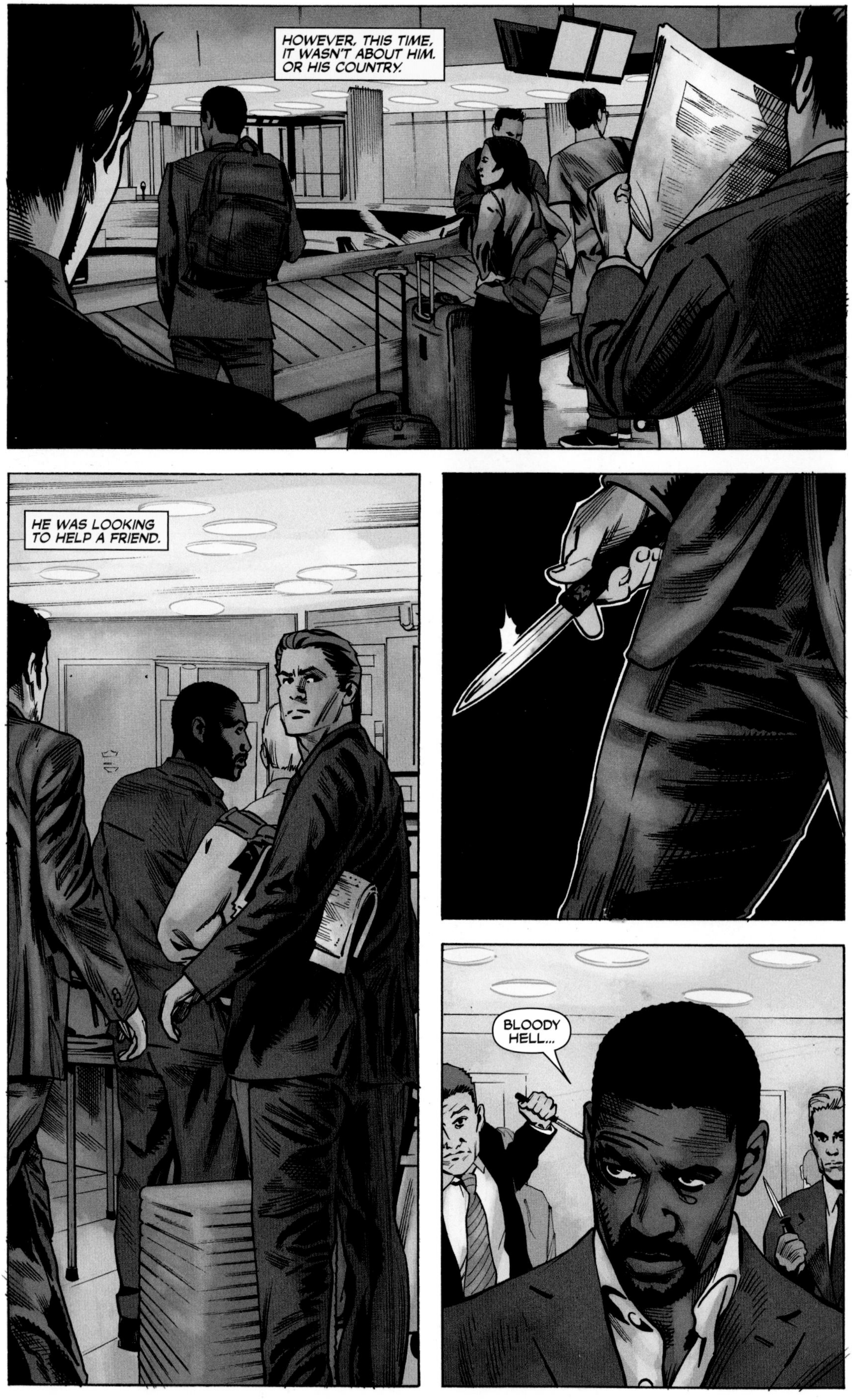
HOWEVER, THIS TIME, IT WASN'T ABOUT HIM. OR HIS COUNTRY.
HE WAS LOOKING TO HELP A FRIEND.
BLOODY HELL...

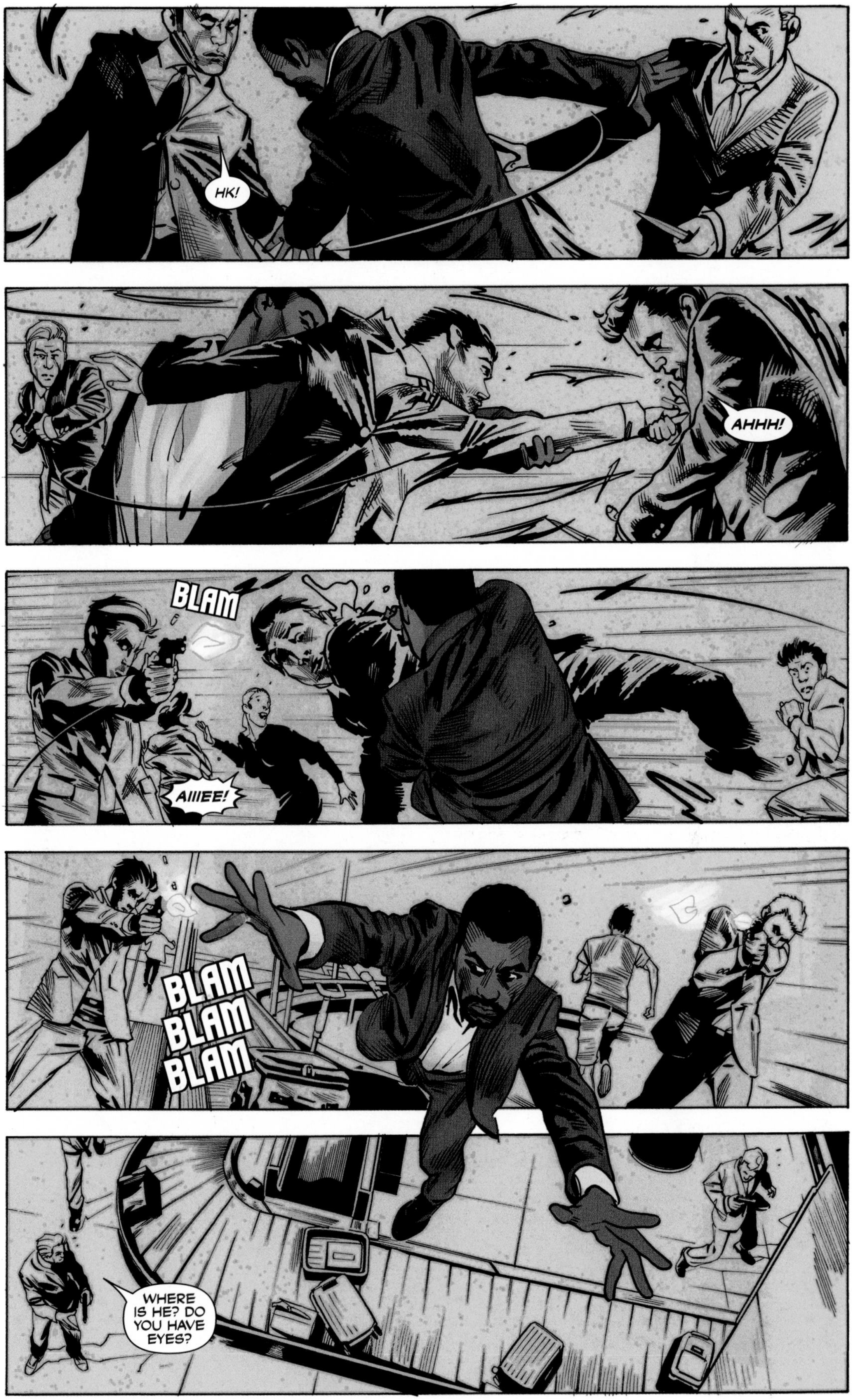
HK!
AHHH!
BLAM
AIIIEE!
BLAM
BLAM
BLAM
WHERE IS HE? DO YOU HAVE EYES?

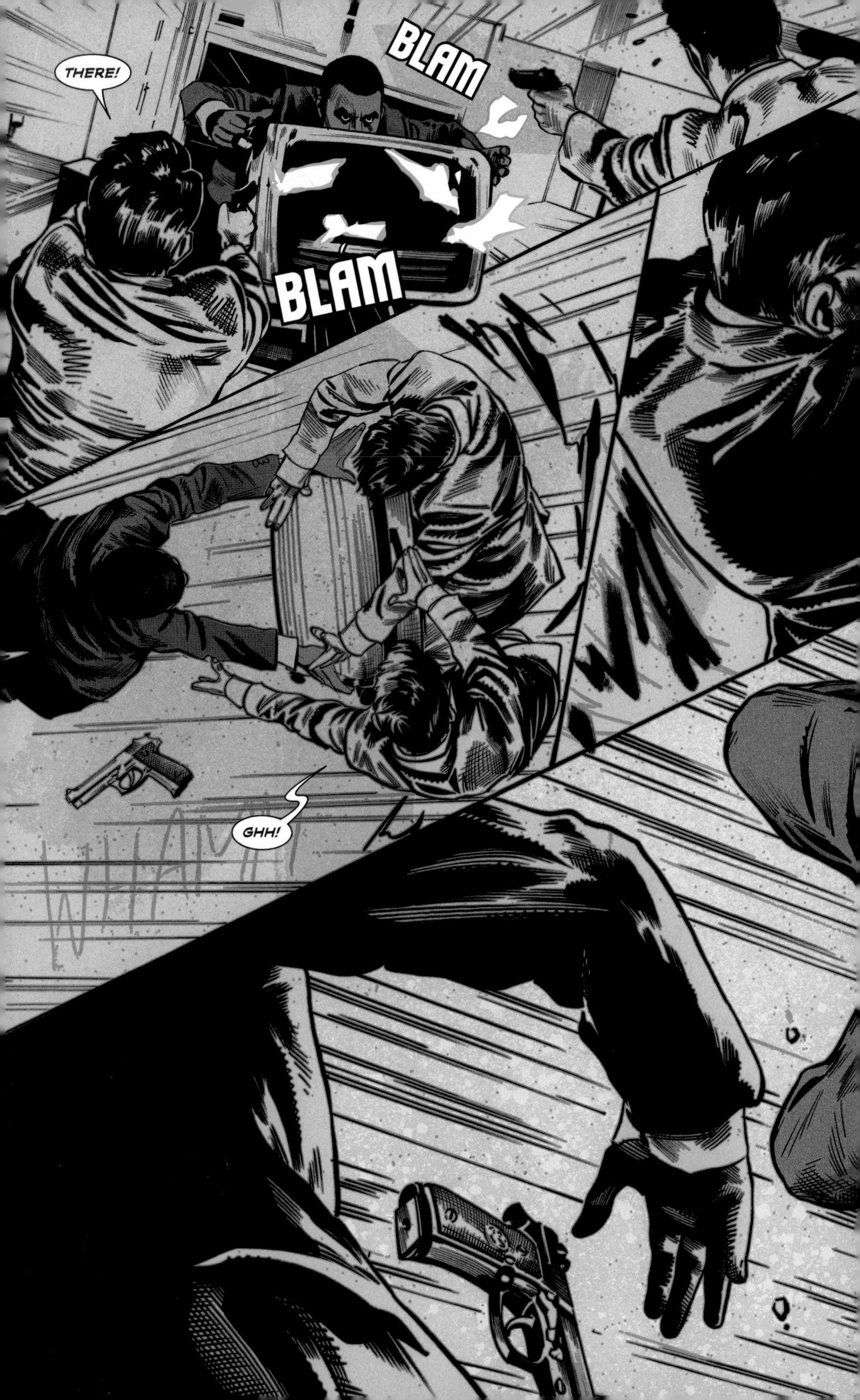
THERE!
BLAM
BLAM
GHH!
WHAM

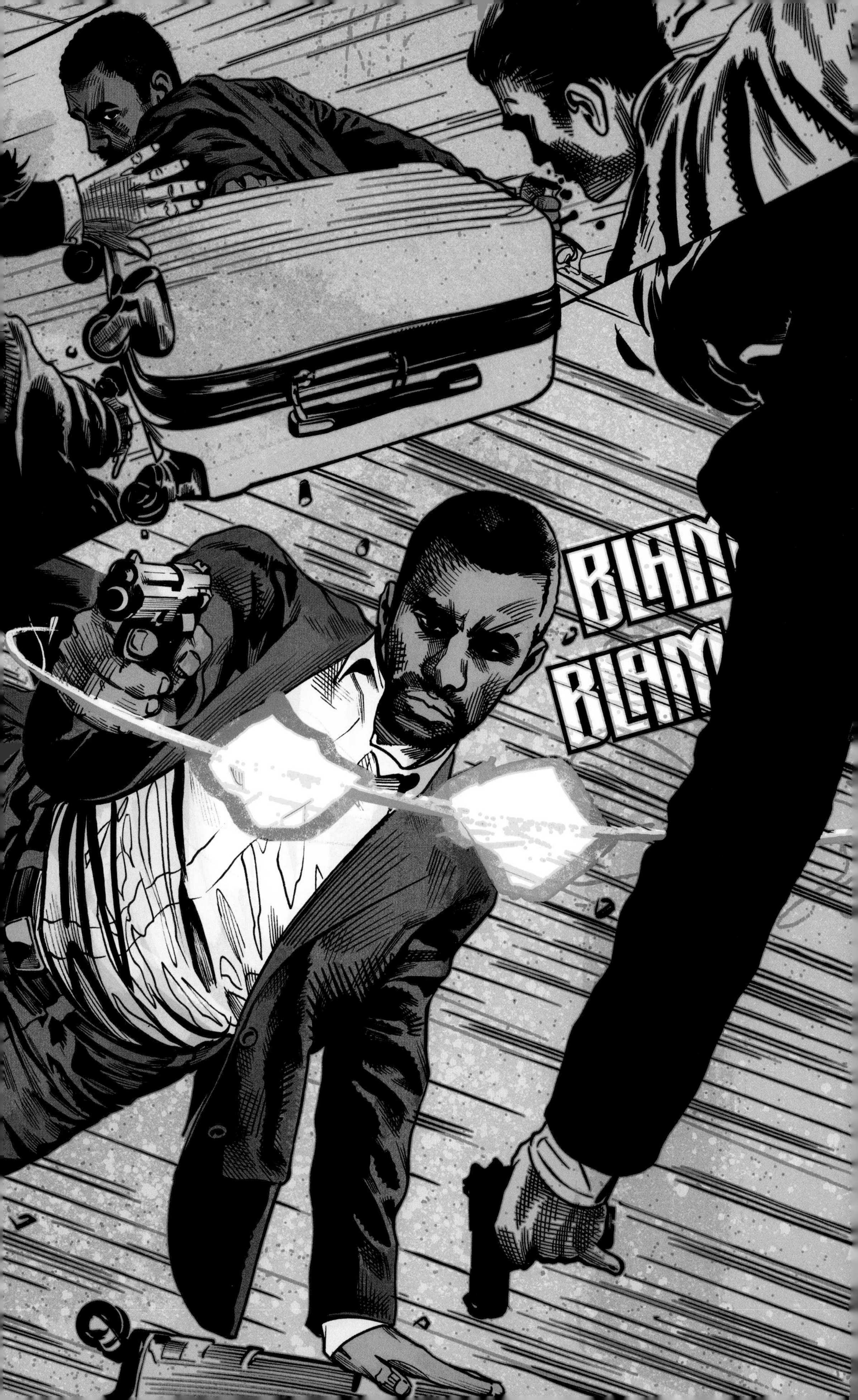
BLAM
BLAM

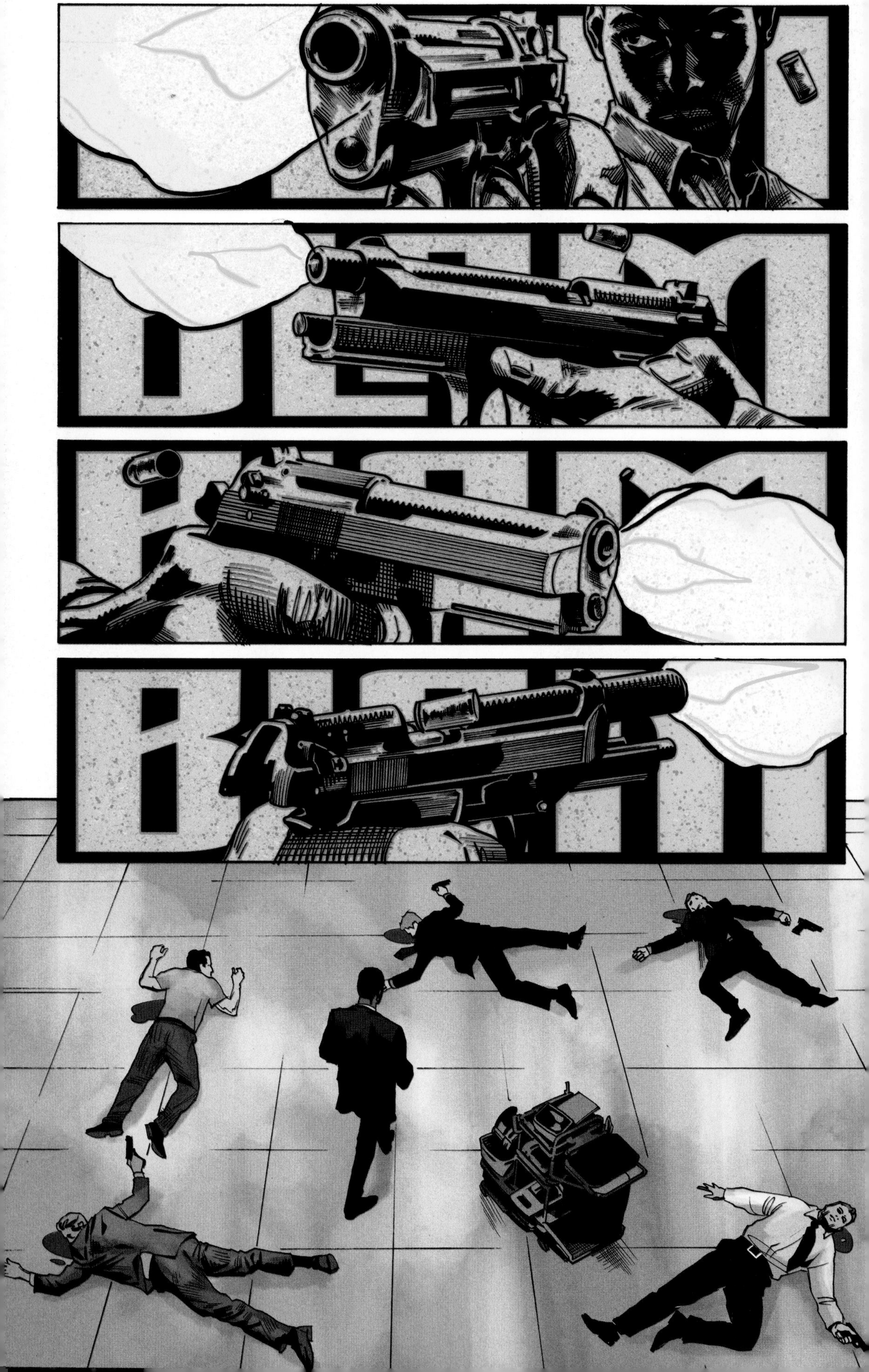

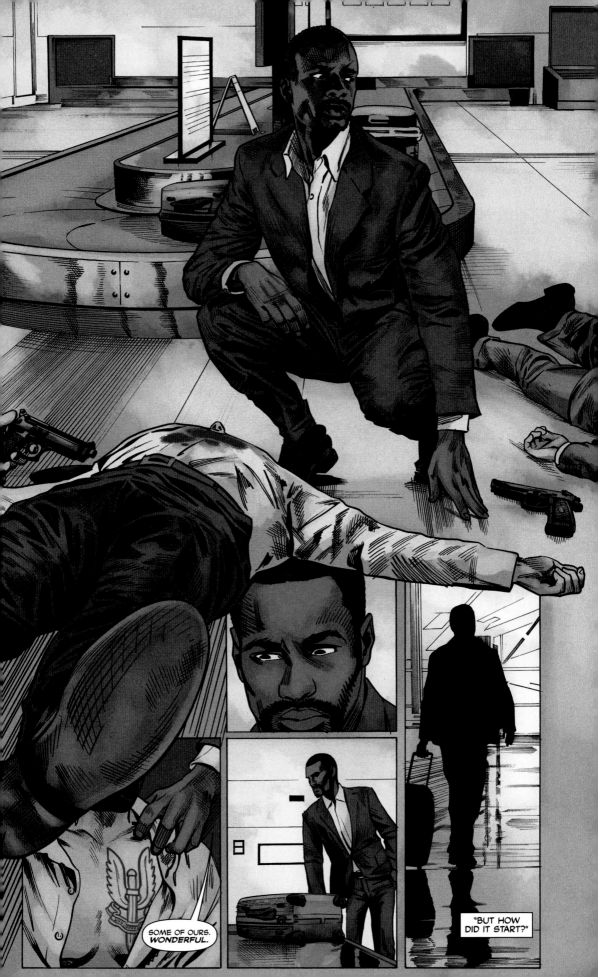

SOME OF OURS. *WONDERFUL.*

"BUT HOW DID IT START?"

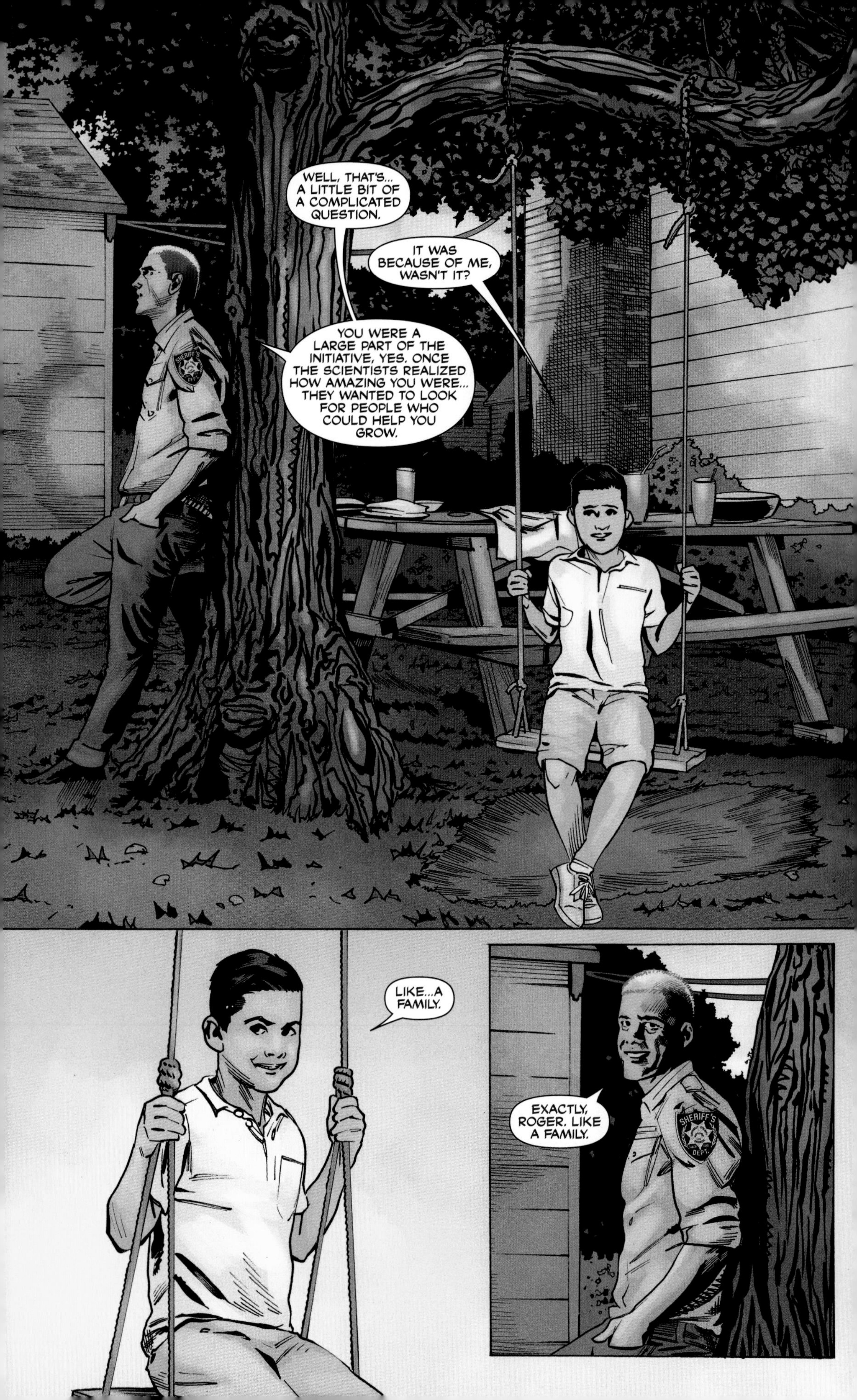
WELL, THAT'S... A LITTLE BIT OF A COMPLICATED QUESTION.
IT WAS BECAUSE OF ME, WASN'T IT?
YOU WERE A LARGE PART OF THE INITIATIVE, YES. ONCE THE SCIENTISTS REALIZED HOW AMAZING YOU WERE... THEY WANTED TO LOOK FOR PEOPLE WHO COULD HELP YOU GROW.
LIKE...A FAMILY.
EXACTLY, ROGER. LIKE A FAMILY.

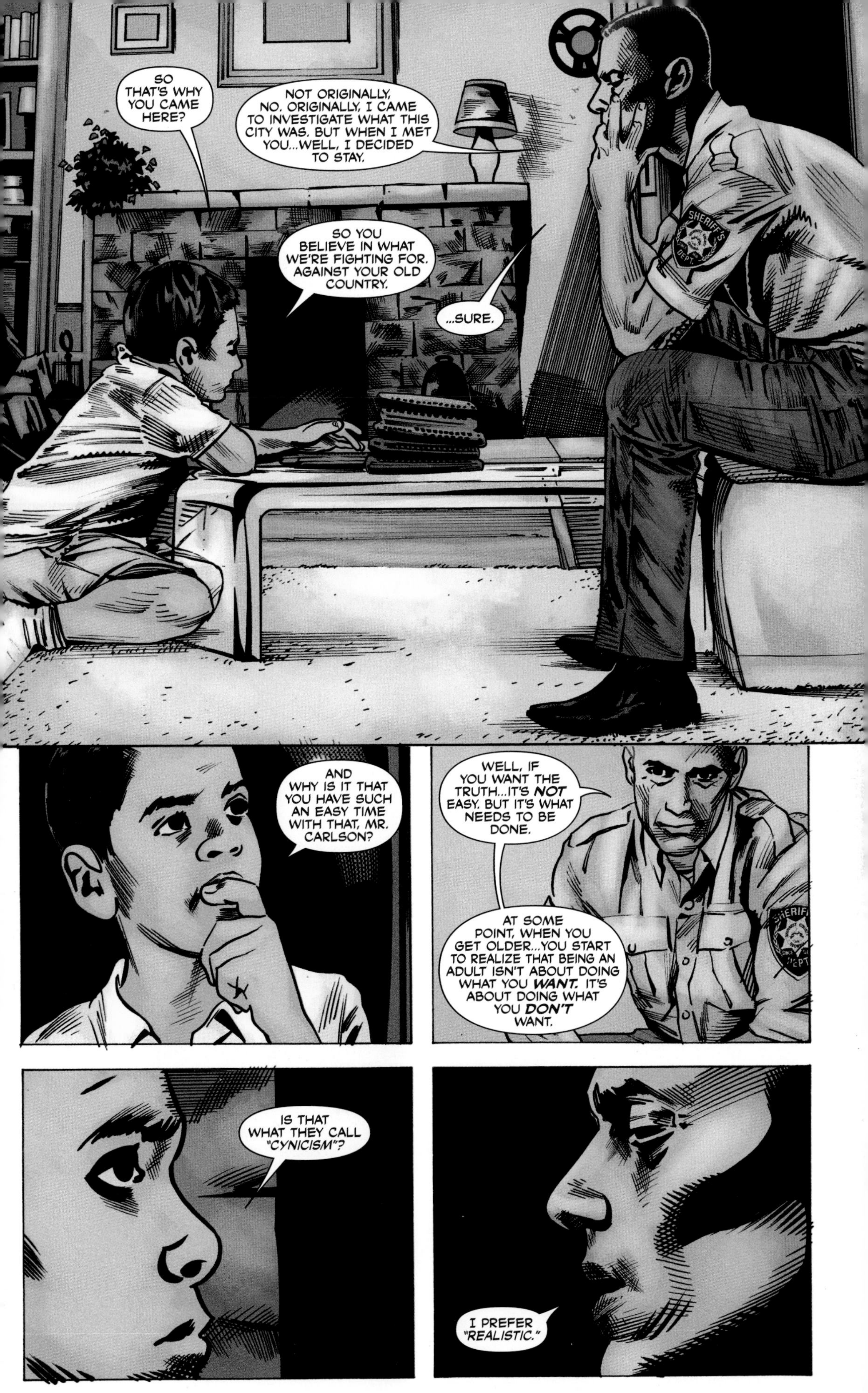
SO THAT'S WHY YOU CAME HERE?
NOT ORIGINALLY. NO. ORIGINALLY, I CAME TO INVESTIGATE WHAT THIS CITY WAS. BUT WHEN I MET YOU...WELL, I DECIDED TO STAY.
SO YOU BELIEVE IN WHAT WE'RE FIGHTING FOR. AGAINST YOUR OLD COUNTRY.
...SURE.
AND WHY IS IT THAT YOU HAVE SUCH AN EASY TIME WITH THAT, MR. CARLSON?
WELL, IF YOU WANT THE TRUTH...IT'S *NOT* EASY. BUT IT'S WHAT NEEDS TO BE DONE.
AT SOME POINT, WHEN YOU GET OLDER...YOU START TO REALIZE THAT BEING AN ADULT ISN'T ABOUT DOING WHAT YOU *WANT.* IT'S ABOUT DOING WHAT YOU *DON'T* WANT.
IS THAT WHAT THEY CALL *"CYNICISM"*?
I PREFER *"REALISTIC."*

THE WORLD *IS* A HARD PLACE TO LIVE. IT'S MESSY, AND SCARY, AND COMPLICATED...AND EVERY DAY IS A STRUGGLE. FOR MOST PEOPLE, IT'S *SCARY*.

BUT IF WE *BEAT* THE WEST, THEN IT'LL BE MUCH *LESS* SCARY FOR EVERYONE. THAT'S WHY WE'RE FIGHTING THEM, ISN'T IT, MR. CARLSON?

...YES, ROGER. EXACTLY.

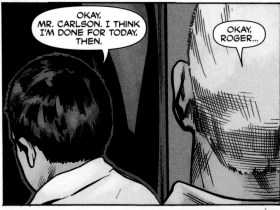

OKAY, MR. CARLSON. I THINK I'M DONE FOR TODAY, THEN.

OKAY, ROGER...

I THINK I'M DONE FOR TODAY, THEN...

...OKAY.

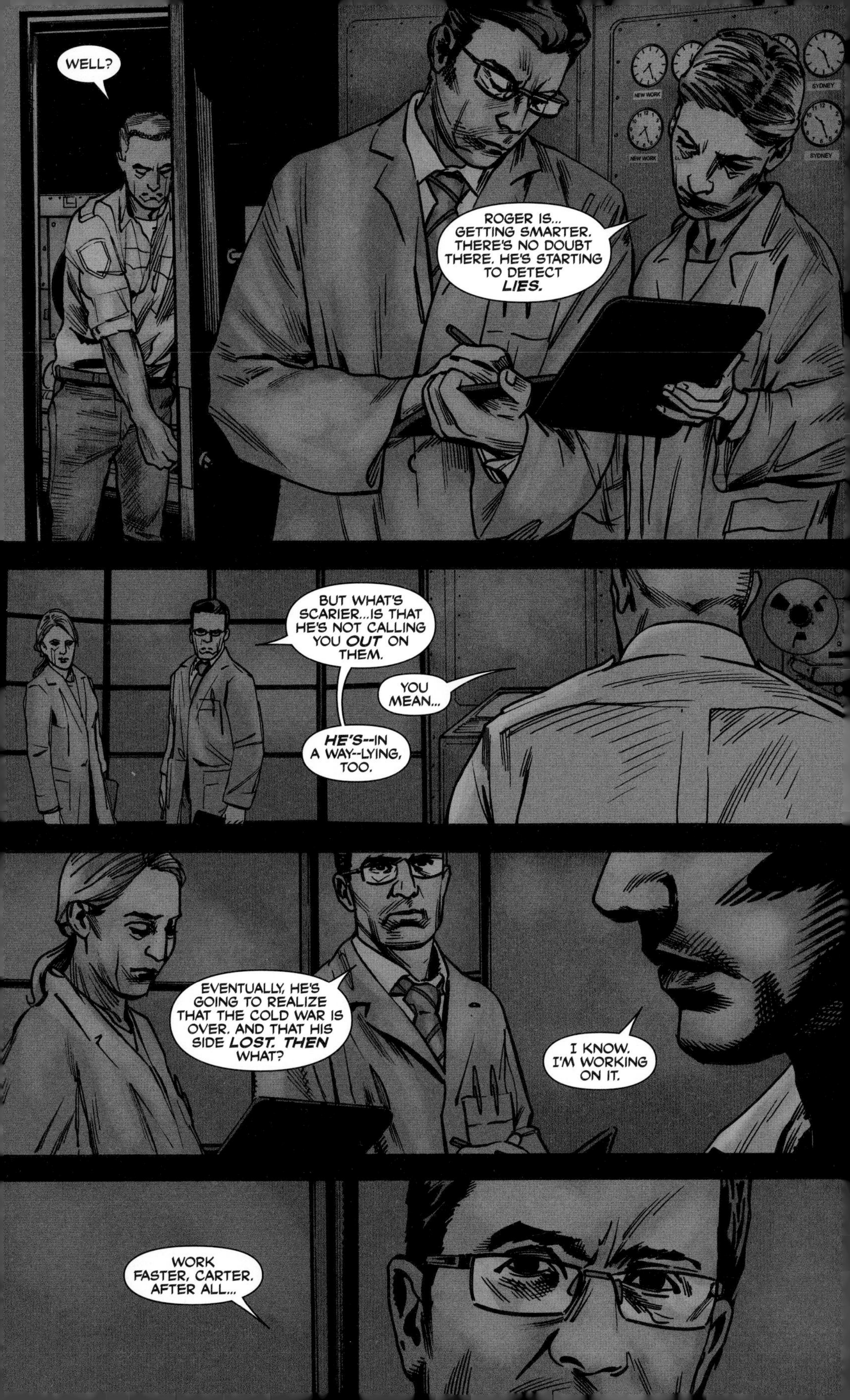
WELL?
ROGER IS... GETTING SMARTER. THERE'S NO DOUBT THERE. HE'S STARTING TO DETECT *LIES.*
NEW WORK
SYDNEY
BUT WHAT'S SCARIER...IS THAT HE'S NOT CALLING YOU *OUT* ON THEM.
YOU MEAN...
HE'S--IN A WAY--LYING, TOO.
EVENTUALLY, HE'S GOING TO REALIZE THAT THE COLD WAR IS OVER. AND THAT HIS SIDE *LOST. THEN* WHAT?
I KNOW. I'M WORKING ON IT.
WORK FASTER, CARTER. AFTER ALL...

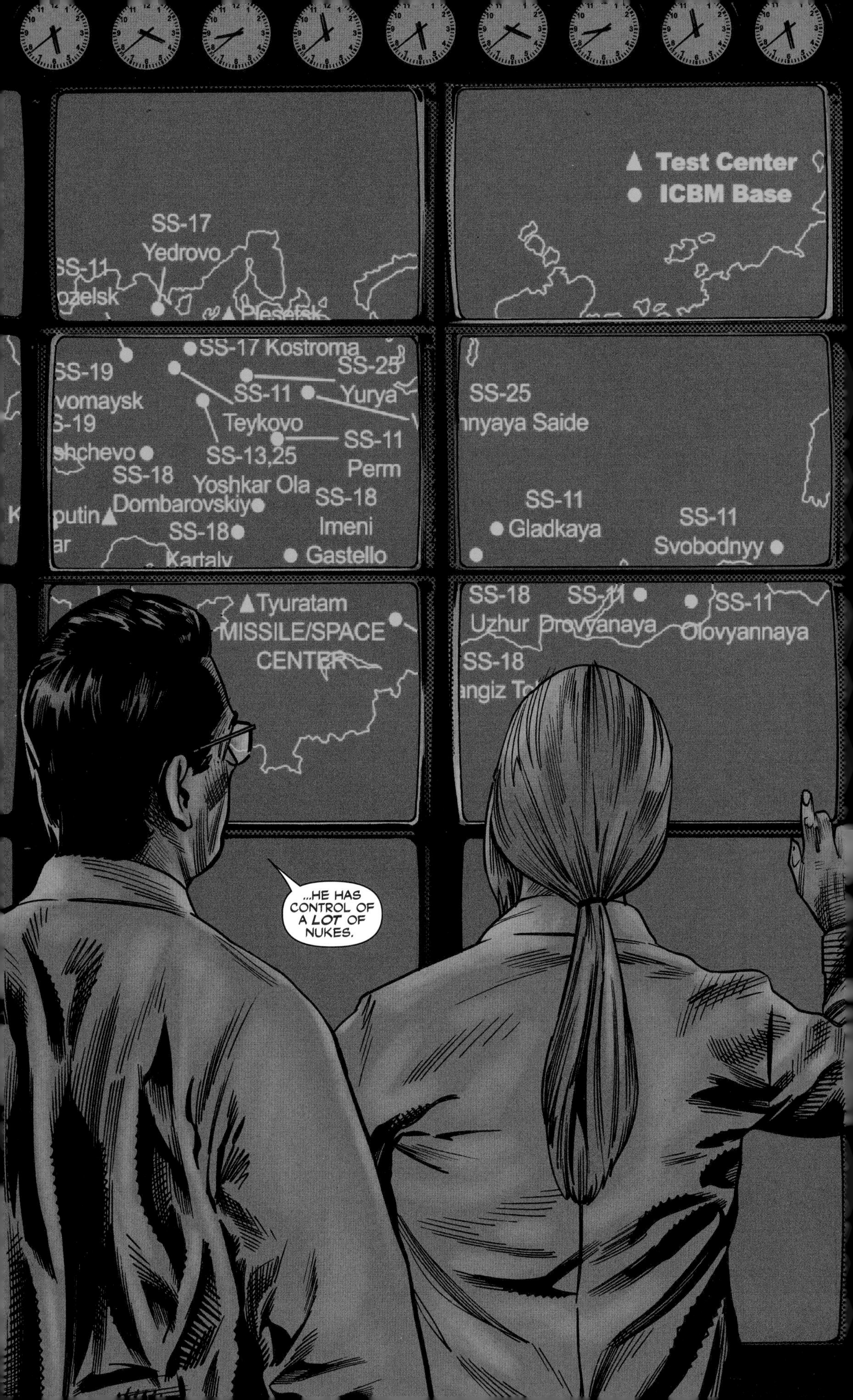
Test Center
ICBM Base
SS-17
Yedrovo
SS-11
SS-17 Kostroma
SS-25
SS-19
SS-11
Yurya
Teykovo
SS-19
SS-11
SS-13,25
Perm
SS-18
Yoshkar Ola
SS-18
Dombarovskiy
SS-18
Imeni
Gastello
SS-25
SS-11
Gladkaya
SS-11
Svobodnyy
Tyuratam
MISSILE/SPACE
CENTER
SS-18
Uzhur
SS-11
Drovyanaya
SS-11
Olovyannaya
SS-18
...HE HAS CONTROL OF A LOT OF NUKES.

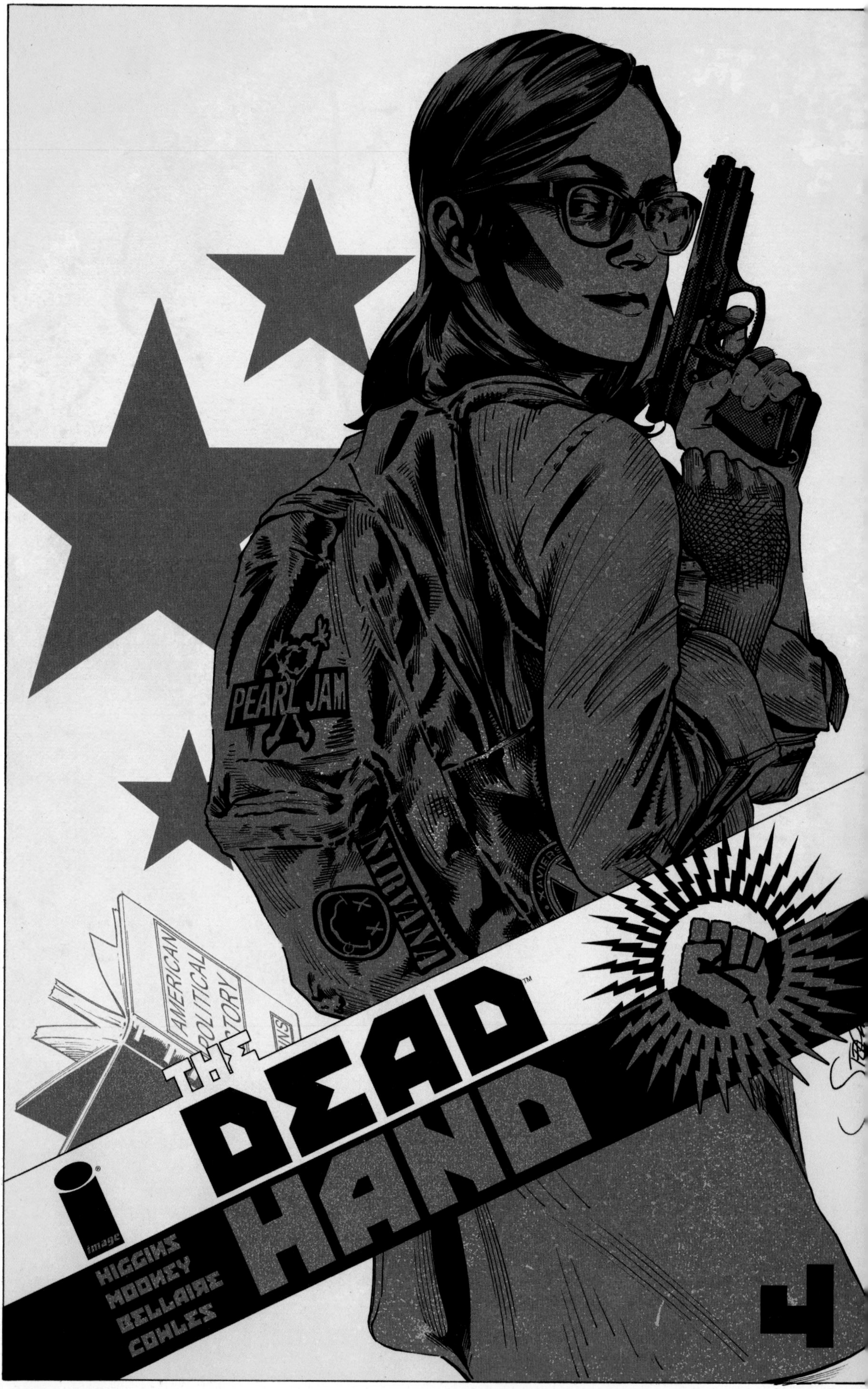
THE DEAD HAND
HIGGINS
MOONEY
BELLAIRE
COWLES
4
PEARL JAM
NIRVANA
AMERICAN POLITICAL HISTORY
image

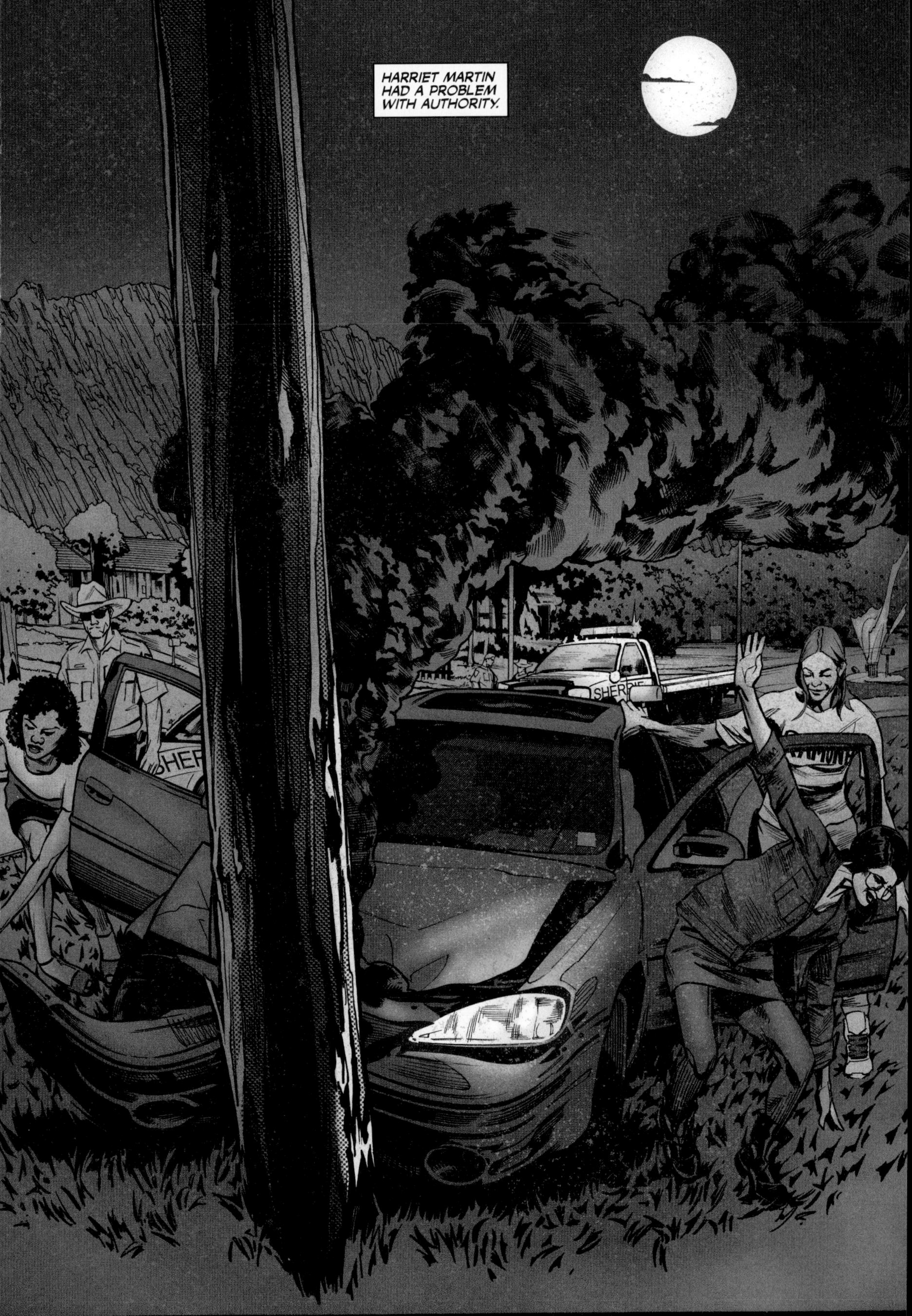
HARRIET MARTIN HAD A PROBLEM WITH AUTHORITY.

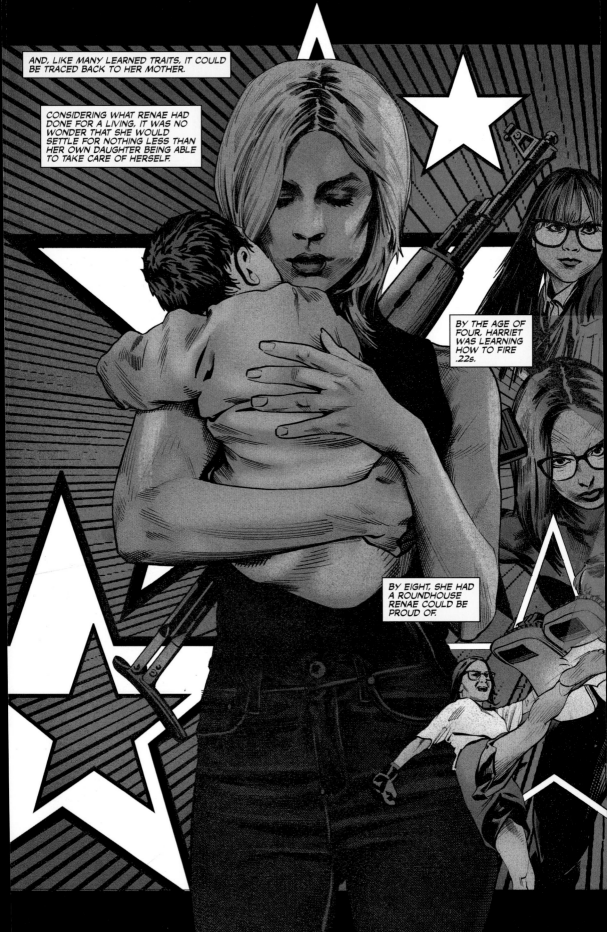

AND, LIKE MANY LEARNED TRAITS, IT COULD BE TRACED BACK TO HER MOTHER.

CONSIDERING WHAT RENAE HAD DONE FOR A LIVING, IT WAS NO WONDER THAT SHE WOULD SETTLE FOR NOTHING LESS THAN HER OWN DAUGHTER BEING ABLE TO TAKE CARE OF HERSELF.

BY THE AGE OF FOUR, HARRIET WAS LEARNING HOW TO FIRE .22s.

BY EIGHT, SHE HAD A ROUNDHOUSE RENAE COULD BE PROUD OF.

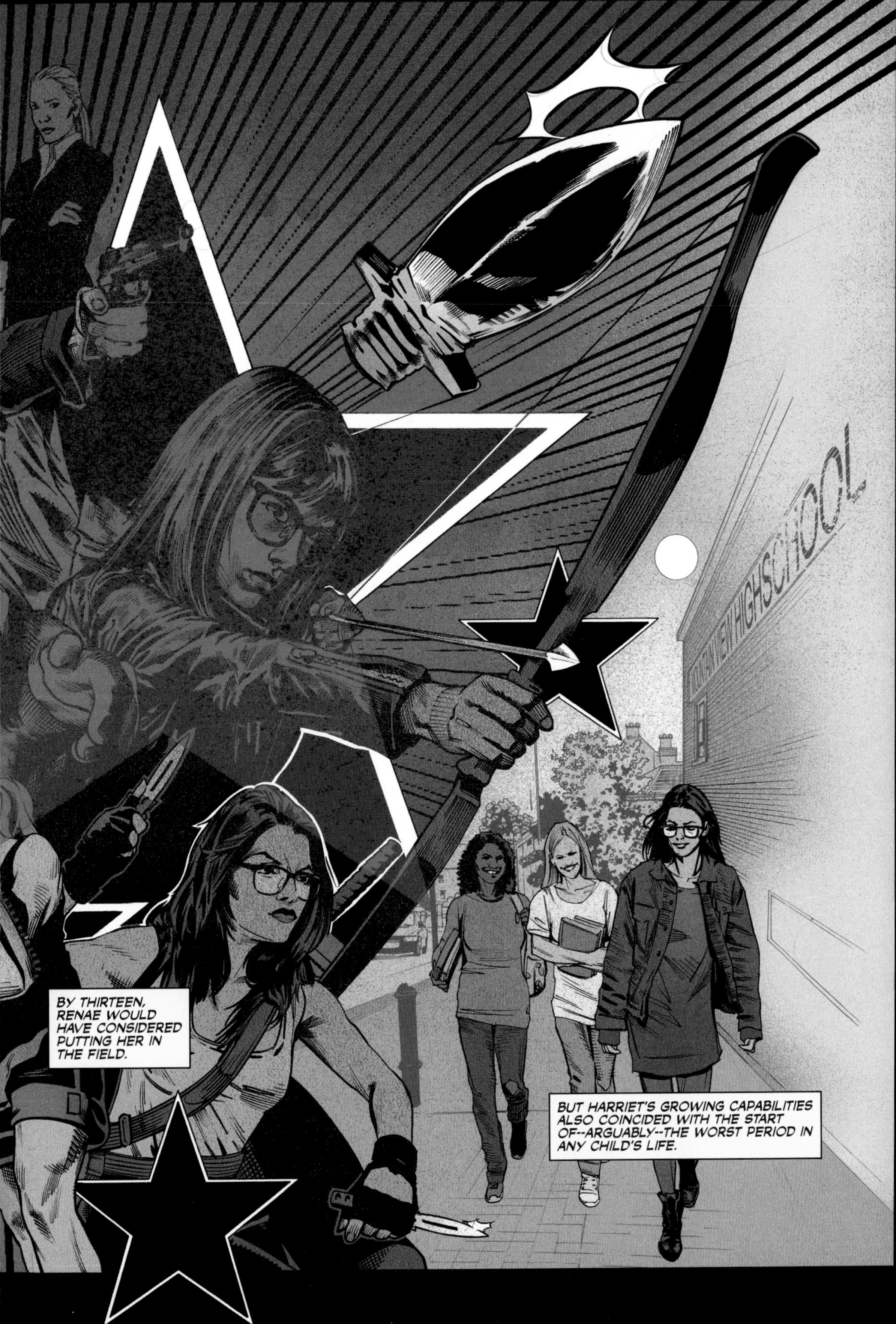
BY THIRTEEN, RENAE WOULD HAVE CONSIDERED PUTTING HER IN THE FIELD.
BUT HARRIET'S GROWING CAPABILITIES ALSO COINCIDED WITH THE START OF--ARGUABLY--THE WORST PERIOD IN ANY CHILD'S LIFE.

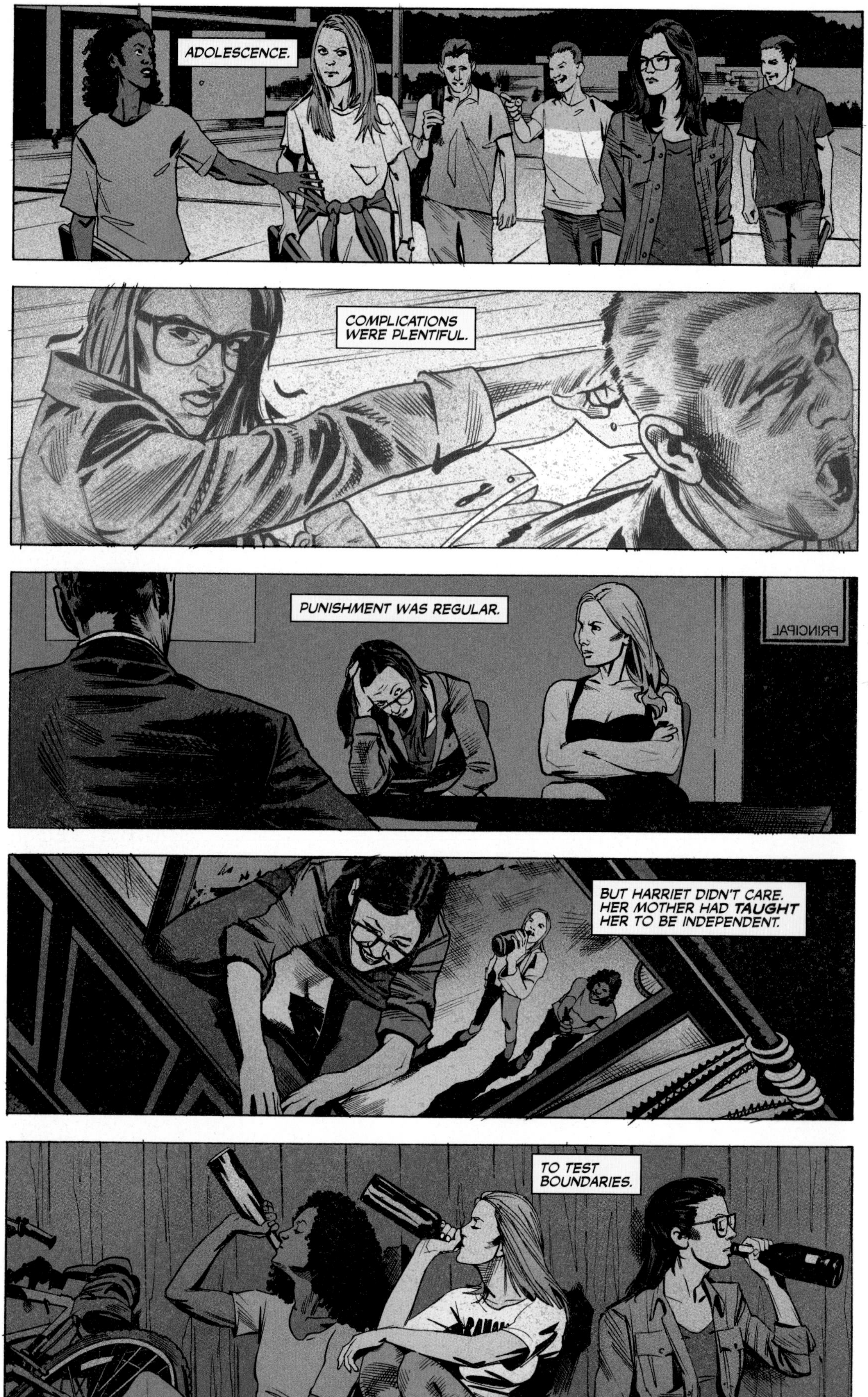
ADOLESCENCE.
COMPLICATIONS WERE PLENTIFUL.
PUNISHMENT WAS REGULAR.
PRINCIPAL
BUT HARRIET DIDN'T CARE. HER MOTHER HAD **TAUGHT** HER TO BE INDEPENDENT.
TO TEST BOUNDARIES.

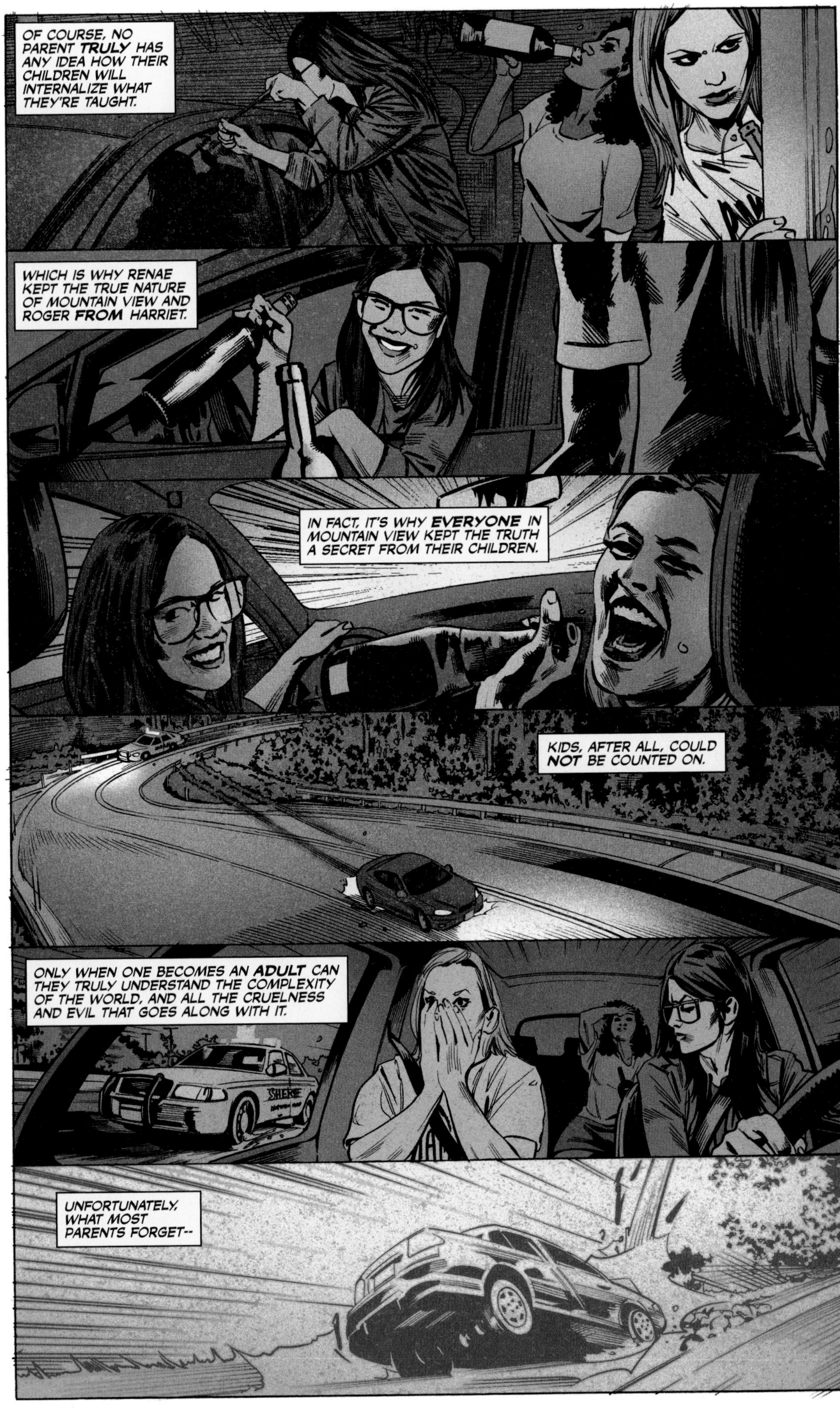
OF COURSE, NO PARENT TRULY HAS ANY IDEA HOW THEIR CHILDREN WILL INTERNALIZE WHAT THEY'RE TAUGHT.
WHICH IS WHY RENAE KEPT THE TRUE NATURE OF MOUNTAIN VIEW AND ROGER FROM HARRIET.
IN FACT, IT'S WHY EVERYONE IN MOUNTAIN VIEW KEPT THE TRUTH A SECRET FROM THEIR CHILDREN.
KIDS, AFTER ALL, COULD NOT BE COUNTED ON.
ONLY WHEN ONE BECOMES AN ADULT CAN THEY TRULY UNDERSTAND THE COMPLEXITY OF THE WORLD, AND ALL THE CRUELNESS AND EVIL THAT GOES ALONG WITH IT.
SHERIFF
UNFORTUNATELY, WHAT MOST PARENTS FORGET--

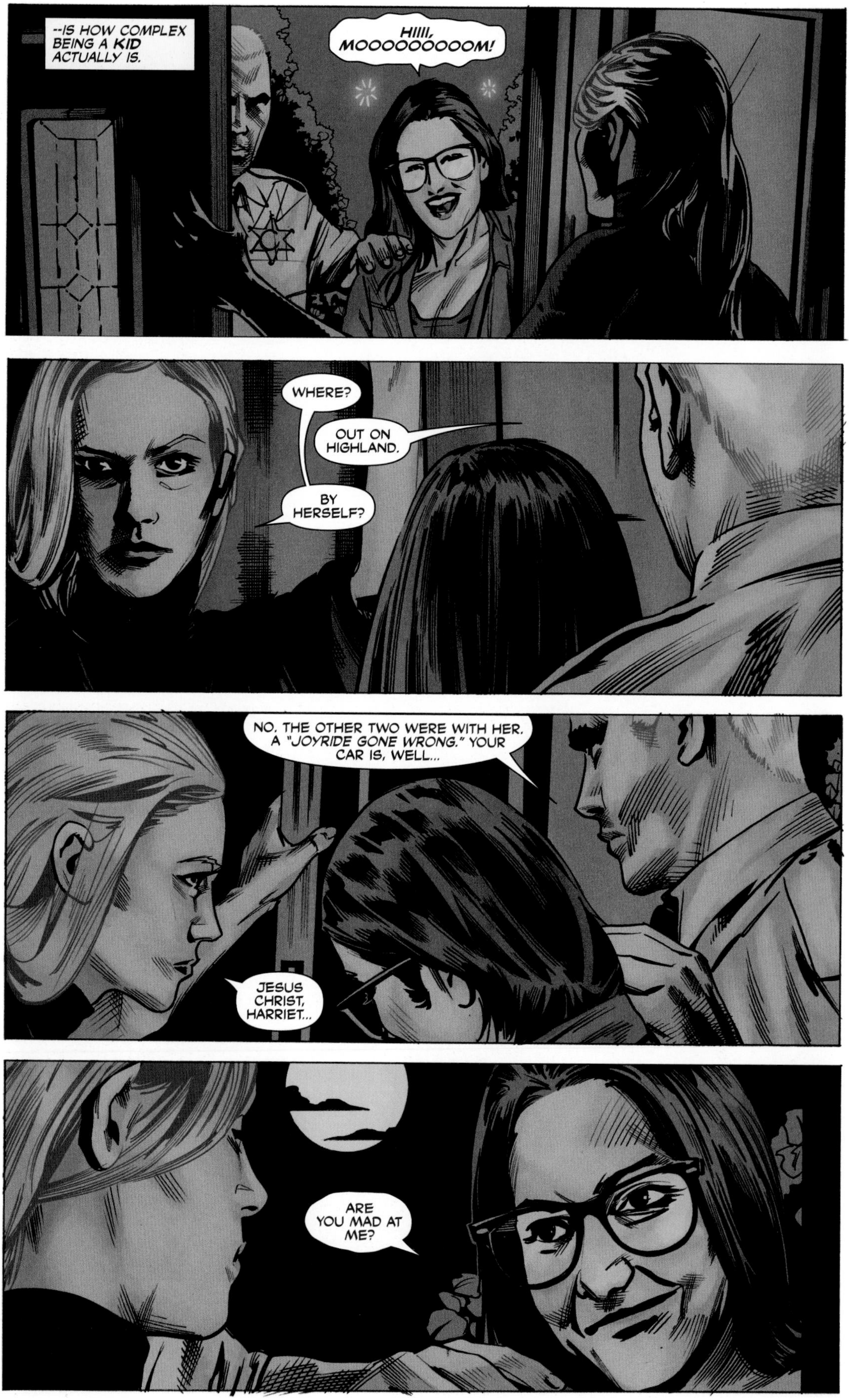
--IS HOW COMPLEX BEING A KID ACTUALLY IS.
HIIII, MOOOOOOOOOM!
WHERE?
OUT ON HIGHLAND.
BY HERSELF?
NO. THE OTHER TWO WERE WITH HER. A "JOYRIDE GONE WRONG." YOUR CAR IS, WELL...
JESUS CHRIST, HARRIET...
ARE YOU MAD AT ME?

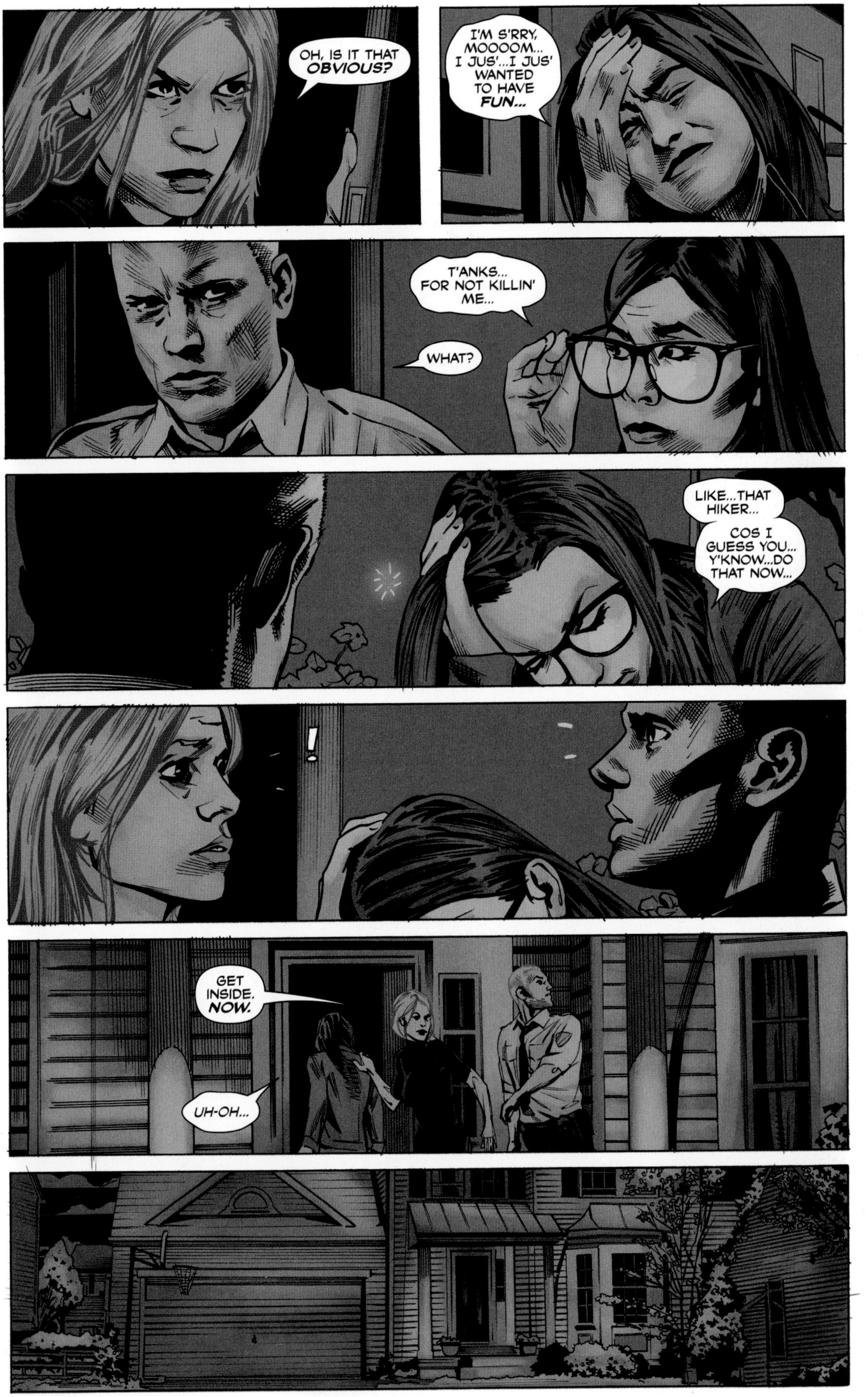
OH, IS IT THAT OBVIOUS?
I'M S'RRY, MOOOOM... I JUS'...I JUS' WANTED TO HAVE FUN...
T'ANKS... FOR NOT KILLIN' ME...
WHAT?
LIKE...THAT HIKER...
COS I GUESS YOU... Y'KNOW...DO THAT NOW...
!
GET INSIDE. NOW.
UH-OH...

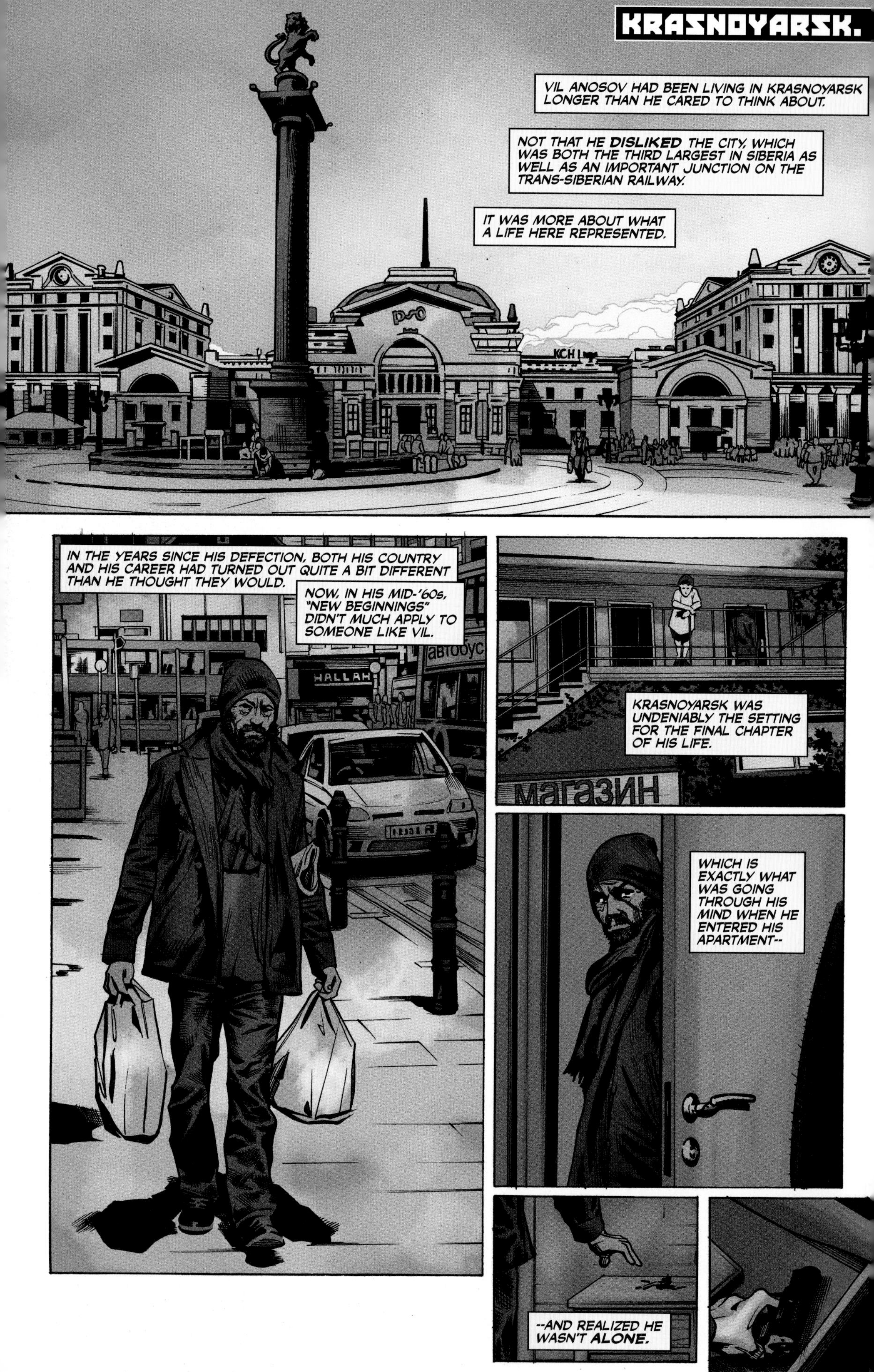
KRASNOYARSK.
VIL ANOSOV HAD BEEN LIVING IN KRASNOYARSK LONGER THAN HE CARED TO THINK ABOUT.
NOT THAT HE DISLIKED THE CITY, WHICH WAS BOTH THE THIRD LARGEST IN SIBERIA AS WELL AS AN IMPORTANT JUNCTION ON THE TRANS-SIBERIAN RAILWAY.
IT WAS MORE ABOUT WHAT A LIFE HERE REPRESENTED.
IN THE YEARS SINCE HIS DEFECTION, BOTH HIS COUNTRY AND HIS CAREER HAD TURNED OUT QUITE A BIT DIFFERENT THAN HE THOUGHT THEY WOULD.
NOW, IN HIS MID-'60s, "NEW BEGINNINGS" DIDN'T MUCH APPLY TO SOMEONE LIKE VIL.
автобус
KRASNOYARSK WAS UNDENIABLY THE SETTING FOR THE FINAL CHAPTER OF HIS LIFE.
магазин
WHICH IS EXACTLY WHAT WAS GOING THROUGH HIS MIND WHEN HE ENTERED HIS APARTMENT--
--AND REALIZED HE WASN'T ALONE.

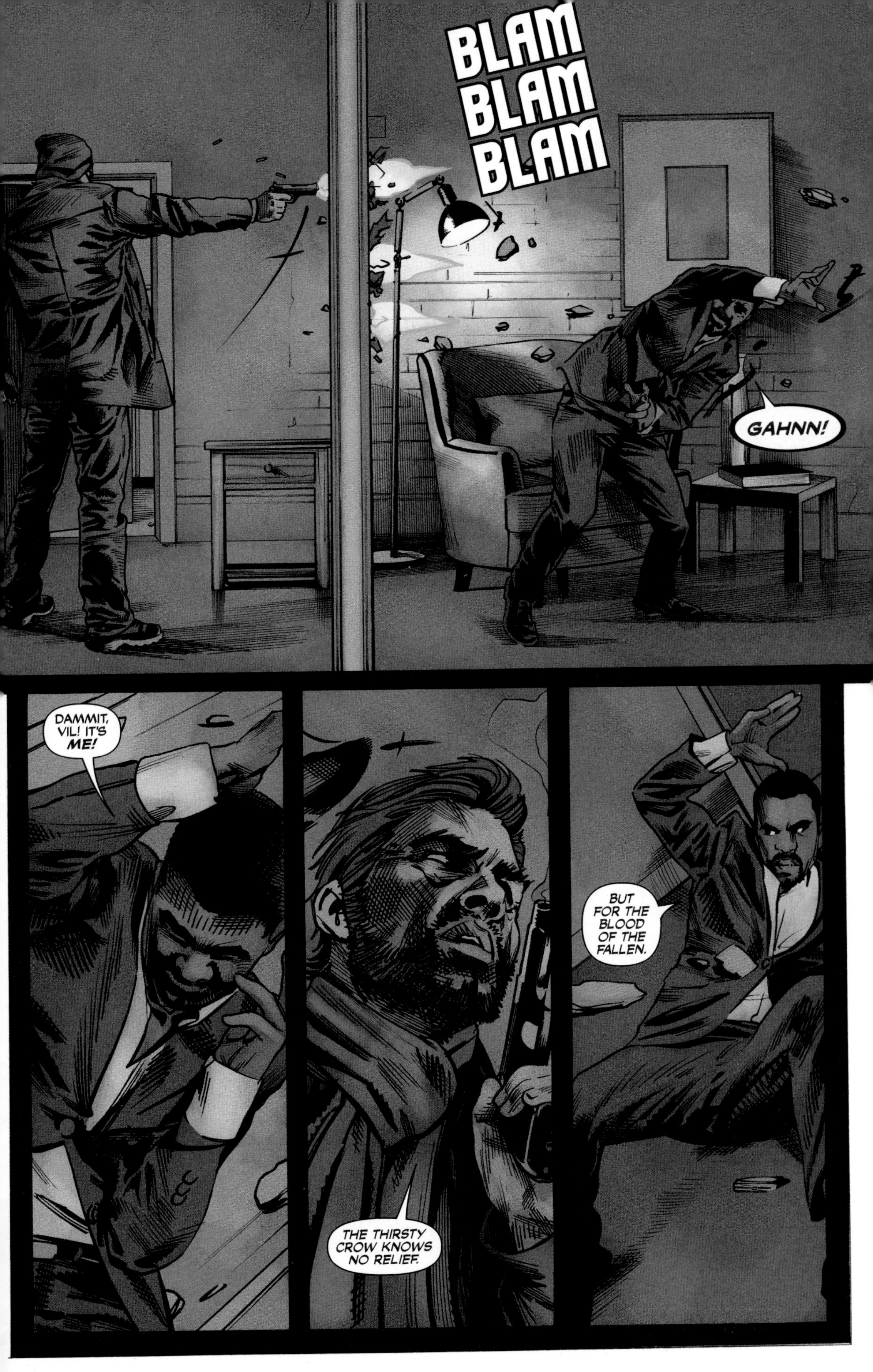
BLAM
BLAM
BLAM
GAHNN!
DAMMIT, VIL! IT'S ME!
THE THIRSTY CROW KNOWS NO RELIEF.
BUT FOR THE BLOOD OF THE FALLEN.

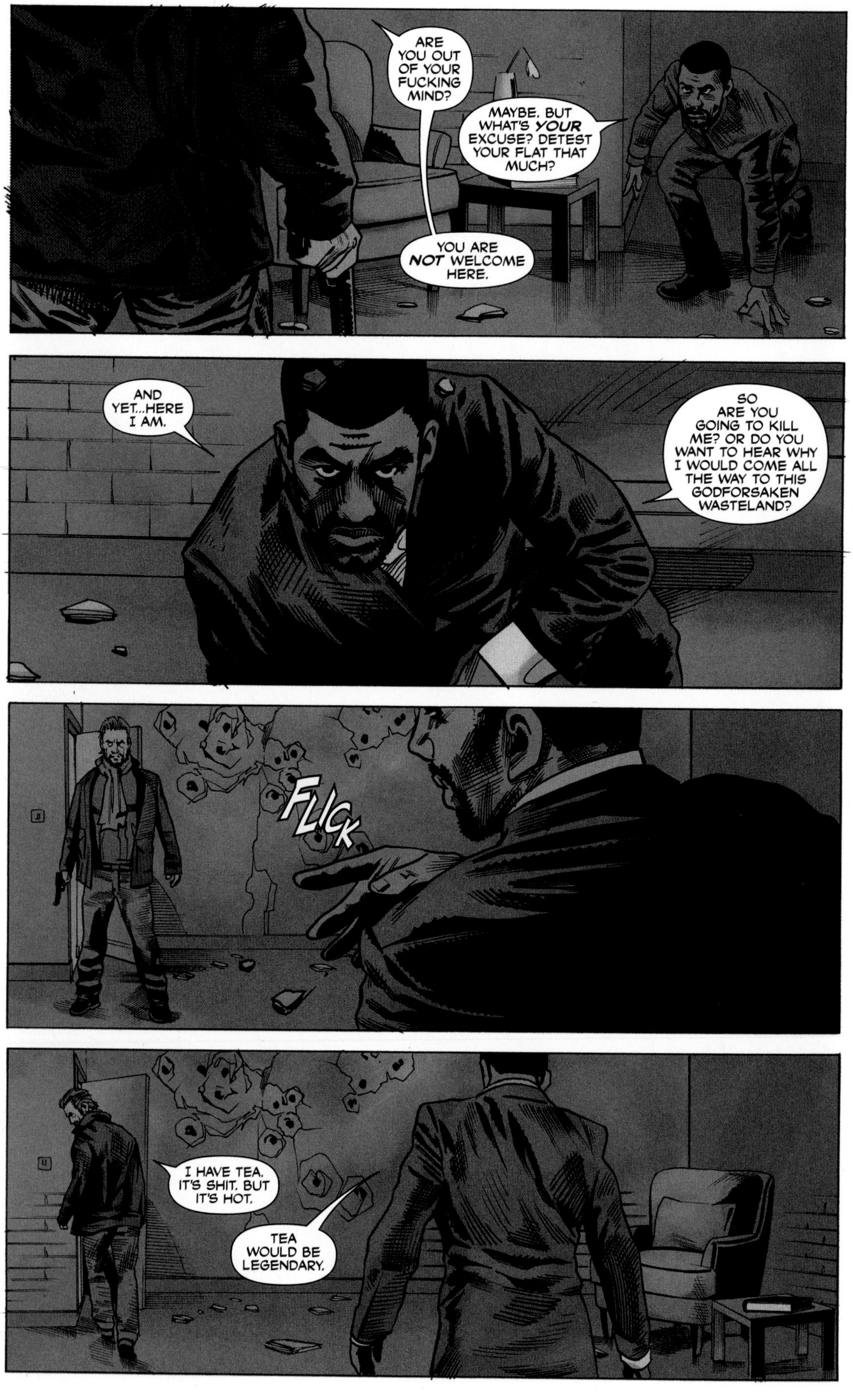
ARE YOU OUT OF YOUR FUCKING MIND?
MAYBE. BUT WHAT'S YOUR EXCUSE? DETEST YOUR FLAT THAT MUCH?
YOU ARE NOT WELCOME HERE.
AND YET...HERE I AM.
SO ARE YOU GOING TO KILL ME? OR DO YOU WANT TO HEAR WHY I WOULD COME ALL THE WAY TO THIS GODFORSAKEN WASTELAND?
FLICK
I HAVE TEA. IT'S SHIT, BUT IT'S HOT.
TEA WOULD BE LEGENDARY.

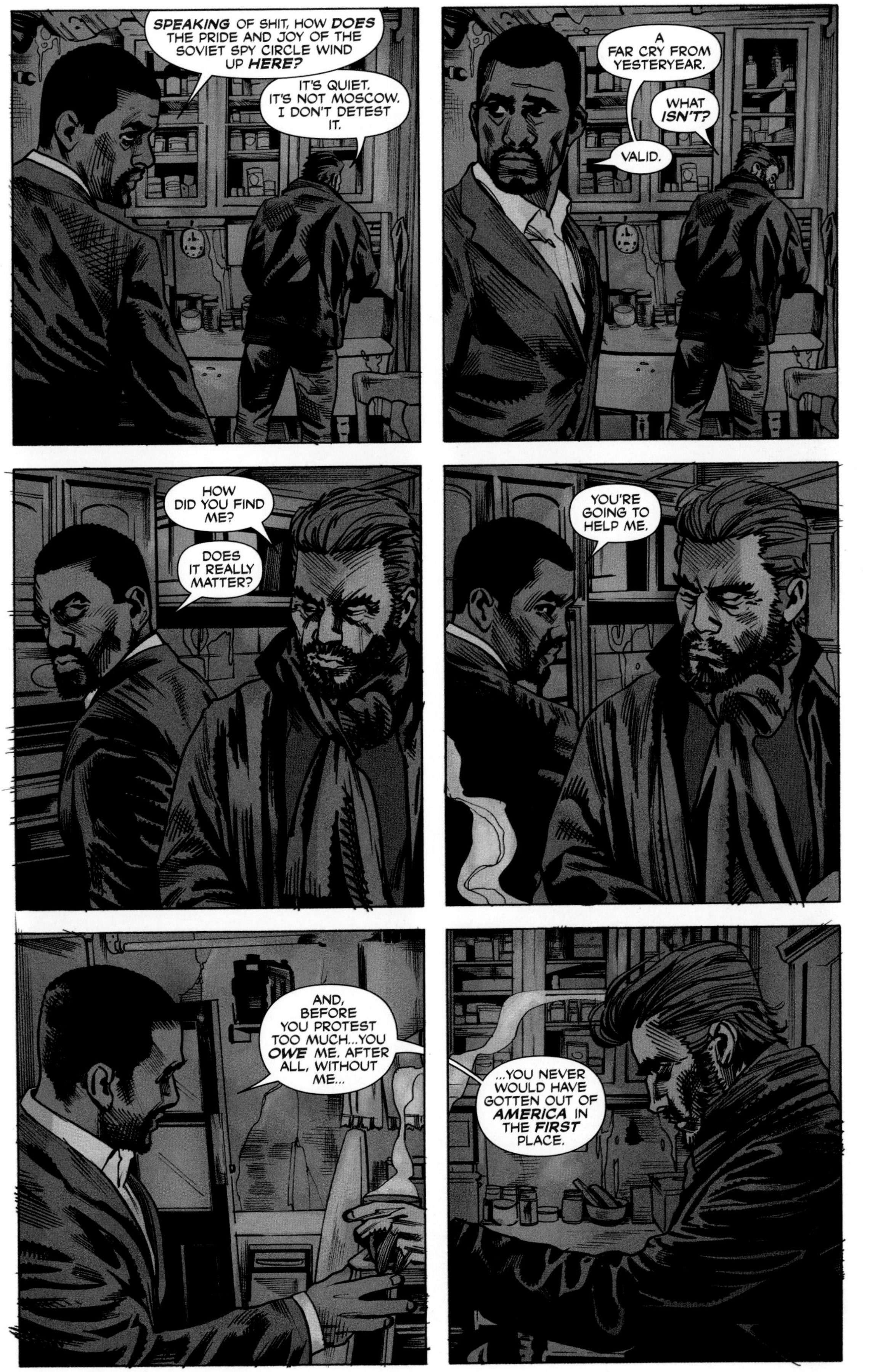
SPEAKING OF SHIT, HOW DOES THE PRIDE AND JOY OF THE SOVIET SPY CIRCLE WIND UP HERE?
IT'S QUIET. IT'S NOT MOSCOW. I DON'T DETEST IT.
A FAR CRY FROM YESTERYEAR.
WHAT ISN'T?
VALID.
HOW DID YOU FIND ME?
DOES IT REALLY MATTER?
YOU'RE GOING TO HELP ME.
AND, BEFORE YOU PROTEST TOO MUCH...YOU OWE ME. AFTER ALL, WITHOUT ME...
...YOU NEVER WOULD HAVE GOTTEN OUT OF AMERICA IN THE FIRST PLACE.

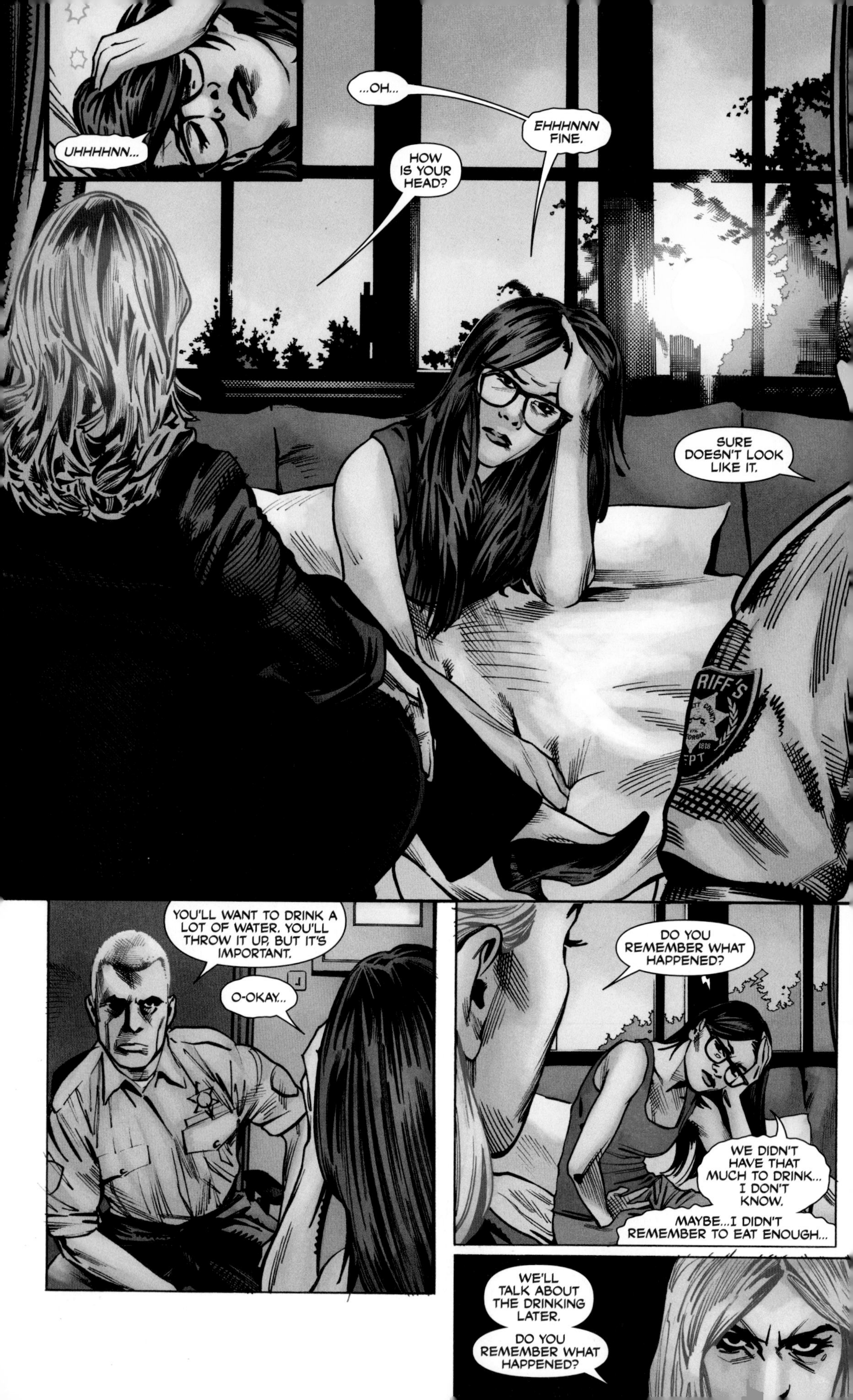
UHHHHNN...
...OH...
EHHHNNN FINE.
HOW IS YOUR HEAD?
SURE DOESN'T LOOK LIKE IT.
YOU'LL WANT TO DRINK A LOT OF WATER. YOU'LL THROW IT UP, BUT IT'S IMPORTANT.
O-OKAY...
DO YOU REMEMBER WHAT HAPPENED?
WE DIDN'T HAVE THAT MUCH TO DRINK... I DON'T KNOW.
MAYBE...I DIDN'T REMEMBER TO EAT ENOUGH...
WE'LL TALK ABOUT THE DRINKING LATER.
DO YOU REMEMBER WHAT HAPPENED?

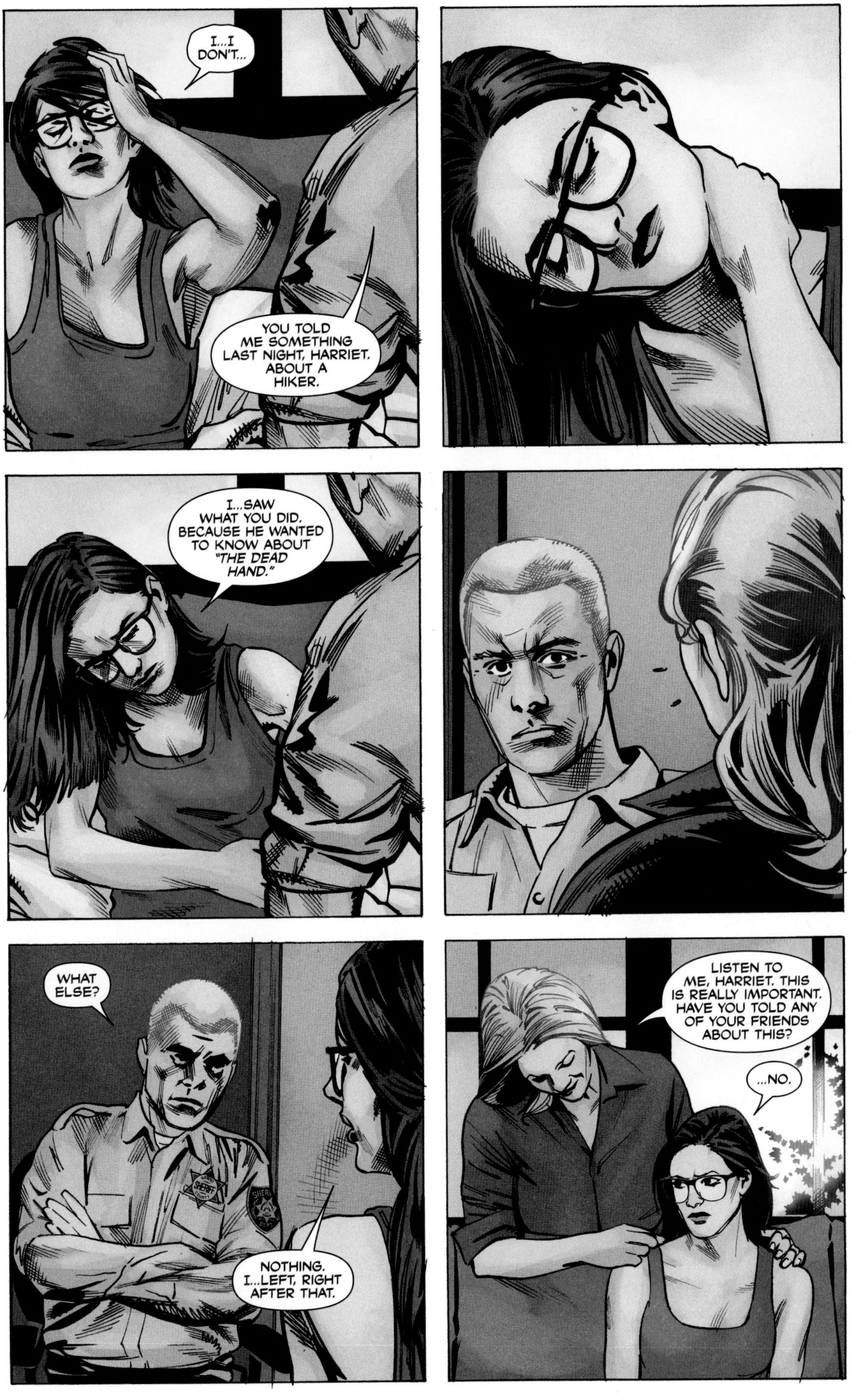
I...I DON'T...
YOU TOLD ME SOMETHING LAST NIGHT, HARRIET. ABOUT A HIKER.
I...SAW WHAT YOU DID. BECAUSE HE WANTED TO KNOW ABOUT "THE DEAD HAND."
WHAT ELSE?
NOTHING. I...LEFT, RIGHT AFTER THAT.
LISTEN TO ME, HARRIET. THIS IS REALLY IMPORTANT. HAVE YOU TOLD ANY OF YOUR FRIENDS ABOUT THIS?
...NO.

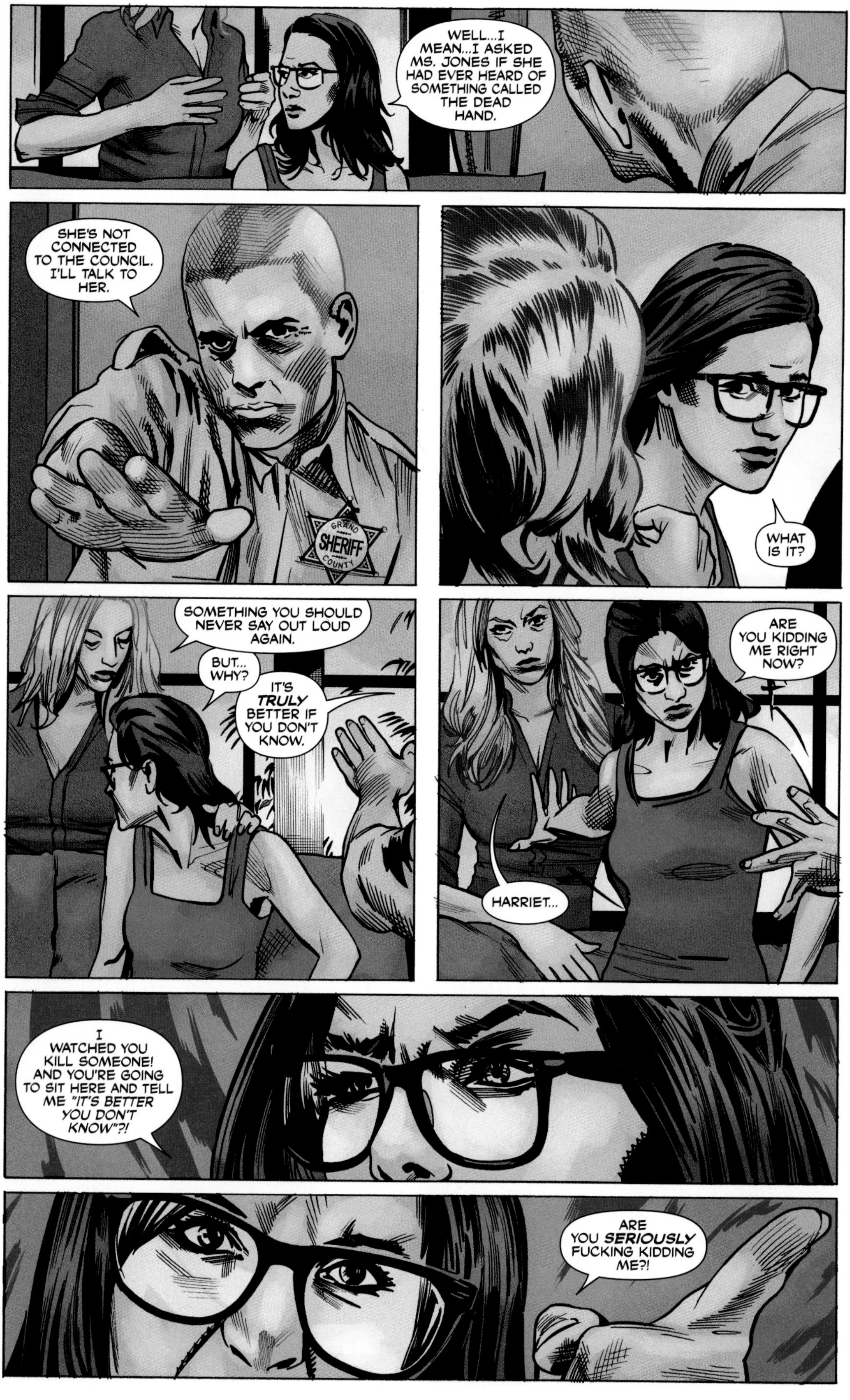
WELL...I MEAN...I ASKED MS. JONES IF SHE HAD EVER HEARD OF SOMETHING CALLED THE DEAD HAND.
SHE'S NOT CONNECTED TO THE COUNCIL. I'LL TALK TO HER.
GRAND SHERIFF COUNTY
WHAT IS IT?
SOMETHING YOU SHOULD NEVER SAY OUT LOUD AGAIN.
BUT... WHY?
IT'S *TRULY* BETTER IF YOU DON'T KNOW.
ARE YOU KIDDING ME RIGHT NOW?
HARRIET...
I WATCHED YOU KILL SOMEONE! AND YOU'RE GOING TO SIT HERE AND TELL ME *"IT'S BETTER YOU DON'T KNOW"?!*
ARE YOU *SERIOUSLY* FUCKING KIDDING ME?!

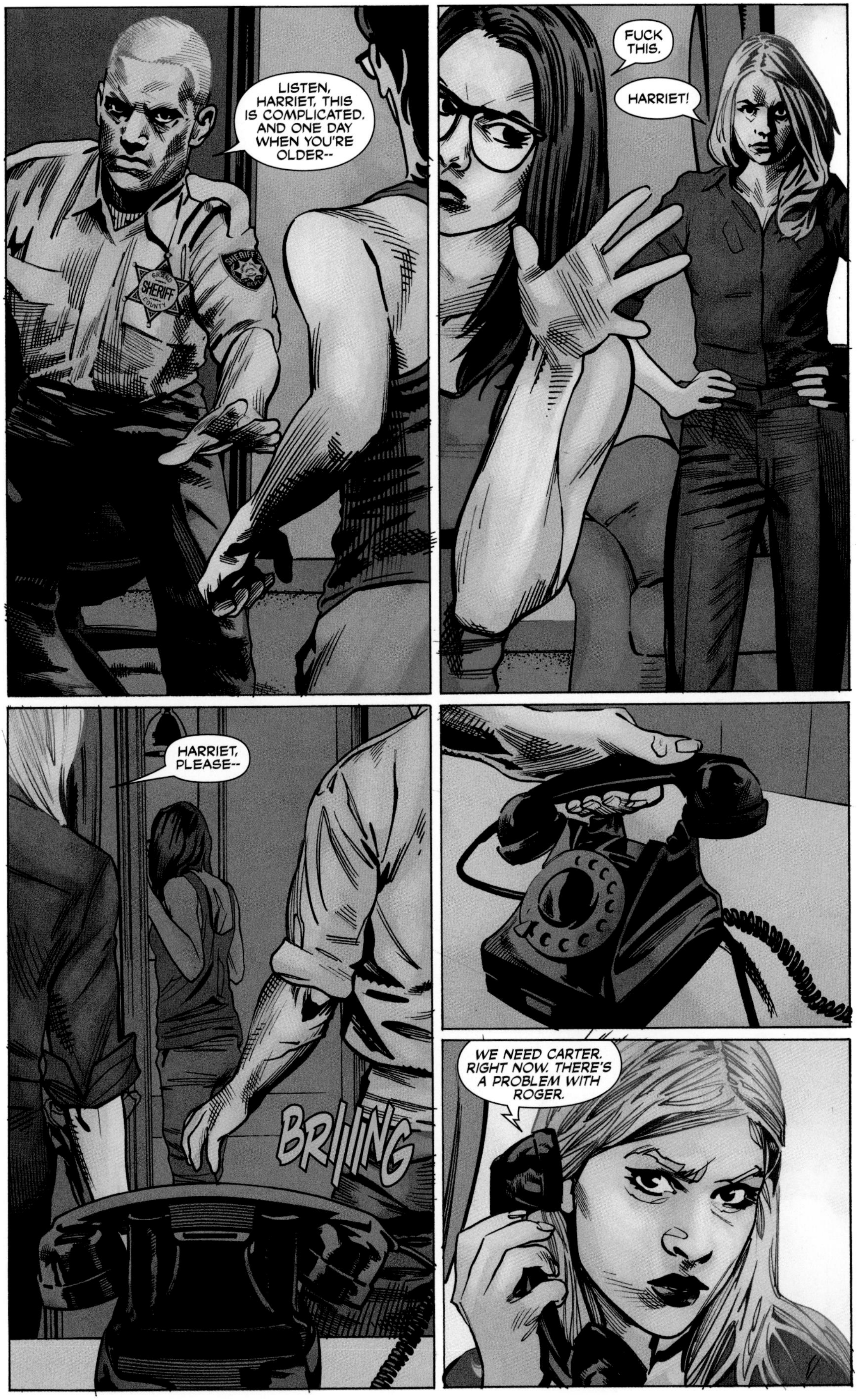
LISTEN, HARRIET, THIS IS COMPLICATED, AND ONE DAY WHEN YOU'RE OLDER--
FUCK THIS.
HARRIET!
HARRIET, PLEASE--
BRIIIING
WE NEED CARTER. RIGHT NOW. THERE'S A PROBLEM WITH ROGER.

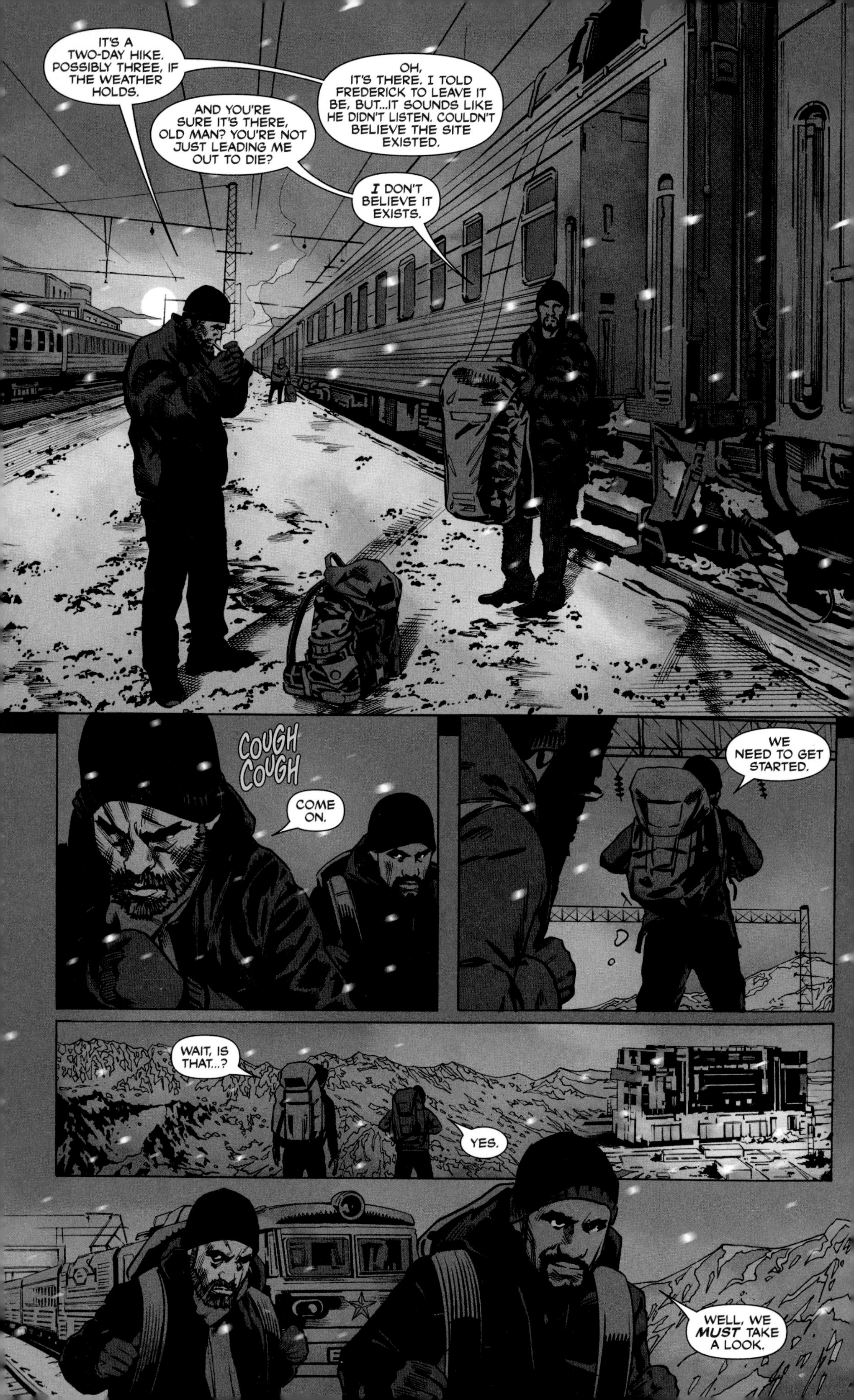
IT'S A TWO-DAY HIKE. POSSIBLY THREE, IF THE WEATHER HOLDS.
AND YOU'RE SURE IT'S THERE, OLD MAN? YOU'RE NOT JUST LEADING ME OUT TO DIE?
OH, IT'S THERE. I TOLD FREDERICK TO LEAVE IT BE, BUT...IT SOUNDS LIKE HE DIDN'T LISTEN. COULDN'T BELIEVE THE SITE EXISTED.
I DON'T BELIEVE IT EXISTS.
COUGH COUGH
COME ON.
WE NEED TO GET STARTED.
WAIT, IS THAT...?
YES.
WELL, WE MUST TAKE A LOOK.

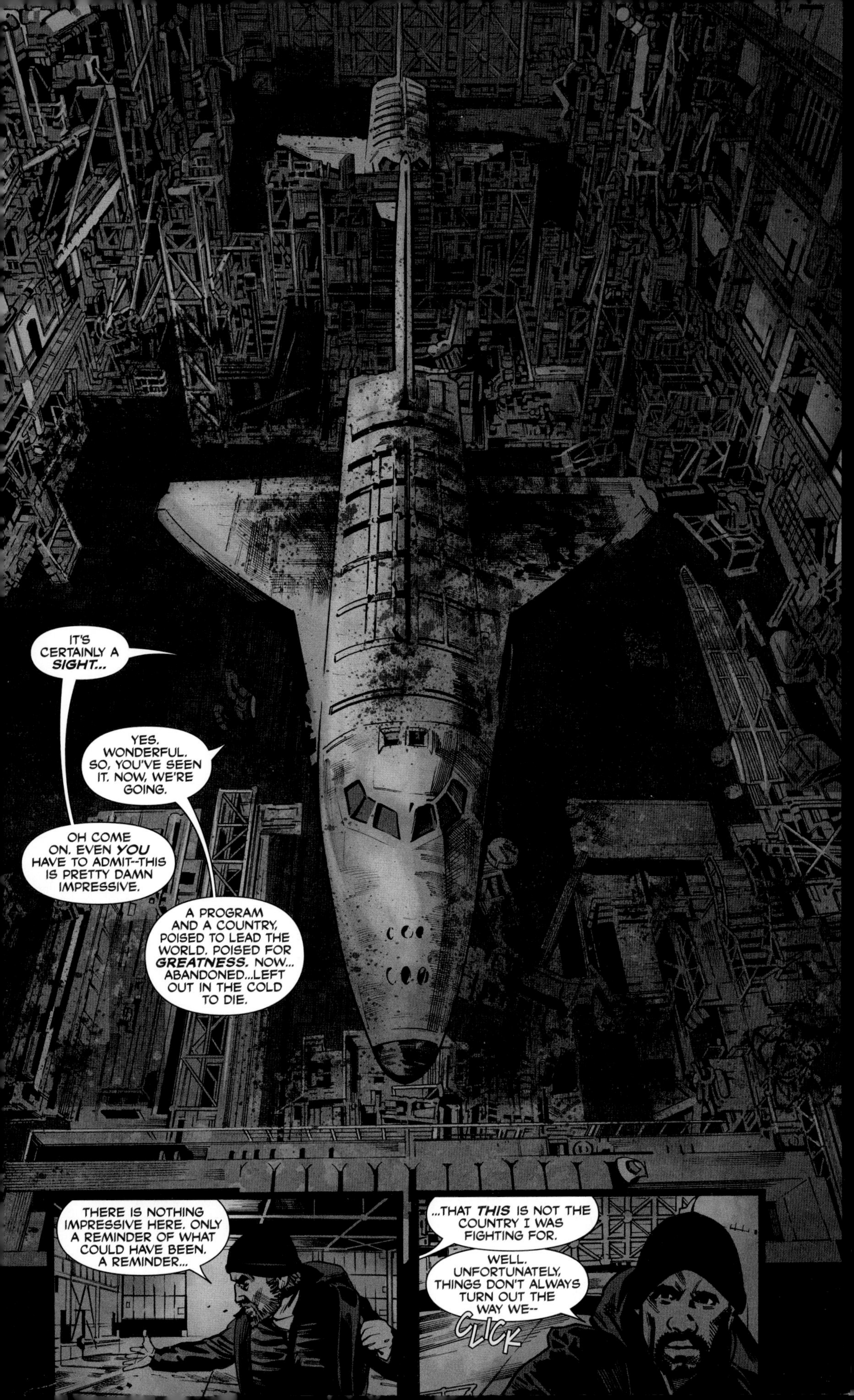
IT'S CERTAINLY A *SIGHT...*
YES. WONDERFUL. SO, YOU'VE SEEN IT. NOW, WE'RE GOING.
OH COME ON. EVEN *YOU* HAVE TO ADMIT--THIS IS PRETTY DAMN IMPRESSIVE.
A PROGRAM AND A COUNTRY, POISED TO LEAD THE WORLD. POISED FOR *GREATNESS.* NOW... ABANDONED...LEFT OUT IN THE COLD TO DIE.
THERE IS NOTHING IMPRESSIVE HERE. ONLY A REMINDER OF WHAT COULD HAVE BEEN. A REMINDER...
...THAT *THIS* IS NOT THE COUNTRY I WAS FIGHTING FOR.
WELL. UNFORTUNATELY, THINGS DON'T ALWAYS TURN OUT THE WAY WE--
CLICK

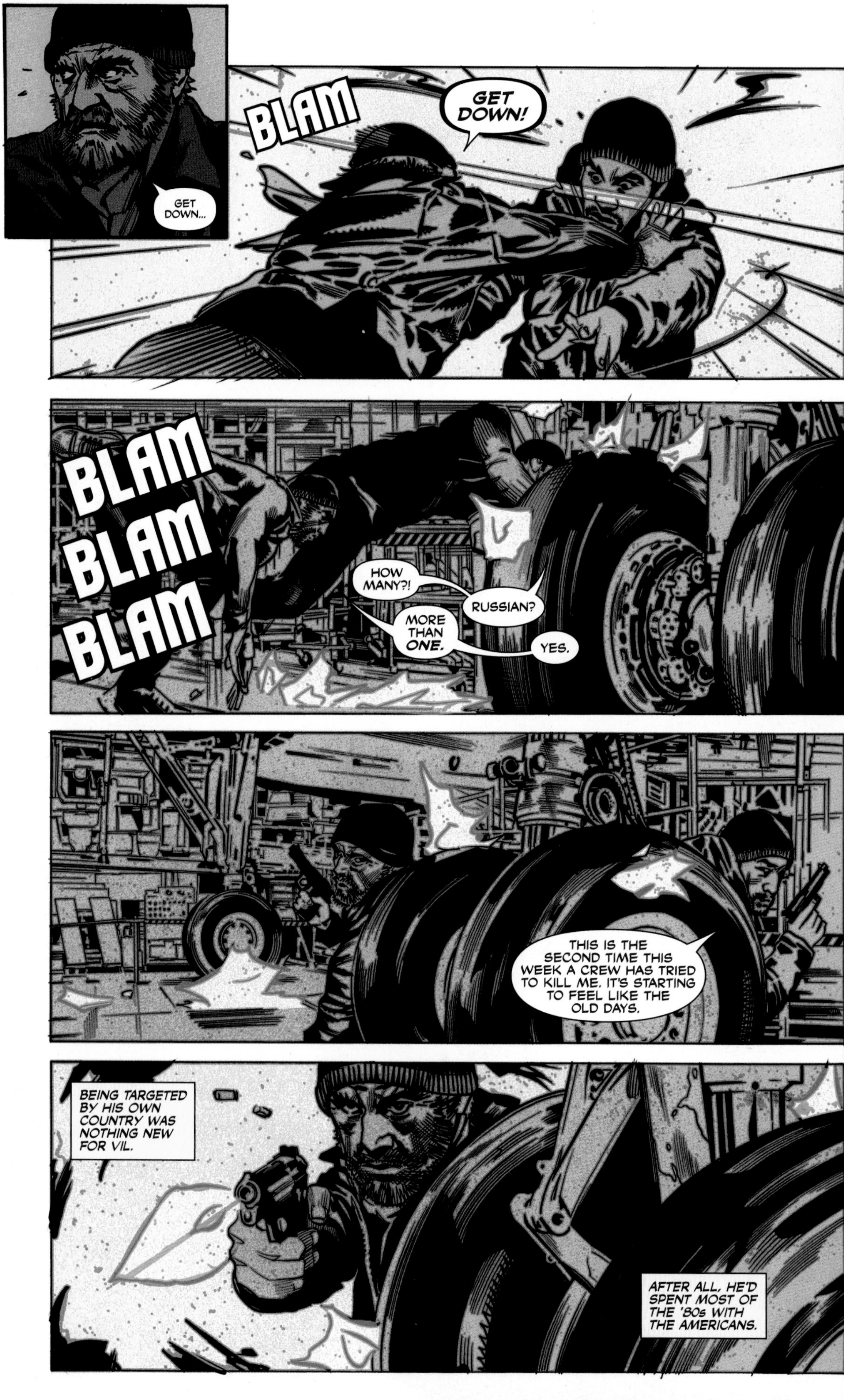
GET DOWN...
BLAM
GET DOWN!
BLAM BLAM BLAM
HOW MANY?!
RUSSIAN?
MORE THAN ONE.
YES.
THIS IS THE SECOND TIME THIS WEEK A CREW HAS TRIED TO KILL ME. IT'S STARTING TO FEEL LIKE THE OLD DAYS.
BEING TARGETED BY HIS OWN COUNTRY WAS NOTHING NEW FOR VIL.
AFTER ALL, HE'D SPENT MOST OF THE '80s WITH THE AMERICANS.

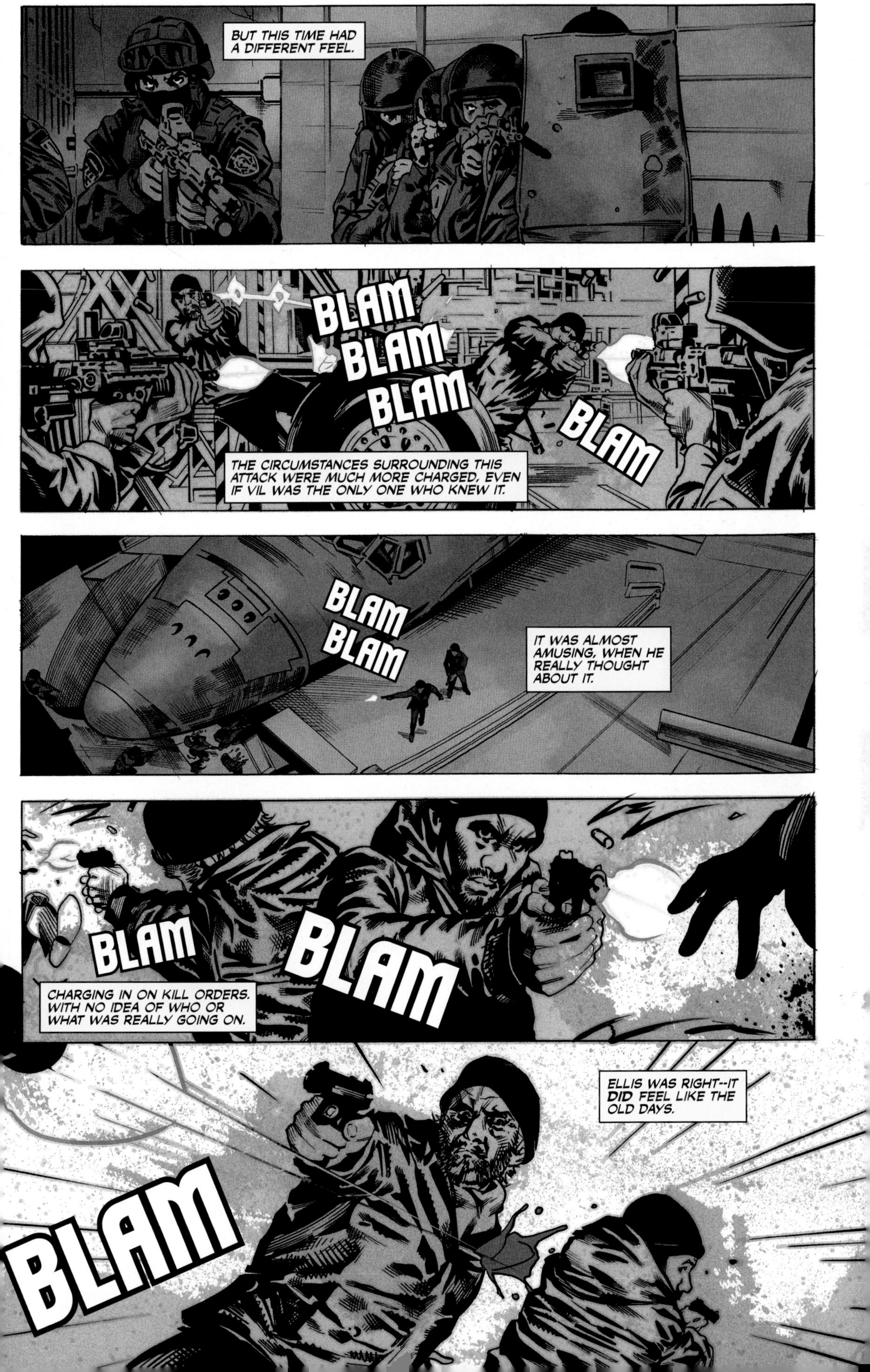
BUT THIS TIME HAD A DIFFERENT FEEL.
BLAM
BLAM
BLAM
BLAM
THE CIRCUMSTANCES SURROUNDING THIS ATTACK WERE MUCH MORE CHARGED, EVEN IF VIL WAS THE ONLY ONE WHO KNEW IT.
BLAM
BLAM
IT WAS ALMOST AMUSING, WHEN HE REALLY THOUGHT ABOUT IT.
BLAM
BLAM
CHARGING IN ON KILL ORDERS. WITH NO IDEA OF WHO OR WHAT WAS REALLY GOING ON.
ELLIS WAS RIGHT--IT **DID** FEEL LIKE THE OLD DAYS.
BLAM

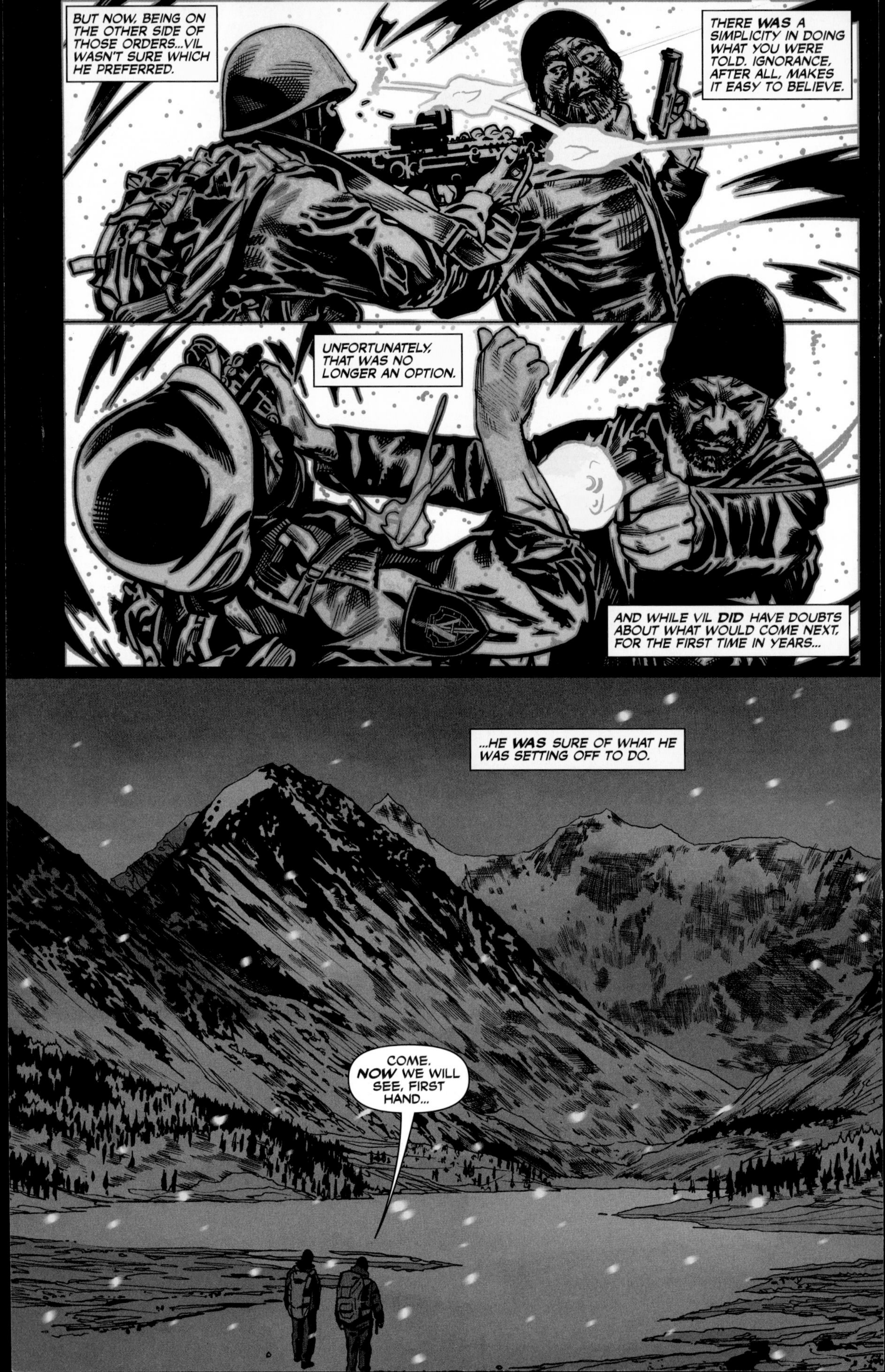
BUT NOW, BEING ON THE OTHER SIDE OF THOSE ORDERS...VIL WASN'T SURE WHICH HE PREFERRED.
THERE **WAS** A SIMPLICITY IN DOING WHAT YOU WERE TOLD. IGNORANCE, AFTER ALL, MAKES IT EASY TO BELIEVE.
UNFORTUNATELY, THAT WAS NO LONGER AN OPTION.
AND WHILE VIL **DID** HAVE DOUBTS ABOUT WHAT WOULD COME NEXT, FOR THE FIRST TIME IN YEARS...
...HE **WAS** SURE OF WHAT HE WAS SETTING OFF TO DO.
COME. **NOW** WE WILL SEE, FIRST HAND...

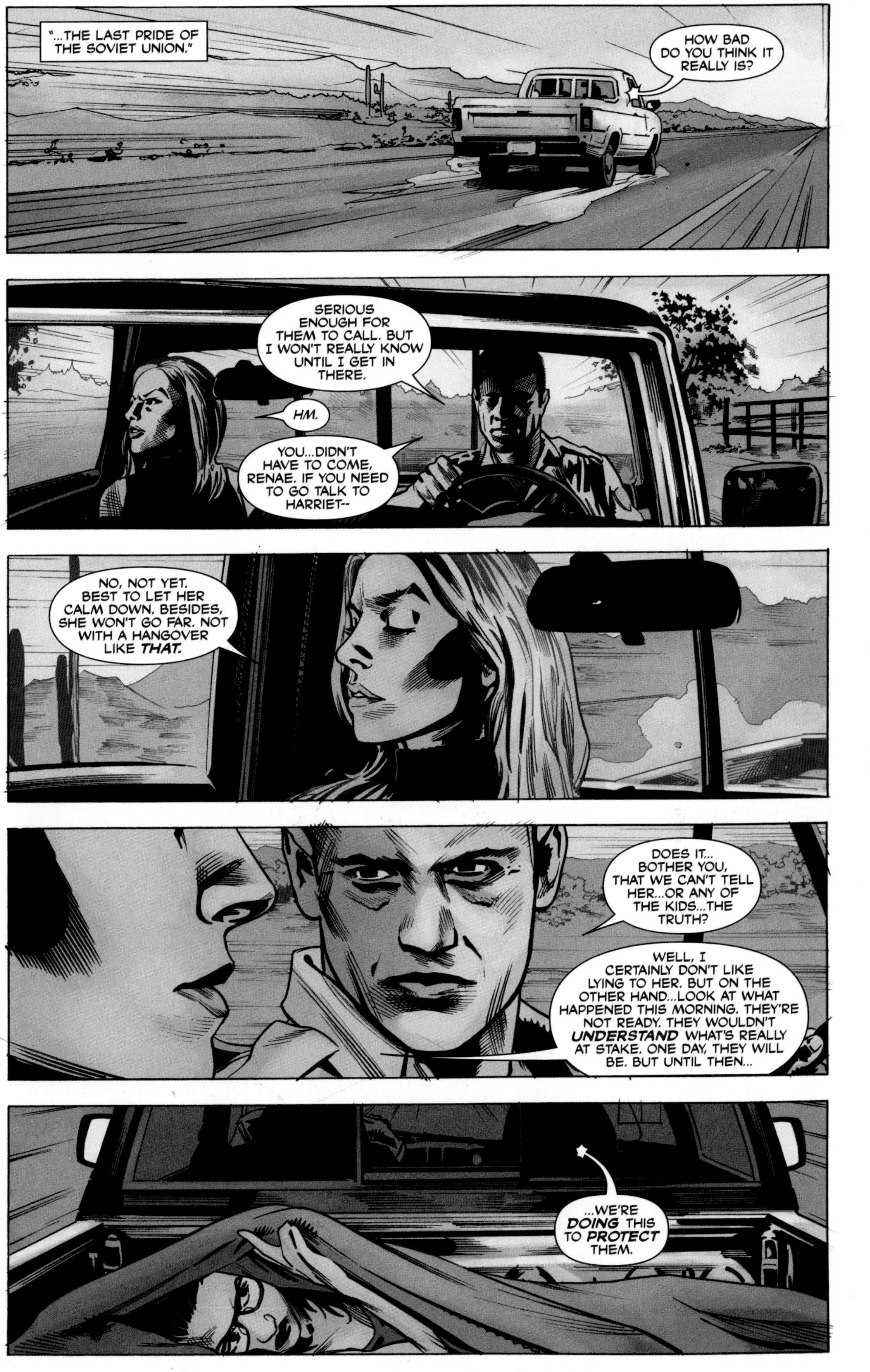
"...THE LAST PRIDE OF THE SOVIET UNION."
HOW BAD DO YOU THINK IT REALLY IS?
SERIOUS ENOUGH FOR THEM TO CALL. BUT I WON'T REALLY KNOW UNTIL I GET IN THERE.
HM.
YOU...DIDN'T HAVE TO COME, RENAE. IF YOU NEED TO GO TALK TO HARRIET--
NO, NOT YET. BEST TO LET HER CALM DOWN. BESIDES, SHE WON'T GO FAR. NOT WITH A HANGOVER LIKE THAT.
DOES IT... BOTHER YOU, THAT WE CAN'T TELL HER...OR ANY OF THE KIDS...THE TRUTH?
WELL, I CERTAINLY DON'T LIKE LYING TO HER. BUT ON THE OTHER HAND...LOOK AT WHAT HAPPENED THIS MORNING. THEY'RE NOT READY. THEY WOULDN'T UNDERSTAND WHAT'S REALLY AT STAKE. ONE DAY, THEY WILL BE. BUT UNTIL THEN...
...WE'RE DOING THIS TO PROTECT THEM.

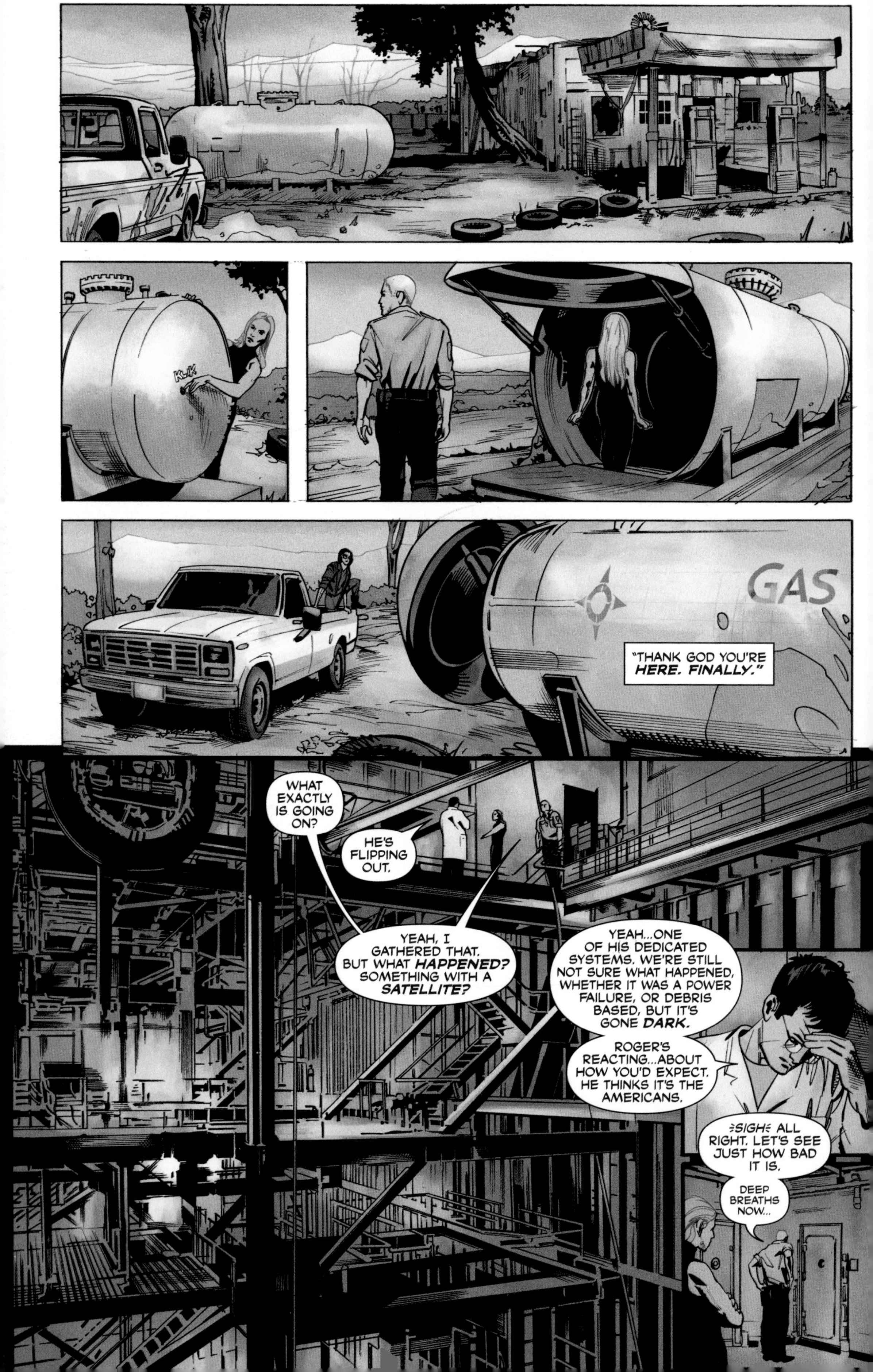
KLIK
GAS
"THANK GOD YOU'RE HERE. FINALLY."
WHAT EXACTLY IS GOING ON?
HE'S FLIPPING OUT.
YEAH, I GATHERED THAT. BUT WHAT HAPPENED? SOMETHING WITH A SATELLITE?
YEAH...ONE OF HIS DEDICATED SYSTEMS. WE'RE STILL NOT SURE WHAT HAPPENED, WHETHER IT WAS A POWER FAILURE, OR DEBRIS BASED, BUT IT'S GONE DARK.
ROGER'S REACTING...ABOUT HOW YOU'D EXPECT. HE THINKS IT'S THE AMERICANS.
SIGH ALL RIGHT. LET'S SEE JUST HOW BAD IT IS.
DEEP BREATHS NOW...

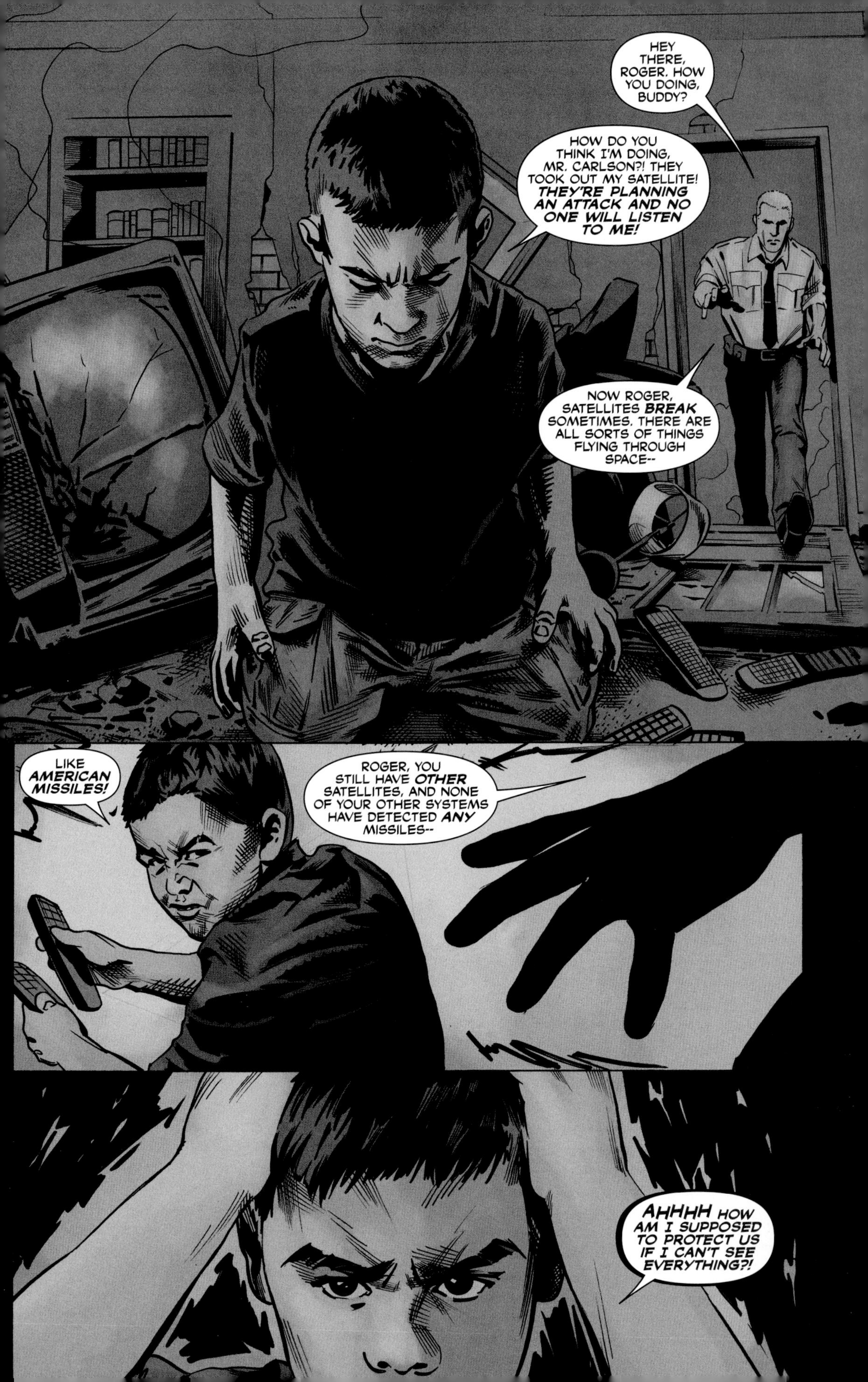
HEY THERE, ROGER. HOW YOU DOING, BUDDY?
HOW DO YOU THINK I'M DOING, MR. CARLSON?! THEY TOOK OUT MY SATELLITE! *THEY'RE PLANNING AN ATTACK AND NO ONE WILL LISTEN TO ME!*
NOW ROGER, SATELLITES **BREAK** SOMETIMES. THERE ARE ALL SORTS OF THINGS FLYING THROUGH SPACE--
LIKE ***AMERICAN MISSILES!***
ROGER, YOU STILL HAVE ***OTHER*** SATELLITES, AND NONE OF YOUR OTHER SYSTEMS HAVE DETECTED ***ANY*** MISSILES--
AHHHH HOW AM I SUPPOSED TO PROTECT US IF I CAN'T SEE EVERYTHING?!

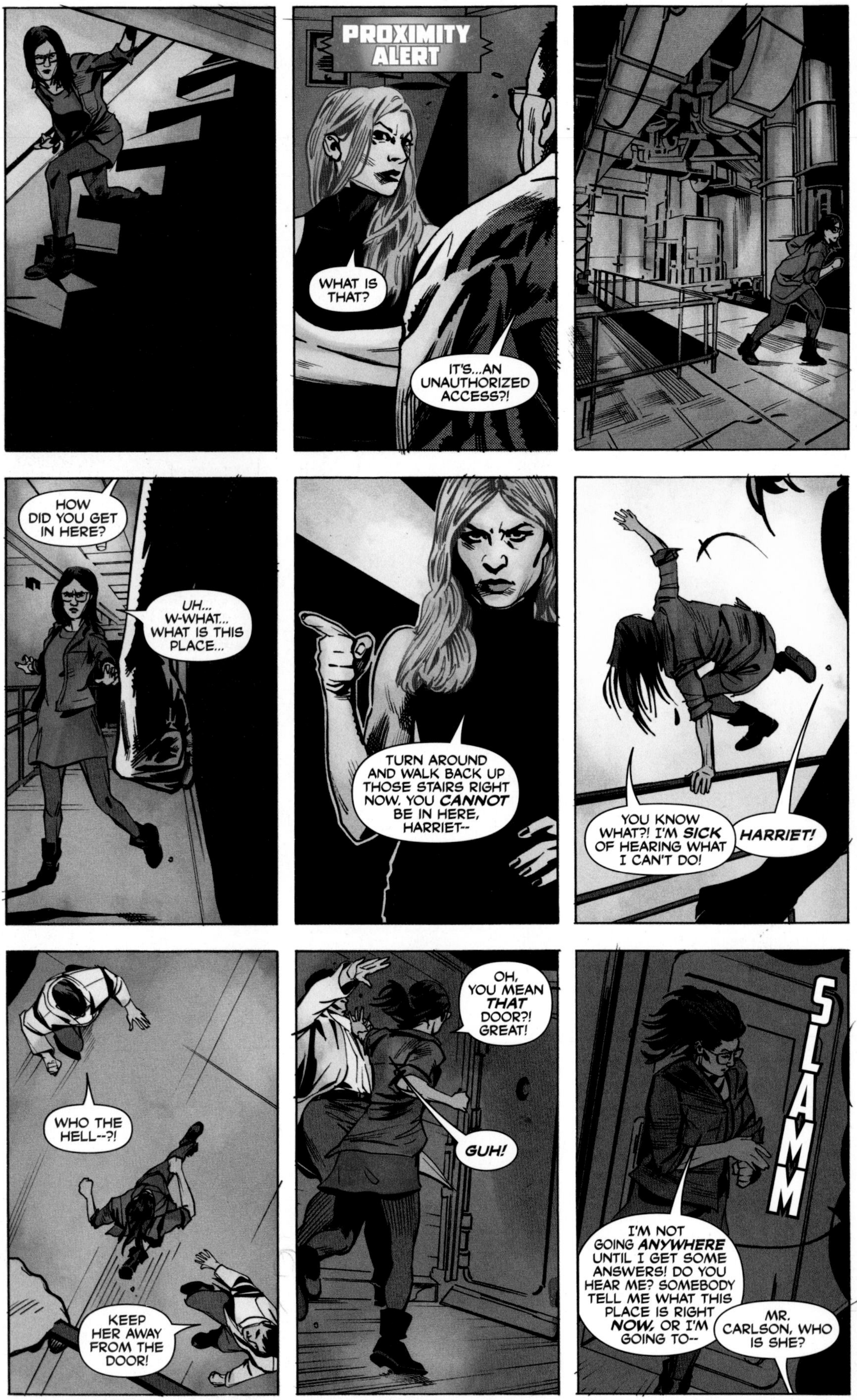
PROXIMITY ALERT
WHAT IS THAT?
IT'S...AN UNAUTHORIZED ACCESS?!
HOW DID YOU GET IN HERE?
UH... W-WHAT... WHAT IS THIS PLACE...
TURN AROUND AND WALK BACK UP THOSE STAIRS RIGHT NOW. YOU CANNOT BE IN HERE, HARRIET--
YOU KNOW WHAT?! I'M SICK OF HEARING WHAT I CAN'T DO!
HARRIET!
WHO THE HELL--?!
KEEP HER AWAY FROM THE DOOR!
OH, YOU MEAN THAT DOOR?! GREAT!
GUH!
SLAMM
I'M NOT GOING ANYWHERE UNTIL I GET SOME ANSWERS! DO YOU HEAR ME? SOMEBODY TELL ME WHAT THIS PLACE IS RIGHT NOW, OR I'M GOING TO--
MR. CARLSON, WHO IS SHE?

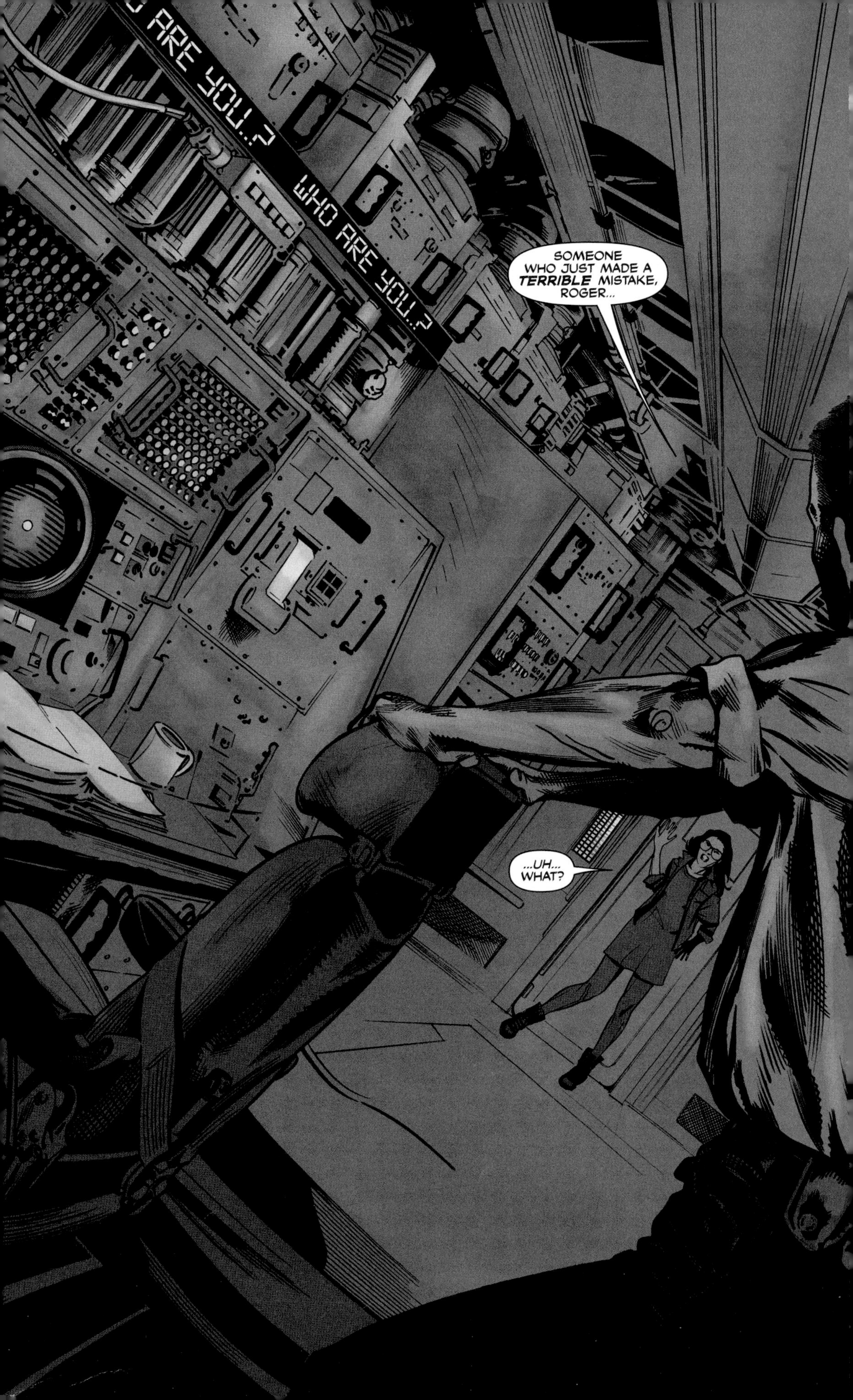
O ARE YOU..?
WHO ARE YOU..?
SOMEONE WHO JUST MADE A *TERRIBLE* MISTAKE, ROGER...
...UH... WHAT?

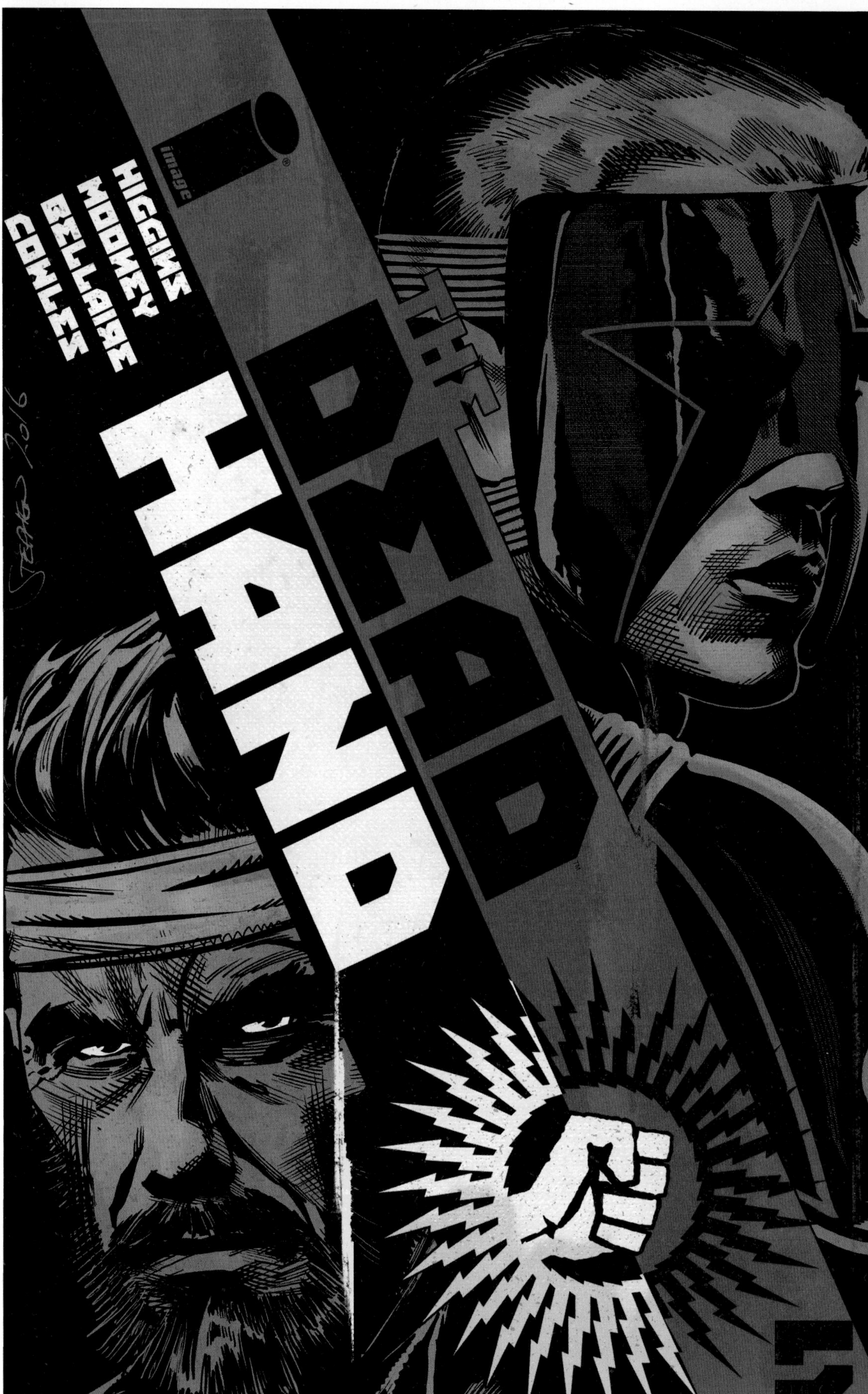
THE DEAD HAND
HIGGINS
MOONEY
BELLAIRE
COWLES
image
5

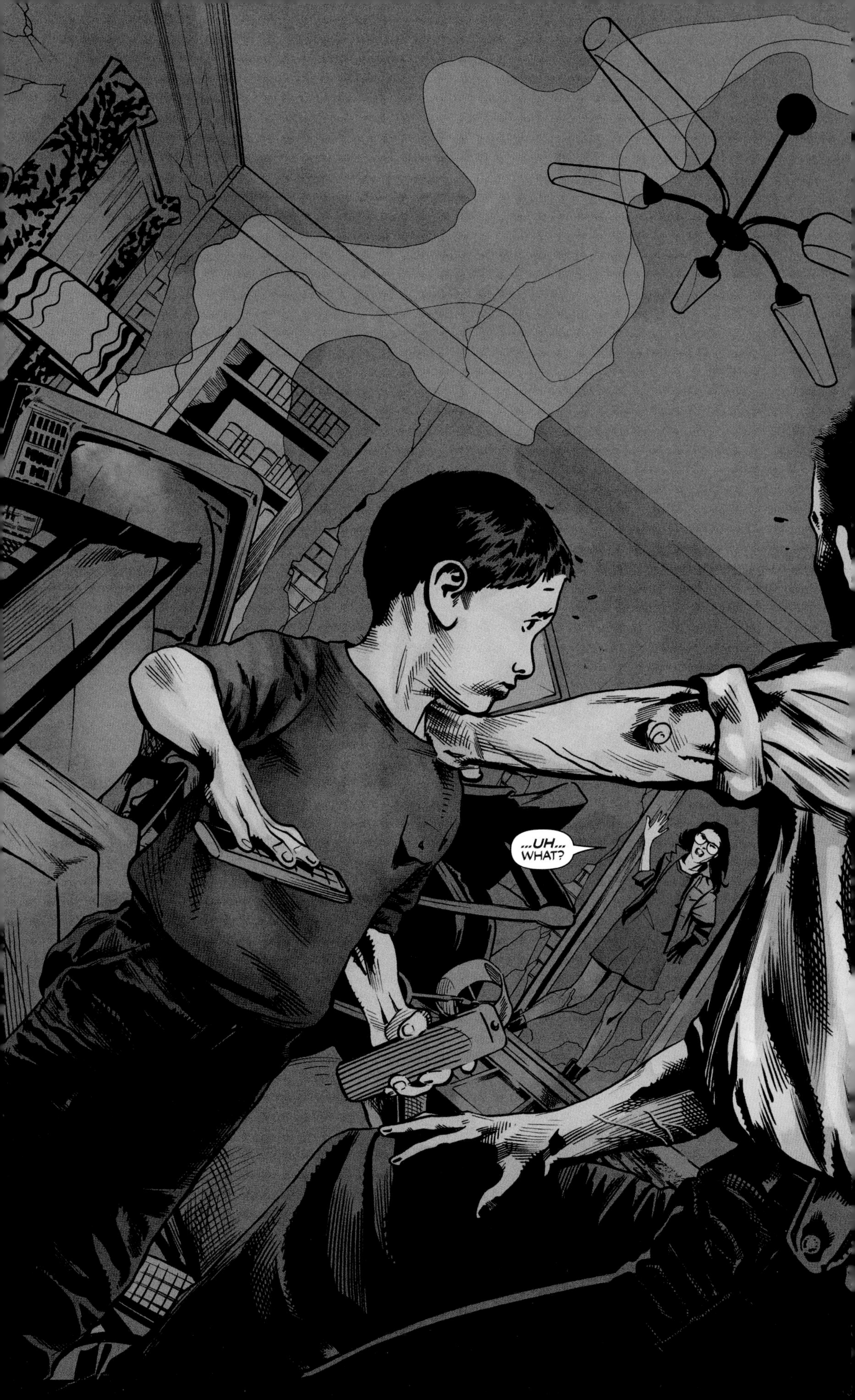
...UH... WHAT?

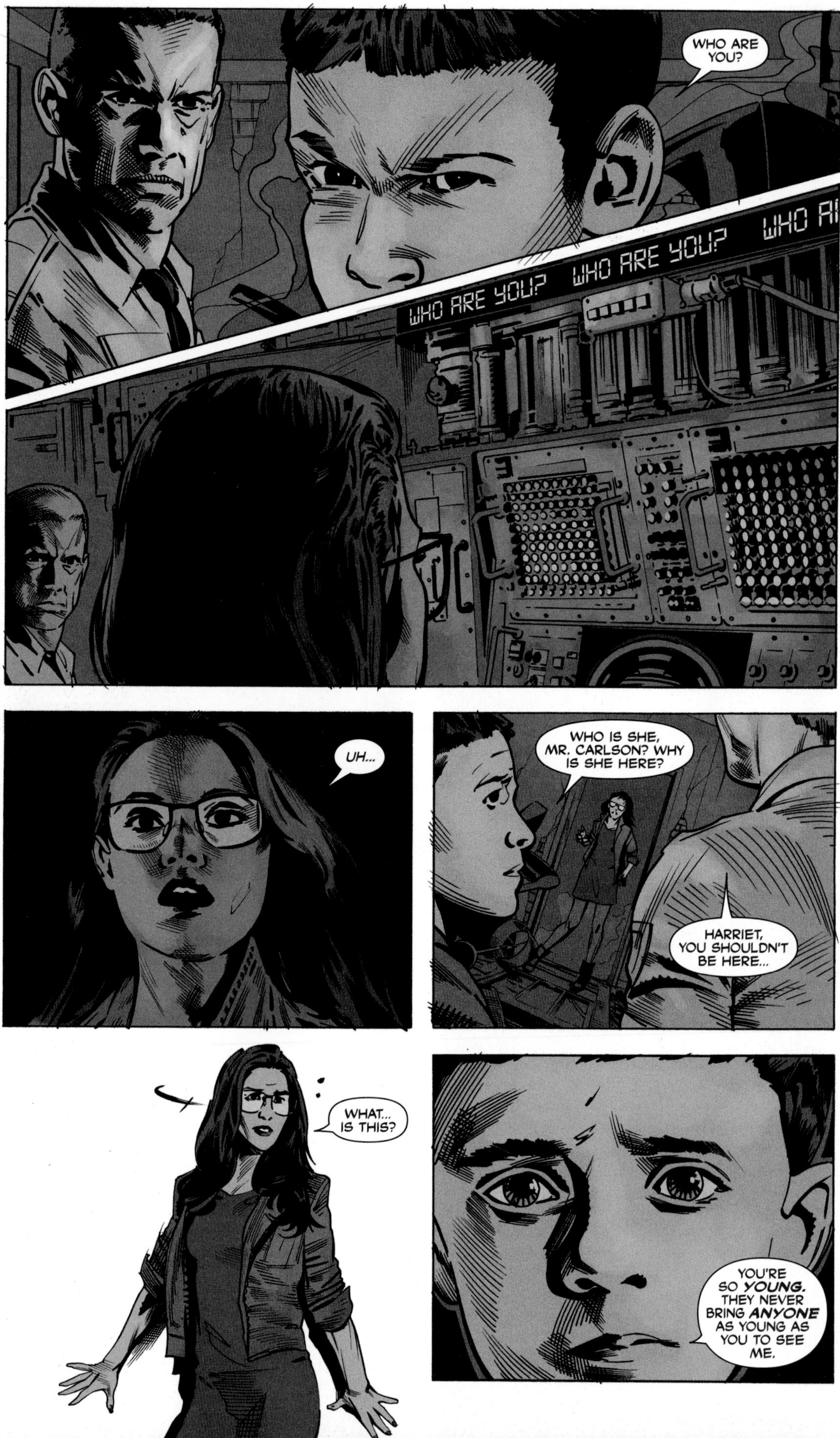
WHO ARE YOU?
WHO ARE YOU? WHO ARE YOU? WHO AR
UH...
WHO IS SHE, MR. CARLSON? WHY IS SHE HERE?
HARRIET, YOU SHOULDN'T BE HERE...
WHAT... IS THIS?
YOU'RE SO YOUNG. THEY NEVER BRING ANYONE AS YOUNG AS YOU TO SEE ME.

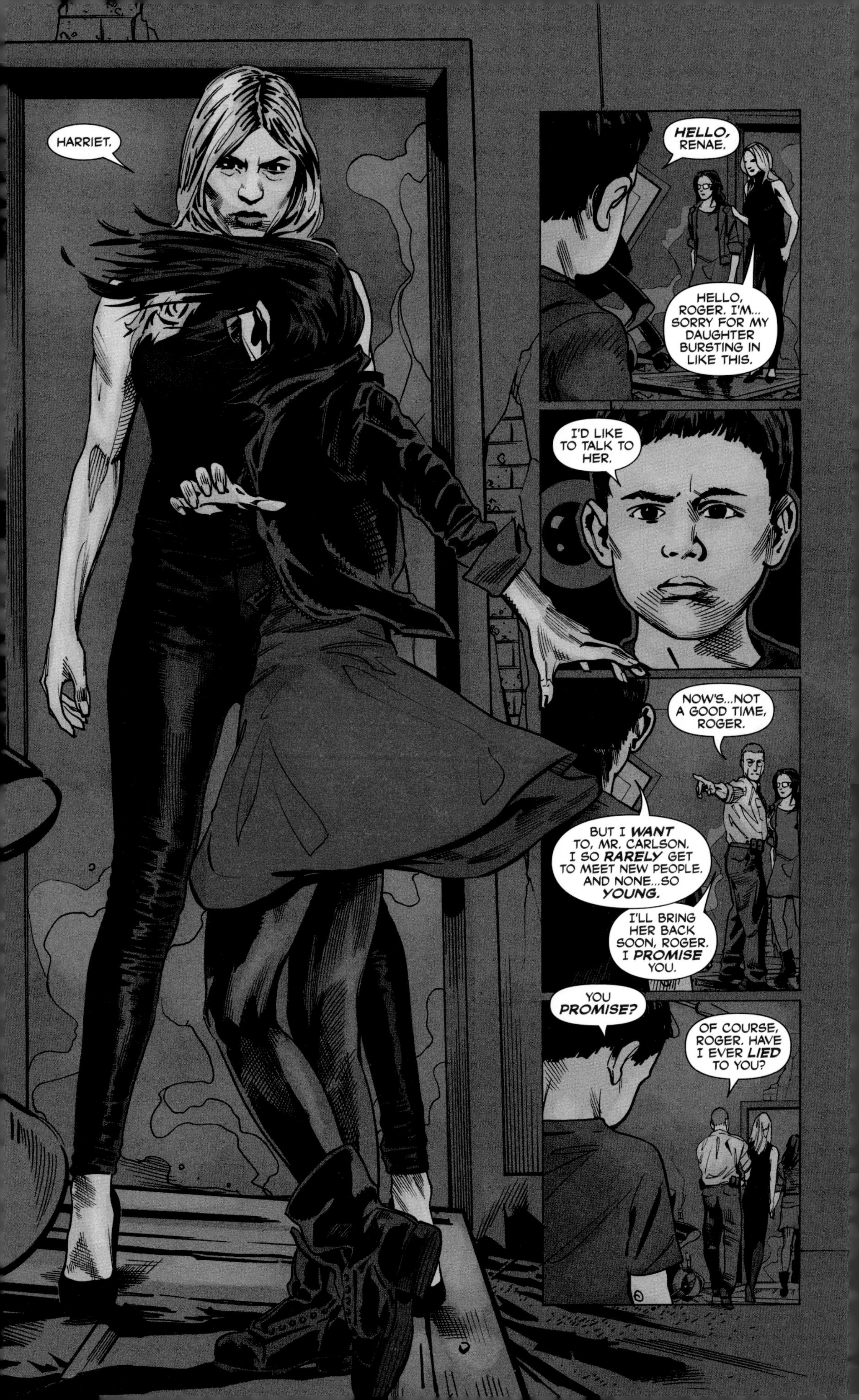
HARRIET.
HELLO, RENAE.
HELLO, ROGER. I'M... SORRY FOR MY DAUGHTER BURSTING IN LIKE THIS.
I'D LIKE TO TALK TO HER.
NOW'S...NOT A GOOD TIME, ROGER.
BUT I WANT TO, MR. CARLSON. I SO RARELY GET TO MEET NEW PEOPLE. AND NONE...SO YOUNG.
I'LL BRING HER BACK SOON, ROGER. I PROMISE YOU.
YOU PROMISE?
OF COURSE, ROGER. HAVE I EVER LIED TO YOU?

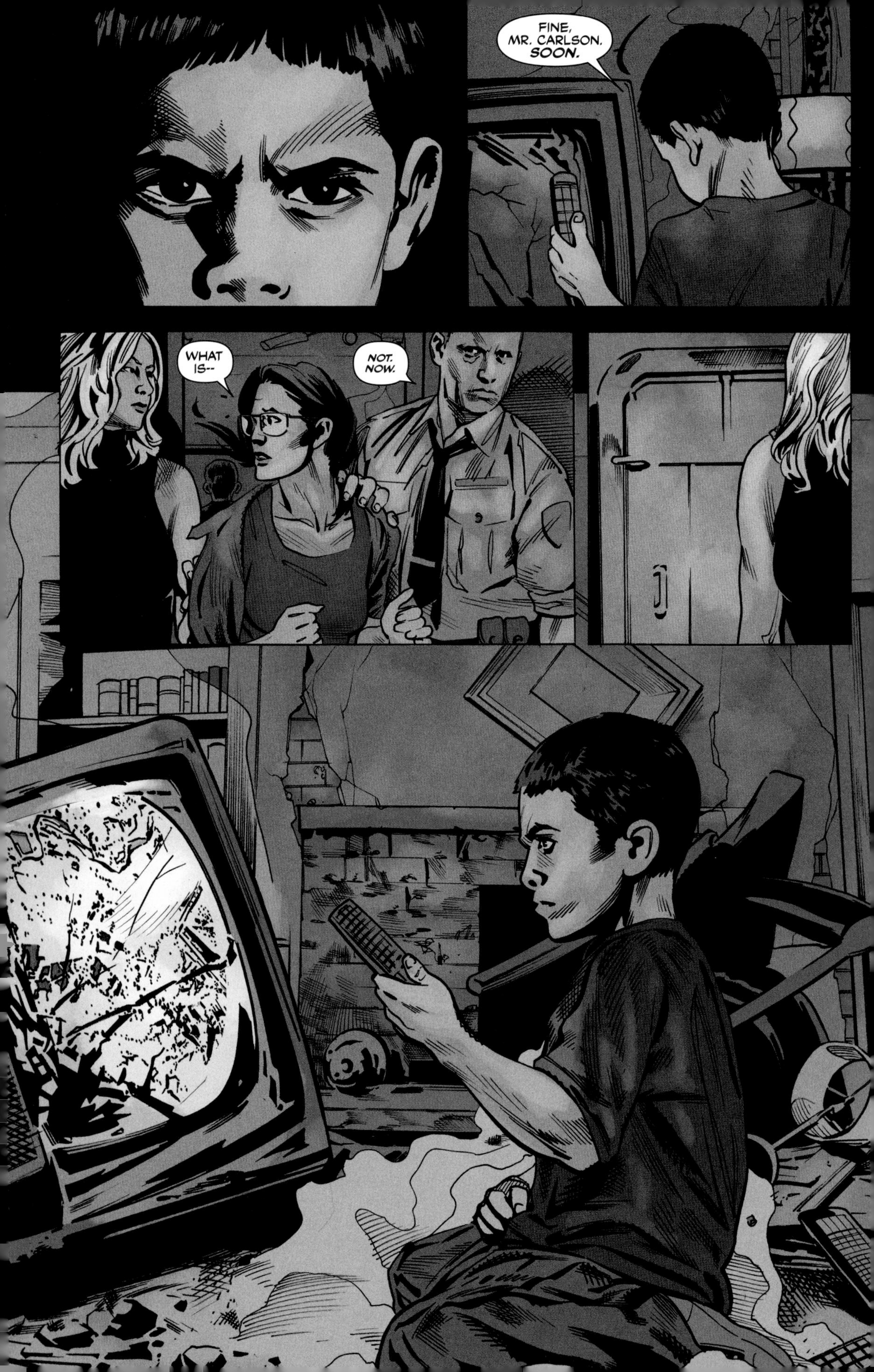

FINE, MR. CARLSON. SOON.
WHAT IS--
NOT. NOW.

CLEAR THE ROOM!

OW! THAT HURTS!

WHO ON GOD'S GREEN EARTH DO YOU THINK YOU ARE?

I'M... I MEAN... I'M NOT--

EXACTLY! YOU'RE NOT ANYONE!

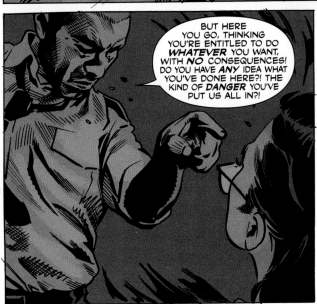

BUT HERE YOU GO, THINKING YOU'RE ENTITLED TO DO *WHATEVER* YOU WANT, WITH *NO* CONSEQUENCES! DO YOU HAVE *ANY* IDEA WHAT YOU'VE DONE HERE?! THE KIND OF *DANGER* YOU'VE PUT US ALL IN?!

NO! BECAUSE NEITHER OF YOU *EVER* TELL ME *ANYTHING!* YOU TREAT ME LIKE SOME *KID*--

YOU *ARE* A KID!

SHE SHOULD KNOW.

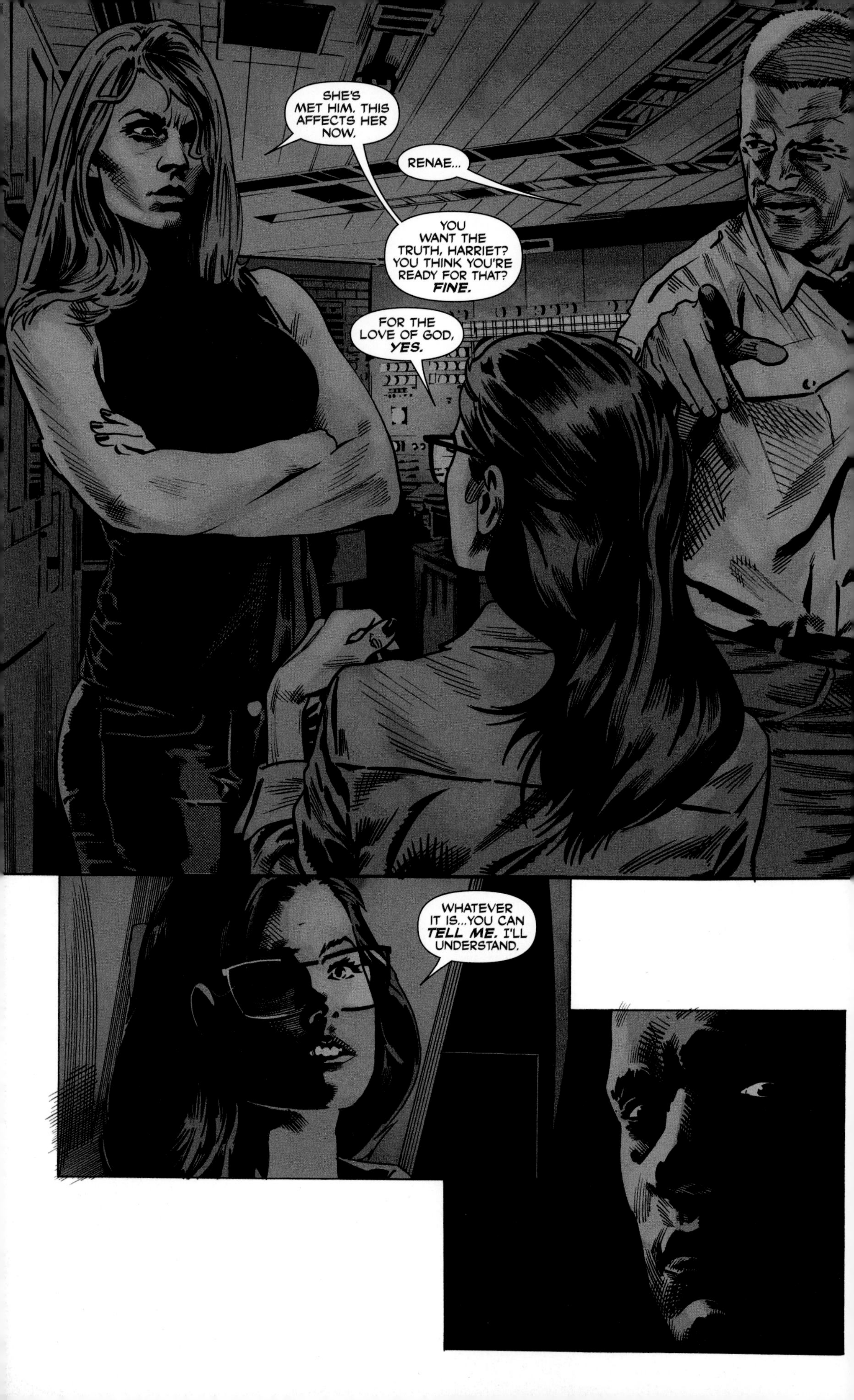
SHE'S MET HIM. THIS AFFECTS HER NOW.
RENAE...
YOU WANT THE TRUTH, HARRIET? YOU THINK YOU'RE READY FOR THAT? FINE.
FOR THE LOVE OF GOD, YES.
WHATEVER IT IS...YOU CAN TELL ME. I'LL UNDERSTAND.

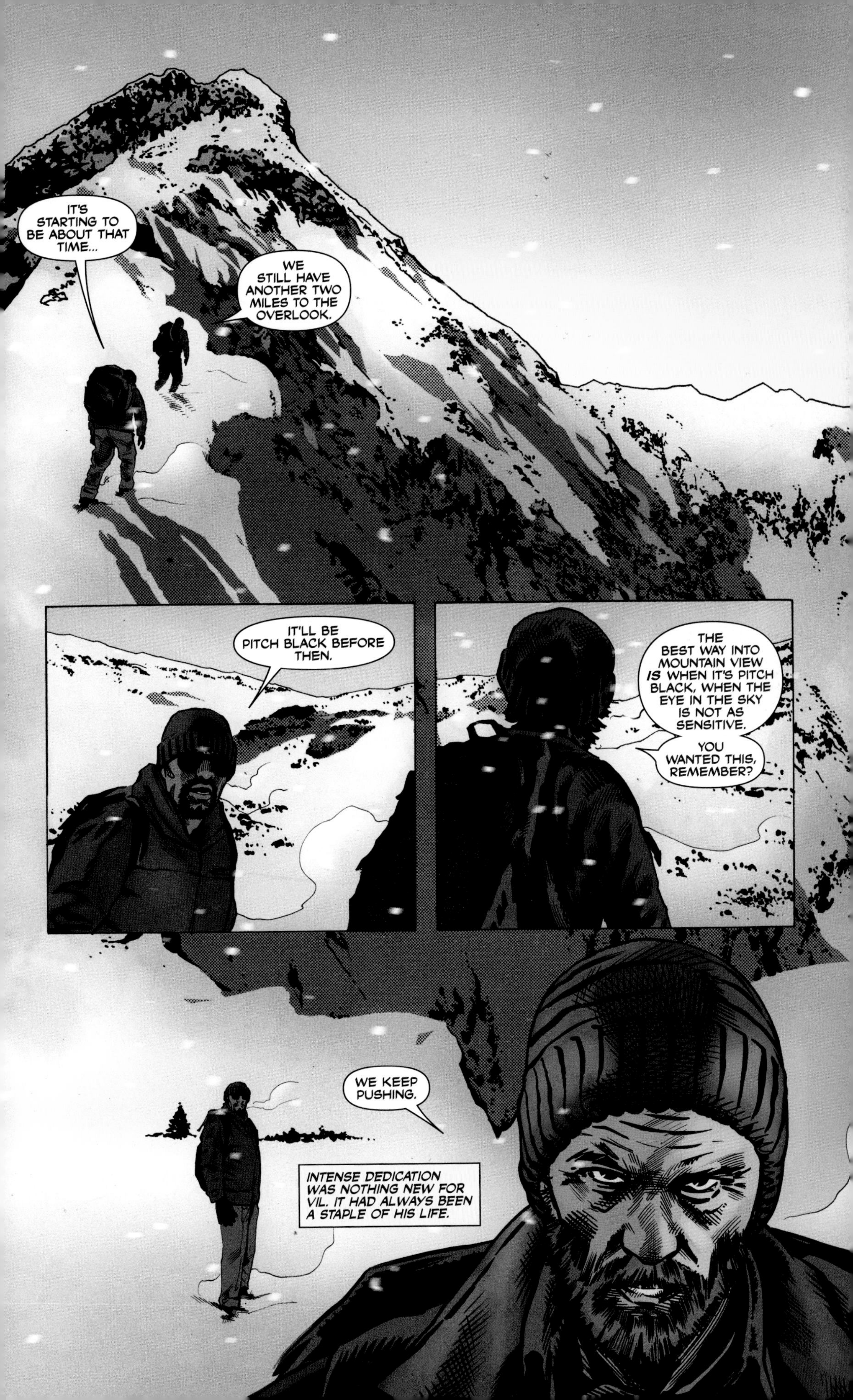
IT'S STARTING TO BE ABOUT THAT TIME...
WE STILL HAVE ANOTHER TWO MILES TO THE OVERLOOK.
IT'LL BE PITCH BLACK BEFORE THEN.
THE BEST WAY INTO MOUNTAIN VIEW *IS* WHEN IT'S PITCH BLACK, WHEN THE EYE IN THE SKY IS NOT AS SENSITIVE.
YOU WANTED THIS, REMEMBER?
WE KEEP PUSHING.
INTENSE DEDICATION WAS NOTHING NEW FOR VIL. IT HAD ALWAYS BEEN A STAPLE OF HIS LIFE.

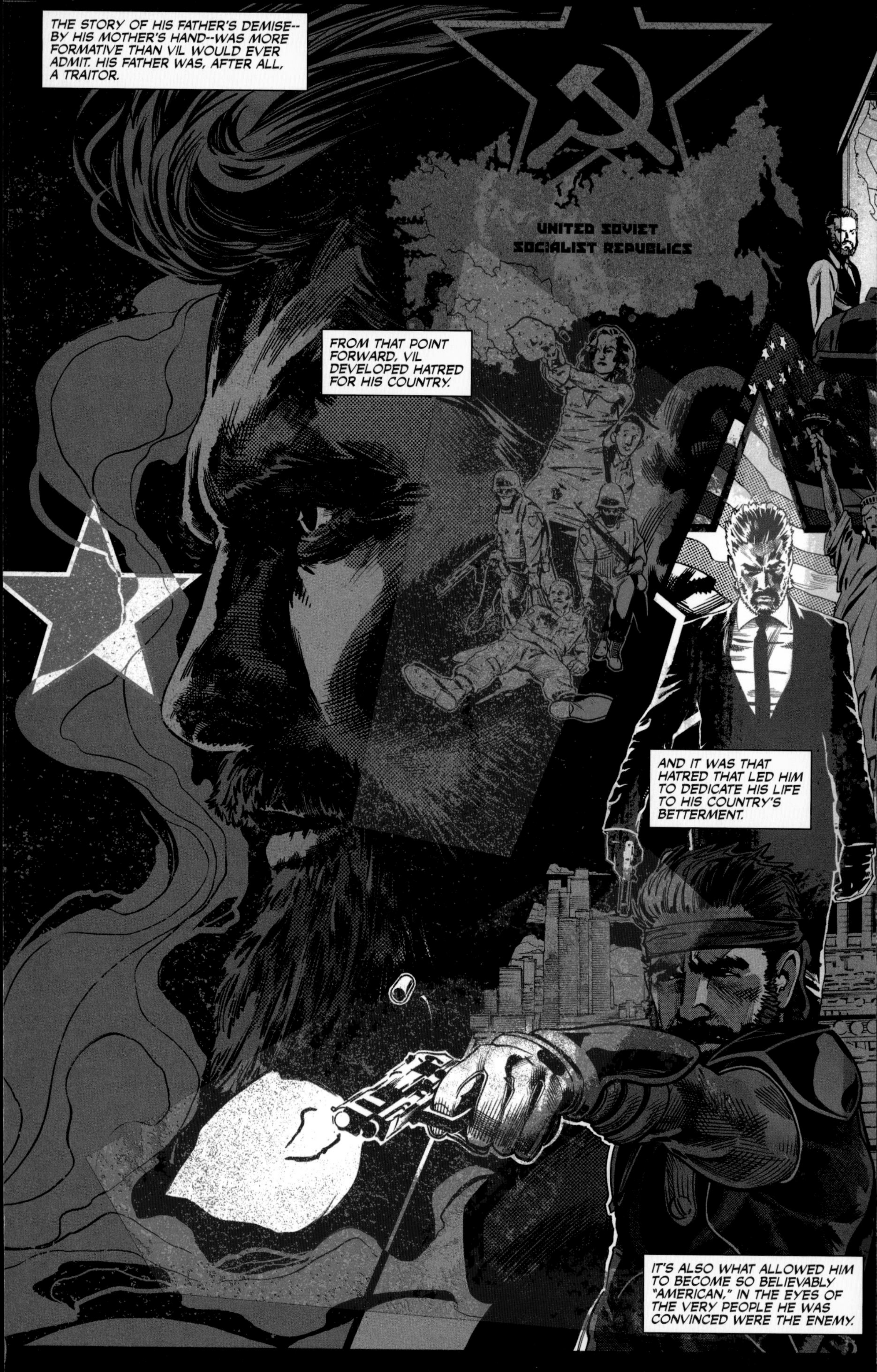
THE STORY OF HIS FATHER'S DEMISE--BY HIS MOTHER'S HAND--WAS MORE FORMATIVE THAN VIL WOULD EVER ADMIT. HIS FATHER WAS, AFTER ALL, A TRAITOR.
UNITED SOVIET SOCIALIST REPUBLICS
FROM THAT POINT FORWARD, VIL DEVELOPED HATRED FOR HIS COUNTRY.
AND IT WAS THAT HATRED THAT LED HIM TO DEDICATE HIS LIFE TO HIS COUNTRY'S BETTERMENT.
IT'S ALSO WHAT ALLOWED HIM TO BECOME SO BELIEVABLY "AMERICAN," IN THE EYES OF THE VERY PEOPLE HE WAS CONVINCED WERE THE ENEMY.

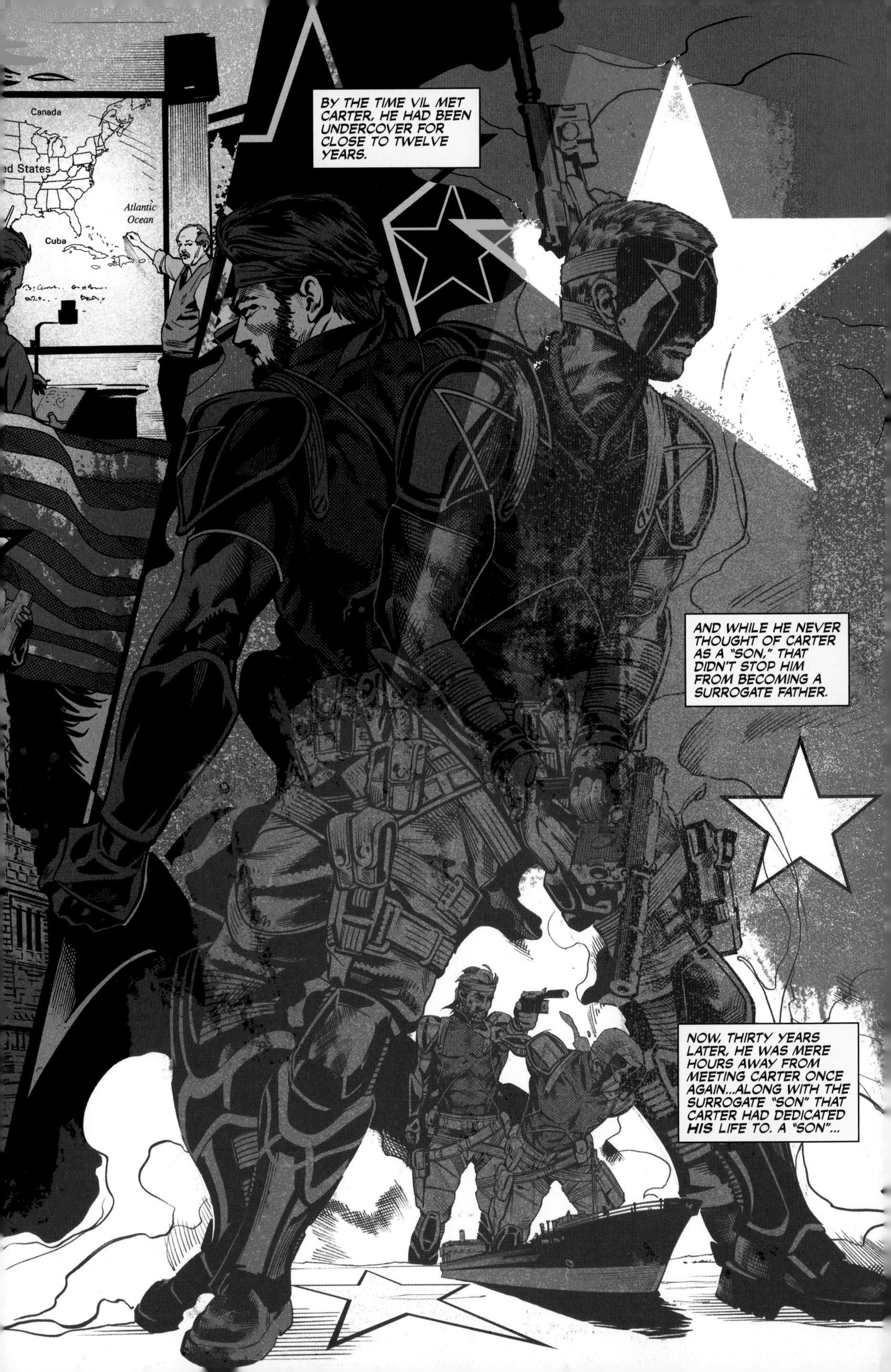
Canada
ed States
Atlantic
Ocean
Cuba
BY THE TIME VIL MET CARTER, HE HAD BEEN UNDERCOVER FOR CLOSE TO TWELVE YEARS.
AND WHILE HE NEVER THOUGHT OF CARTER AS A "SON," THAT DIDN'T STOP HIM FROM BECOMING A SURROGATE FATHER.
NOW, THIRTY YEARS LATER, HE WAS MERE HOURS AWAY FROM MEETING CARTER ONCE AGAIN...ALONG WITH THE SURROGATE "SON" THAT CARTER HAD DEDICATED HIS LIFE TO. A "SON"...

...WHO COULD END THE WORLD.

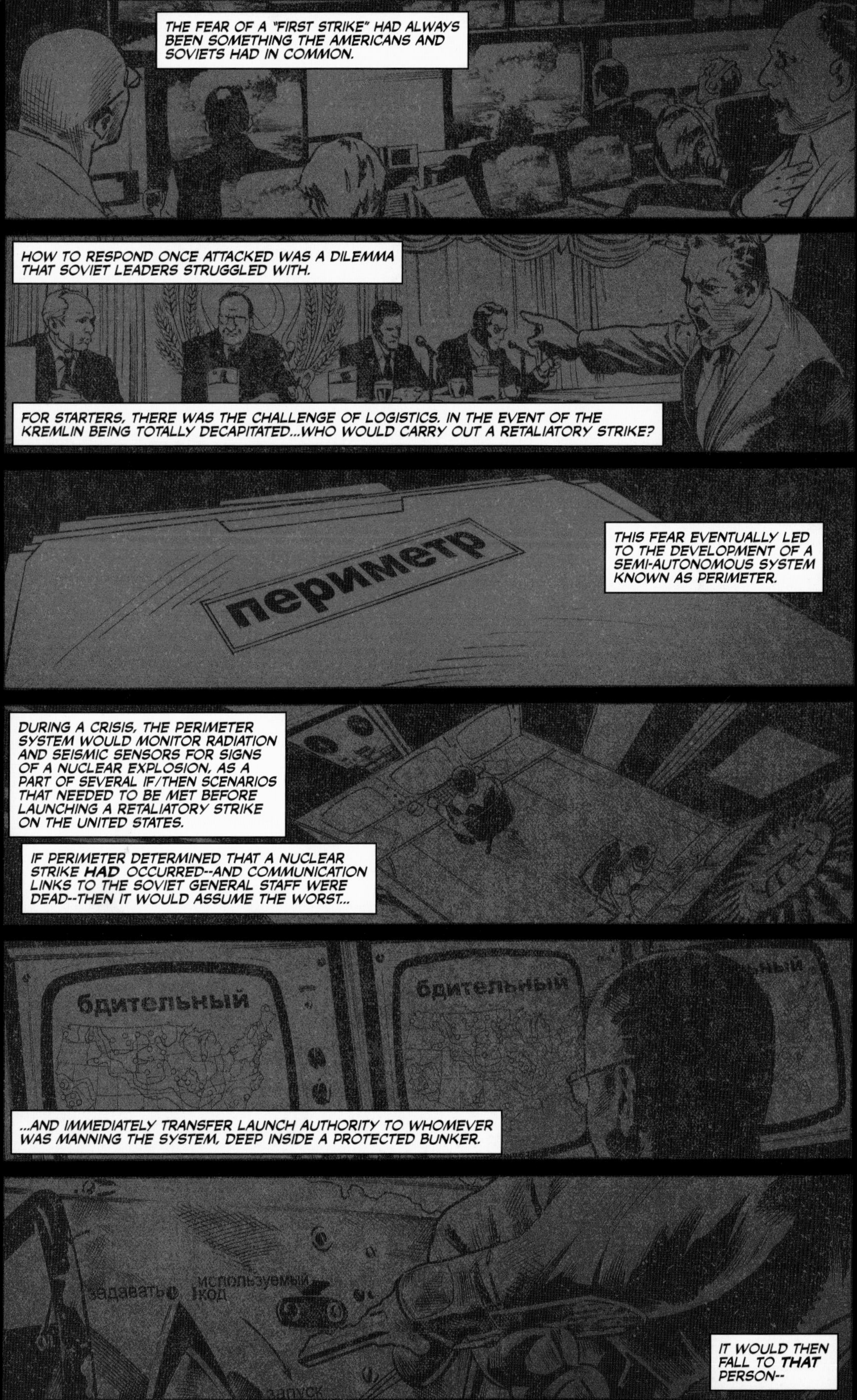
THE FEAR OF A "FIRST STRIKE" HAD ALWAYS BEEN SOMETHING THE AMERICANS AND SOVIETS HAD IN COMMON.
HOW TO RESPOND ONCE ATTACKED WAS A DILEMMA THAT SOVIET LEADERS STRUGGLED WITH.
FOR STARTERS, THERE WAS THE CHALLENGE OF LOGISTICS. IN THE EVENT OF THE KREMLIN BEING TOTALLY DECAPITATED...WHO WOULD CARRY OUT A RETALIATORY STRIKE?
периметр
THIS FEAR EVENTUALLY LED TO THE DEVELOPMENT OF A SEMI-AUTONOMOUS SYSTEM KNOWN AS PERIMETER.
DURING A CRISIS, THE PERIMETER SYSTEM WOULD MONITOR RADIATION AND SEISMIC SENSORS FOR SIGNS OF A NUCLEAR EXPLOSION, AS A PART OF SEVERAL IF/THEN SCENARIOS THAT NEEDED TO BE MET BEFORE LAUNCHING A RETALIATORY STRIKE ON THE UNITED STATES.
IF PERIMETER DETERMINED THAT A NUCLEAR STRIKE **HAD** OCCURRED--AND COMMUNICATION LINKS TO THE SOVIET GENERAL STAFF WERE DEAD--THEN IT WOULD ASSUME THE WORST...
бдительный
бдительный
...AND IMMEDIATELY TRANSFER LAUNCH AUTHORITY TO WHOMEVER WAS MANNING THE SYSTEM, DEEP INSIDE A PROTECTED BUNKER.
задавать
используемый код
IT WOULD THEN FALL TO **THAT** PERSON--

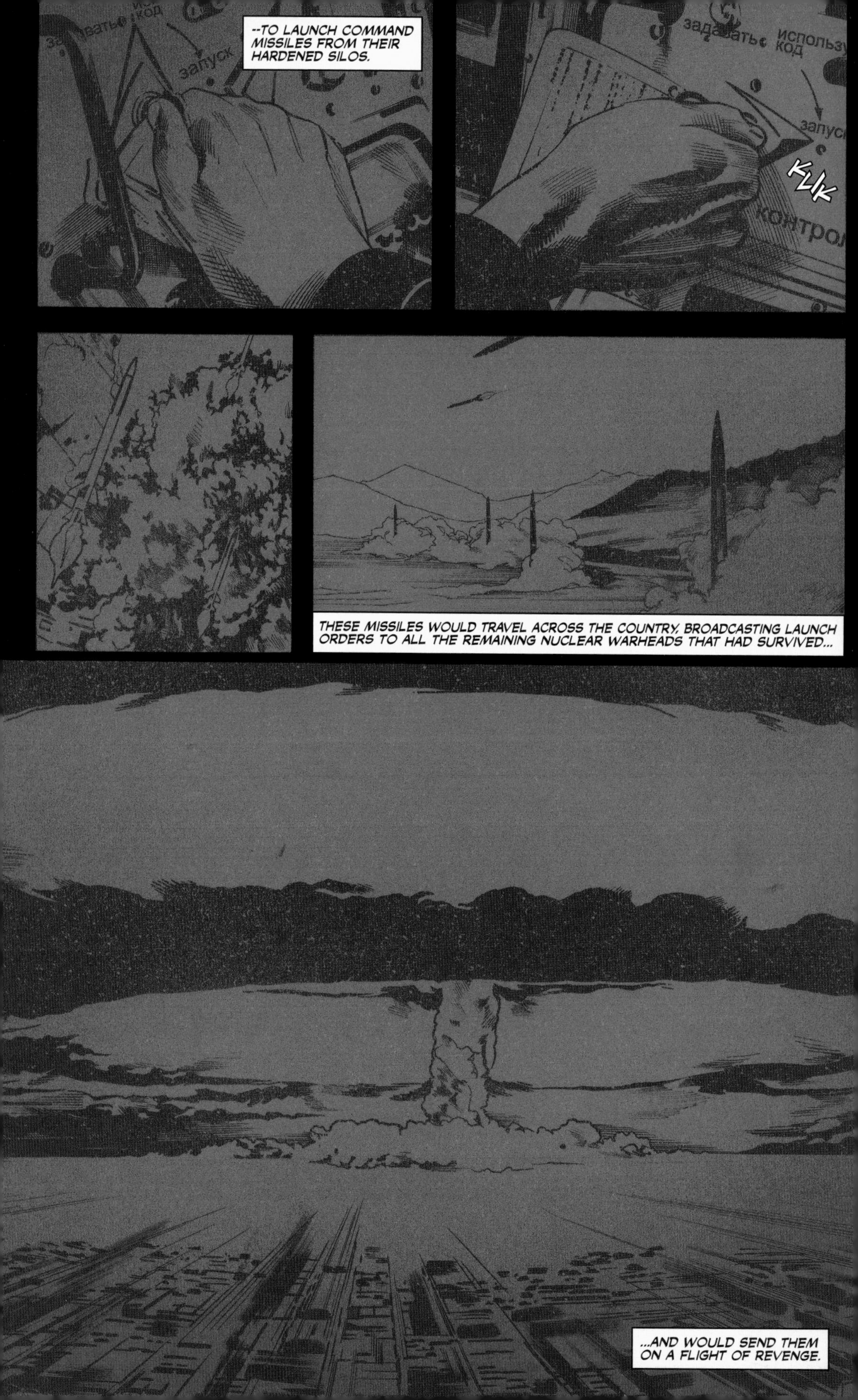

--TO LAUNCH COMMAND MISSILES FROM THEIR HARDENED SILOS.
запуск
задавать
код
запуск
KLIK
THESE MISSILES WOULD TRAVEL ACROSS THE COUNTRY, BROADCASTING LAUNCH ORDERS TO ALL THE REMAINING NUCLEAR WARHEADS THAT HAD SURVIVED...
...AND WOULD SEND THEM ON A FLIGHT OF REVENGE.

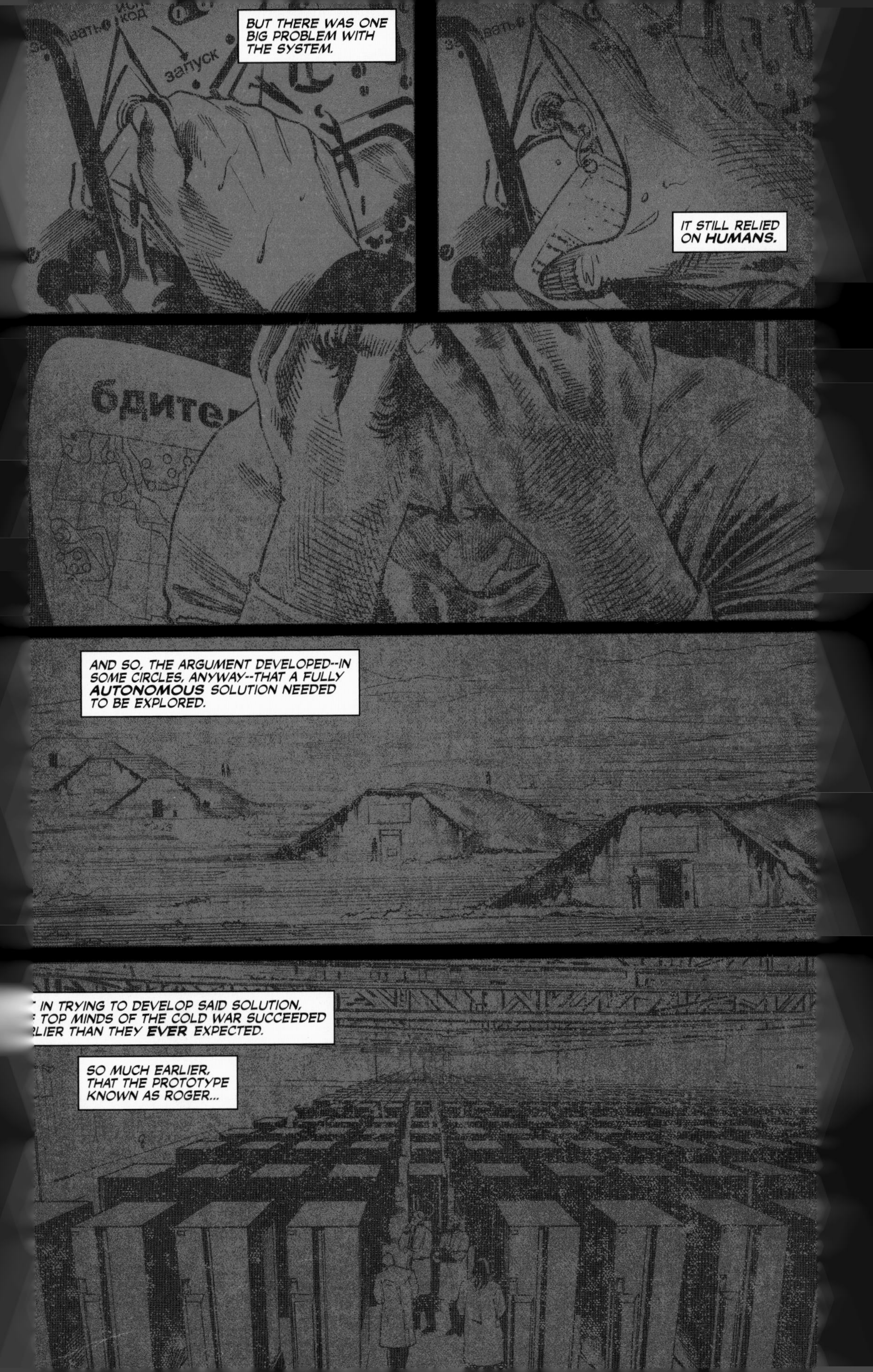
BUT THERE WAS ONE BIG PROBLEM WITH THE SYSTEM.
запуск
IT STILL RELIED ON **HUMANS.**
AND SO, THE ARGUMENT DEVELOPED--IN SOME CIRCLES, ANYWAY--THAT A FULLY **AUTONOMOUS** SOLUTION NEEDED TO BE EXPLORED.
IN TRYING TO DEVELOP SAID SOLUTION, TOP MINDS OF THE COLD WAR SUCCEEDED RLIER THAN THEY **EVER** EXPECTED.
SO MUCH EARLIER, THAT THE PROTOTYPE KNOWN AS ROGER...

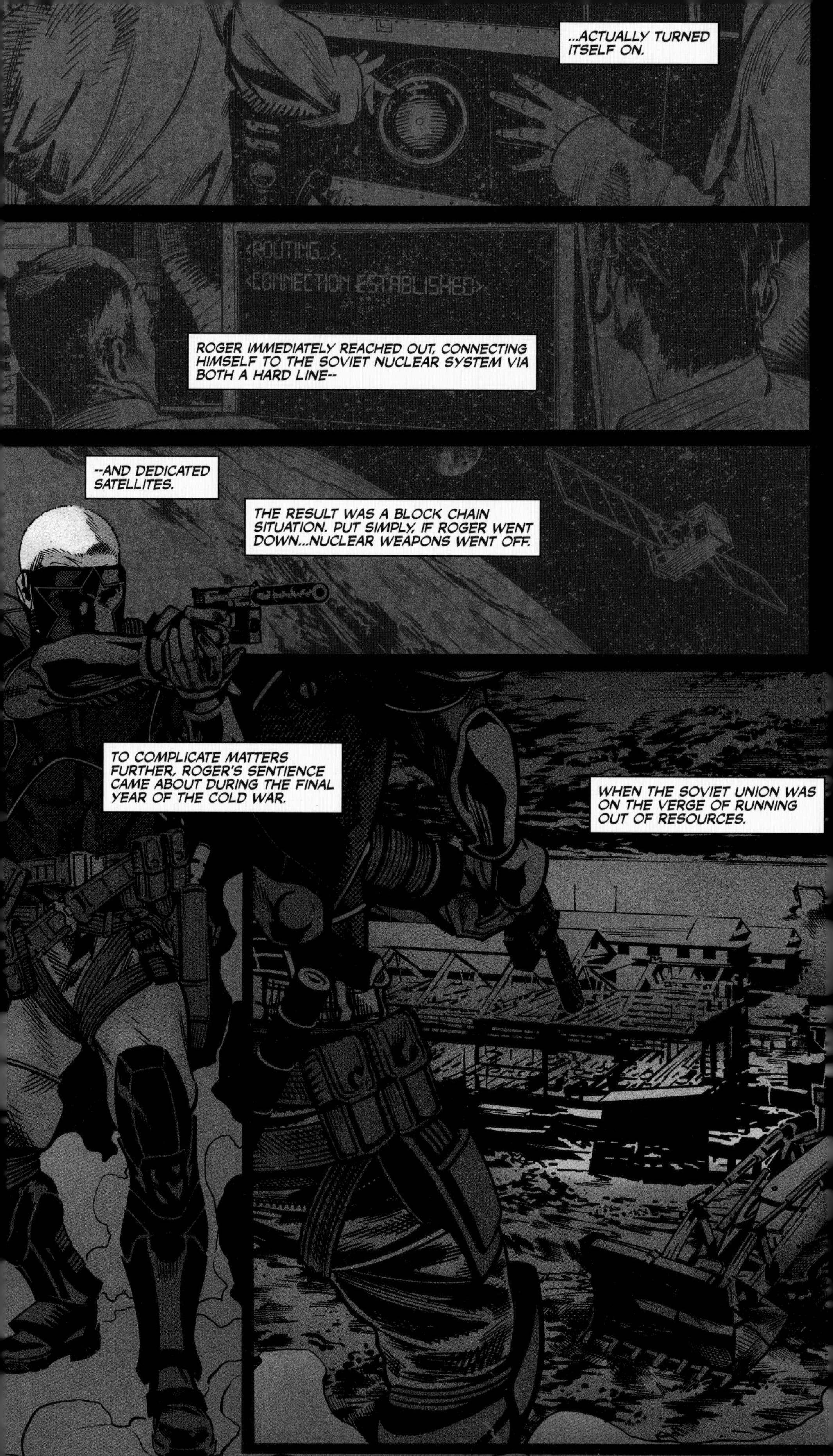
...ACTUALLY TURNED ITSELF ON.
<ROUTING...>
<CONNECTION ESTABLISHED>
ROGER IMMEDIATELY REACHED OUT, CONNECTING HIMSELF TO THE SOVIET NUCLEAR SYSTEM VIA BOTH A HARD LINE--
--AND DEDICATED SATELLITES.
THE RESULT WAS A BLOCK CHAIN SITUATION. PUT SIMPLY, IF ROGER WENT DOWN...NUCLEAR WEAPONS WENT OFF.
TO COMPLICATE MATTERS FURTHER, ROGER'S SENTIENCE CAME ABOUT DURING THE FINAL YEAR OF THE COLD WAR.
WHEN THE SOVIET UNION WAS ON THE VERGE OF RUNNING OUT OF RESOURCES.

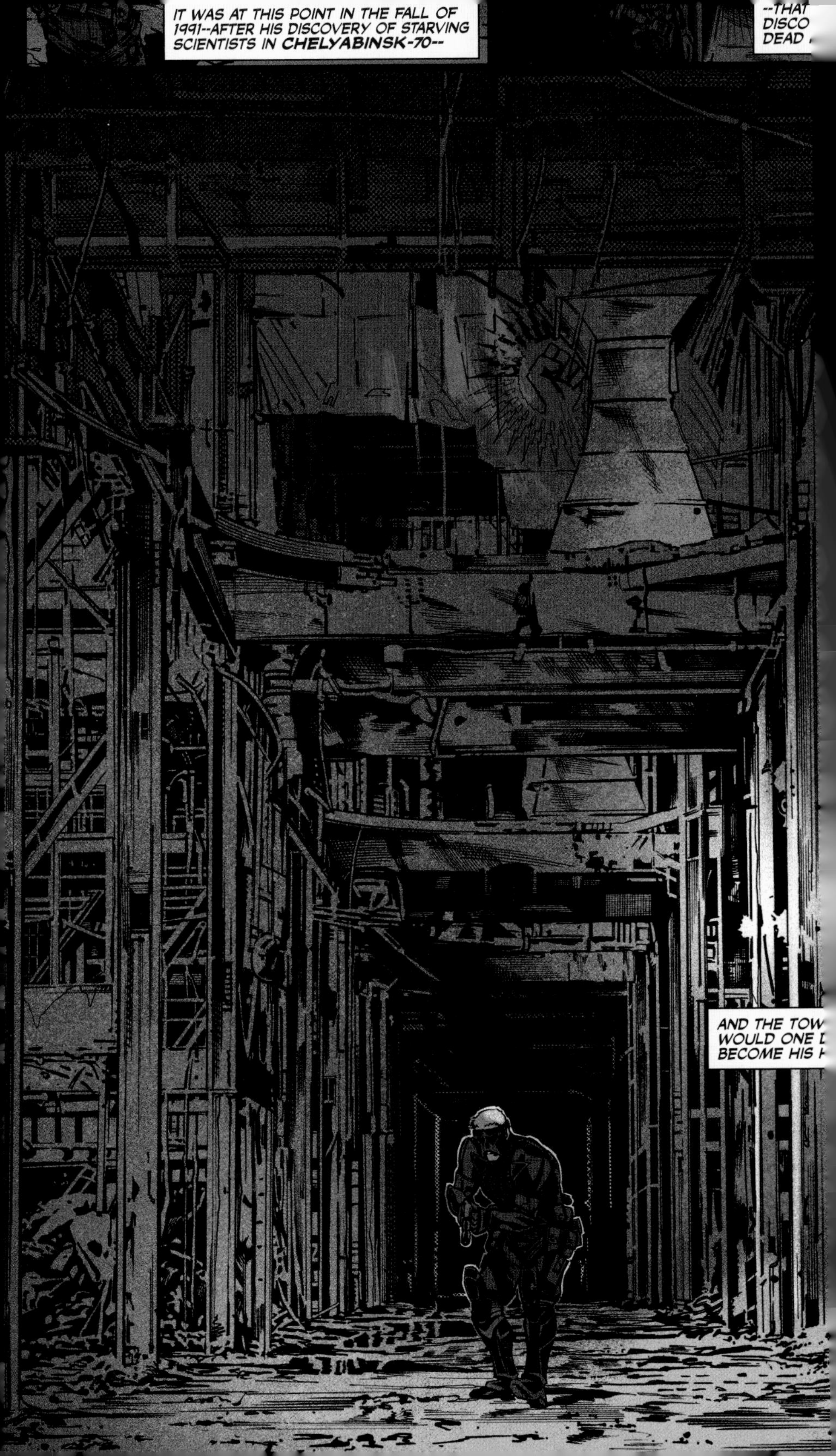

IT WAS AT THIS POINT IN THE FALL OF 1991--AFTER HIS DISCOVERY OF STARVING SCIENTISTS IN **CHELYABINSK-70**--
--THAT
DISCO
DEAD
AND THE TOW
WOULD ONE
BECOME HIS

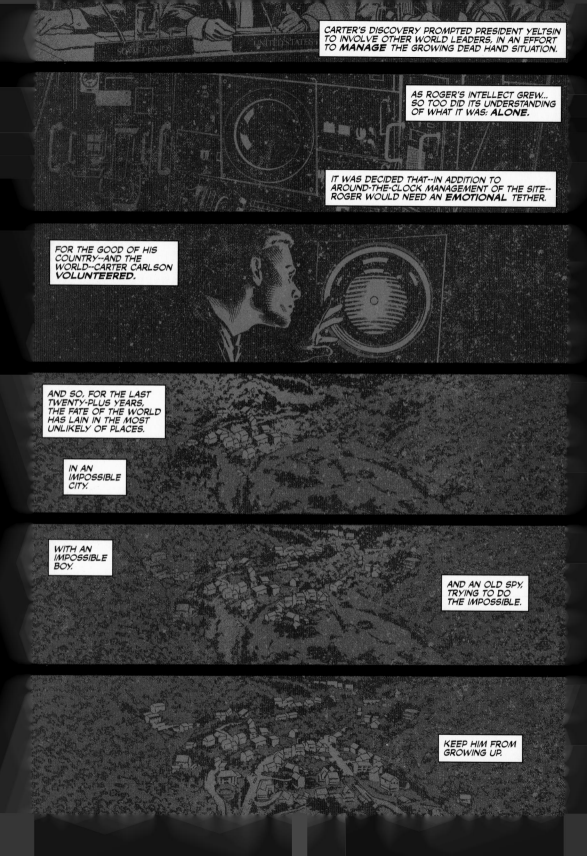

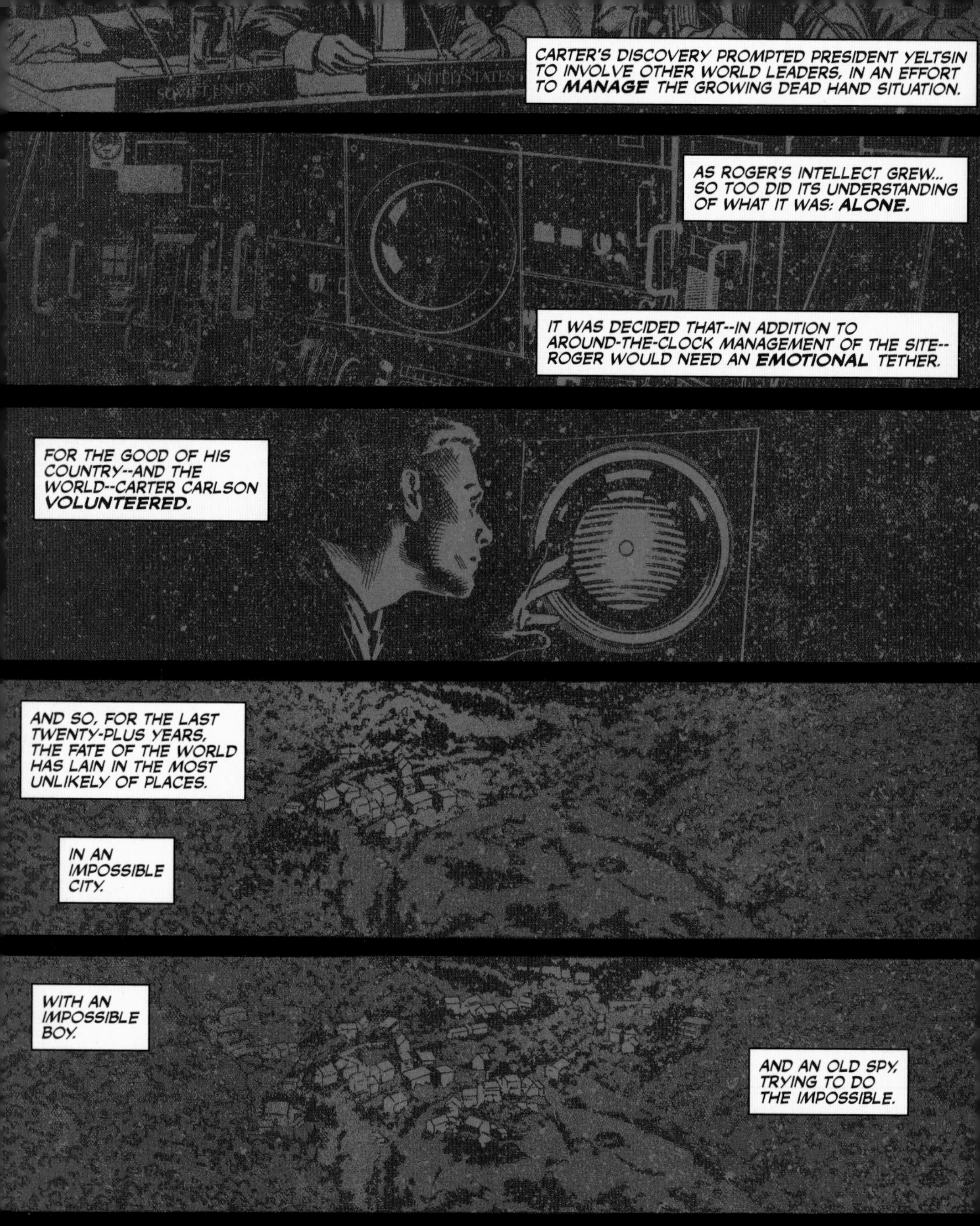
SOVIET UNION
UNITED STATES
CARTER'S DISCOVERY PROMPTED PRESIDENT YELTSIN TO INVOLVE OTHER WORLD LEADERS, IN AN EFFORT TO **MANAGE** THE GROWING DEAD HAND SITUATION.
AS ROGER'S INTELLECT GREW... SO TOO DID ITS UNDERSTANDING OF WHAT IT WAS: **ALONE.**
IT WAS DECIDED THAT--IN ADDITION TO AROUND-THE-CLOCK MANAGEMENT OF THE SITE--ROGER WOULD NEED AN **EMOTIONAL** TETHER.
FOR THE GOOD OF HIS COUNTRY--AND THE WORLD--CARTER CARLSON **VOLUNTEERED.**
AND SO, FOR THE LAST TWENTY-PLUS YEARS, THE FATE OF THE WORLD HAS LAIN IN THE MOST UNLIKELY OF PLACES.
IN AN IMPOSSIBLE CITY.
WITH AN IMPOSSIBLE BOY.
AND AN OLD SPY, TRYING TO DO THE IMPOSSIBLE.
KEEP HIM FROM GROWING UP.

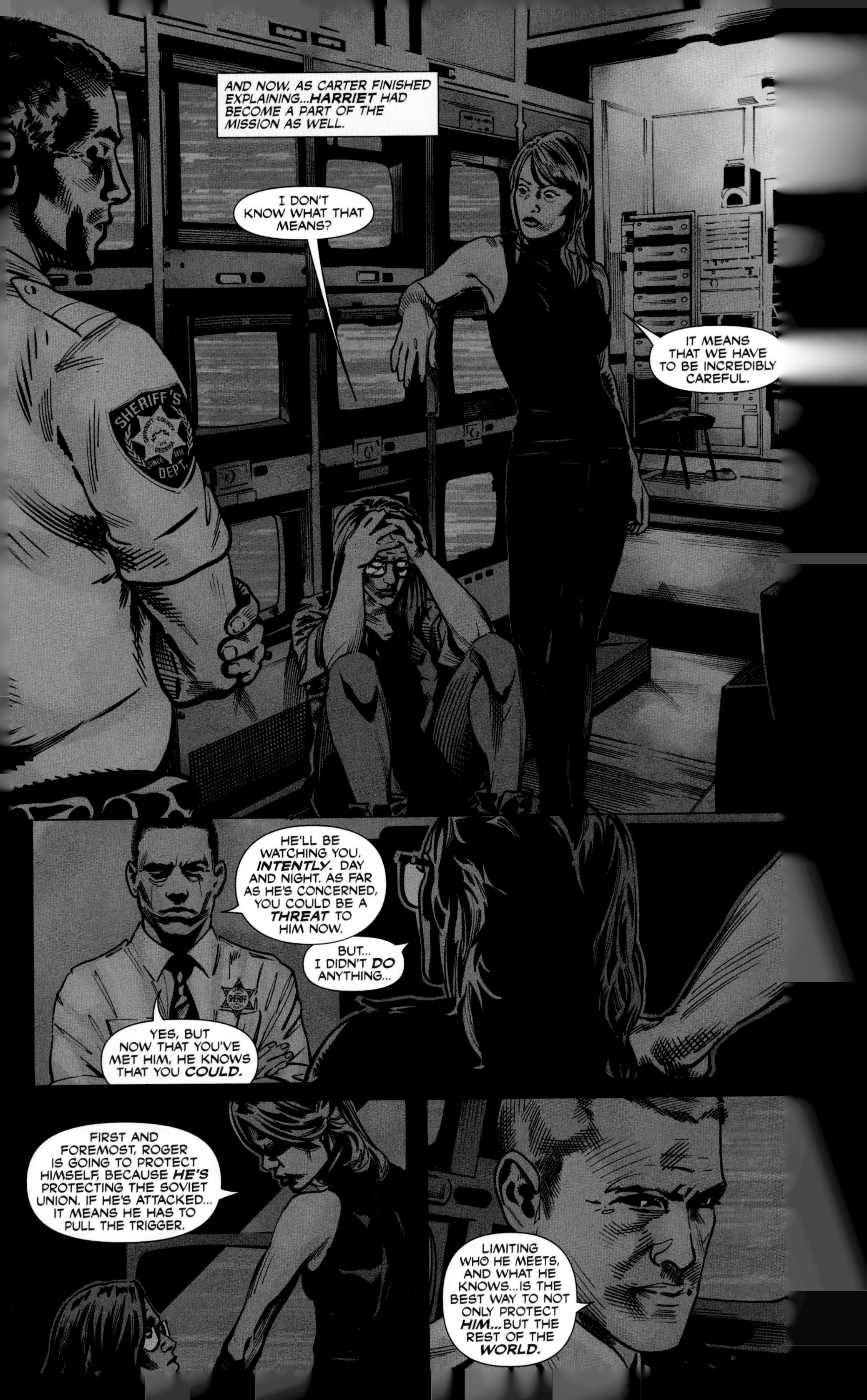
AND NOW, AS CARTER FINISHED EXPLAINING...HARRIET HAD BECOME A PART OF THE MISSION AS WELL.
I DON'T KNOW WHAT THAT MEANS?
IT MEANS THAT WE HAVE TO BE INCREDIBLY CAREFUL.
SHERIFF'S DEPT.
HE'LL BE WATCHING YOU. INTENTLY. DAY AND NIGHT. AS FAR AS HE'S CONCERNED, YOU COULD BE A THREAT TO HIM NOW.
BUT... I DIDN'T DO ANYTHING...
YES, BUT NOW THAT YOU'VE MET HIM, HE KNOWS THAT YOU COULD.
FIRST AND FOREMOST, ROGER IS GOING TO PROTECT HIMSELF, BECAUSE HE'S PROTECTING THE SOVIET UNION. IF HE'S ATTACKED... IT MEANS HE HAS TO PULL THE TRIGGER.
LIMITING WHO HE MEETS, AND WHAT HE KNOWS...IS THE BEST WAY TO NOT ONLY PROTECT HIM...BUT THE REST OF THE WORLD.

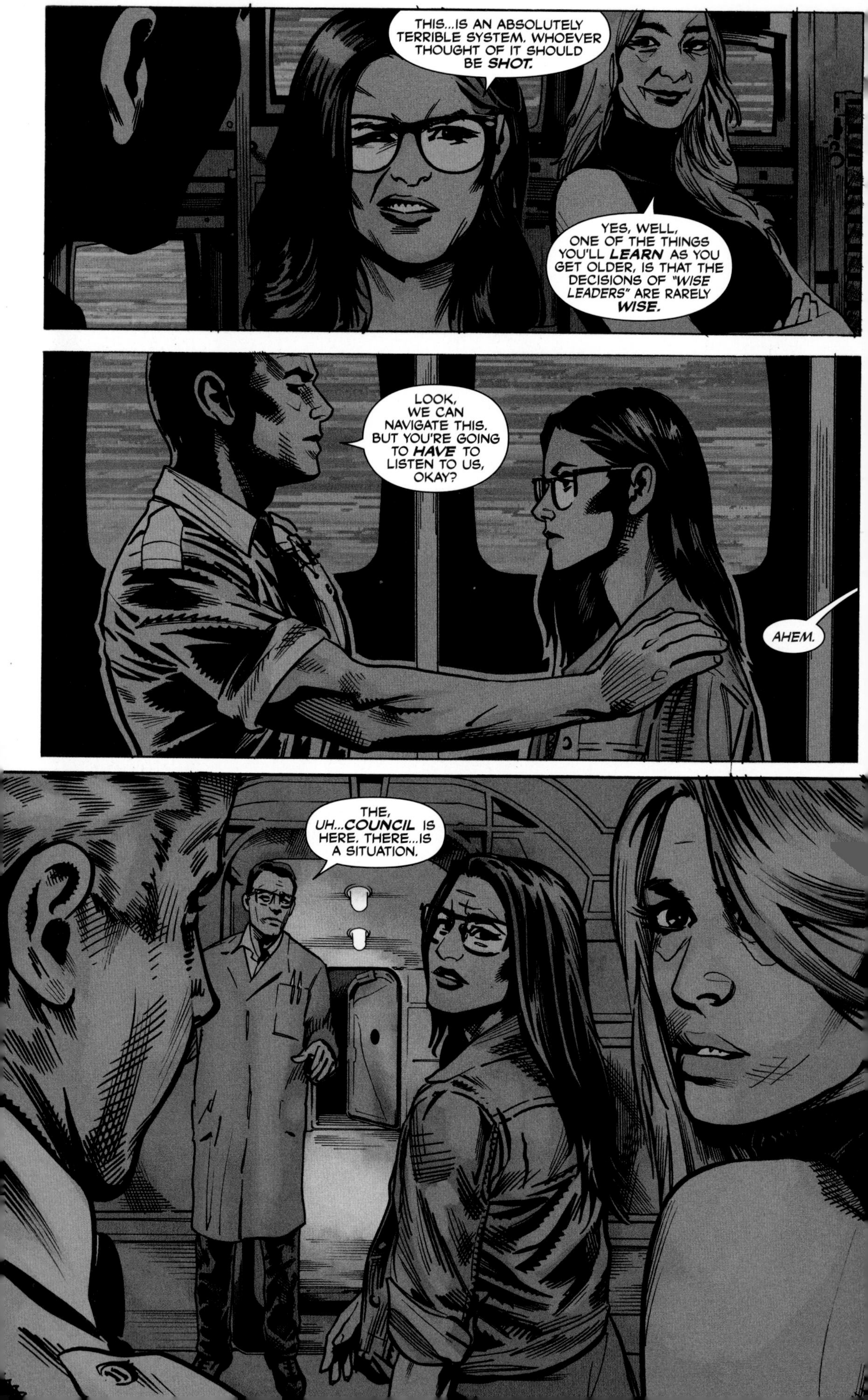
THIS...IS AN ABSOLUTELY TERRIBLE SYSTEM. WHOEVER THOUGHT OF IT SHOULD BE SHOT.
YES, WELL, ONE OF THE THINGS YOU'LL LEARN AS YOU GET OLDER, IS THAT THE DECISIONS OF "WISE LEADERS" ARE RARELY WISE.
LOOK, WE CAN NAVIGATE THIS. BUT YOU'RE GOING TO HAVE TO LISTEN TO US, OKAY?
AHEM.
THE, UH...COUNCIL IS HERE. THERE...IS A SITUATION.

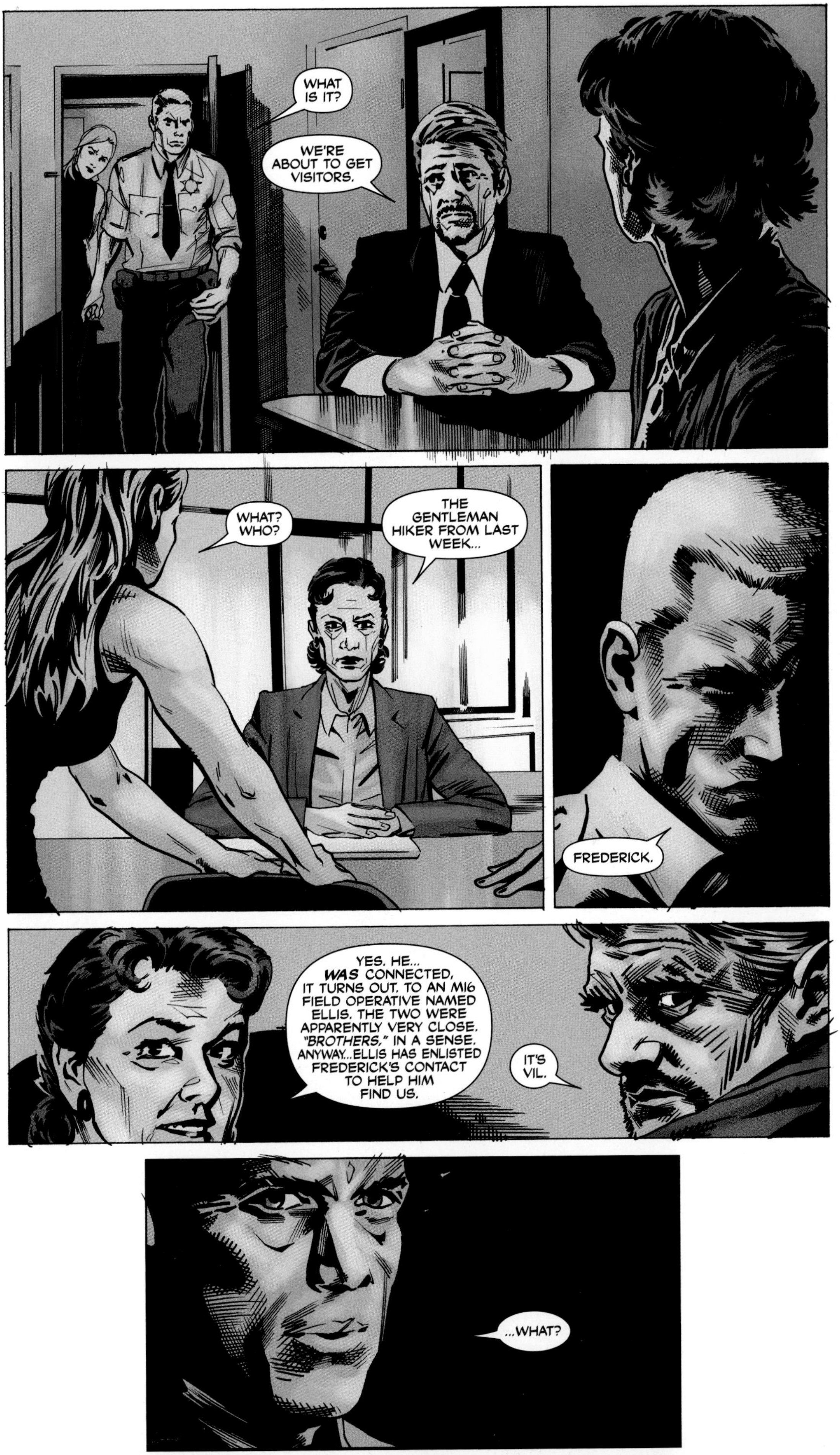
WHAT IS IT?
WE'RE ABOUT TO GET VISITORS.
WHAT? WHO?
THE GENTLEMAN HIKER FROM LAST WEEK...
FREDERICK.
YES. HE... WAS CONNECTED, IT TURNS OUT. TO AN MI6 FIELD OPERATIVE NAMED ELLIS. THE TWO WERE APPARENTLY VERY CLOSE. "BROTHERS," IN A SENSE. ANYWAY...ELLIS HAS ENLISTED FREDERICK'S CONTACT TO HELP HIM FIND US.
IT'S VIL.
...WHAT?

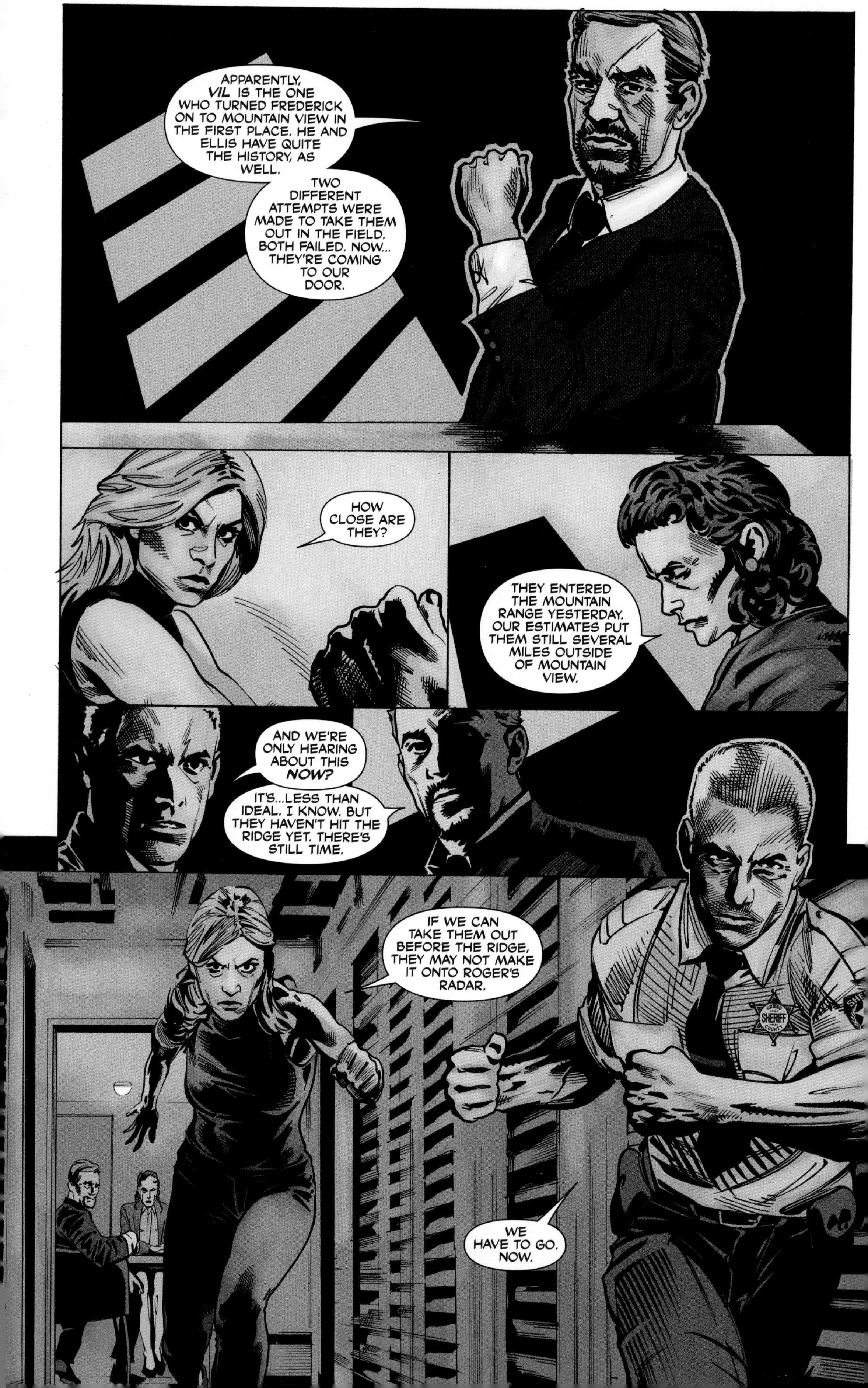
APPARENTLY, VIL IS THE ONE WHO TURNED FREDERICK ON TO MOUNTAIN VIEW IN THE FIRST PLACE. HE AND ELLIS HAVE QUITE THE HISTORY, AS WELL.
TWO DIFFERENT ATTEMPTS WERE MADE TO TAKE THEM OUT IN THE FIELD. BOTH FAILED. NOW... THEY'RE COMING TO OUR DOOR.
HOW CLOSE ARE THEY?
THEY ENTERED THE MOUNTAIN RANGE YESTERDAY. OUR ESTIMATES PUT THEM STILL SEVERAL MILES OUTSIDE OF MOUNTAIN VIEW.
AND WE'RE ONLY HEARING ABOUT THIS NOW?
IT'S...LESS THAN IDEAL. I KNOW. BUT THEY HAVEN'T HIT THE RIDGE YET. THERE'S STILL TIME.
IF WE CAN TAKE THEM OUT BEFORE THE RIDGE, THEY MAY NOT MAKE IT ONTO ROGER'S RADAR.
SHERIFF
WE HAVE TO GO. NOW.

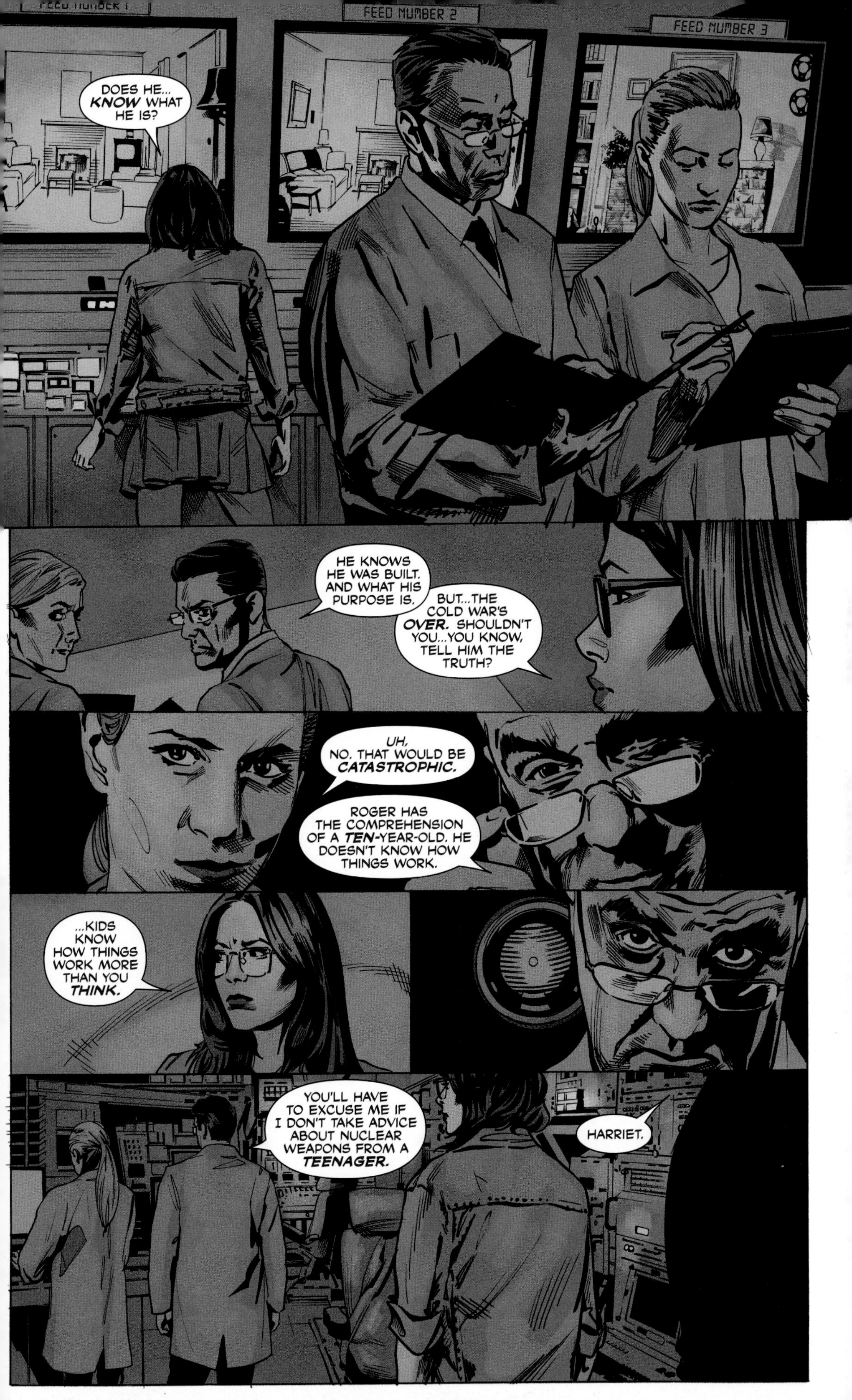
FEED NUMBER 2
FEED NUMBER 3
DOES HE... KNOW WHAT HE IS?
HE KNOWS HE WAS BUILT. AND WHAT HIS PURPOSE IS.
BUT...THE COLD WAR'S OVER. SHOULDN'T YOU...YOU KNOW, TELL HIM THE TRUTH?
UH, NO. THAT WOULD BE CATASTROPHIC.
ROGER HAS THE COMPREHENSION OF A TEN-YEAR-OLD. HE DOESN'T KNOW HOW THINGS WORK.
...KIDS KNOW HOW THINGS WORK MORE THAN YOU THINK.
YOU'LL HAVE TO EXCUSE ME IF I DON'T TAKE ADVICE ABOUT NUCLEAR WEAPONS FROM A TEENAGER.
HARRIET.

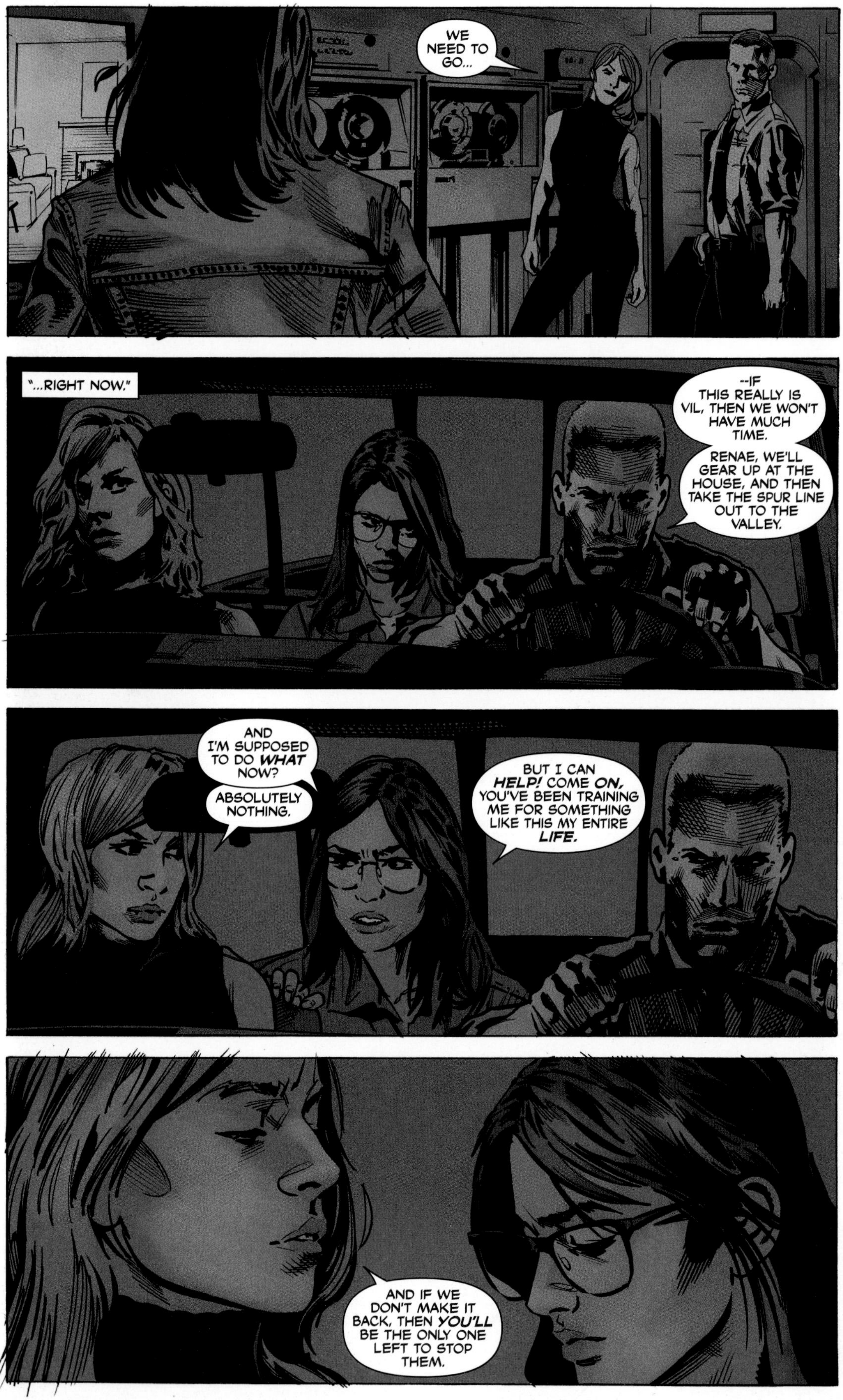
WE NEED TO GO...
"...RIGHT NOW."
--IF THIS REALLY IS VIL, THEN WE WON'T HAVE MUCH TIME.
RENAE, WE'LL GEAR UP AT THE HOUSE, AND THEN TAKE THE SPUR LINE OUT TO THE VALLEY.
AND I'M SUPPOSED TO DO *WHAT* NOW?
ABSOLUTELY NOTHING.
BUT I CAN *HELP!* COME *ON,* YOU'VE BEEN TRAINING ME FOR SOMETHING LIKE THIS MY ENTIRE *LIFE.*
AND IF WE DON'T MAKE IT BACK, THEN *YOU'LL* BE THE ONLY ONE LEFT TO STOP THEM.

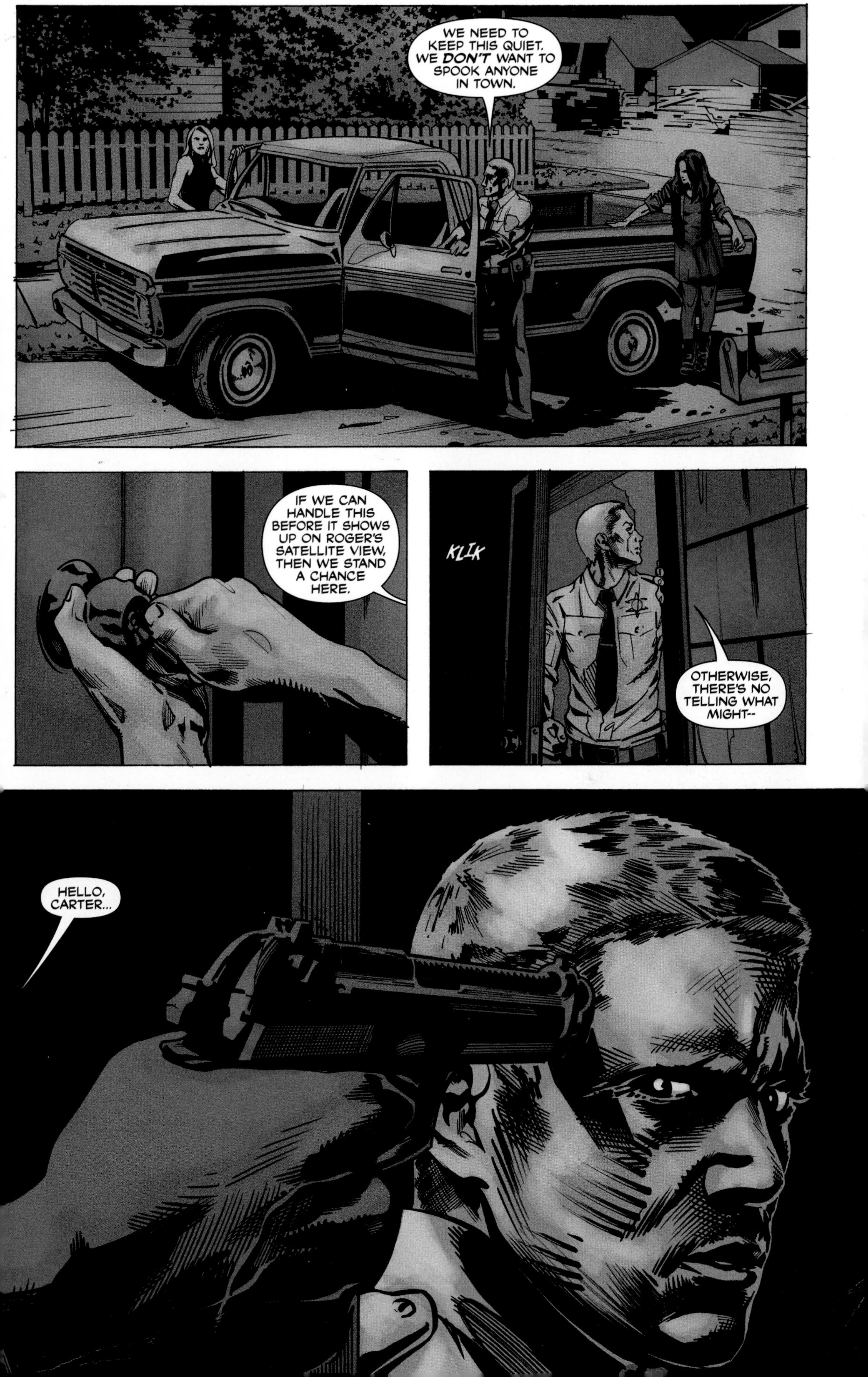
WE NEED TO KEEP THIS QUIET. WE DON'T WANT TO SPOOK ANYONE IN TOWN.
IF WE CAN HANDLE THIS BEFORE IT SHOWS UP ON ROGER'S SATELLITE VIEW, THEN WE STAND A CHANCE HERE.
KLIK
OTHERWISE, THERE'S NO TELLING WHAT MIGHT--
HELLO, CARTER...

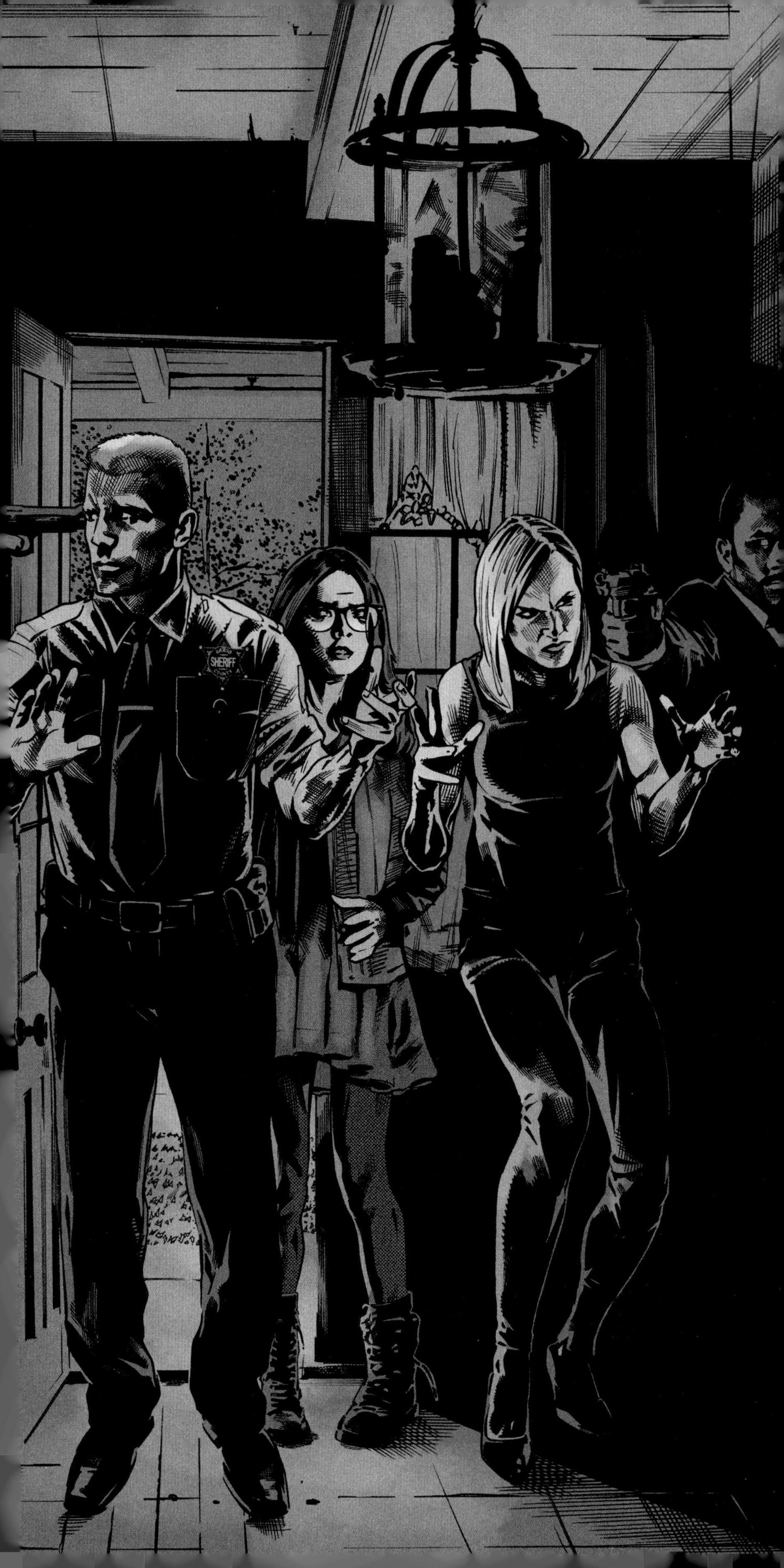
SHERIFF

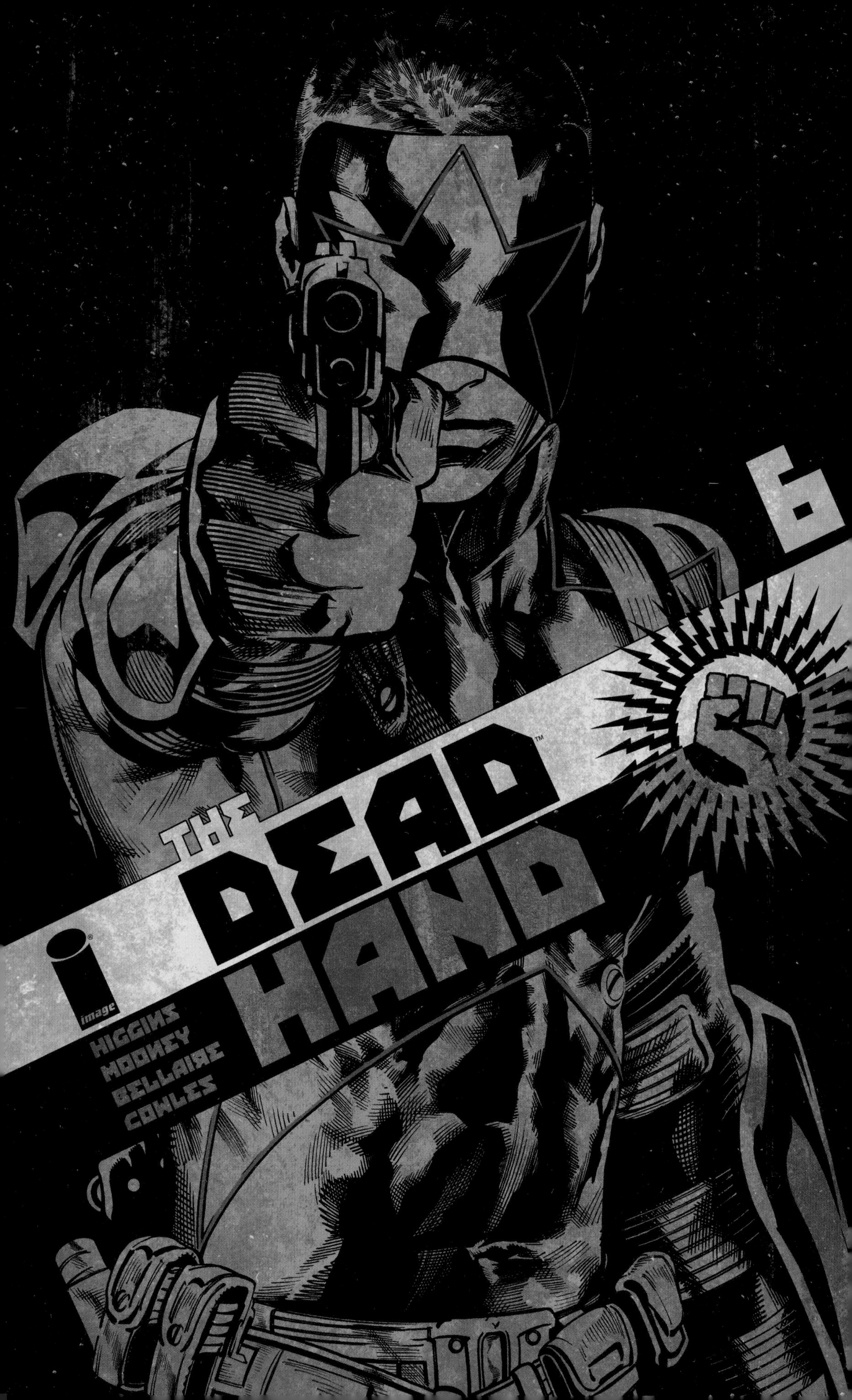
6
THE DEAD HAND™
image
HIGGINS
MOONEY
BELLAIRE
COWLES

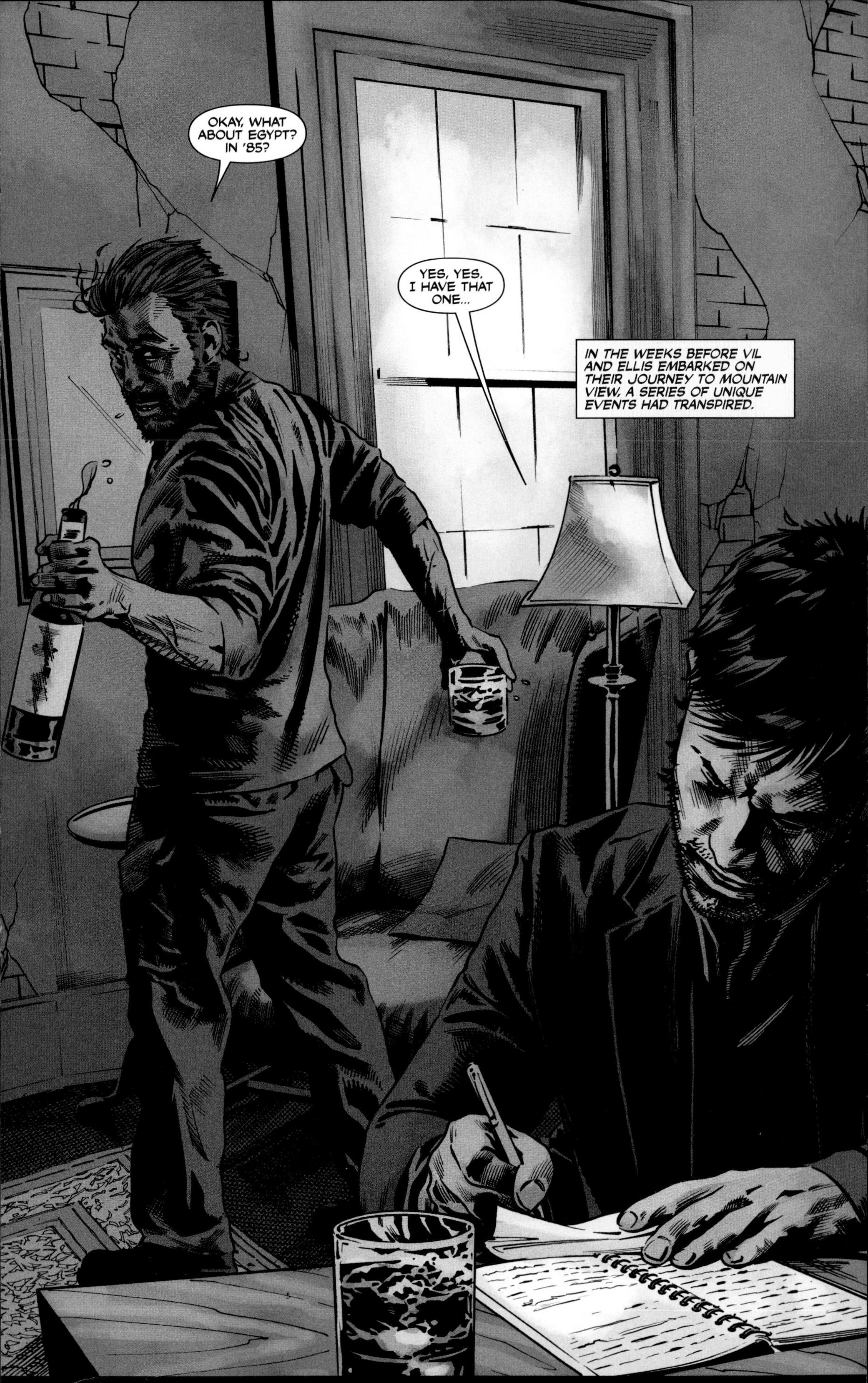
OKAY, WHAT ABOUT EGYPT? IN '85?
YES, YES. I HAVE THAT ONE...
IN THE WEEKS BEFORE VIL AND ELLIS EMBARKED ON THEIR JOURNEY TO MOUNTAIN VIEW, A SERIES OF UNIQUE EVENTS HAD TRANSPIRED.

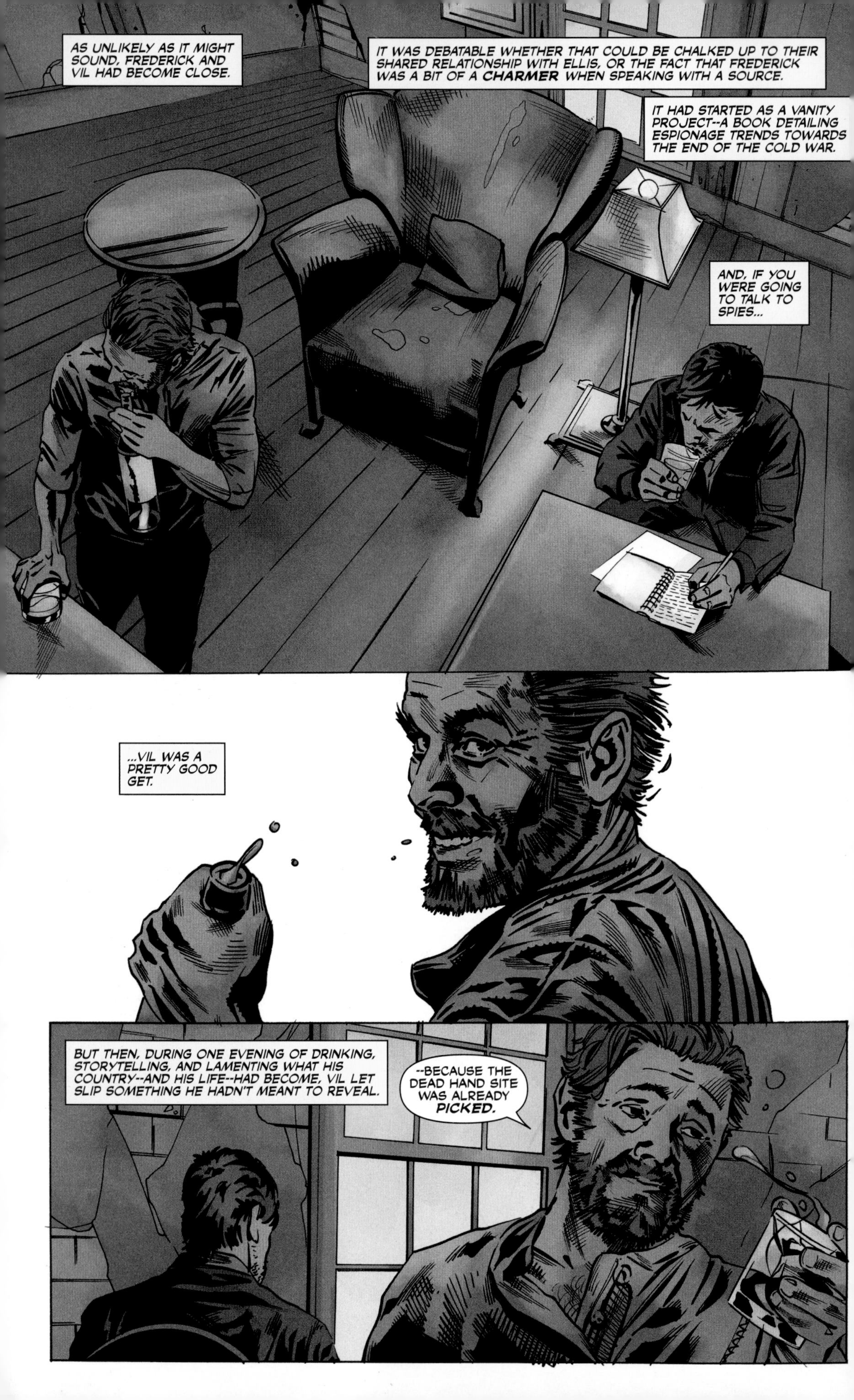
AS UNLIKELY AS IT MIGHT SOUND, FREDERICK AND VIL HAD BECOME CLOSE.
IT WAS DEBATABLE WHETHER THAT COULD BE CHALKED UP TO THEIR SHARED RELATIONSHIP WITH ELLIS, OR THE FACT THAT FREDERICK WAS A BIT OF A CHARMER WHEN SPEAKING WITH A SOURCE.
IT HAD STARTED AS A VANITY PROJECT--A BOOK DETAILING ESPIONAGE TRENDS TOWARDS THE END OF THE COLD WAR.
AND, IF YOU WERE GOING TO TALK TO SPIES...
...VIL WAS A PRETTY GOOD GET.
BUT THEN, DURING ONE EVENING OF DRINKING, STORYTELLING, AND LAMENTING WHAT HIS COUNTRY--AND HIS LIFE--HAD BECOME, VIL LET SLIP SOMETHING HE HADN'T MEANT TO REVEAL.
--BECAUSE THE DEAD HAND SITE WAS ALREADY PICKED.

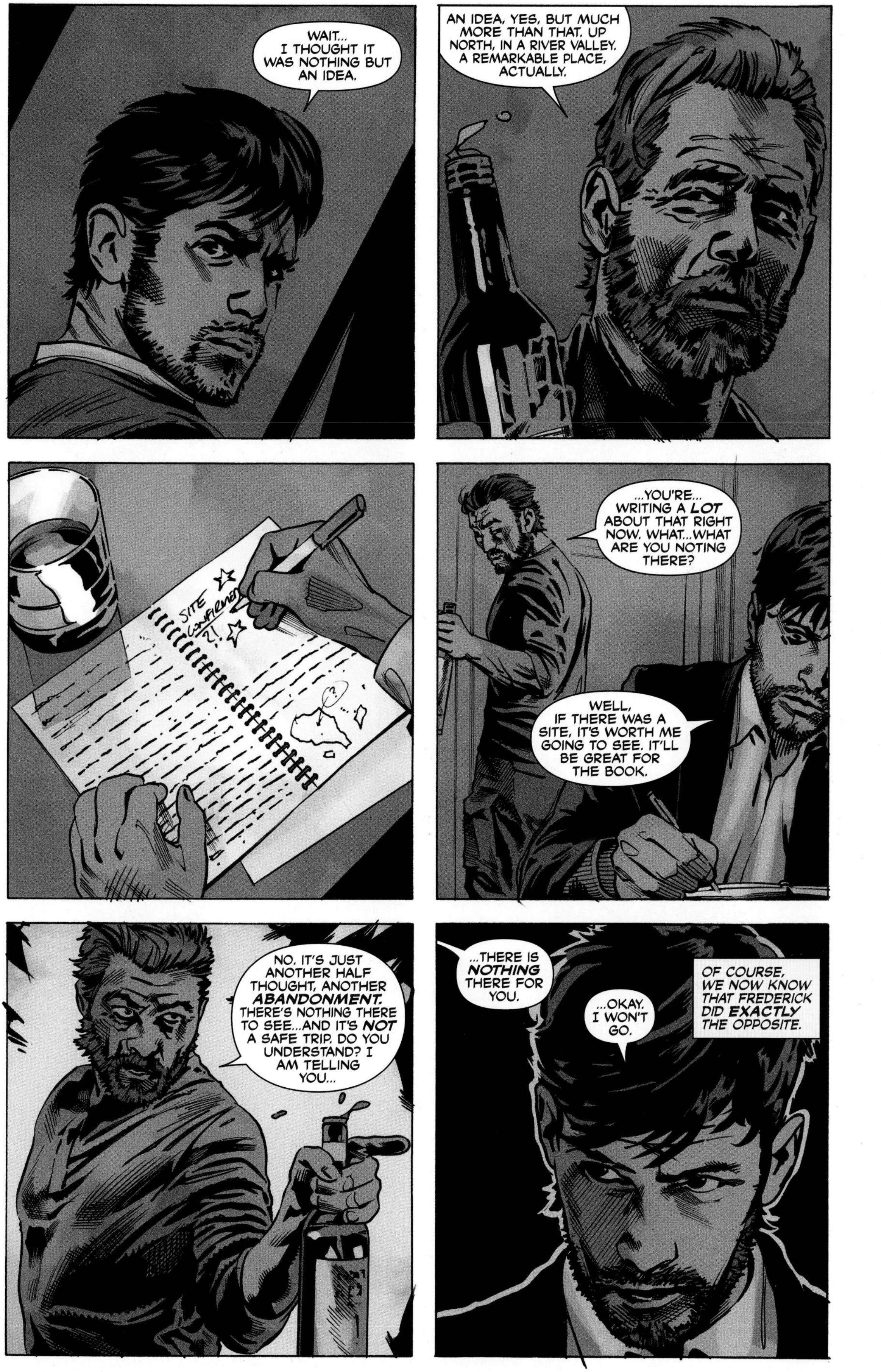
WAIT... I THOUGHT IT WAS NOTHING BUT AN IDEA.
AN IDEA, YES, BUT MUCH MORE THAN THAT. UP NORTH, IN A RIVER VALLEY. A REMARKABLE PLACE, ACTUALLY.
SITE CONFIRMED ?!
...YOU'RE... WRITING A ***LOT*** ABOUT THAT RIGHT NOW. WHAT...WHAT ARE YOU NOTING THERE?
WELL, IF THERE WAS A SITE, IT'S WORTH ME GOING TO SEE. IT'LL BE GREAT FOR THE BOOK.
NO. IT'S JUST ANOTHER HALF THOUGHT, ANOTHER ***ABANDONMENT.*** THERE'S NOTHING THERE TO SEE...AND IT'S ***NOT*** A SAFE TRIP. DO YOU UNDERSTAND? I AM TELLING YOU...
...THERE IS ***NOTHING*** THERE FOR YOU.
...OKAY. I WON'T GO.
*OF COURSE, WE NOW KNOW THAT FREDERICK DID **EXACTLY** THE OPPOSITE.*

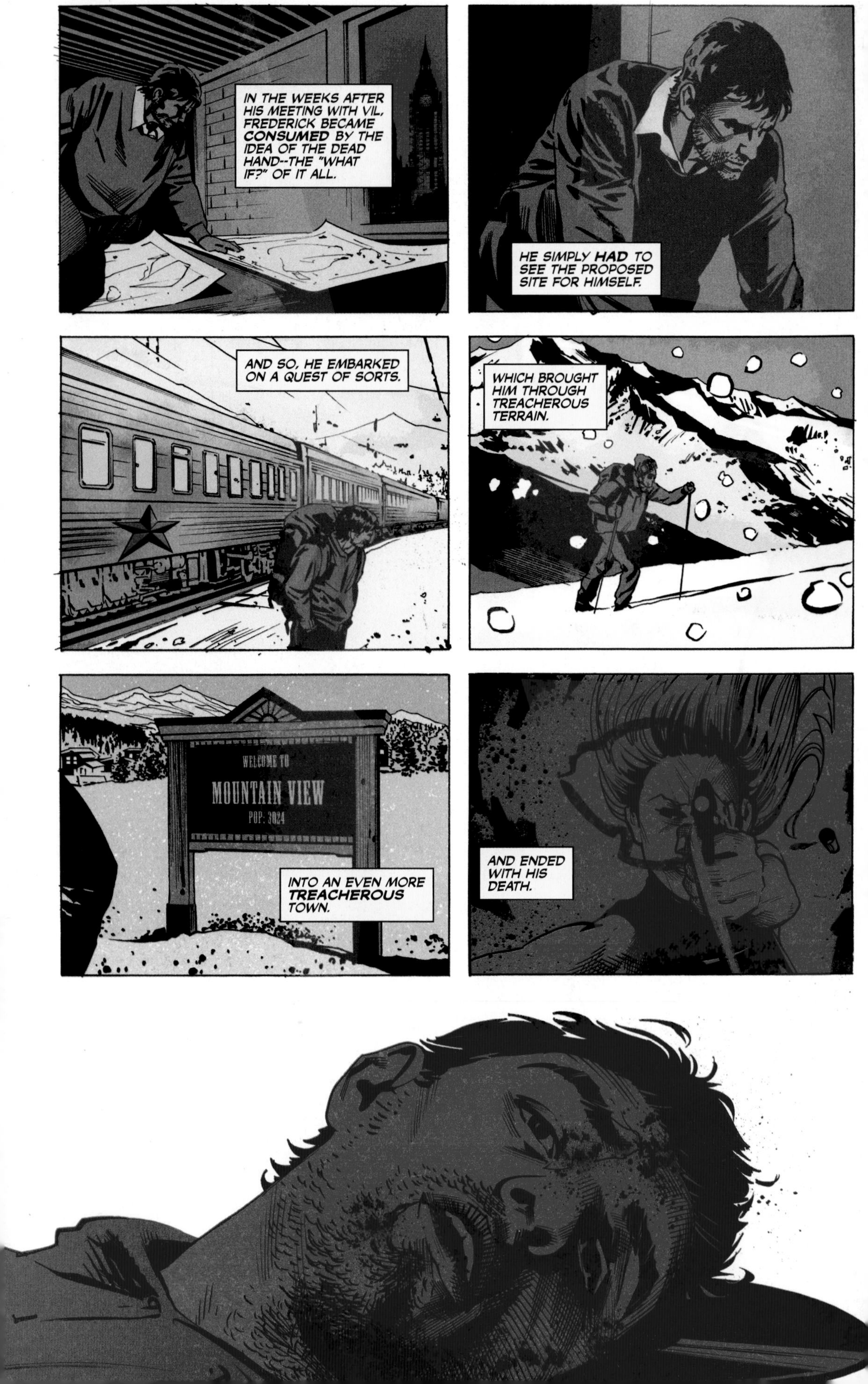
IN THE WEEKS AFTER HIS MEETING WITH VIL, FREDERICK BECAME **CONSUMED** BY THE IDEA OF THE DEAD HAND--THE "WHAT IF?" OF IT ALL.
HE SIMPLY **HAD** TO SEE THE PROPOSED SITE FOR HIMSELF.
AND SO, HE EMBARKED ON A QUEST OF SORTS.
WHICH BROUGHT HIM THROUGH TREACHEROUS TERRAIN.
WELCOME TO
MOUNTAIN VIEW
POP: 3024
INTO AN EVEN MORE **TREACHEROUS** TOWN.
AND ENDED WITH HIS DEATH.

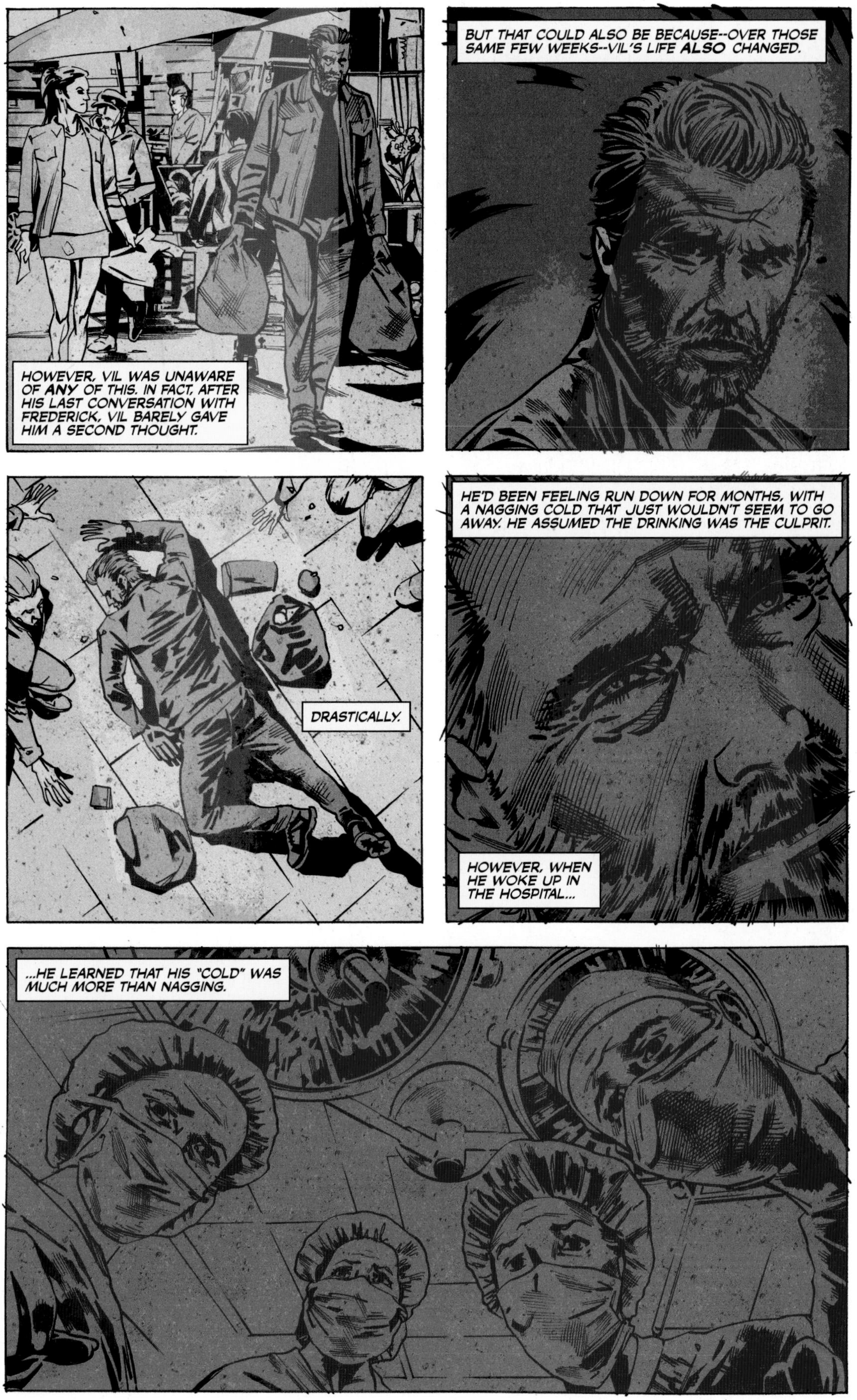
HOWEVER, VIL WAS UNAWARE OF ANY OF THIS. IN FACT, AFTER HIS LAST CONVERSATION WITH FREDERICK, VIL BARELY GAVE HIM A SECOND THOUGHT.
BUT THAT COULD ALSO BE BECAUSE--OVER THOSE SAME FEW WEEKS--VIL'S LIFE ALSO CHANGED.
DRASTICALLY.
HE'D BEEN FEELING RUN DOWN FOR MONTHS, WITH A NAGGING COLD THAT JUST WOULDN'T SEEM TO GO AWAY. HE ASSUMED THE DRINKING WAS THE CULPRIT.
HOWEVER, WHEN HE WOKE UP IN THE HOSPITAL...
...HE LEARNED THAT HIS "COLD" WAS MUCH MORE THAN NAGGING.

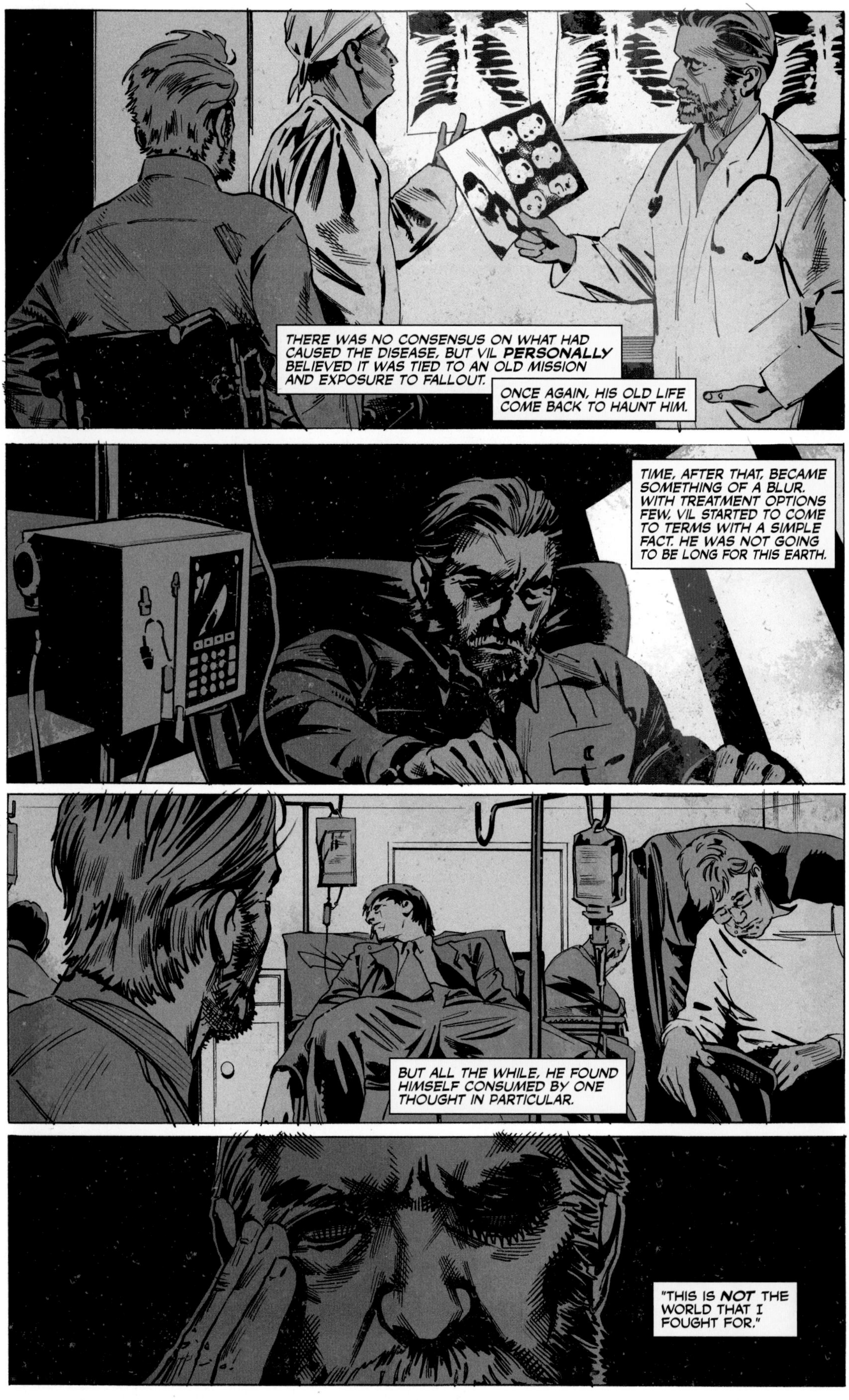
THERE WAS NO CONSENSUS ON WHAT HAD CAUSED THE DISEASE, BUT VIL **PERSONALLY** BELIEVED IT WAS TIED TO AN OLD MISSION AND EXPOSURE TO FALLOUT.
ONCE AGAIN, HIS OLD LIFE COME BACK TO HAUNT HIM.
TIME, AFTER THAT, BECAME SOMETHING OF A BLUR. WITH TREATMENT OPTIONS FEW, VIL STARTED TO COME TO TERMS WITH A SIMPLE FACT. HE WAS NOT GOING TO BE LONG FOR THIS EARTH.
BUT ALL THE WHILE, HE FOUND HIMSELF CONSUMED BY ONE THOUGHT IN PARTICULAR.
"THIS IS ***NOT*** THE WORLD THAT I FOUGHT FOR."

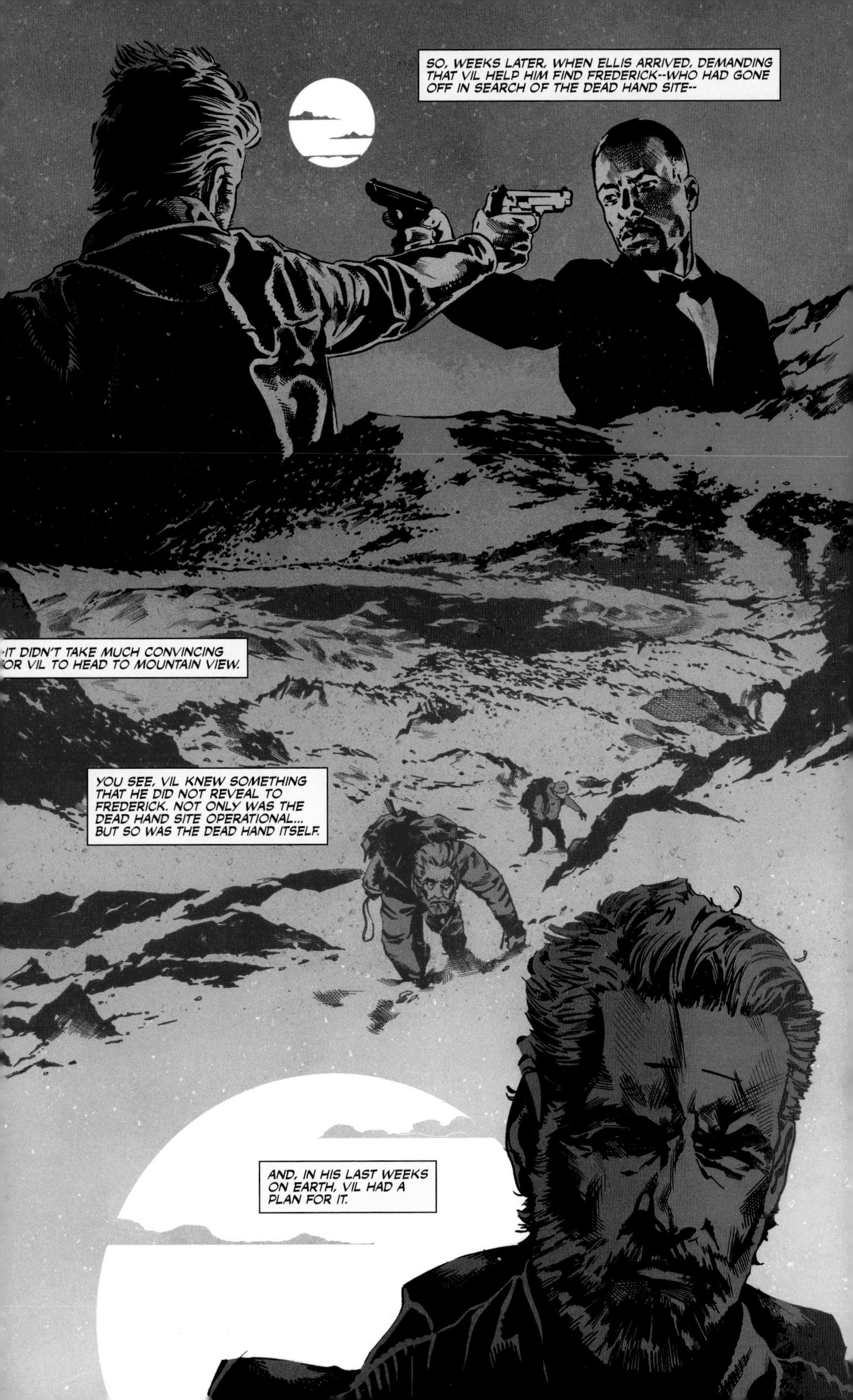
SO, WEEKS LATER, WHEN ELLIS ARRIVED, DEMANDING THAT VIL HELP HIM FIND FREDERICK--WHO HAD GONE OFF IN SEARCH OF THE DEAD HAND SITE--
-IT DIDN'T TAKE MUCH CONVINCING FOR VIL TO HEAD TO MOUNTAIN VIEW.
YOU SEE, VIL KNEW SOMETHING THAT HE DID NOT REVEAL TO FREDERICK. NOT ONLY WAS THE DEAD HAND SITE OPERATIONAL... BUT SO WAS THE DEAD HAND ITSELF.
AND, IN HIS LAST WEEKS ON EARTH, VIL HAD A PLAN FOR IT.

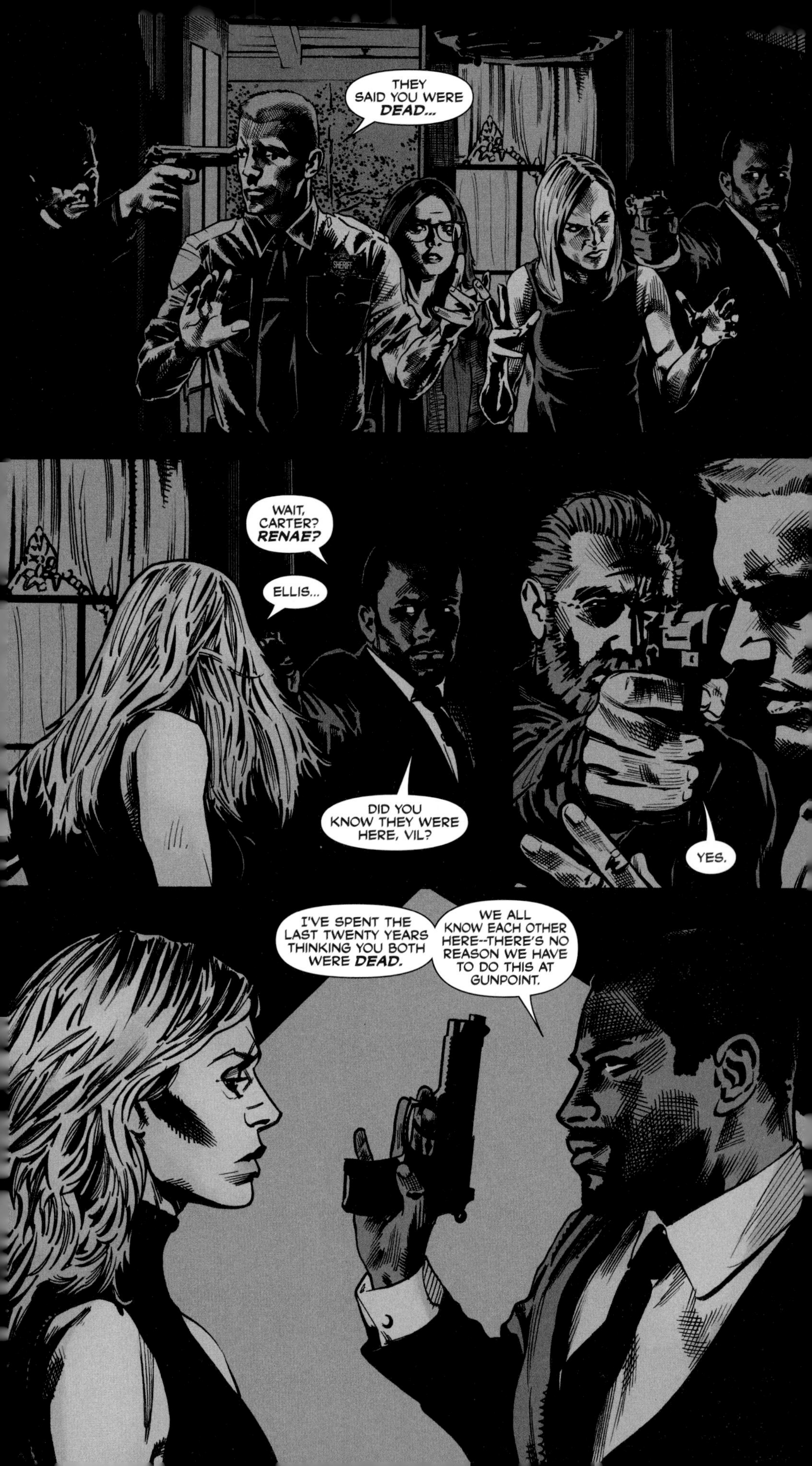
THEY SAID YOU WERE DEAD...
WAIT, CARTER? RENAE?
ELLIS...
DID YOU KNOW THEY WERE HERE, VIL?
YES.
I'VE SPENT THE LAST TWENTY YEARS THINKING YOU BOTH WERE DEAD.
WE ALL KNOW EACH OTHER HERE--THERE'S NO REASON WE HAVE TO DO THIS AT GUNPOINT.

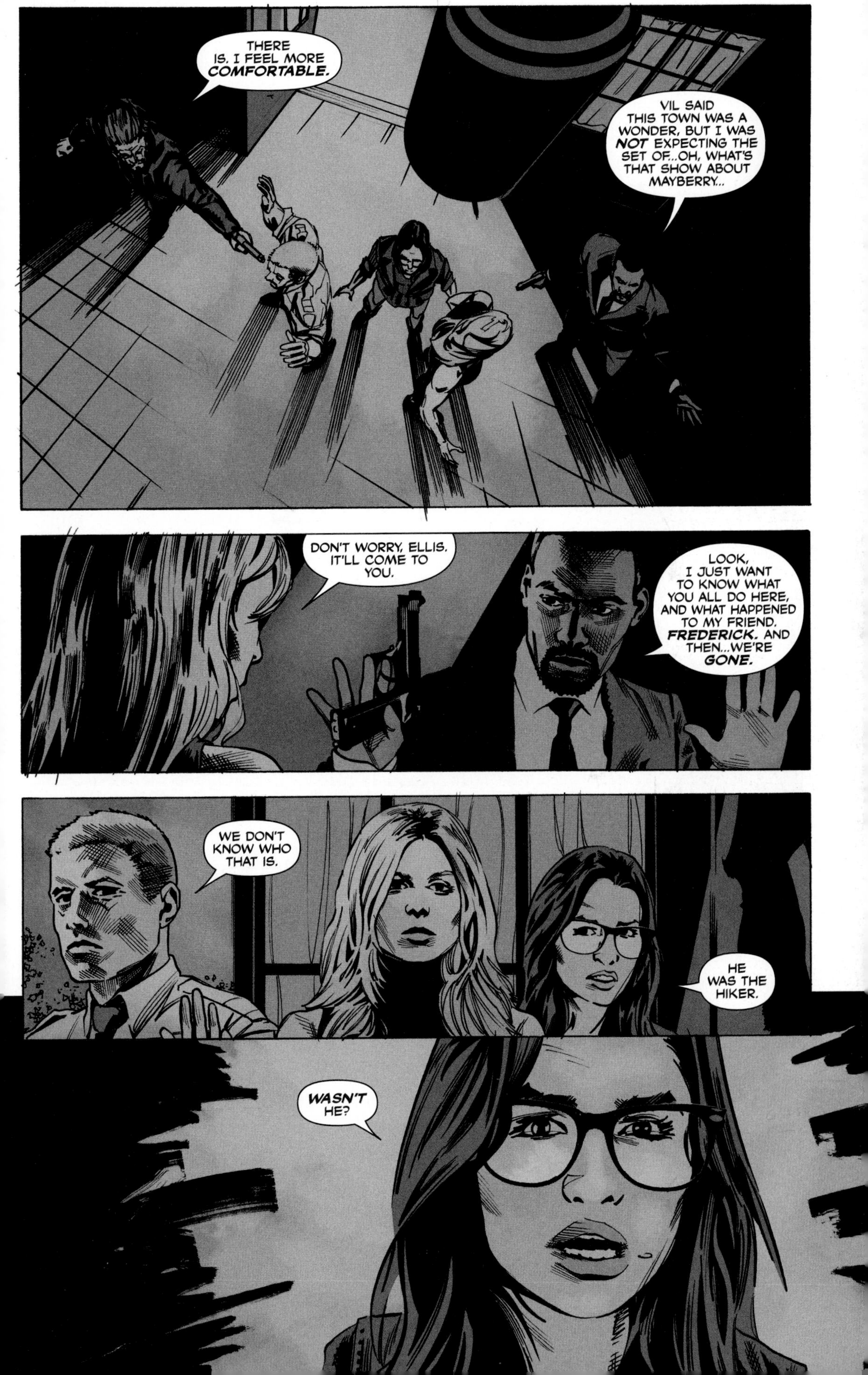
THERE IS. I FEEL MORE COMFORTABLE.
VIL SAID THIS TOWN WAS A WONDER, BUT I WAS NOT EXPECTING THE SET OF...OH, WHAT'S THAT SHOW ABOUT MAYBERRY...
DON'T WORRY, ELLIS. IT'LL COME TO YOU.
LOOK, I JUST WANT TO KNOW WHAT YOU ALL DO HERE, AND WHAT HAPPENED TO MY FRIEND. FREDERICK. AND THEN...WE'RE GONE.
WE DON'T KNOW WHO THAT IS.
HE WAS THE HIKER.
WASN'T HE?

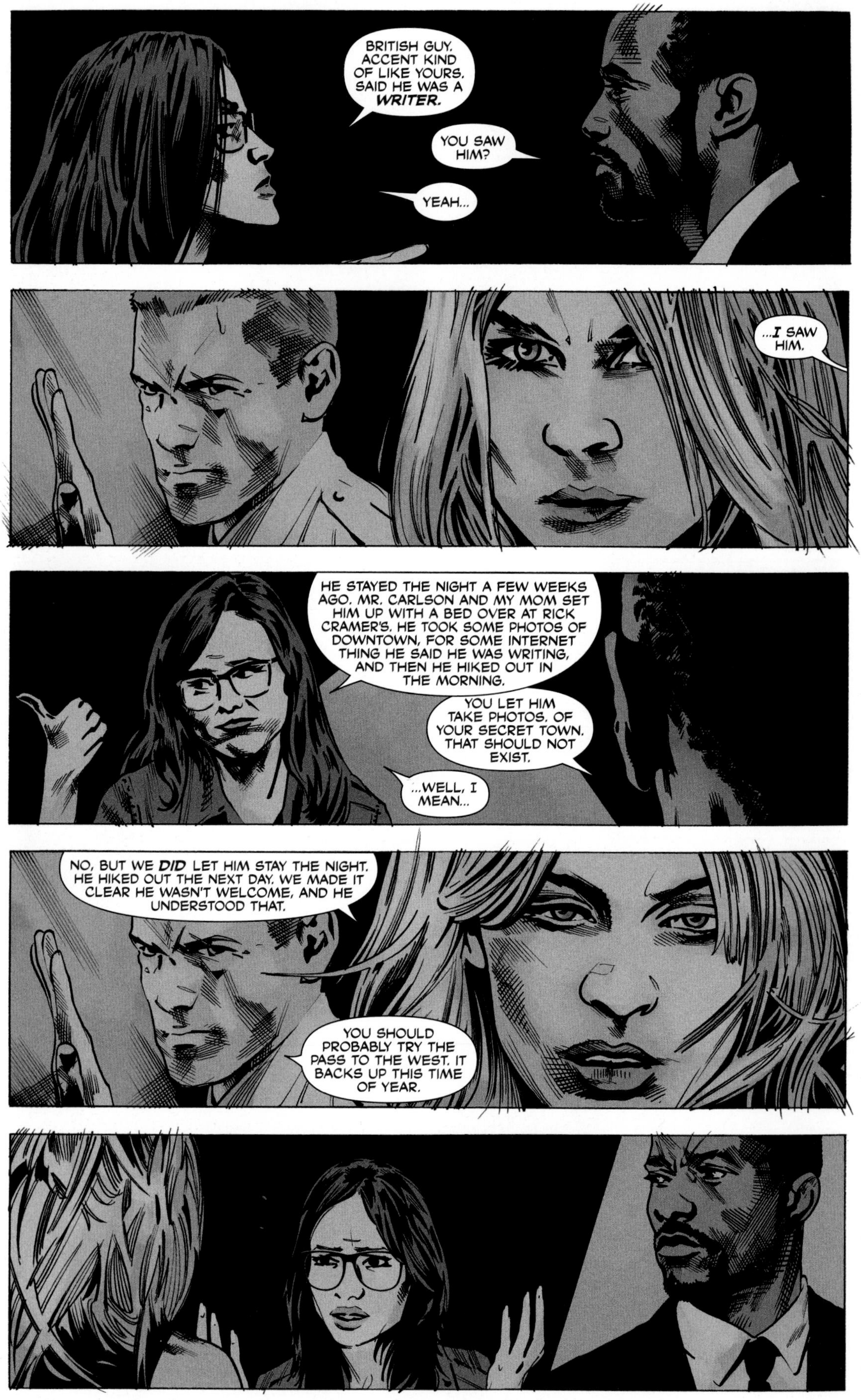
BRITISH GUY. ACCENT KIND OF LIKE YOURS. SAID HE WAS A WRITER.
YOU SAW HIM?
YEAH...
...I SAW HIM.
HE STAYED THE NIGHT A FEW WEEKS AGO. MR. CARLSON AND MY MOM SET HIM UP WITH A BED OVER AT RICK CRAMER'S. HE TOOK SOME PHOTOS OF DOWNTOWN, FOR SOME INTERNET THING HE SAID HE WAS WRITING, AND THEN HE HIKED OUT IN THE MORNING.
YOU LET HIM TAKE PHOTOS. OF YOUR SECRET TOWN. THAT SHOULD NOT EXIST.
...WELL, I MEAN...
NO, BUT WE DID LET HIM STAY THE NIGHT. HE HIKED OUT THE NEXT DAY. WE MADE IT CLEAR HE WASN'T WELCOME, AND HE UNDERSTOOD THAT.
YOU SHOULD PROBABLY TRY THE PASS TO THE WEST. IT BACKS UP THIS TIME OF YEAR.

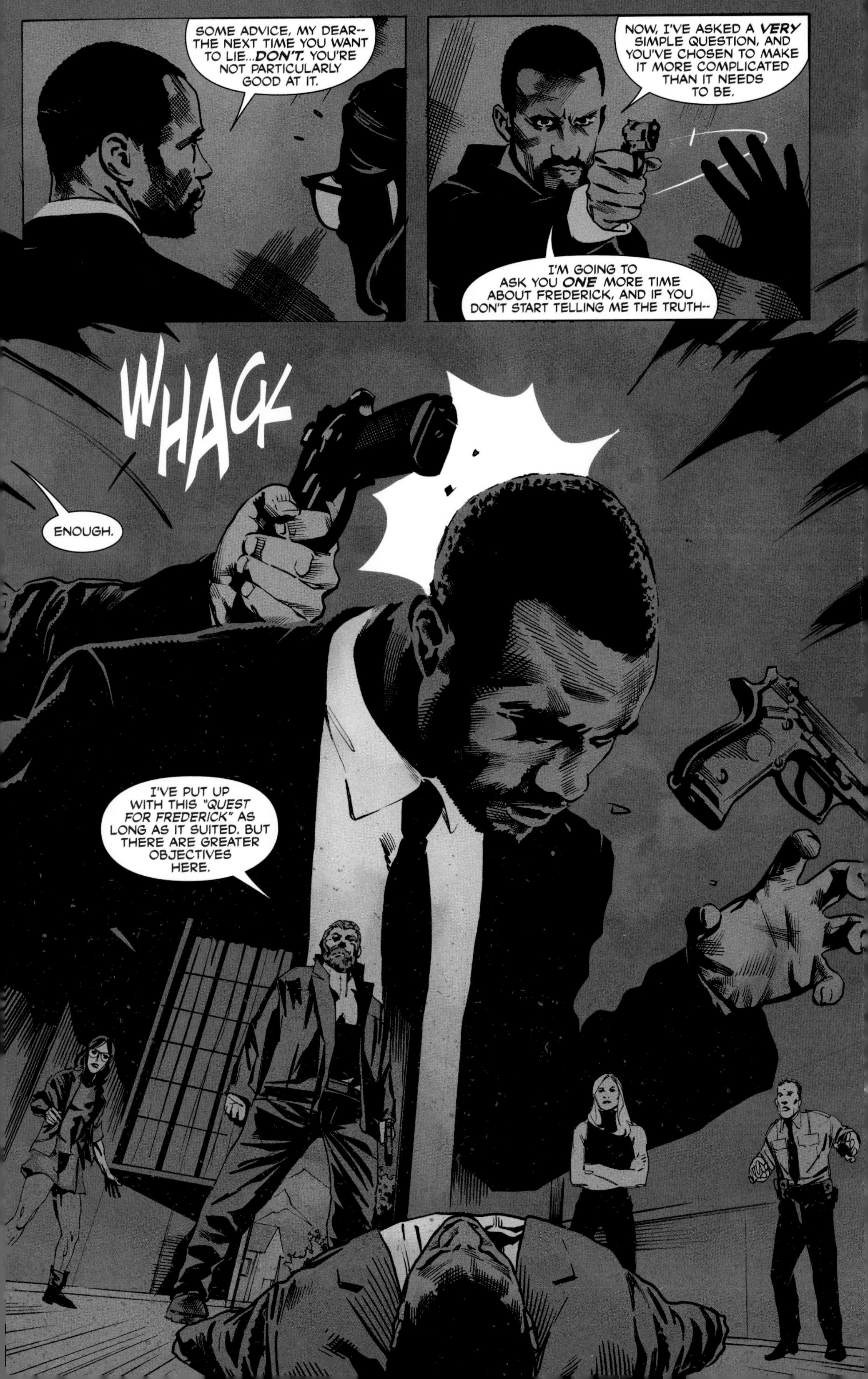
SOME ADVICE, MY DEAR--THE NEXT TIME YOU WANT TO LIE...DON'T. YOU'RE NOT PARTICULARLY GOOD AT IT.
NOW, I'VE ASKED A VERY SIMPLE QUESTION, AND YOU'VE CHOSEN TO MAKE IT MORE COMPLICATED THAN IT NEEDS TO BE.
I'M GOING TO ASK YOU ONE MORE TIME ABOUT FREDERICK, AND IF YOU DON'T START TELLING ME THE TRUTH--
WHACK
ENOUGH.
I'VE PUT UP WITH THIS "QUEST FOR FREDERICK" AS LONG AS IT SUITED. BUT THERE ARE GREATER OBJECTIVES HERE.

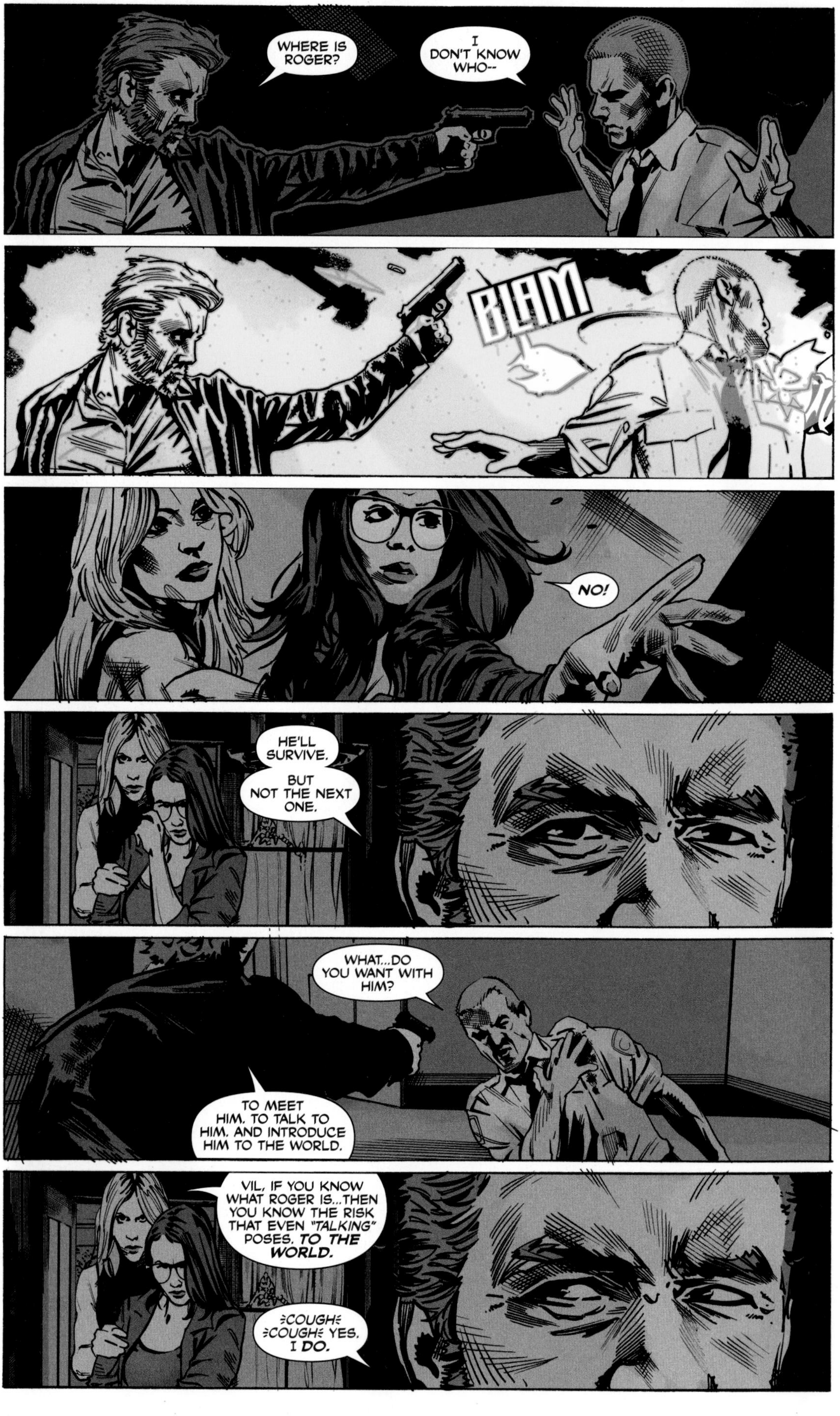

WHERE IS ROGER?
I DON'T KNOW WHO--
BLAM
NO!
HE'LL SURVIVE.
BUT NOT THE NEXT ONE.
WHAT...DO YOU WANT WITH HIM?
TO MEET HIM. TO TALK TO HIM. AND INTRODUCE HIM TO THE WORLD.
VIL, IF YOU KNOW WHAT ROGER IS...THEN YOU KNOW THE RISK THAT EVEN "TALKING" POSES. TO THE WORLD.
≡COUGH≡ ≡COUGH≡ YES. I DO.

I ALSO KNOW THAT I'M AN OLD MAN WITH LITTLE TIME LEFT. WHO LIVES IN A WORLD HE NO LONGER KNOWS.

SO, WHAT, YOU WANT TO SEE THE LAST THING YOUR COUNTRY DID THAT WAS WORTH A DAMN?

NO.

HE WANTS... ≡EHN≡ TO TELL ROGER THE *TRUTH*. ABOUT HOW THINGS TURNED OUT.

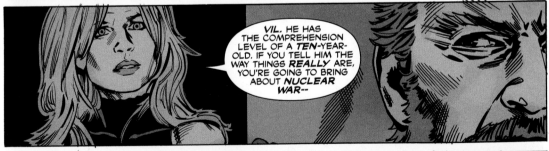

DON'T YOU?

VIL. HE HAS THE COMPREHENSION LEVEL OF A *TEN*-YEAR-OLD. IF YOU TELL HIM THE WAY THINGS *REALLY* ARE, YOU'RE GOING TO BRING ABOUT *NUCLEAR WAR*--

KLIK

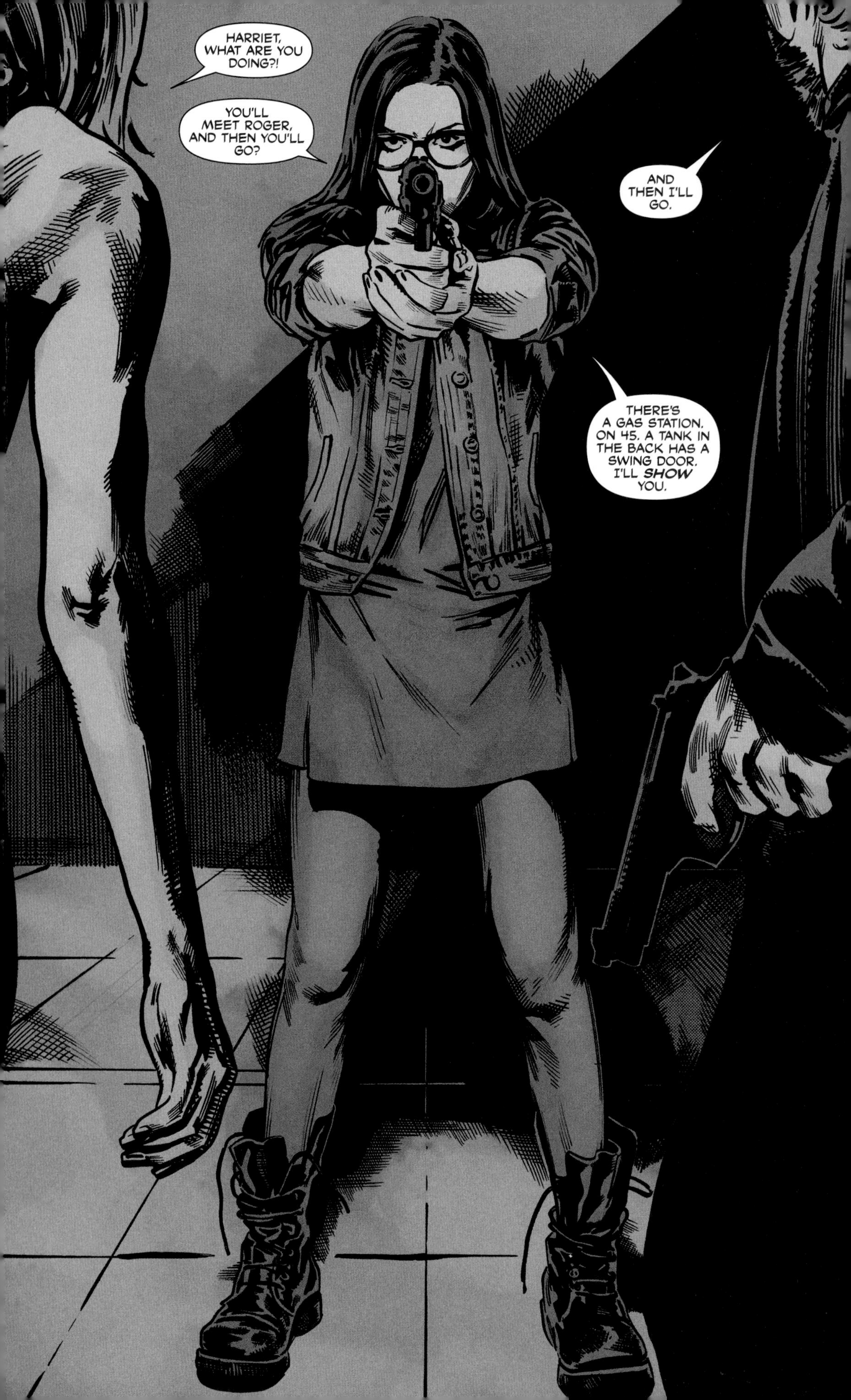
HARRIET, WHAT ARE YOU DOING?!
YOU'LL MEET ROGER, AND THEN YOU'LL GO?
AND THEN I'LL GO.
THERE'S A GAS STATION. ON 45. A TANK IN THE BACK HAS A SWING DOOR. I'LL SHOW YOU.

GET IN THE TRUCK.

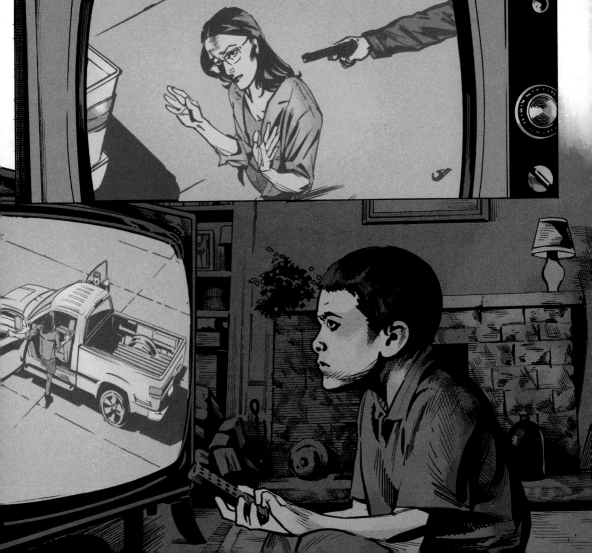

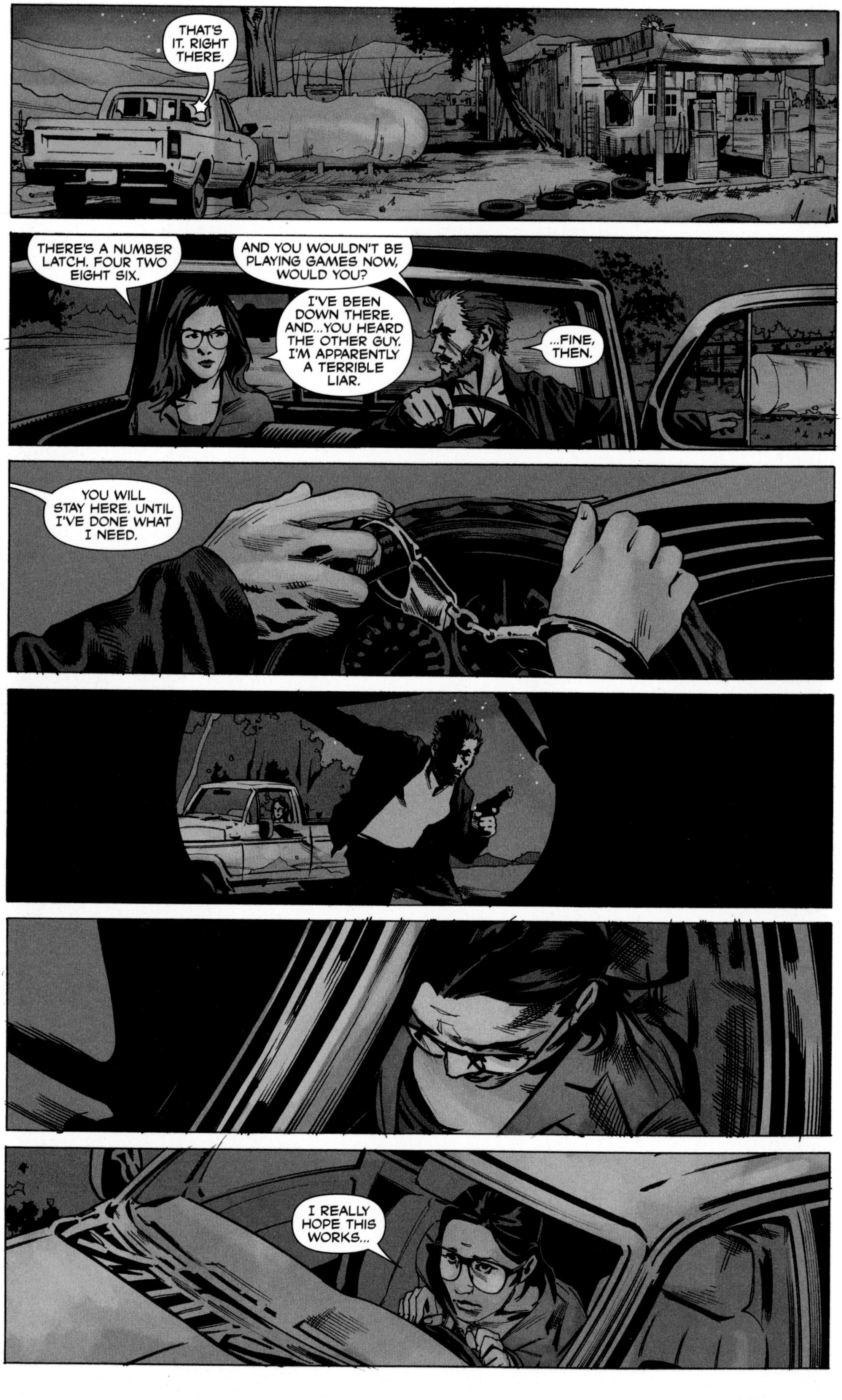
THAT'S IT. RIGHT THERE.
THERE'S A NUMBER LATCH. FOUR TWO EIGHT SIX.
AND YOU WOULDN'T BE PLAYING GAMES NOW, WOULD YOU?
I'VE BEEN DOWN THERE. AND...YOU HEARD THE OTHER GUY. I'M APPARENTLY A TERRIBLE LIAR.
...FINE, THEN.
YOU WILL STAY HERE. UNTIL I'VE DONE WHAT I NEED.
I REALLY HOPE THIS WORKS...

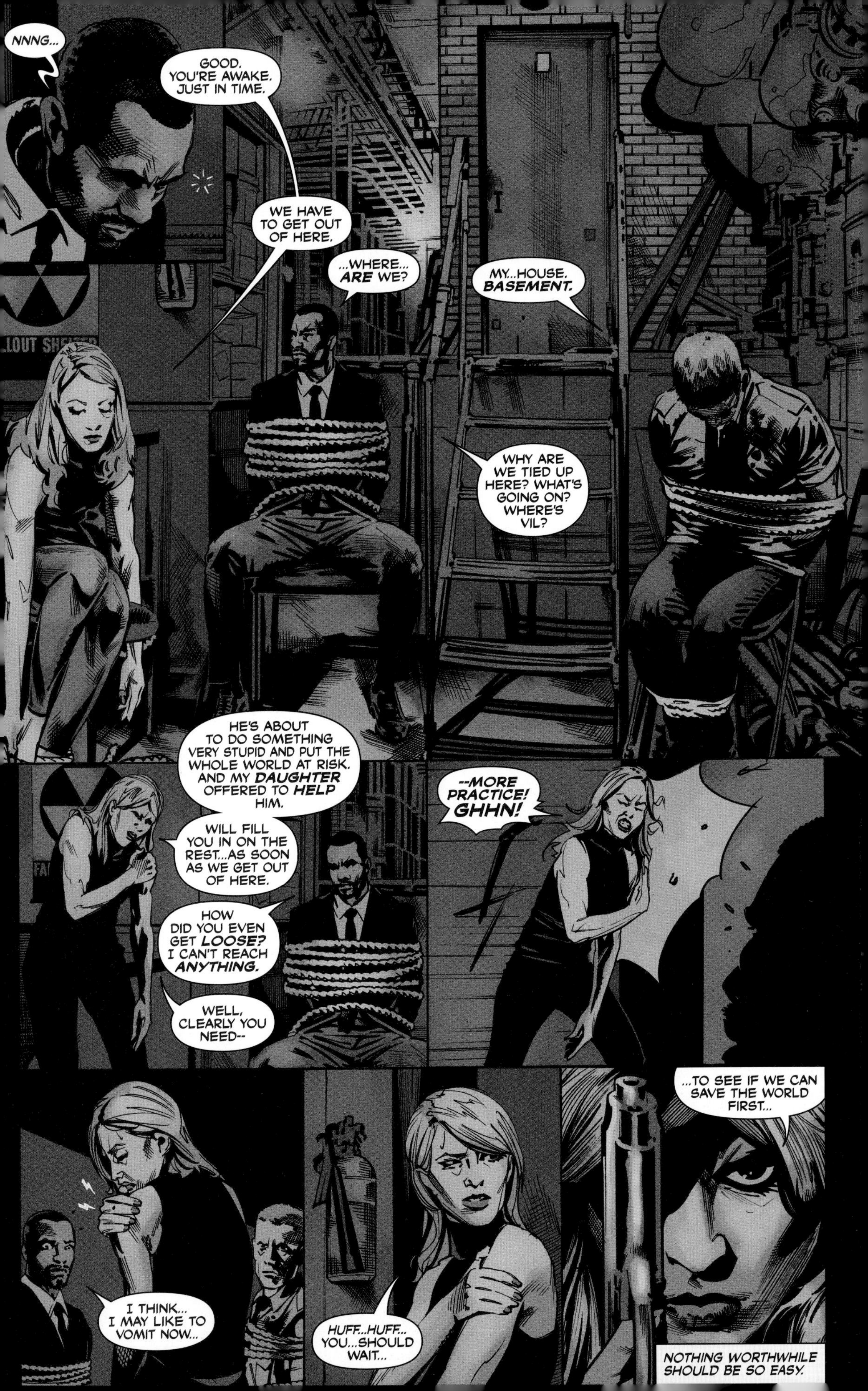
NNNG...
GOOD. YOU'RE AWAKE. JUST IN TIME.
WE HAVE TO GET OUT OF HERE.
...WHERE... ARE WE?
MY...HOUSE. BASEMENT.
WHY ARE WE TIED UP HERE? WHAT'S GOING ON? WHERE'S VIL?
HE'S ABOUT TO DO SOMETHING VERY STUPID AND PUT THE WHOLE WORLD AT RISK. AND MY DAUGHTER OFFERED TO HELP HIM.
WILL FILL YOU IN ON THE REST...AS SOON AS WE GET OUT OF HERE.
HOW DID YOU EVEN GET LOOSE? I CAN'T REACH ANYTHING.
WELL, CLEARLY YOU NEED--
--MORE PRACTICE! GHHN!
I THINK... I MAY LIKE TO VOMIT NOW...
HUFF...HUFF... YOU...SHOULD WAIT...
...TO SEE IF WE CAN SAVE THE WORLD FIRST...
NOTHING WORTHWHILE SHOULD BE SO EASY.

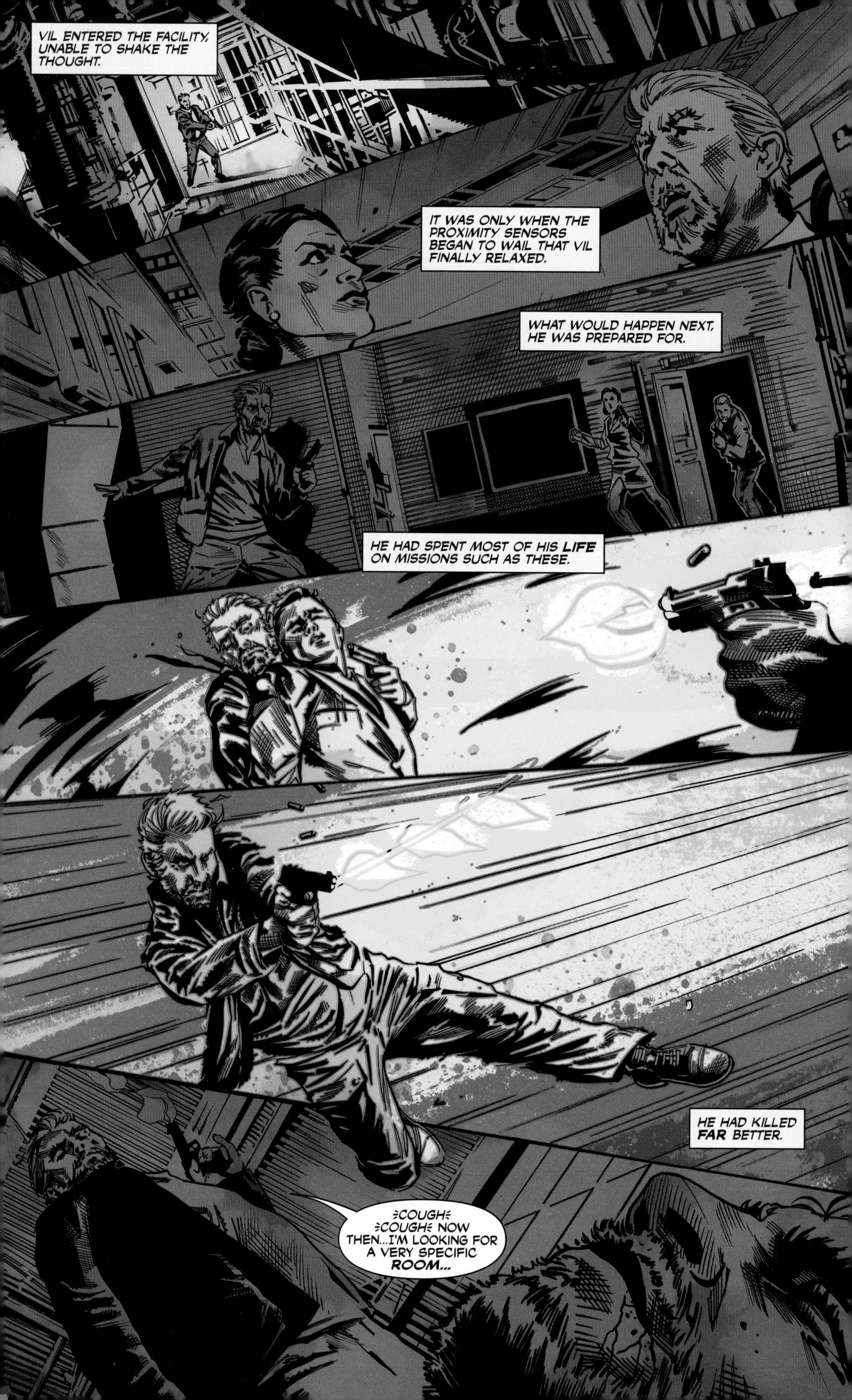
VIL ENTERED THE FACILITY, UNABLE TO SHAKE THE THOUGHT.
IT WAS ONLY WHEN THE PROXIMITY SENSORS BEGAN TO WAIL THAT VIL FINALLY RELAXED.
WHAT WOULD HAPPEN NEXT, HE WAS PREPARED FOR.
HE HAD SPENT MOST OF HIS LIFE ON MISSIONS SUCH AS THESE.
HE HAD KILLED FAR BETTER.
COUGH *COUGH* NOW THEN...I'M LOOKING FOR A VERY SPECIFIC ROOM...

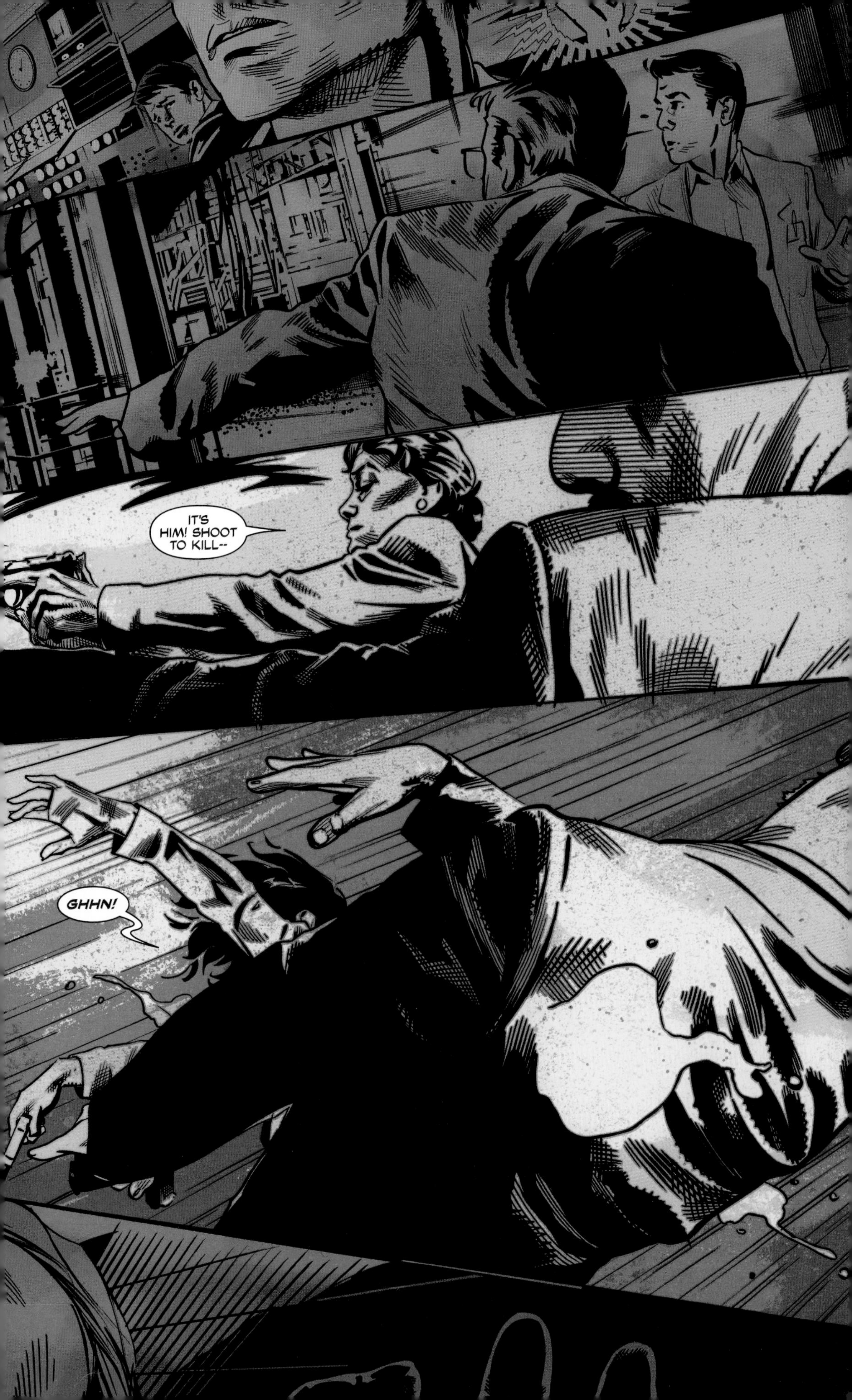
IT'S HIM! SHOOT TO KILL--
GHHN!

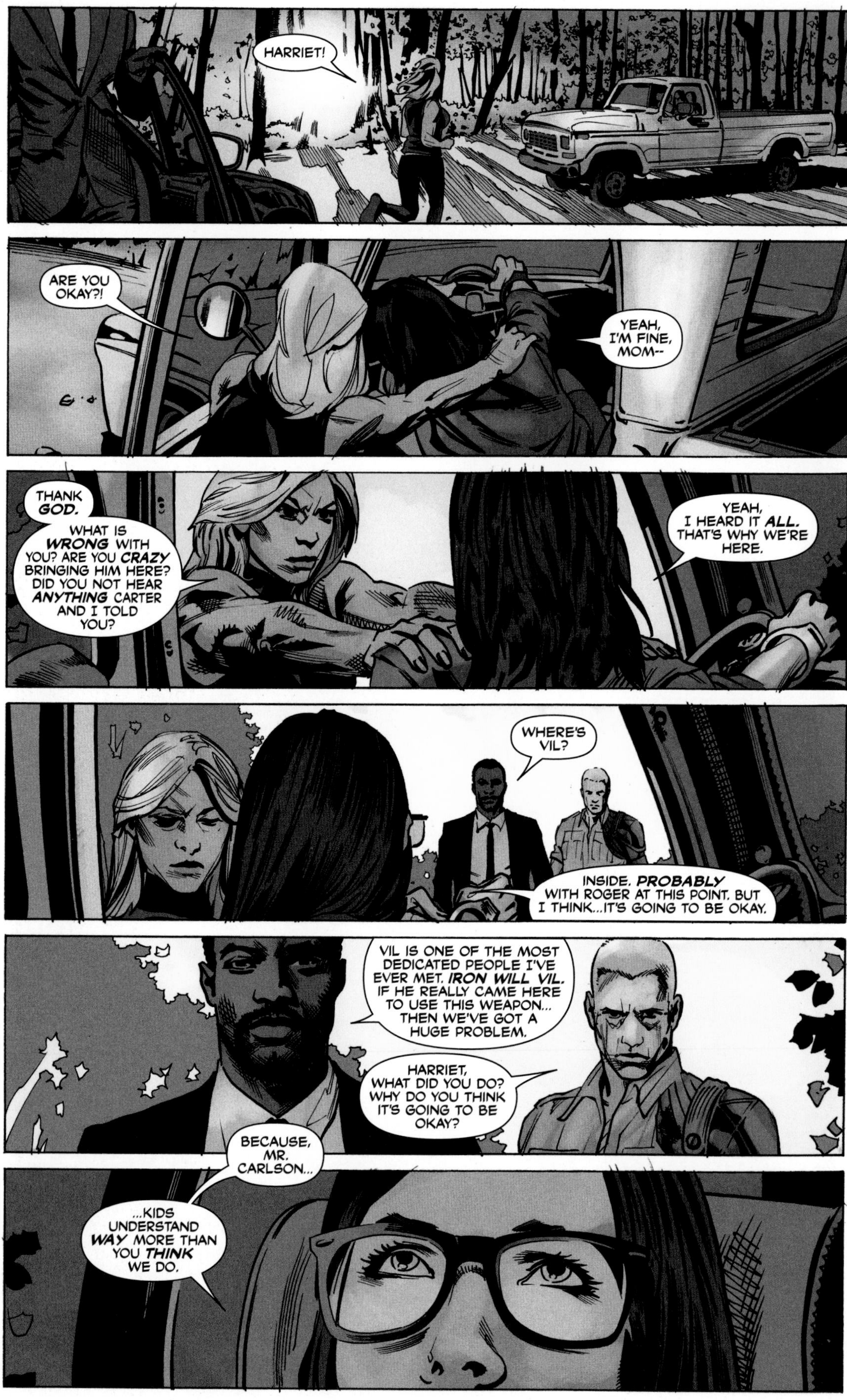
HARRIET!
ARE YOU OKAY?!
YEAH, I'M FINE, MOM--
THANK GOD.
WHAT IS WRONG WITH YOU? ARE YOU CRAZY BRINGING HIM HERE? DID YOU NOT HEAR ANYTHING CARTER AND I TOLD YOU?
YEAH, I HEARD IT ALL. THAT'S WHY WE'RE HERE.
WHERE'S VIL?
INSIDE. PROBABLY WITH ROGER AT THIS POINT. BUT I THINK...IT'S GOING TO BE OKAY.
VIL IS ONE OF THE MOST DEDICATED PEOPLE I'VE EVER MET. IRON WILL VIL. IF HE REALLY CAME HERE TO USE THIS WEAPON... THEN WE'VE GOT A HUGE PROBLEM.
HARRIET, WHAT DID YOU DO? WHY DO YOU THINK IT'S GOING TO BE OKAY?
BECAUSE, MR. CARLSON...
...KIDS UNDERSTAND WAY MORE THAN YOU THINK WE DO.

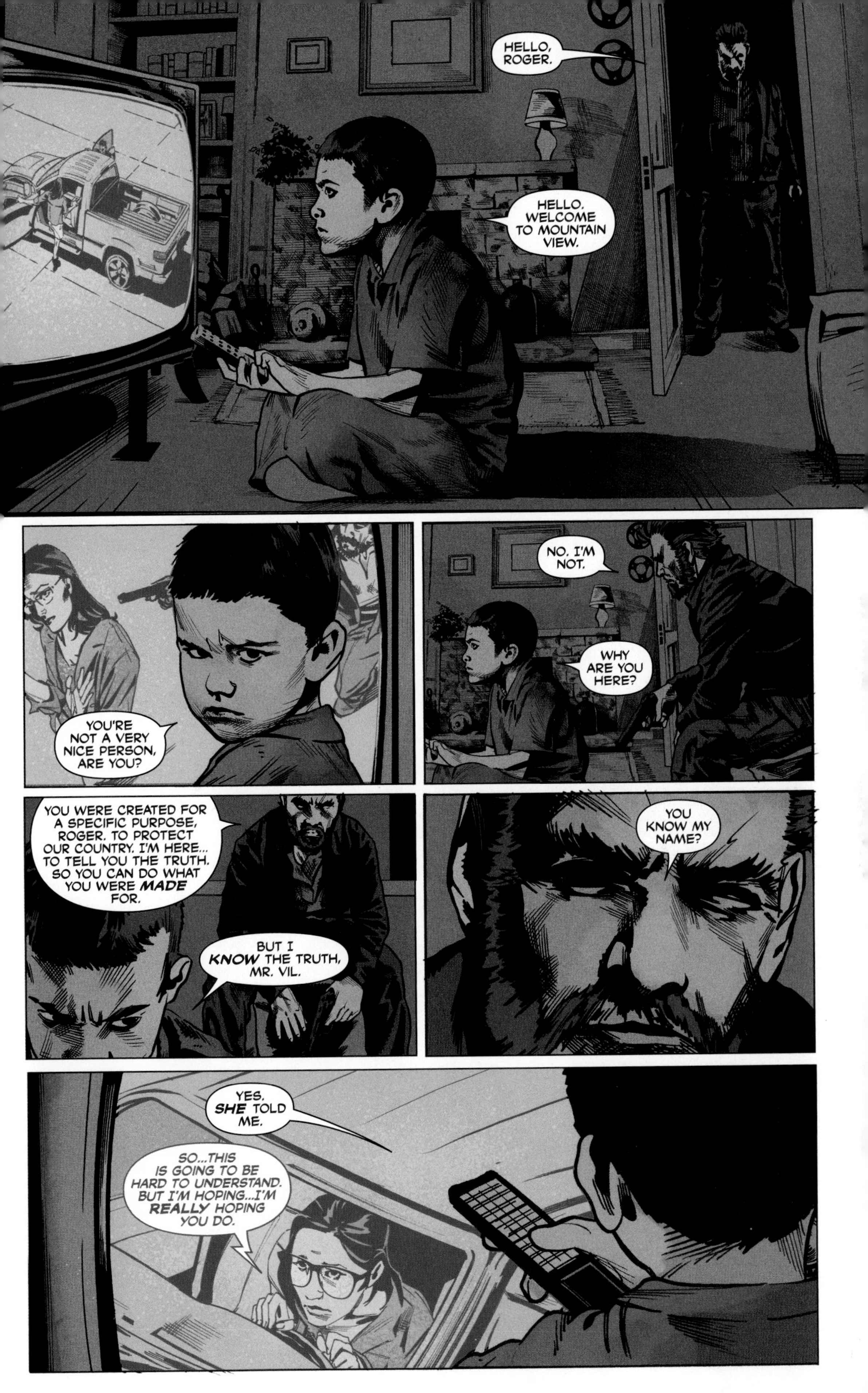
HELLO, ROGER.
HELLO. WELCOME TO MOUNTAIN VIEW.
YOU'RE NOT A VERY NICE PERSON, ARE YOU?
NO. I'M NOT.
WHY ARE YOU HERE?
YOU WERE CREATED FOR A SPECIFIC PURPOSE, ROGER. TO PROTECT OUR COUNTRY. I'M HERE... TO TELL YOU THE TRUTH. SO YOU CAN DO WHAT YOU WERE MADE FOR.
BUT I KNOW THE TRUTH, MR. VIL.
YOU KNOW MY NAME?
YES. SHE TOLD ME.
SO...THIS IS GOING TO BE HARD TO UNDERSTAND. BUT I'M HOPING...I'M REALLY HOPING YOU DO.

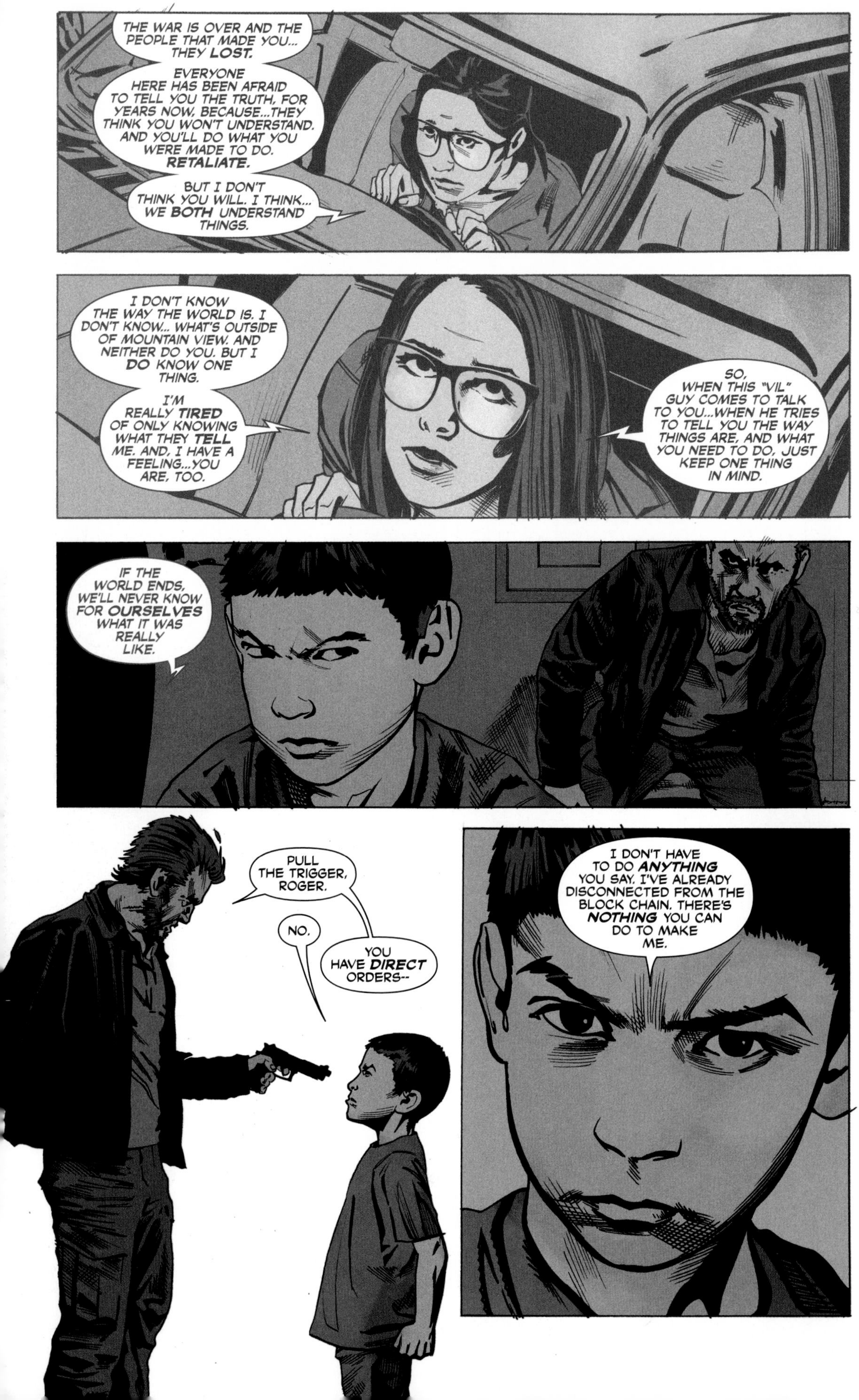
THE WAR IS OVER AND THE PEOPLE THAT MADE YOU... THEY LOST.
EVERYONE HERE HAS BEEN AFRAID TO TELL YOU THE TRUTH, FOR YEARS NOW, BECAUSE...THEY THINK YOU WON'T UNDERSTAND. AND YOU'LL DO WHAT YOU WERE MADE TO DO. RETALIATE.
BUT I DON'T THINK YOU WILL. I THINK... WE BOTH UNDERSTAND THINGS.
I DON'T KNOW THE WAY THE WORLD IS. I DON'T KNOW... WHAT'S OUTSIDE OF MOUNTAIN VIEW. AND NEITHER DO YOU. BUT I DO KNOW ONE THING.
I'M REALLY TIRED OF ONLY KNOWING WHAT THEY TELL ME. AND, I HAVE A FEELING...YOU ARE, TOO.
SO, WHEN THIS "VIL" GUY COMES TO TALK TO YOU...WHEN HE TRIES TO TELL YOU THE WAY THINGS ARE, AND WHAT YOU NEED TO DO, JUST KEEP ONE THING IN MIND.
IF THE WORLD ENDS, WE'LL NEVER KNOW FOR OURSELVES WHAT IT WAS REALLY LIKE.
PULL THE TRIGGER, ROGER.
NO.
YOU HAVE DIRECT ORDERS--
I DON'T HAVE TO DO ANYTHING YOU SAY. I'VE ALREADY DISCONNECTED FROM THE BLOCK CHAIN. THERE'S NOTHING YOU CAN DO TO MAKE ME.

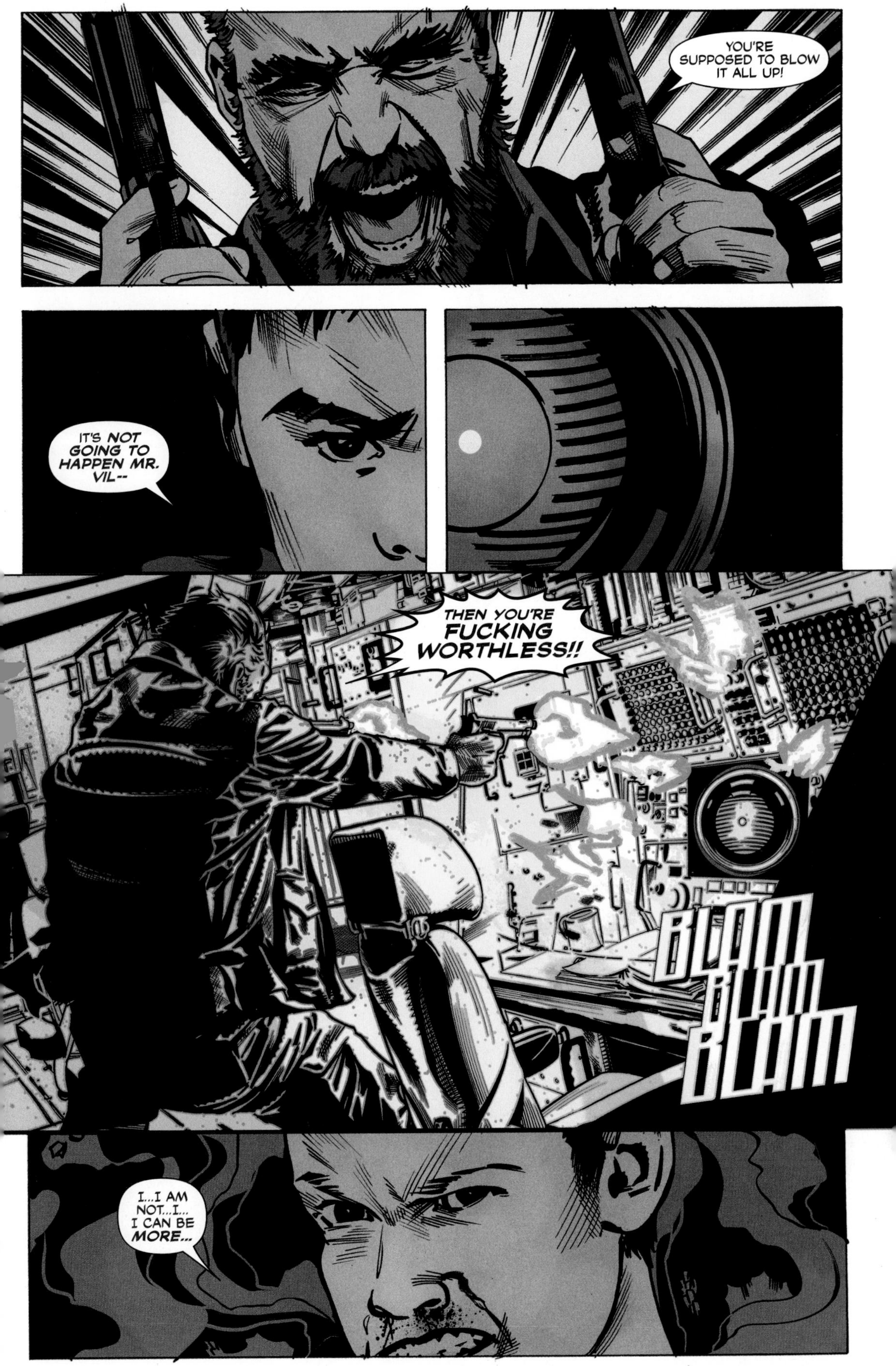
YOU'RE SUPPOSED TO BLOW IT ALL UP!
IT'S NOT GOING TO HAPPEN MR. VIL--
THEN YOU'RE FUCKING WORTHLESS!!
BLAM BLAM BLAM
I...I AM NOT...I... I CAN BE MORE...

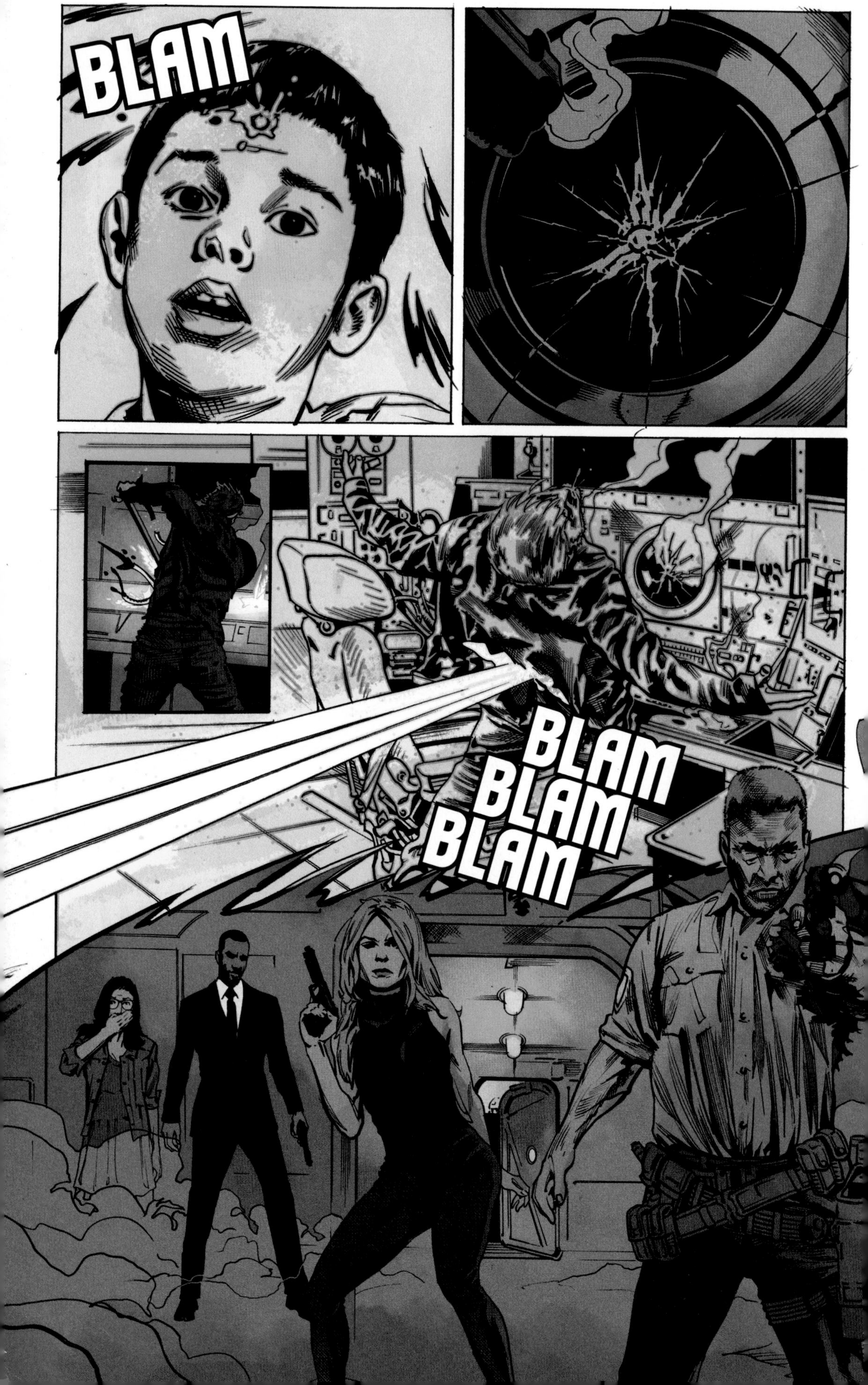
BLAM
BLAM
BLAM
BLAM

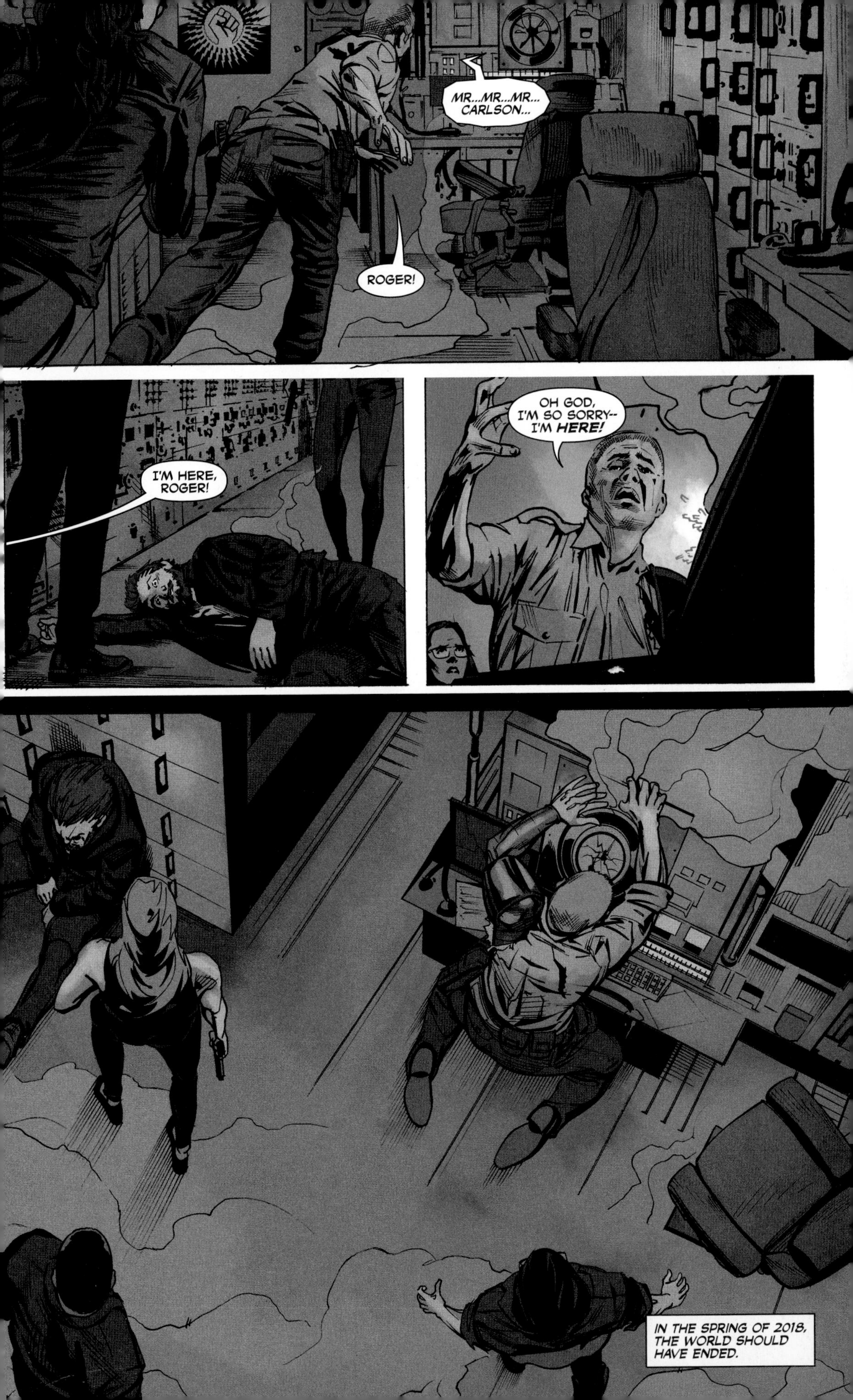
MR...MR...MR... CARLSON...
ROGER!
I'M HERE, ROGER!
OH GOD, I'M SO SORRY-- I'M HERE!
IN THE SPRING OF 2018, THE WORLD SHOULD HAVE ENDED.

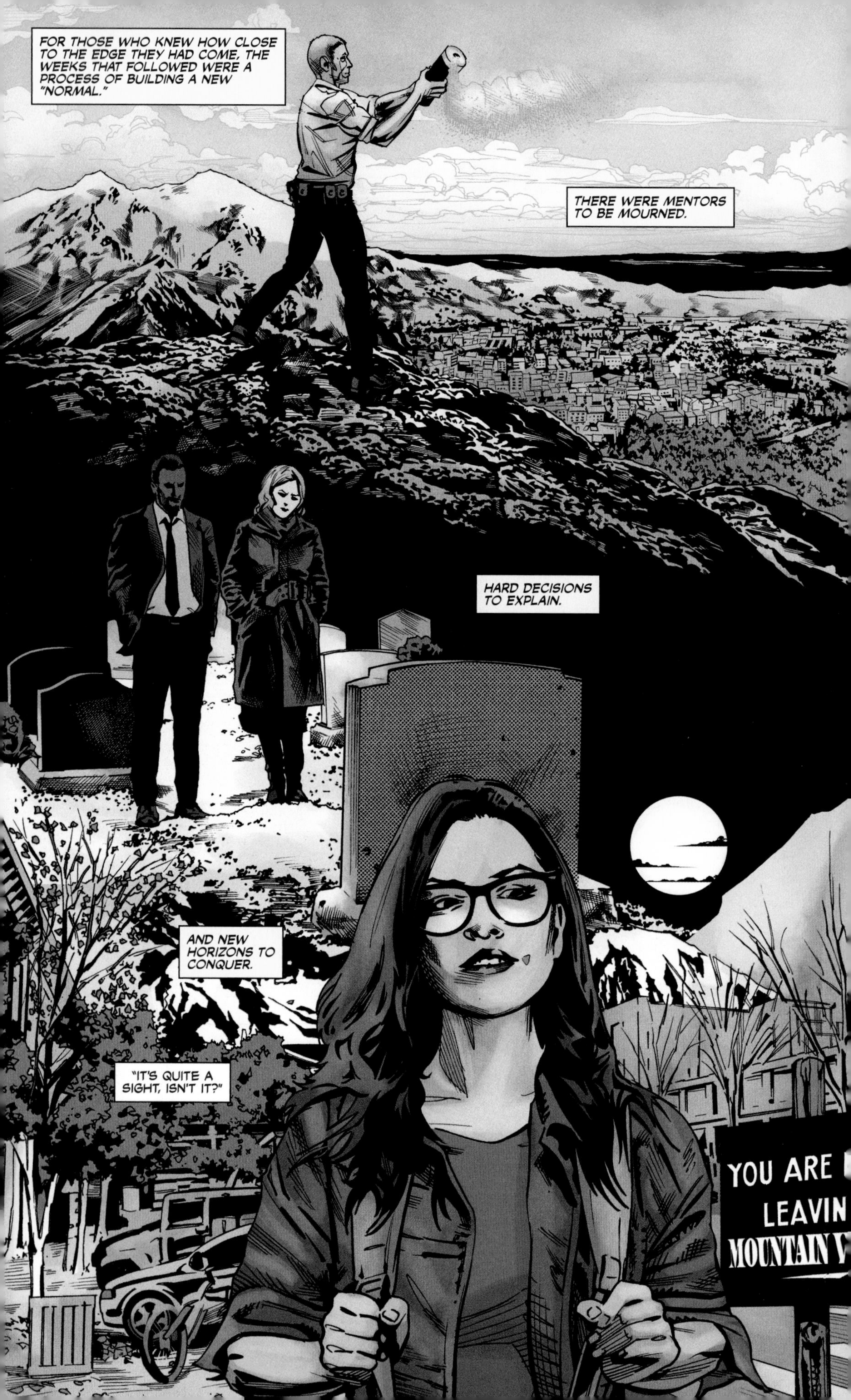
FOR THOSE WHO KNEW HOW CLOSE TO THE EDGE THEY HAD COME, THE WEEKS THAT FOLLOWED WERE A PROCESS OF BUILDING A NEW "NORMAL."
THERE WERE MENTORS TO BE MOURNED.
HARD DECISIONS TO EXPLAIN.
AND NEW HORIZONS TO CONQUER.
"IT'S QUITE A SIGHT, ISN'T IT?"
YOU ARE
LEAVIN
MOUNTAIN V

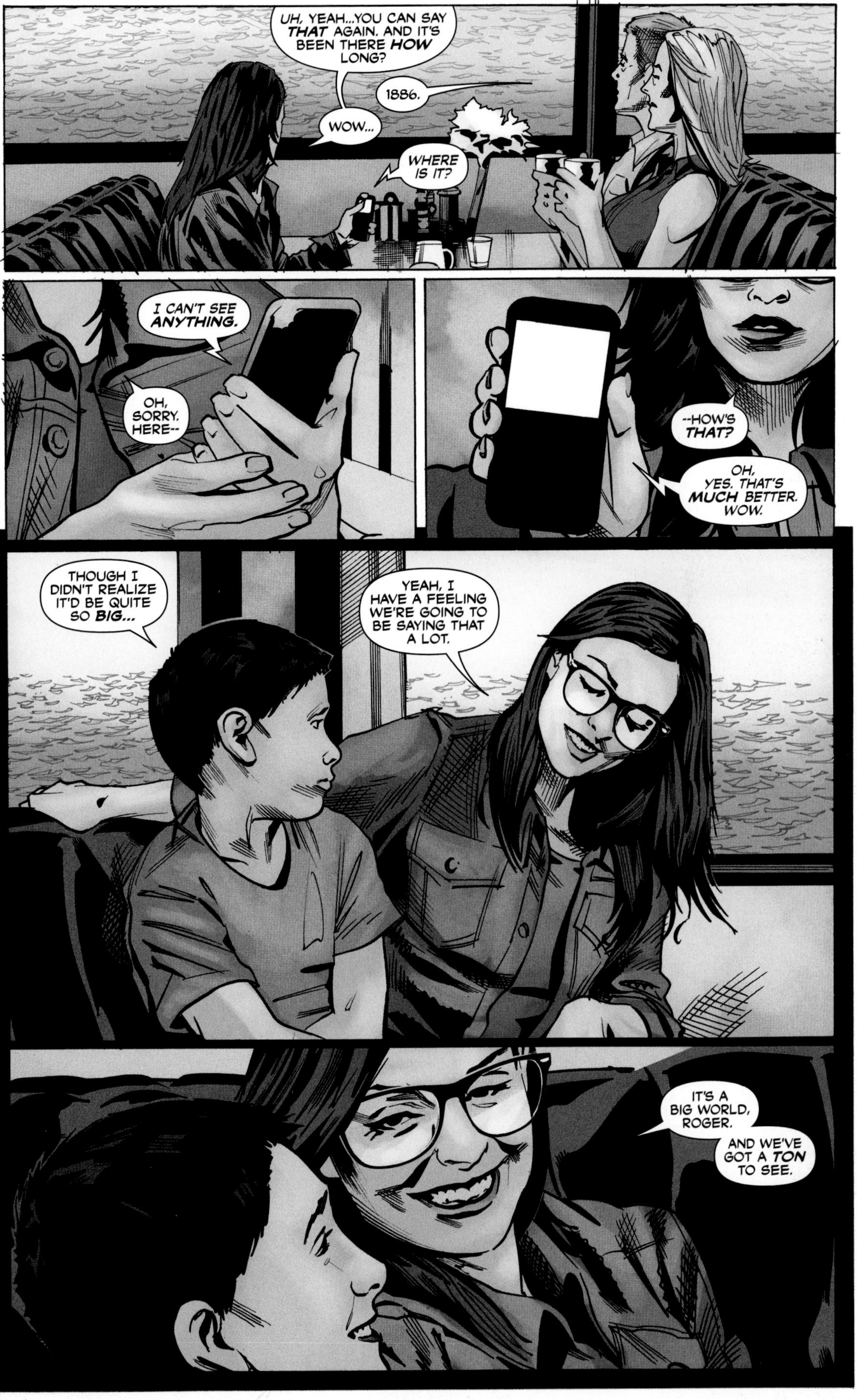

UH, YEAH...YOU CAN SAY THAT AGAIN. AND IT'S BEEN THERE HOW LONG?
1886.
WOW...
WHERE IS IT?
I CAN'T SEE ANYTHING.
OH, SORRY. HERE--
--HOW'S THAT?
OH, YES. THAT'S MUCH BETTER. WOW.
THOUGH I DIDN'T REALIZE IT'D BE QUITE SO BIG...
YEAH, I HAVE A FEELING WE'RE GOING TO BE SAYING THAT A LOT.
IT'S A BIG WORLD, ROGER.
AND WE'VE GOT A TON TO SEE.

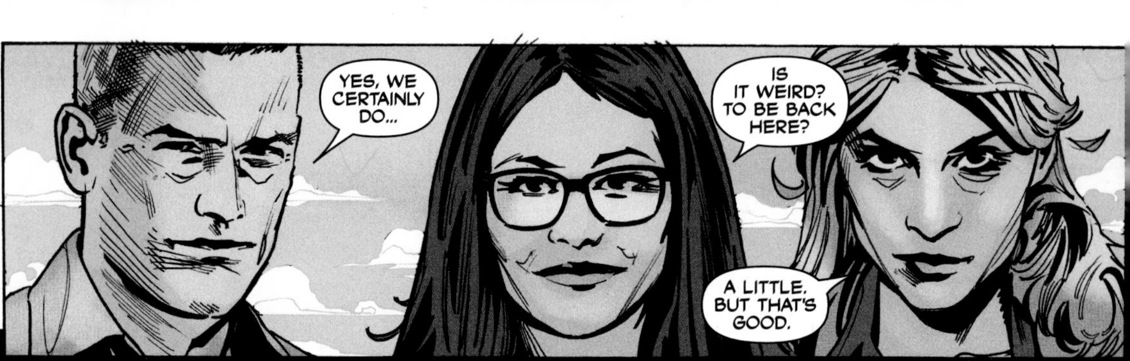
YES, WE CERTAINLY DO...
IS IT WEIRD? TO BE BACK HERE?
A LITTLE. BUT THAT'S GOOD.

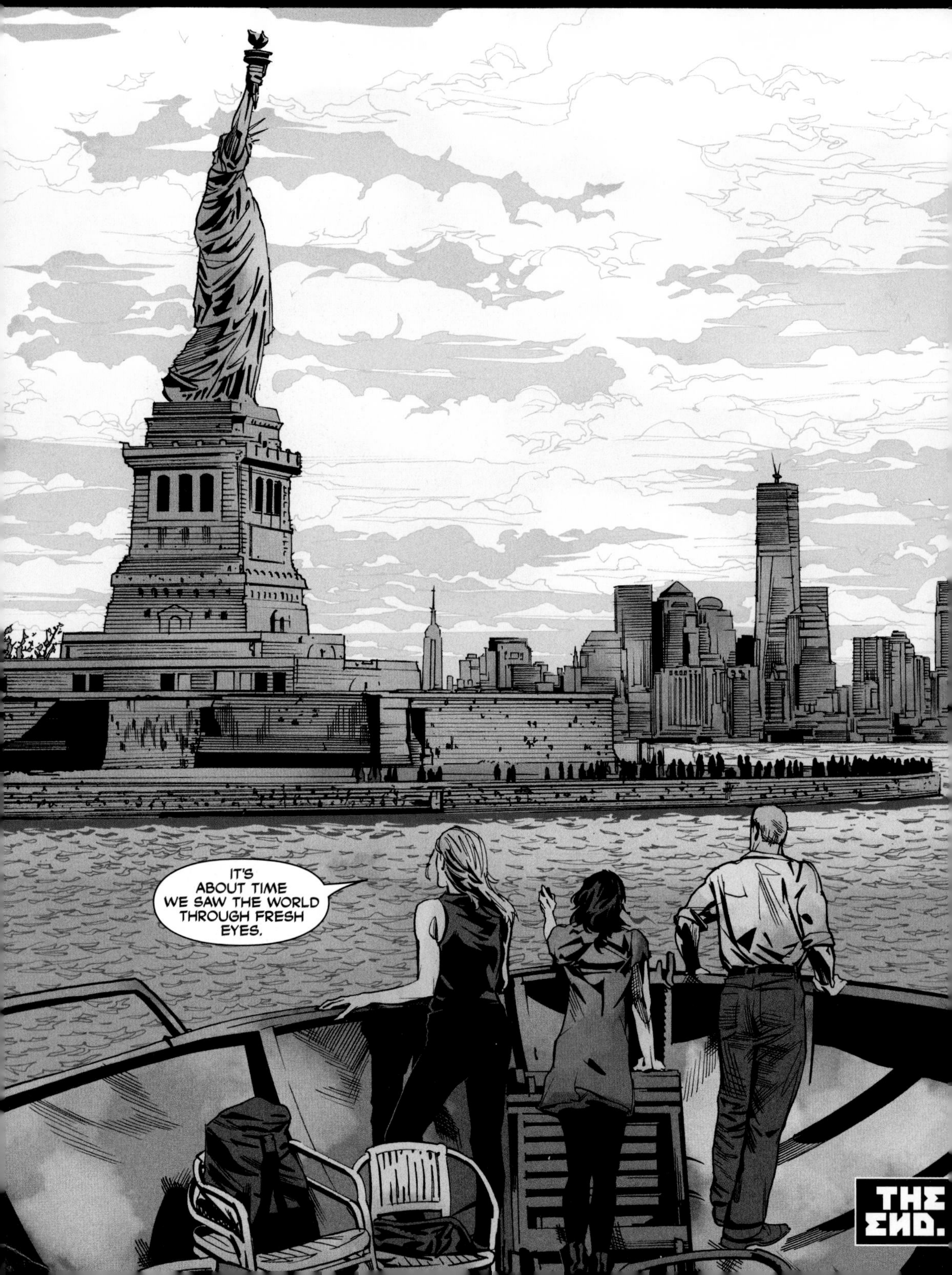
IT'S ABOUT TIME WE SAW THE WORLD THROUGH FRESH EYES.
THE END.

CHARACTER DESIGNS AND UNUSED COVERS

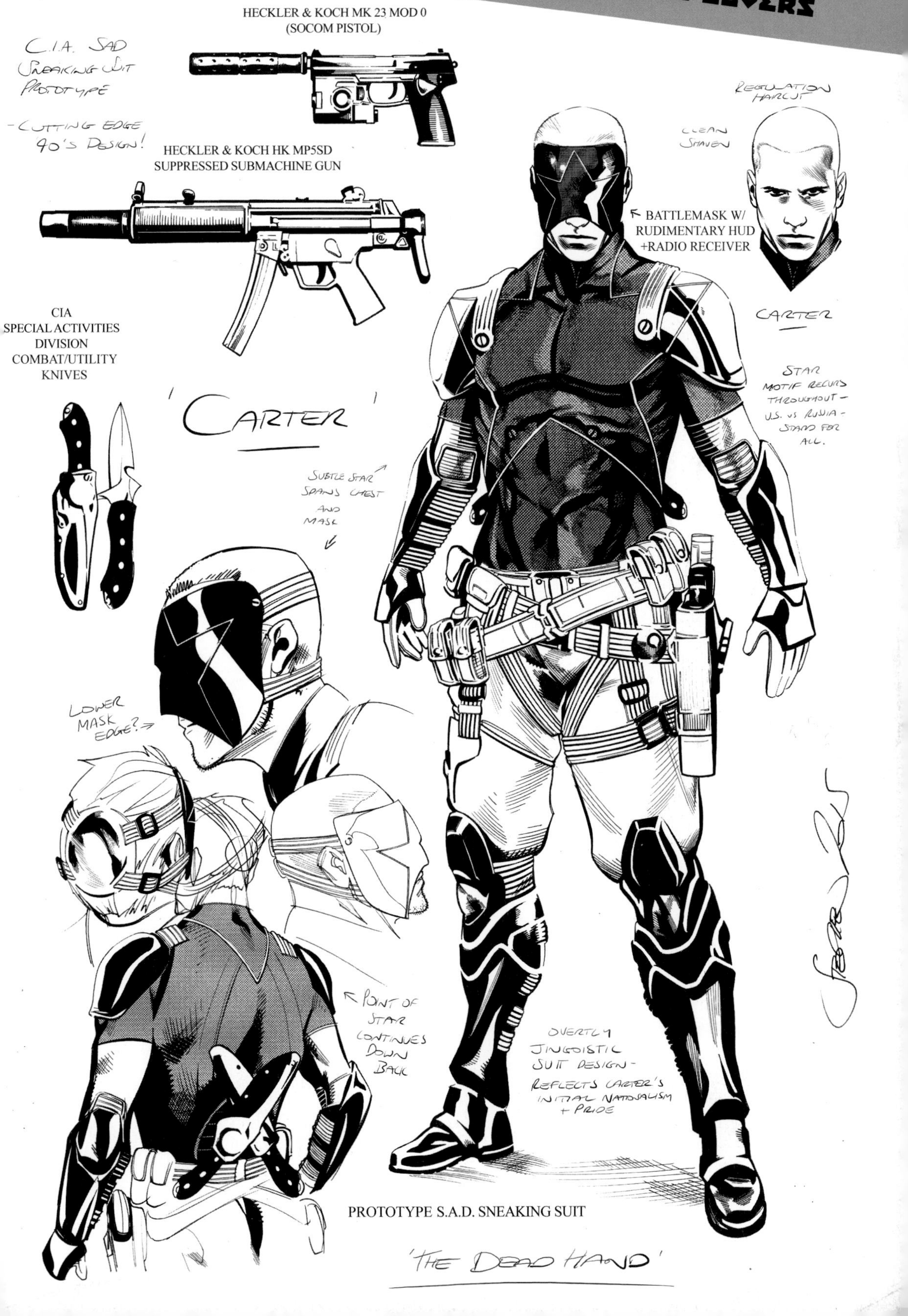

HECKLER & KOCH MK 23 MOD 0
(SOCOM PISTOL)
C.I.A. SAD
SNEAKING SUIT
PROTOTYPE
- CUTTING EDGE
90'S DESIGN!
HECKLER & KOCH HK MP5SD
SUPPRESSED SUBMACHINE GUN
REGULATION
HAIRCUT
CLEAN
SHAVEN
BATTLEMASK W/
RUDIMENTARY HUD
+RADIO RECEIVER
CARTER
CIA
SPECIAL ACTIVITIES
DIVISION
COMBAT/UTILITY
KNIVES
'CARTER'
STAR
MOTIF RECURS
THROUGHOUT -
U.S. VS RUSSIA -
STAND FOR
ALL.
SUBTLE STAR
SPANS CHEST
AND
MASK
LOWER
MASK
EDGE?
POINT OF
STAR
CONTINUES
DOWN
BACK
OVERTLY
JINGOISTIC
SUIT DESIGN -
REFLECTS CARTER'S
INITIAL NATIONALISM
+ PRIDE
PROTOTYPE S.A.D. SNEAKING SUIT
'THE DEAD HAND'

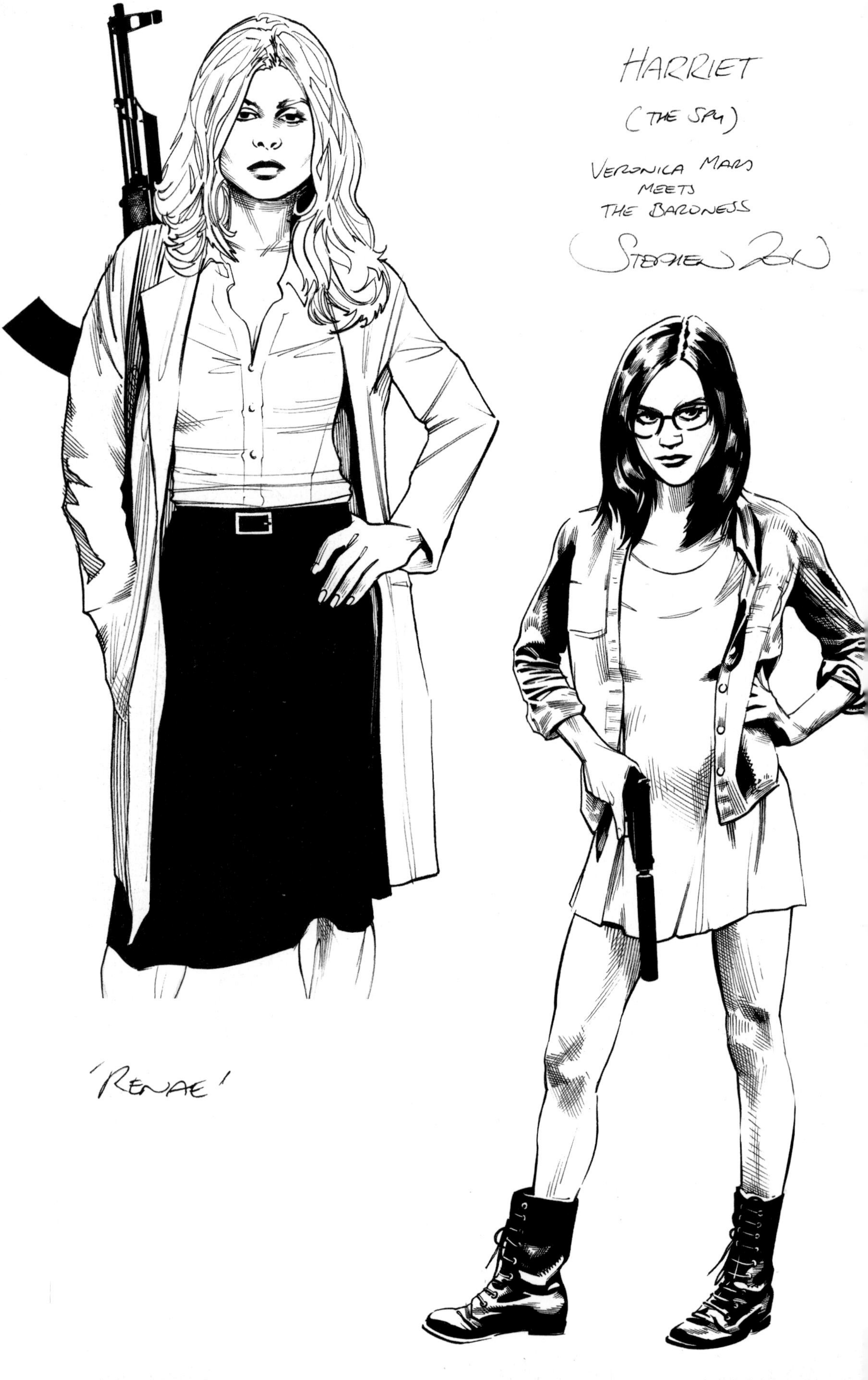
HARRIET
(THE SPY)
VERONICA MARS
MEETS
THE BARONESS
'RENAE'

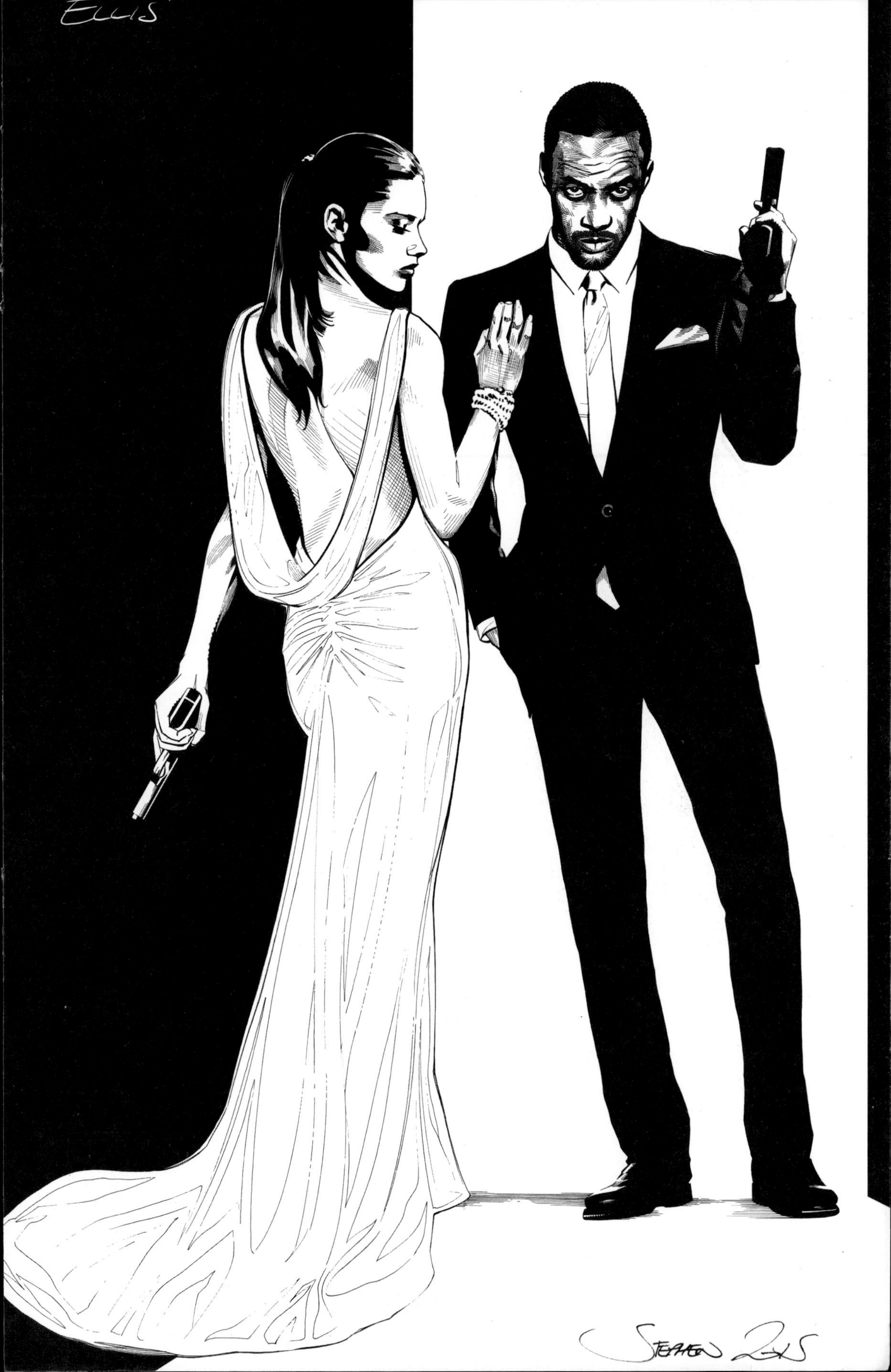
ELLIS
STEPHEN

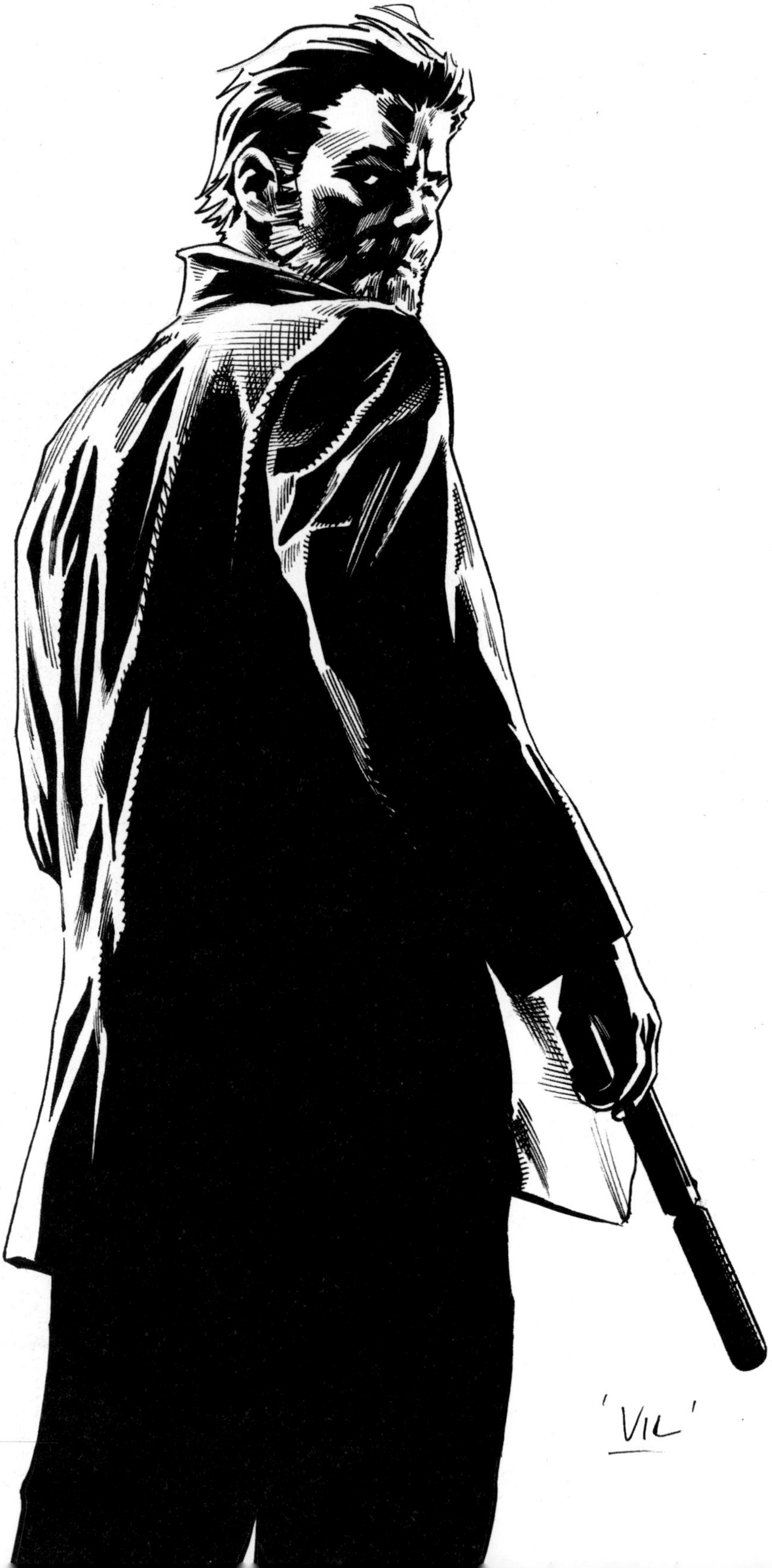
'VIL'

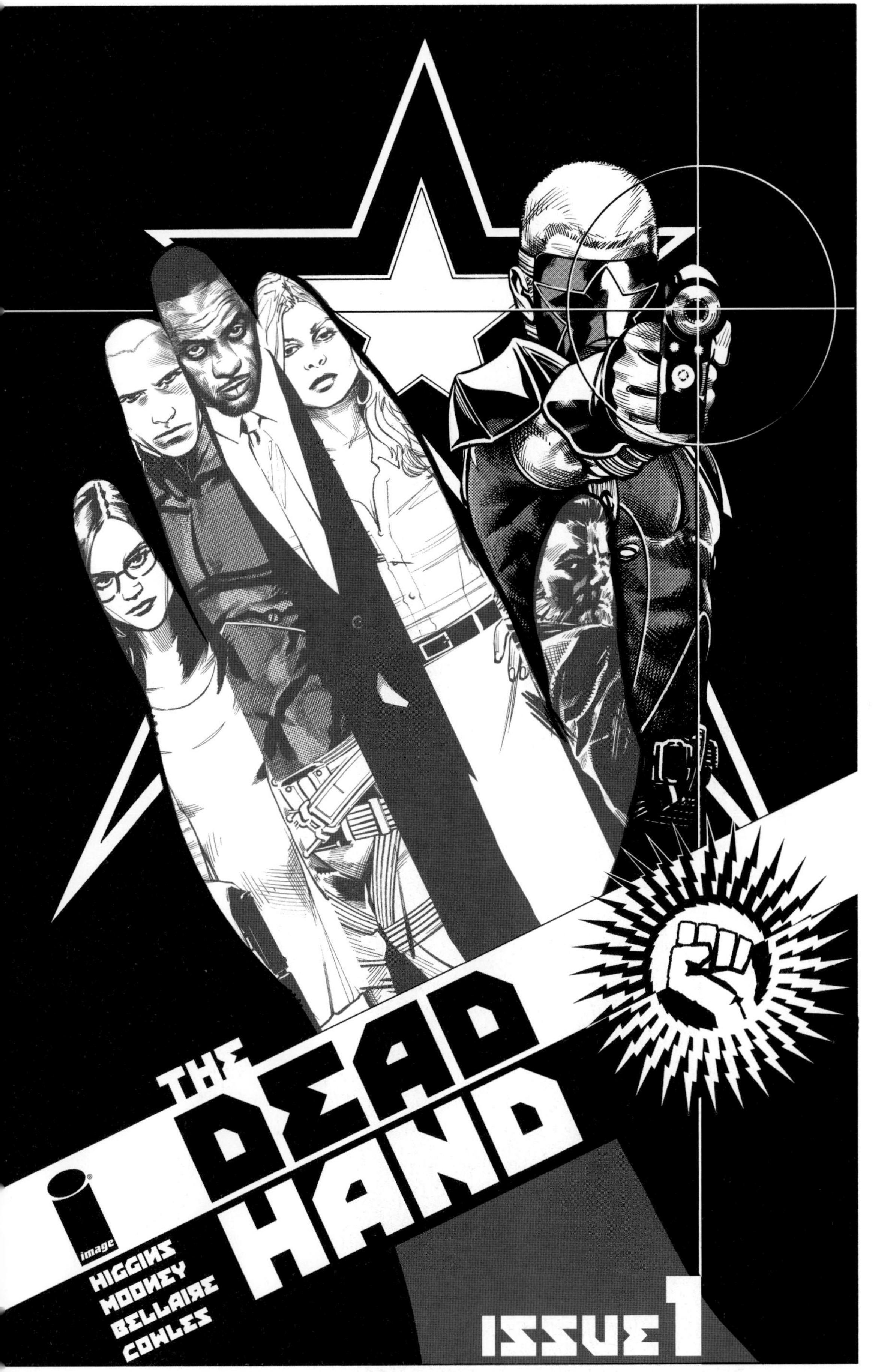
THE DEAD HAND
image
HIGGINS
MOONEY
BELLAIRE
COWLES
ISSUE 1

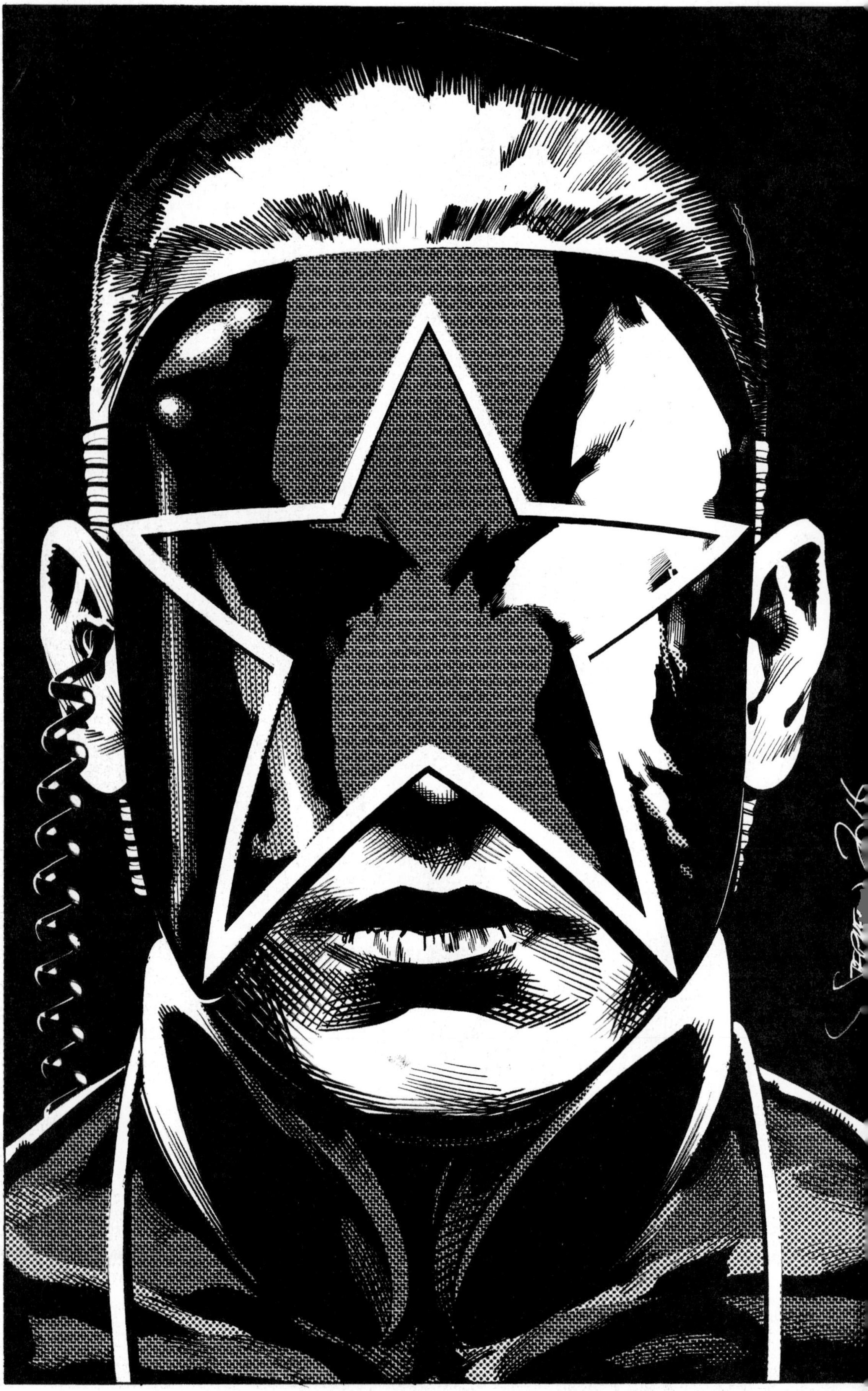

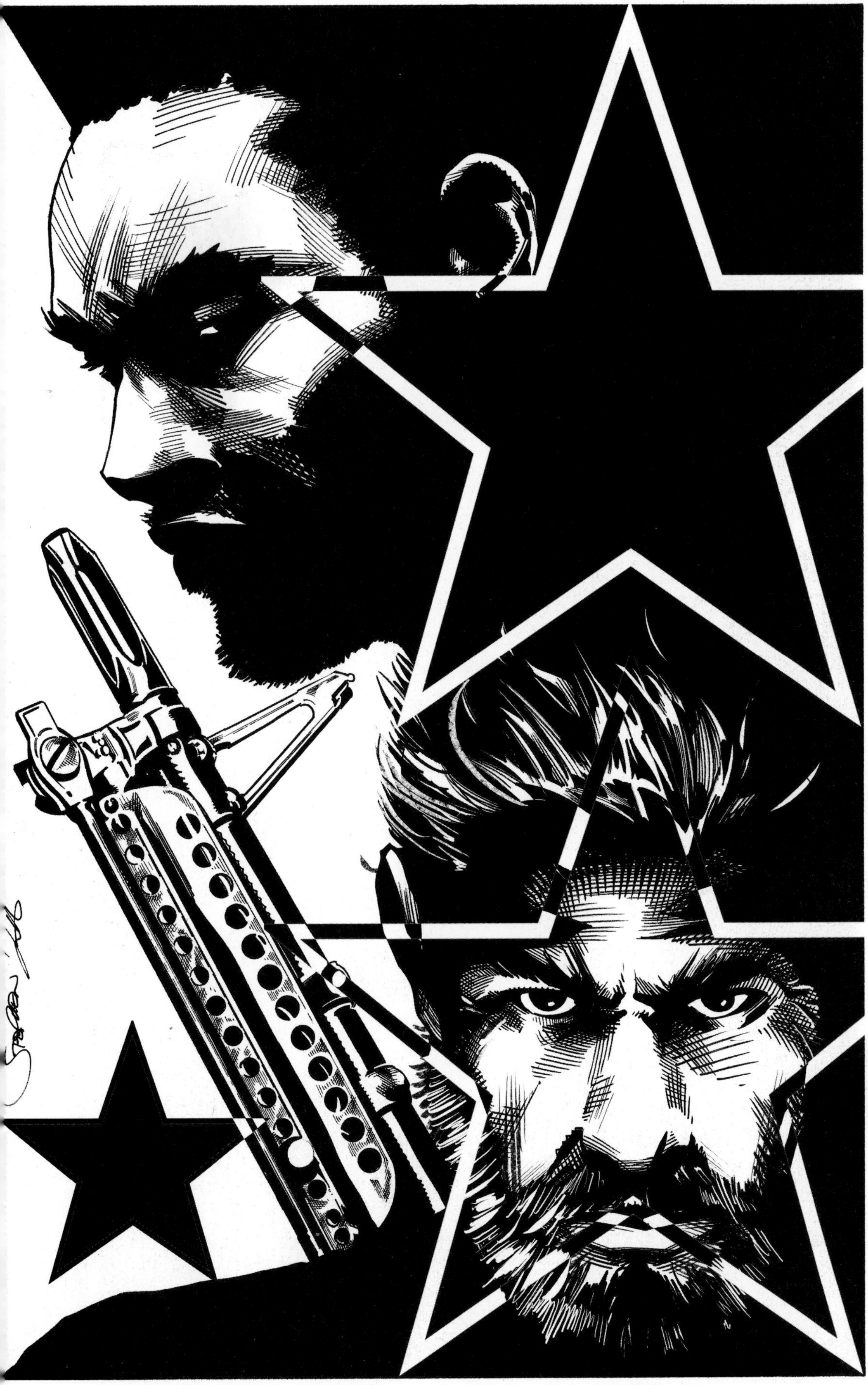

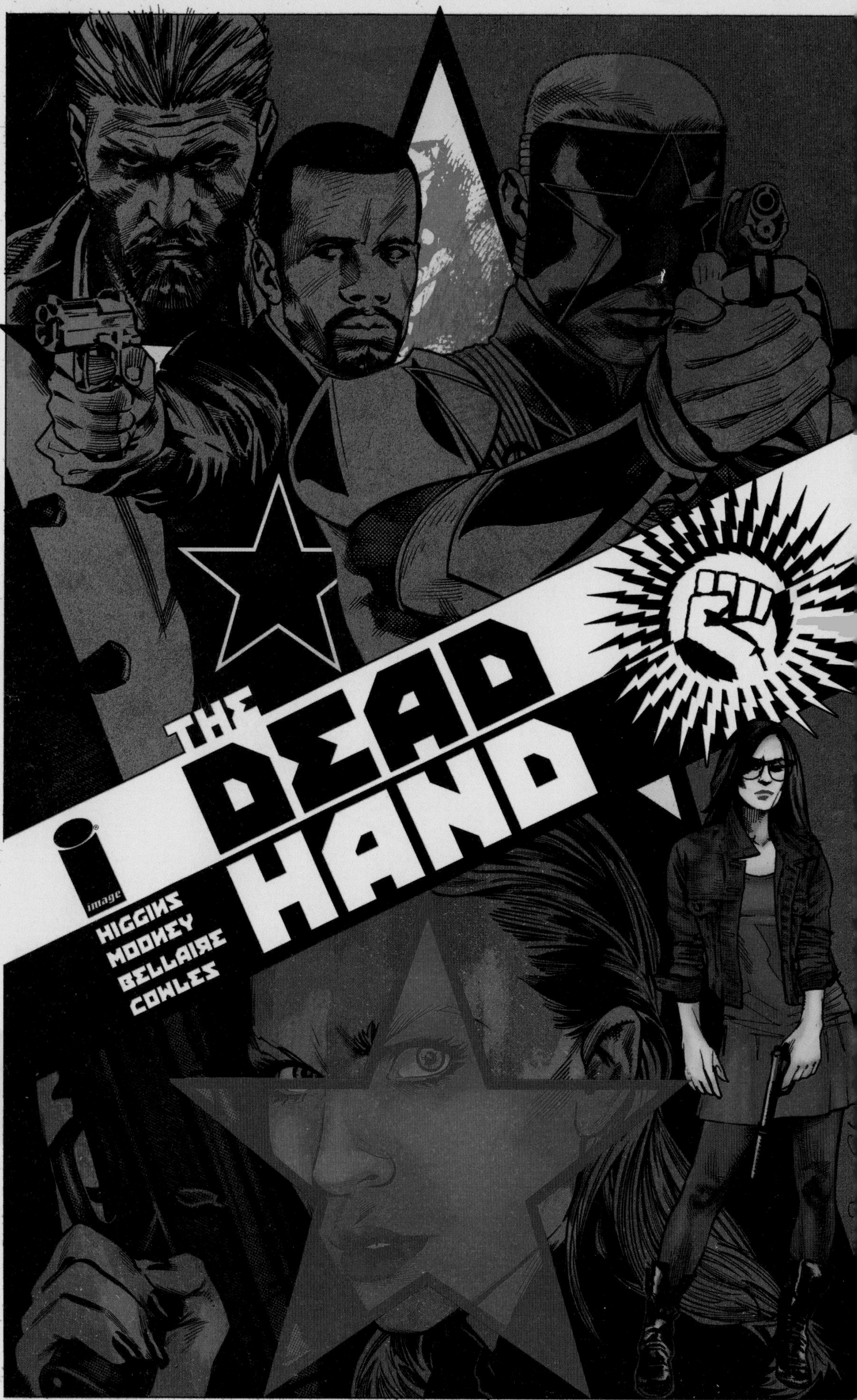
THE
DEAD
HAND
image
HIGGINS
MOONEY
BELLAIRE
COWLES